Panda Books
The Desert Wolf

Guo Xuebo was born in Kunlun Banner on Inner Mongolia's Horqin Sandland in 1948. After graduating from technical school, Guo Xuebo worked for seven years in Kesuoshou Banner about two hundred kilometres from Kunlun Banner, as editor at the county broadcasting station, and as scriptwriter for the prefecture's cultural centre and its song and dance ensemble. In 1977 he entered the Beijing Central Institute of Drama and was awarded a research fellowship at the Literary Research Institute of the Chinese Academy of Social Sciences upon graduation in 1980. He made his literary debut in 1975, and "The Sand Fox", his first short story about the desert, was published in 1985, followed by "The Desert Wolf", "Sand Burial", "Sand Rites", "The Fiery Residence" and "The Goddess of Xiling River". He is currently associated with a publishing house in Beijing.

Panda Books
First Edition 1996
Copyright © 1996 CHINESE LITERATURE PRESS
ISBN 7-5071-0344-7
ISBN 0-8351-3180-7

Published by CHINESE LITERATURE PRESS
Beijing 100037, China
Distributed by China International Book Trading Corporation
35 Chegongzhuang Xilu, Beijing 100044, China
P.O. Box 399, Beijing, China
Printed in the People's Republic of China

GUO XUEBO

THE DESERT WOLF

Panda Books

Foreword

Some months ago my friend Jin Jianfan, who knows my interest in books that will be of value to young people — and also to older men and women — gave me the translation in French of three short stories by Guo Xuebo. One of them was "The Sand Fox" ("La renarde du desert" in French). I was fascinated, reading it, by the skill, the mastery of style, the economy of words (which denotes true talent in a writer) and the evocative power of this short tale. There were other tales written by Guo Xuebo which I then started to read. I agree with my good friend the great and renowned writer Wang Meng, who in his preface wrote: "We need such a writer as Guo Xuebo."

Since then I have also read "Sand Rites", and the translation of this short novel in the English version (*Chinese Literature*, Winter 1995).

I think that Guo's work does bring new life, a new perspective to modern Chinese writing. Reading "Sand Rites", I felt the sand under my feet. I was walking in the desert, knowing it, and I could hear the Song of Andai in my ears. Just as in the short story of the mother fox, I felt that I was transported there on the scene. The people in the story were real, alive. And always, there is also compassion, not only for the animals, but also for the human being. As in the short story, he makes one feel how abhorrent wanton killing of an animal is, so in "Sand Rites" he bares the soul of the men and women he writes about, until one feels that one knows them, and one wants to go on knowing them, talking with them. He makes the desert itself, those vast stretches of pitiless sand, stir with a soul of its own.

This is great art, great writing. It is also, on reading, sheer poetry. Poetry unforced, untamed, which rises from the desert sands, and grips the heart. Well does Guo Xuebo in "Sand Rites" compare the desert to a woman, a woman unrelenting and untamed, fierce and fickle, and to be conquered, untiringly. I find here a relationship to great old Asian tales, which in India, for instance, have given rise to wonderful songs and hymns to the power of woman. But Guo does not stop there. He makes music out of hardship, out of suffering. He brings us back also the traditions of the desert, in song, in poetry.

I feel privileged to have met Guo Xuebo, although very briefly. I write these few lines to express my admiration for a young and gifted master of the word. Master also of the music of words. I can still hear the Song of Andai, although I have never really HEARD it ... but it is there, and it makes my heart beat faster.

I am very glad that *Chinese Literature* is bringing out many many writers like Guo Xuebo. I look forward to meeting them and reading them. I hope the translation in English and in French and other languages will also bring him a wide readership abroad.

Han Suyin
February 5, 1996

Indispensable Guo Xuebo

Wang Meng

One wonders if it is because of the transformation of contemporary society at such supersonic speed, that human existence and human relations have become so enormously complex. Both our literature and our very nerves have been seized and held in thrall by the harmonies and dissonances playing out in the high-rise pigeon-coops of our urbanised environment. Contributing to this fascination is the long history of our civilisation, particularly the over-burgeoning nature of our population and the cultural traditions which have impinged upon human relations, the frequent and violent social changes that have occurred over the last several centuries, the "academic major" of class struggle in which we were steeped in recent decades, and finally the increasing tendency for people to gravitate towards the cities. Indeed, sometimes, upon reading one literary work after another, it is impossible to imagine how their protagonists would live in a natural environment. It is impossible to imagine any other existence for them outside their incessant involvement in intrigues and love-hate relationships.

Yet, we human beings are Nature's offspring, at one and the same time her favourite and her "unfilial" sons. We are irrevocably linked to the sun, moon and stars, the four seasons, the rain and snow and clouds, the mountains and rivers and plains, the grasslands and the deserts, the oceans and lakes, the forests and marshlands, the birds and insects and beasts, all of which are, always and ever, integral parts of nature. If we have become out of touch with nature, it only goes to show our own perverseness and stupidity. If we have forgotten how to revere nature and love her, we are displaying our spiritual and emotional impoverishment. If we commit crimes against nature, it reveals a serious imbalance in our mentality that needs urgent redress, for we face an impending disaster of our own making avertible only through immediate rectification. Poignant inspiration and eloquent warnings abide in the contrast between man and nature, and between civilisation and the simpler lifestyles and folkways that harken back to more primitive times. It is incumbent upon us to heed the messages therein. We need to seize the day while there is still time. We need to seriously re-think our priorities and repent of our ways. And we need the invaluable contributions of writers like Guo Xuebo.

Guo Xuebo who has come to the fore in recent years, writes of the desert. In his portrayals, we find not merely the flora and fauna of the desert, but her very body and soul, a living entity intimately involved in the nurturance of her subjects, our brother nationalities who make the desert their home. Herein lies a new regionalism that Guo Xuebo has contributed to our body of literature. Presented from a viewpoint both daring and devotional, austere and passionate, realistic and romantic, his is a regionalism that opens our eyes to a uniquely grand and sweeping spectacle that alters utterly our view of nature and the desert.

We need Guo Xuebo and his works. The more we

modernise the more we need the redemptive supplementation and challenge of literature. Prosperity, of course, stands as essential to our aspirations. We need industry, a market economy, science and technology. We need buildings of function and beauty, an infrastructure upon which to base development. But these material concerns can not in and of themselves completely fulfill the yearnings of our hearts, nor do they comprise the total aspect of modernisation. We need to reflect anew upon our history and geography and our relationship to nature. We need great skies and sweeping swathes of earth — including desert. Those who count among our friends are not merely our own kind, but also the beasts. In the quest for the new fruits of civilisation, we must not forget the virtues of our essential nature as humans and guard ourselves against new imbalances in our thinking. We must not be oblivious to the fact that we are too, the product of nature. The more we modernise, the more we need Guo Xuebo. We need him to transport us into a simpler, more rudimental world, a world less neglected by our jaded sensibilities, imbued with greater romanticism and more capable of exercising our imagination, a world that is gentler and more hospitable than the one in which we find ourselves now.

Beijing, June 6, 1992

Contents

The Desert Wolf   1

The Sand Fox   86

Sand Rites   109

Sand Burial   218

Spring on the Horqin Sandland —— *Ji Cheng*   348

The Desert Wolf

> Since born into the wilderness of this antique desert
> You've been looking for
> A world of green
>
> — Author's Note

The emissary of the deer went to see God to complain about the wolf. He indignantly recounted to God how the wolf was always chasing the deer in the forests and the wastelands. The deer were forever running away, there was no peace in their lives, they were always on tenterhooks. And the wolf was eating the deer's family members one by one. This was totally unfair. Since God had created deer, why had he also created the wolf to chase them?

God stroked his beard and after a silence smiled slightly and agreed to the deer's request. He called the wolf back to Heaven. From then on, the deer clan lived a peaceful life as they no longer needed to be afraid or spend their days running away. They lived in the forest on the edge of a lake. When they were hungry they ate grass, when they were thirsty they drank water, and when they had eaten and drunk their fill they slept. Because they no longer ran around, they grew lazy and fat. Gradually they lost the strong bodies they had forged during the days when they were rushing about. Because there was no wolf, there was no one to dispose of the deer when they died, so the bodies rotted where they fell. One day a pestilence erupted in the deer's home, and herd after herd dropped down dead. Even more died from disease than had been eaten by the wolf. The whole clan was on the brink of extinction.

There was nothing they could do, so the envoy of the deer returned to God to recount to him their suffering and to ask him to send the wolf back. Otherwise, laziness and comfort would destroy the whole clan!

From then on, once again there were wolves in the forests and the wastelands. And, pursued by the wolf, the deer flourished as in days past.

1

He looked like a turtle.

The bronze-coloured pack on his back looked like a heavy turtle shell.

The panther struck out a red tongue and licked the blood from the corners of his mouth.

The hairless wolf cub glanced in panic at the panther. The panther had torn open the stomach of the black-eyed wolf cub and savoured bite after bite of its delicious, bloody innards. The hairless cub and his furry brother had shrunk into a ball at the edge of the cliff. They were scared out of their wits. They had forgotten to run away and were trembling all over. The hairless cub's short, pointed snout pressed against the furry one and let out an agonised, low howl. Their predicament was all the result of his vicious wolf brother. He had teamed up with his green-eyed brother to attack him and force him out of the lair. They wanted to take advantage of the mother wolf's absence when she was out looking for food to drive away this strange tailless, hairless brother of theirs. As a result, there were spotted by the panther when they started to fight at the entrance of the lair and had brought this disaster upon themselves. Now, the fate of the green-eyed wolf also awaited them. The hairless cub angrily bared his teeth.

That piebald panther indolently turned around. He stretched and let out a vicious roar. He stared rapaciously at the two pathetic little creatures. He stretched out his tail and walked slowly towards them, as if he were going to a banquet. The two cubs remained motionless. In an instant, the panther swooped down on them like the wind, but the hairless cub agilely leapt out of the way and with his forepaws grasped a white poplar tree that was off to one side. He shuffled up it. The panther, caught by surprise, was infuriated, and his tail swept angrily towards the remaining cub. This was an attack with the power of a thunderbolt. The furry cub let out a cry and rolled onto the ground. The panther charged, and in a second his sharp teeth split open the cub's chest and he stuck in his jaws and casually began to eat.

There was a sad, shrill howl. A grey blur flew towards the panther and latched onto its throat.

The panther let out a startled cry and swung his head back and forth at the same time using his front paws to push it away. The grey thing was knocked off, rolled on the ground, and then leapt about ten metres away from where it stopped and stood. It was a mother wolf. Seeing her cubs eaten alive by the panther, she was filled with fury and attacked without regard for her own life. At first her surprise attack was successful. She had torn away a piece of flesh from the panther's neck and blood was pouring out. But she had also been wounded. The panther had injured one of her legs. She bared her teeth, her face towards the ground, and let out a low growl as she waited for her chance to attack again. The panther was enraged. It coiled and then sprang through the air towards the mother wolf.

The mother wolf dared not to wage battle to the death so she fled. She had no chance to launch another attack. With one of her legs was injured, so she could only dodge the panther's assault on three legs. She retreated again and again until she was forced to the edge of the cliff. The mother wolf let out a desperate howl and bared her teeth as she waited for the final battle. Suddenly, a black shape flashed like a sharp arrow from the white poplar tree. It was the hairless cub. He landed squarely on the neck of the panther and viciously bit and clawed at him. The panther shook his head back and forth but could not toss him off. He let out several howls and then suddenly rolled onto the ground. The hairless cub adroitly darted off to the side to avoid being crushed by the rolling panther. The enraged animal left the mother wolf alone and went to attack the cub. The hairless cub agilely leapt away, trying to lead the panther over the cliff. The panther bounded after him and almost caught him. In a flash the cub was pressed up against the edge of the cliff. Below was a gorge a hundred metres deep.

Fear froze him to the spot. He saw the panther leap into the air from several metres away. There was no place for the cub to run. His life hung in the balance, and he recklessly dove over the cliff. His two front paws suddenly hit a clump of vines, which he grasped tightly. The panther landed on the ground, but his two front paws went over the edge, and, unable to stop the momentum, somersaulted and plunged into the gorge. The hairless cub used the vines to pull himself back up the cliff. He was terrified. The mother wolf ran over and touched him with her pointy snout. Then she let out a howl of happiness.

She swiftly led him away, towards the Manges Desert in the west.

From then on, two ferocious wolves appeared on the dunes at the edge of the Manges Desert. It was a mother wolf with a lame leg leading a hairless young wolf who sometimes ran along on four legs and sometimes walked on two. They came and went like shadows, attacking cattle and sheep and even villagers. When hunters chased them, they disappeared without a trace, making the rough and desolate stretch of dunes even more wild and terrifying.

He grew out of breath carrying his turtle-like bag. At a glance it appeared as if he were carrying a brown boulder. The two straps of the bag went over this shoulders, and in his hand he grasped a walking stick he had picked up along the way. He walked slowly and lethargically, as if he were trudging through a swamp. As he dragged his feet across the dunes he left two tracks in the sand behind him. There was no path ahead of him, and in the light of dawn the boundless dunes seemed to unfold endlessly into the horizon. It was a labyrinth designed by the Devil. He had wandered through this maze for three days. He knew he was lost.

Three days before he had asked directions from a man looking for his camel. This man was old and had grey stubble on his face. He looked up out of one eye, glanced coldly at him, and then stared into the distance where the sun was setting. He told him to walk towards the setting sun. All the paths that way would lead him into the Manges Desert. The young man wondered if the old man missed his other eye or whether he just thought that in this world he needed only one eye. Meanwhile, the old man stared at him strangely with his one good eye and said, "My friend, what are you doing going alone into that damned desert?"

He pushed back the glasses pressing on the bridge of his nose. He did not know how to answer him. If he told him directly that he was looking for some cradle of mankind, that he was searching for the "Holy Land of Bomb", the place that had caused incessant bickering and divided the whole research institute into feuding camps, what would the old man think? Would he understand? Would he scoff at him for his craziness, for being out of his mind?

He lacked the courage to tell the truth to the old man with the one needle-like eye. He pulled out his canteen to take a drink. But the canteen was already empty. He smacked his dry lips together.

The old man shifted his "needle" and sat on the sand. He gazed lazily towards the vast and boundless Manges Desert in the west.

"Old man, is it true that on the edge of the desert there is still a small village?"

"A small village? Eh, you must mean the Jin family shack!" The old man squinted that "needle" and said laconically, "Are you going to that village?"

"That's right."

"Why the hell are you doing going to that dirt-poor place? The sand there goes right up to your crotch and those people are so poor they've all gone crazy."

He rubbed his shoulders where the straps of the backpack had made them red, and hesitated.

"I'm looking for somebody. If that place is so poor, why haven't they moved away?" he asked.

"I've wondered that myself, but those villagers are strange. They say that they have lived there for thousands of years, that their ancestors' bones are all buried there. They can't bear to leave. If you ask me, they're just waiting to die! A sandstorm, would completely bury them in half a god-damned second! Ha ha ha." The old man laughed dryly and then asked, "So who are you looking for?"

"I'm looking for an old hunter named Jingad." As he looked at the old man the youth palpitated with fear.

The old man raised his thick eyebrows.

"You're looking for him? Do you know him?"

"No." The youth feared that he would continue cross-examining him so he stood up and lifted his copper-coloured backpack.

The old man's one good eye fixed on his heavy pack. Only then did he see that what the old man was holding in his hand and using as a walking stick was actually a hunting rifle! His heart skipped a beat.

"Young man, go home! That old man is crazy. Nothing good will come out of looking for him!"

The old man's one eye again gazed out at the desert. He pulled up a blade of withered grass, stuck it into his mouth and began chewing on it.

"Old man, can you tell me how to get to that village?" he asked deferentially. He stood there, keeping his distance.

The old man ignored him for a time. He finally answered, "At the base of that high dune in front of us there is a small trail."

"Thank you." He turned and started walking towards the tall sand dune that almost resembled a snow drift.

"Come back!" the old man yelled.

"Eh?" He stopped, turned and saw the hunting rifle in the old man's hands and walked back obediently. "Old man, I don't have anything valuable in my bag. It's all books and materials, along with a few pieces of bread."

The one-eyed old man seemed not to hear him and continued to gaze indifferently off into the desert in the west. "Hey, untie your canteen and toss it over here!" he ordered.

He did as he was told.

The old man's hand left his hunting rifle and reached into his bag for something. Slowly he pulled out a leather gourd, pulled out the stopper, and poured the contents into the iron canteen. What flowed out was water. The youth was greatly moved.

The old man tossed back the canteen and said,

"The Jin family shack is still fifty or sixty *li* away along the dune path and there is no water along the way. If you die of thirst, what am I supposed to do when the god in the nether world accuses me of seeing someone dying and not trying to save them? Ha ha ha."

The young man looked sheepishly at the old man. His throat was hot and clogged. But once again the old man's one good eye drifted off towards the desert, so he did not notice that the young man was almost moved to tears.

He looked back once, and he saw the eccentric old man stretched out motionless on the sand. Several hungry crows circled in the sky. He did not know if the old man had tricked him or if he himself were just useless, but in the end he was unable to find that small path. At the base of the tall dune were all sorts of animal tracks, but he was afraid of running into a desert wolf or desert panther or some other wild animal, so he did not dare follow those footprints. So, for three whole days he walked round and round on the maze-like dune. He lost hope, thinking that he would spend the rest of his life wandering through this labyrinth. He was surrounded by endless, monochrome dunes. Sometimes the sun was in the north, sometimes in the south, sometimes it rose in the west, and sometimes it set in the east. He feared that he was going crazy. In his family genealogy there were records of ancestors who had gone insane. Were those latent genes showing themselves now?

He withered like a dry blade of grass. He sat on a tree stump, puffing like a bellows, his throat on fire. The early morning light was just spreading across the sand, and the dawn mist slowly rose to envelop him.

Sometimes it left his head exposed, sometimes it did not cover his arms or legs. The effect was to make it appear as if he had been dismembered. He stuck out his tongue and licked the traces of blood oozing from his cracked lips.

He had long ago drunk the water the one-eyed old man gave him. He had finished the bread he had carried with him. He was so hungry and thirsty that his throat was on fire and stars flashed before his eyes. Where the hell was that Jin family shack? And where was the "Holy Land of Bomb", the thing that had led him into this desperate situation?

From his backpack he pulled out a book. It was a hand-bound volume covered in green cloth. On the front in gilded characters was the name: *Jiangar*.

A bitter smile appeared on his face. He drunkenly groped at the book. His two lips quivering, trance-like he began to recite:

In that ancient, golden century,
The orphan Jiangar
Was born in the holy land of Bomb.
Jiangar's holy city of Bomb,
It was a happy heaven on earth,
The people there were eternally young,
They did not grow old, they did not die.
They treated each other like brothers,
There was no war, there was always peace...

He stumbled off the stump with a thud. In his dizziness, the stars in his eyes became a blur. He grasped a thread of clear-headedness to pick up the ancient book and with great effort stuffed it back into his backpack.

He let out a long sigh.

Suddenly, a long shadow appeared in his confused line of vision. It was hurrying along on two legs and had the shape of a person. It was rushing towards a depression in front of him. At that moment he vaguely discerned that in that depression were flashes of enchanting water.

Water! He grinned and let out a laugh. The scabs on his lips again cracked open, and drops of thick blood oozed out. His body lacked water, so his blood had thickened. He wanted to stand and walk like that person, but he did not succeed. Not in the least bit discouraged, thereupon he began to crawl towards the enchanting water. He pulled himself along like an earthworm. He recited lines from that ancient book:

In the happy land of Jiangar,
The four seasons are like spring.
There is no baking heat,
There is no bone-chilling cold.
A cool wind soughs like song,
A sweet rain sprinkles down.
Flowers are brilliant and grasses fragrant.
  ......

He seemed to have been crawling forever.

His chest gouged out a wide ditch in the sand. The call of water stimulated his desiccated blood. His four limbs and his chest had no other feeling than the desire to continue crawling. Thorns from the puncture vines growing in the sand pierced his palms and his chest, leaving a line of blood that was swallowed up by the sand. He also had a large wound on his knee. The blood was too much for the sand to cover; drops of blood fell into the wide path.

Thank God, he had finally crawled to the edge of the clear water.

Once again he saw that long figure. It was there, its head lowered as it drank water. Before he said anything, he hurriedly dropped his head to drink. But for some reason his mouth could not reach the water. He desperately reached out his hand to touch the water, but he could not touch even a drop. He crawled forward a little more, but the water retreated a step. He grasped the calf of the man next to him and pleaded, "Save me..."

"Arr!" The form let out a howl, jumped back and bared its teeth at him. Only then did he vaguely discover that the form was a strange wild animal. Its body was hairless and its penis swung back and forth between its legs. Its skin was the colour of coal, as thick as bark, and covered with callouses. It looked like elephant skin.

"Aah!" he cried out in terror as he pulled back his hand.

The strange creature bounded away with a rush, but now it had four, not two, legs on the ground. It ran like a wolf, as fast as the wind and as nimble as an ape. He closed his eyes in terror, wishing he could break free from this fearsome hallucination.

Water, water, water ... he opened his mouth and licked the sand, and in a low, halting voice recited:

Jiangar's Holy Land of Bomb,
Spring water bubbles forth,

The green grass...

He lost consciousness.

The old man walked out from the blood-red setting sun. The brown rays beat savagely upon his naked back. With his cloth robe wrapped around his waist and his powder bag, his shot bag, and his pipe pouch hanging from his belt, he looked like the chieftan of some primitive tribe.

The solitary old man continued to walk with the sun behind him. The crooked path of his footsteps remained on the sand. He turned and gazed back at the sun, already half-swallowed by the desert. He narrowed his good eye as if he were taking aim at something. Damn, only the setting sun in the desert would be the thick red colour of blood. He bent his head and laughed. The still desert, like an enormous, somnolent beast, its boundless, vast monotone, along with the sinister, hideous tranquillity produced by its dull colour all foretold that here belonged to hell, that here was part of the world of the dead. He was not completely sure which world he had walked out of. In fact, he had walked no more than ten *li* into the desert.

Those god-damned markings from the blowing tumbleweed!

Perhaps the hungry ghosts in the sand dunes were playing tricks on him. Otherwise, how would the tumbleweed roll against the wind? Strange. What were all those markings? What kind of mystery did they hide?

He discovered these strange tracks at the base of a crooked tree. A clump of dried tumbleweed had scuffed over the original markings in the sand as the wind rolled them into the desert. After he examined them closely, he decided that the prints resembled both wolf tracks and human footprints. They also did not seem to resemble anything at all. What was bizarre was that the tumbleweed had rolled into the desert against the wind. Strange. He followed them for ten *li* and then did not dare to go any further. He did not have enough water or rations. Going further into the desert was just looking for death. He forced himself to go back.

He arrived again at the base of the crooked tree.

The tracks of tumbleweed started again on a small strip of naked sand. The clump of tumbleweed seemed to have fallen from the sky. Except for some scattered bushes of Chinese mugwort and desert wormwood, there was no tumbleweed or anything else growing. There were not even dried and dead plants from years past. He looked all around and saw only the vast desert. It was the work of a ghost, it had to be. There were certainly enough hungry ghosts out here in the desert. Wanting to take a rest, he climbed up onto a bank off to the side that had some plants growing on it. But when he reached it he was greatly startled. With his good eye he stared intensely at the mugwort and desert wormwood growing on the bank. The plants had been bent down. His hunter's keen perception told him that some kind of animal had passed through here. He focussed his senses and followed the path of the bent branches. He walked a few steps, stopped to examine the traces, then walked some more, all the while searching and trying to determine what kind of creature it was. He wanted to find the tracks in the sand so he could determine their source. But the creature must have been purposely trying to frustrate him. It moved stealthily on the dune, never leaving the bushes, and not once did it set foot into the open sand.

He searched patiently. He bent over and poked through the grass as beads of sweat formed on his copper-coloured back and then rolled down it. He used the hunting rifle as a walking stick. In fact, he had already been searching like this for seven or eight years. He had left his tracks on every mound and sand dune in the surrounding one hundred square *li* of desert. He had examined just about every blade of grass, every tree, and every footprint left by man or beast. Of course, no one knew what he was looking for. Some said he was seeking a gold mine in the desert, some that he was looking for a kind of magical plant, and some said that he was just crazy.

The bizarre tracks meandered along the slope. They headed up and off to the left and then circled back around. The old man discovered that there was a depression at the bottom of the slope. No grass grew here, but there were also no tracks. Only the strange traces of the rolling tumbleweed appeared. The old man silently told himself that things were strange, then he followed the tracks of the tumbleweed into the depression.

Thereupon he discovered the unconscious young man.

The old man was not at all surprised; he seemed to have anticipated this long before. But his brow wrinkled and his good eye flashed when he saw the tremendous suffering the young man had endured. His mouth was full of sand, his hands had left furrows where they had clutched at the sand, but his face had a strange, seemingly satisfied expression. What a peculiar young man! He had had that feeling when he saw him for the first time three days before. He remembered back to his youth, when on the public road he had seen the faithful men and women going to the Xiaokulun Temple to worship. They were dressed in rags. As they walked they placed a brick in front of them, knelt down and knocked their heads on the brick, and as they stretched their bodies forward, they pushed their bricks to the front. They stood again, walked forward to the brick, and then knelt again. That was how they travelled, with a kneel and a kowtow, using their bodies to measure the long public road. They came from border areas and poor, remote villages to gather in front of the dusty temple in Xiaokulun. They listened to a living Buddha read from the sutra, spun their well-oiled prayer wheels, and then placed the money they had earned with their blood and sweat in a gilded cabinet in front of a gold Buddha. He did not understand these faithful men and women, but he clearly remembered these worshippers' tortured way of walking. They looked just like earthworms, first stretching their torsos and then pulling their legs along behind as they simultaneously extended their upper bodies again. Wherever the living Buddha was to read from the sutra, the public road, the animal tracks on the side of the public road, in fact all of the trails leading to the Xiaokulun Temple were overflowing with these standing and kneeling "earthworms".

The old man looked the youth up and down. It was almost as if he were watching one of the "earthworms". The young man's body was lying stretched out in the dry, soft sand. His two hands had dug furrows as they clutched at the sand, his backpack looked like a rock pressing him down. He looked exactly like a large turtle in front of the temple carrying a stone tablet as punishment for his sins.

"Ha ha ha." Again the dry laugh emanated from the old man's throat. "This is what you get for trying to find that old fox Jingad!" The old man's one good eye shot out a cold gaze.

He lifted the young man into a sitting position, pulled out the leather gourd and poured water into the young man's throat. The young man swallowed the sand in his mouth along with the water. Water, the essence of all life. It worked just like the Devil's magic as it brought the young man back to consciousness.

"Eh, old man, is it you?" The young man's vision was blurred.

"It looks as if fate is between us." The old man tossed him a piece of flat bread. "Eat this, it's a bit better than the sand."

The young man fixed his gaze on the depression in front of him. There was absolutely no water there, there was no enchanting reflection of light off the water. It was only an empty stretch of dry, cracked, light brown sand. Bewildered, he mumbled, "I saw a ghost. There was clearly water here, but I couldn't reach it. How did it just disappear like that?"

The young man walked two steps, and then, puzzled, stared at the sand in front of him. He did not believe that what he had just seen was a mirage. And then there was that strange animal. He had touched its calf, had felt its skin, thick as bark, and he had felt its cool body temperature and its twitching animal strength. He clearly remembered its savage snarl. Was it all not real, was it a mirage just as he lost consciousness? No, no.

He shook his head in bewilderment. Grains of sand flew from his hair.

The old man saw his queer expression and said, "I wasn't lying to you. There really is a path to the Jin family shack at the bottom of that dune."

"Bullshit! There are only tracks at the bottom of that dune!" the young man said indignantly.

"Ha ha ha..." The old man started laughing and then suddenly stopped. His good eye stared at him dagged-like. "Stupid fellow, those animal tracks are the path you were looking for!"

"Ah, that..."

"The trails on the dunes aren't separated for people or animals. Everybody travels along the same path, they just avoid running into each other. Trouble starts when they run into each other."

"Give me a little more water!" He pleaded. "Old man, thank you for saving my life."

The old man passed him the water gourd and asked, "What's your name?"

"Ahm."

"Where are you from?"

"The provincial capital. I'm in the literature department of the Academy of Social Sciences."

"Why did you come into the desert instead of staying back at your warm-water* department in the provincial capital?"

---

*This is a pun on the word "wenxue" meaning "literature" and "wenshui" meaning "warm water".

"Old man, if I told you you would not understand. I came to look for something— "

"Look for something?"

"No, it's not really a thing, it's an ancient, sacred place called the Holy Land of Bomb. It was a Utopia. I want to find the ruins. According to analyses of relevant historical materials, those ruins lie somewhere in the Manges Desert, buried under the sand." Ahm stuttered as he explained. The old man kept his good eye fixed on him.

Ahm gave a simplified explanation of that Utopia that was the "cradle of mankind" — the Holy Land of Bomb.

In ancient times, a hero named Jiangar appeared in the north. When he was three years old, he "leapt on the steed Ahlanzhaer and breached the three great fortresses and conquered the evil Manges demons". When he was four years old he "breached the four great fortresses and made the yellow demon Dulijiefan mend his evil ways". When he was five years old he "captured alive the five demons of the sea of Ta". When he was six he "defeated the six great countries in the east and his name spread far and near". From this he constructed his beautiful and richly endowed Holy Land of Bomb. The people there never aged, the four seasons were like spring, there were no disasters, there were no wars, and it was eternally happy and peaceful.

"Ha ha ha! My silly friend, you are talking about Heaven! You should go to Heaven to look for this place. This is the desert. There is no green grass, there are no birds and flowers, there are no damnable places with bubbling springs." The old man chuckled loudly.

"Some of the scholars in our department also believe that this place never existed. They say it is an imaginary place produced by the difficult lives of the members of the working class. I do not believe that." Ahm raised his voice and began to earnestly argue his case. "I have investigated and verified many relevant historical materials, and the area of the Holy Land of Bomb lies within the Manges Desert. I want to find its ruins, prove its existence, and remind people of the wonderful world of that 'cradle of mankind'. I must find that lost world, that lost 'cradle of mankind' ... "

Ahm grew silent.

The old man stared at him for a long time. He did not know if he were mulling over his words or his actual person. After a while he said coldly, "If I were you, I would first solve my drinking and eating problems and make sure that I wouldn't be buried here. Only then would I start talking about other things. You bookworms!"

Ahm laughed in embarrassment.

"What is that?" the old man asked, discovering footprints on the right bank and walked over to examine them. "What kind of feet made those? What thing walked through here?"

Ahm said, "I saw it. It looked like a wolf, but it had no hair on its body and it could walk on two legs. No, it was some kind of strange creature. It ran incredibly fast on four legs ... I'm really not sure what it was." He told the old man what he had seen just as he was losing consciousness.

Suddenly the old man's expression changed. His good eye flashed. He did not say a word but grabbed his hunting rifle, his countenance serious and tense. He started to follow the part-wolf-like, part-man-like footprints. He had not gone far when those footprints merged with the traces of the tumbleweed and disappeared.

Eh, so what those traces of tumbleweed were covering were the tracks of some strange creature!

The old man looked off into the vast and mysterious desert in the west. In the silence his good eye became cold and fierce.

Ahm was about to ask something, but the old man angrily ordered him, "Shut your mouth! Don't ask anything, just come with me!"

Ahm discovered that they were walking along the narrow path at the base of the dune. It was heading towards the mysterious Jin family shack.

2

In the scorching light of dusk the two of them stumbled exhausted into the village.

"Kaboom!"

The roar of thunder rolled across the desert sky. A jagged, snake-like flash of lightning rent the sky asunder, and raindrops the size of coins poured forth, crashing onto the desert floor and sending up puffs of white smoke. The thundering, desiccated desert was satisfied, assuaged, like a well-behaved child peacefully lying down, as it sucked up the sweet liquid dropped from the sky. Its most pleasant time was approaching.

Under the cover of darkness and the torrential downpour, an old wolf stole across the desert. Carrying a cub in her mouth, she struggled step by step to approach the dark black mass in front of her. It was very difficult for the old wolf to carry the unconscious, hairless cub. The rain had soaked her fur, and she had tucked her tail tightly between her two back legs. Although one leg was lame, she still appeared strong and healthy. The hairless cub was strange and pathetic. Its chest and back were covered with wounds. It looked as if it had been attacked by the sharp talons and beak of some bird of prey. Its blood mixed with the rain and dripped to the ground. Its hairless body was soaked through by the rain, making it look slippery and naked. As the old wolf dragged it along in her mouth its body left a furrow in the sand.

They had taken advantage of the darkness to steal vulture chicks, but they were discovered and attacked by the female vulture. The hairless cub had neither sharp teeth nor hard claws, his body had no thick fur to protect him, so after a vicious assault by the vulture's talons and beak he was wounded all over and had passed out. The old wolf was unscathed, and she waited for her chance to charge the vulture, but she did not dare to engage in a full-scale battle. She was afraid of attracting the attention of the whole flock of vultures. She picked up the wounded cub in her mouth and hurriedly retreated from the battlefield.

A bolt of lightning flashed across the sky, the deep blue light illuminating sky and earth and the upright mass ahead. It was the ruined walls of an ancient city, covered by the desert and then exposed by the wind. The mother wolf stole between the ruined ramparts and stopped at the base of a weather-beaten, crumbling earthen wall. There was a black opening at the bottom of this wall. The old wolf looked around vigilantly, her green eyes flashing alertly and fiercely in the pitch-black night. She listened for a moment, and only then did she turn around and crawl backwards into the hole, the cub still in her mouth. Her eyes disappeared into the darkness of the hole.

This was their lair.

Deep in the desert, and within the ancient ruins, she had dug this lair, far from mankind or the desert plain where other animals roamed. It was the cunning and skilled mother wolf's masterpiece. Not only was it far from man, more importantly it was in a place where even the vulture, the king of the desert, dared not tread. Apart from the deathly stillness of the desert and the ruins, there was nothing else to keep them company. After she had fought with the panther and lost two cubs and the use of one leg, she resolutely led her one fortunate, remaining pup — the hairless one — into these ancient ruins in the heart of the desert. It was safe and warm there. The ruins of that magnificent civilisation served as a natural screen, and they were the earliest discoverers and occupiers of the site. Of course, when they needed to search for food it was somewhat distant because so deep in the desert there were no small animals for them to prey on. However, the cunning and clever old mother wolf found a way to overcome this problem. In summer and autumn, after the grass had grown tall and the wild animals had grown fat, she went out of the desert to hunt. She carried back with her hares, pheasants, field mice, and even fat pigs and sheep from surrounding farms and buried them in the sand near her lair. The desert sand was most effective at preserving meat. It was a wonderful "refrigerator".

The old mother wolf carried the hairless cub as she stepped back into the recesses of the hole. The further in she went, the wider it became. After she had walked for about twenty metres she reached the end. At this point it was almost as large as a room. The old mother wolf seemed to have tunnelled into one of the rooms of the ruined city. There was a thick layer of straw on the ground. It was extremely comfortable.

The mother wolf placed the hairless cub on the hay and pushed against him with her pointy snout. But the cub remained motionless. The mother wolf let out several mournful howls. Blood still flowed from the wound on the cub's chest, and the mother wolf licked at it with her long rough tongue. She also licked the wounds on his back. She kept at it until the bleeding stopped. But the cub was still unconscious, his body curled into a ball and trembling incessantly.

The old mother wolf stood up, arched her neck and let out a long howl. Her sharp and sorrowful cry resounded like frozen metal scraping against the walls of the cave and carried out of her lair and echoed throughout the ruins of the ancient city and the surrounding desert. Everything in range of that frightful howl was stilled and cowed.

The shocking cry startled the hairless cub. He trembled more and then eventually pulled back from the black edge of death. He opened his eyes slightly. What looked like two tears flowed from the filth around his eyes. The old mother wolf licked them away. The hairless cub struggled to reach out and stroke the mother wolf, but he could not. He just let out two weak cries and then slipped back into unconsciousness.

The old mother wolf was extremely agitated. With her red tongue hanging out, she ran back and forth inside the lair and circled the cub. She let out a long series of terrible howls. However, her calls were unable to rouse the hairless cub from its death-like coma.

The old mother wolf sniffed at the cub's hot mouth, let out another anxious cry, and then rushed towards the opening of her lair. She bounded out into the open and flew like a black arrow towards the boundless east.

The desert remained still through the torrential rain. The torrents were like infinite whips lashing at the naked body of the exposed desert. This enormous beast appeared to have been broken. Occasionally a blue streak of lightning flashed across the sky, illuminating the serene ferocity of the desert and making one suddenly aware of its horrible outline. The peak-like drifting sand, the precipitous dunes, places with names like Sleeping Tiger Dune, Coiling Snake Mound, were quietly filling themselves with the rain and waiting for the wind to return and carry off sand, covering the sky and blocking the sun as it blew towards the green world in the east. That was its eternal duty, and it remained eternally unfulfilled.

The sky brightened. The black sky first cracked in the east, and the fissure gradually expanded. The thick curtain of rain eventually shattered. Finally, a light, fresh wind blew up and pushed them away. The sky was suddenly clear and clean.

Just then, the old mother wolf, taking advantage of the darkness before dawn, rushed home from the east. Her mouth was tightly shut, she moved as if she had wings, and her thick and long tail dragged along behind her. It acted as a broom, sweeping over her footprints as she ran along. The traces that remained looked just as if a clump of tumbleweed had rolled across the sand. The old mother wolf relied on this clever scheme to cover her tracks, evade her numerous pursuers, and fool the eyes of the hunters. At the same time she wanted to guarantee the secrecy of her lair in the ancient city and ensure that she and her cub could live in peace.

As usual the old mother wolf backed into her lair. She rushed urgently over to the cub, nuzzled him, and then opened her mouth and smeared a sticky, black, viscous liquid on the life-threatening wound on his chest. It was a mixture of some kind of black liquid and partially chewed grass stems. She watched him for a while and then sniffed at him. After a rest she once again sped out of the lair and headed off towards the east.

When she returned at dusk she carried in her mouth a hare and a pheasant. Just as she entered the lair the hairless cub rolled over and let out a weak cry.

There were thirty or forty households in the village.

Mud houses were scattered at the base of the dunes. Around some of the houses the owners had dug a trench, making their version of a courtyard; some had planted a screen of trees. Some had nothing around them but bare sand and one or two wooden hitching posts stuck in the ground. There were several naked children playing in the sand on the edge of the village road. They looked like dirty monkeys, their thin little bodies burned by the sun to the colour of black, dried fish. Their faces, torsos and little penises were coated in sand. One of the children, probably eleven or twelve, also naked, pulled strongly at the thing between his legs and peed on one of the dirty monkeys playing in the sand. The hot urine dribbled down the youngster's darkened neck, but not only was he not angry he actually found it funny, as if what was flowing were not urine but sugar-water or milk.

At that moment a woman of about thirty appeared at the side of the dripping child and pulled him away. She angrily scolded the bigger child, "Ergou, you are always bullying this poor creature. If your mother and father were dead and someone peed on your neck, would you find it so funny?" As she was scolding him she took her scarf and wiped the urine off the little boy. She muttered to herself: "If little Maomao were still alive, he'd be just as useless, always being pushed around…"

The one-eyed old man yelled forcefully to the young woman, "Aim, come home and make dinner. Stop worrying about other people's kids!"

"Pa, you're back! I already made the food a while ago." The young woman released the child and walked over to the one-eyed old man.

"We have an extra person. This young man is a guest from the city." The old man introduced Ahm to the woman.

"From the city?" Aim seemed seized with terror and she grew silent. She lowered her head as if some sorrow in her heart had been stirred.

Ahm was taken aback when he saw the woman's reaction. Her expression went blank and seemed to drift off to some distant place. Her dark face was pallid and sallow. Ahm intuitively sensed that this was the face of someone whose heart had been dealt a terrible blow.

"Old man, I'm sorry, but would you first take me to see old Jingad!" Ahm said,

"Who? Old ... Jin?" Aim looked at Ahm in surprise. "You haven't asked the name of the 'old man' who led you here?"

"What? Old man, you?..." Only then did Ahm realise.

"Ha ha ha..." the old man laughed coarsely and heartily. "I'm Jingad, that forsaken, old 'one-eyed ghost! Ha ha ha."

Ahm chuckled awkwardly. "Old man, you can really draw things out. You let me wander around vainly for three days on that dune and almost die."

"I gave you water, just enough for three days, so that you wouldn't die of thirst. Let's go, we can chat in my house." The old man invited Ahm in.

A three-room earthen house was stuck crookedly at the base of a dune in the northwestern corner of the village. The west and east rooms belonged to father and daughter, respectively, and the middle room was the kitchen and the corridor. There were two dilapidated rooms attached to the east side, and a yard was surrounded by a wattle fence. The old man put Ahm in his own room on the west side. After he washed his face Aim brought in the food. There was a plate of corn-flour pancakes, a small pot of soup, and several pieces of salted vegetables. The soup really was soup: a few leeks and a pinch of salt had been added to the clear water. Ahm had worked on a production team, so the big, hard pancakes did not scare him. He drank some of the clear soup and wolfed down two and a half pancakes. While he was eating Aim stood off to the side, staring at him. She seemed to again be thinking of whatever was weighing on her heart.

After they finished the old man told Ahm to rest a while. Without allowing him to respond, he strode out of the room to take care of something.

Ahm had a strange feeling. Since he had walked into this three-room earthen house, he was vaguely aware of some strange atmosphere pervading the house. For the time being he could not work out the reason, but it was just like the atmosphere you felt if by chance you walked into an ancient temple on a mountainside. Did it come from the woman's dazed expression and her silent apathy? Or did this dark, cold atmosphere spring from that one-eyed old man's uncouth and disagreeable laugh? Yes, it was a dark, cold atmosphere. Something cold and dark was concealed within these three rooms. Did it have something to do with the grieved, wounded Aim? What was it? Did she have a husband or children? From the happiness she showed being around children, he could see that either she had now or had once had a child.

On several occasions Ahm wanted to ask, but each time he stopped himself. Aim seemed aware of his curiosity and so avoided having to talk with him.

Suspicious, he left the house and walked out to the village road. This was really a desert village that the world had forgotten. The village was exceptionally quiet as if the deathly stillness of the desert in the west had spread there. He could not even hear chickens squawking or dogs barking. By the crumbling earth wall on the side of the road, a woman was grinding corn with a roller. A baby was strapped on her back.

This baby was also exceptionally well-behaved. The child was not making a sound. The only noise came from the heavy millstone as it rolled over the white corn kernels. A tall man was just returning from ploughing in the dunes. On his shoulders he carried a curved, wooden plough, so heavy that it bent his tall, thin body into a bow shape. The ox he was leading also looked as if it were suffering greatly. Its ribs protruded and it swayed as it walked.

The only road linking the village with the world was quickly swallowed up by the desert grass growing on both sides, making it seem as if neither man nor machine had ever travelled down it. What proved that the village was alive and had some links with the outside world was a single telephone line. The telegraph poles stretched in a crooked line across the tops of the dunes. Some had been blown down by the wind and were now lying there with the telephone line, parts of which had been buried under the drifting sand and were rusting. He did not know if this phone line actually connected with the outside world. The blood-red sun had partially disappeared in the west. Its once searing rays now painted the village in the dark red glow of its passing. As the village dissolved into twilight, it seemed more lifeless and empty than ever. He could not help but feel that he was seeing an illusion: it was only a picture of lifeless brown paint that a painter had casually spread on a canvas, it was not actually a living village.

Ahm silently admired the stubbornness of these villagers. They were willing to be lonely and to live in a difficult place totally isolated from the world. Their fates were in the hands of the heavens, the sands and the winds. The inhabitants here had completely lost touch with the desires of other men.

Ahm discovered a verdant patch of land on the northern edge of the village. He went over to examine it and was startled by what he saw. It was a cemetery, a relatively large one, with close to a thousand earthen mounds pressed close together. Each tomb was well-maintained, with fresh earth added and paper money placed on top. Trees and green grass grew around it. It was quite full of life. Ahm sighed as he thought to himself that the village itself was like a tomb, while the graveyard seemed like a lively town. Everything here was unbelievably distorted and reversed. He did not want to look anymore. It was too oppressive.

By the time he had walked back to old Jingad's home, the lamps inside were already burning. The old man had not returned. Aim was probably in her room. From his bag he pulled out the ancient book *Jiangar*. For a long time he had worked to translate this book into modern Chinese. This was a long and difficult task. Legend had it that several years before a professor had undertaken this job, but when he reached a certain chapter he had been suddenly seized by an impulse to search for the ruins of the Holy Land of Bomb. He packed up the book and set out, but he never returned. At the time it made the news and was considered no less noteworthy than the disappearance of Peng Jimu, a scientist who disappeared into thin air during a survey trip in the desert. Ever since then Ahm had been enthralled by *Jiangar*. What was strange was that when he reached that chapter he too was struck by a sudden desire to search for the ruins. There seemed to be some magic symbols hidden in that chapter. As soon as he read them he felt compelled to search out the ruins and examine them for himself. He did not know if, like that professor, he too would disappear without a trace, but something out there was calling to him. He wanted to make no mistake and solve the mystery. He needed to search courageously for the city.

He opened the book and read carefully.

Aim carried in a basin of hot water for him to wash his feet. He was very thankful but also quite puzzled. How did she know that people in the city had the habit of washing their feet? The people of the dunes did not even wash their faces every day, let alone wash their feet and shower. Only when rainwater accumulated into pools would they jump in and wash.

She stared at him blankly for a while and then suddenly said, "You really look like him."

"Look like whom?"

"At that time, some people from the city came here, and then afterwards they all left," she said.

"Oh, I understand. Some 'educated youths' came to the village, and there was one who looked a lot like me, right?" Ahm felt he was nearing the source of her wound.

"Uh-uhh," she admitted as she lowered her head.

"Who was he?"

"He ... was my man."

"The two of you were married?"

"No."

Ahm was puzzled. He looked questioningly at the wooden-faced Aim.

"Why not?"

"My dad caught the two of us together and grabbed his gun and chased him. He ran off to the city and never returned."

"Oh, so the old man is a little short-tempered."

"No, no. Later, he grabbed his gun again and went to the city to look for him and make him come back and marry me. But he had lost an arm in an accident at his factory. When he saw my dad he wept and knelt down and pleaded with him, saying that there was no way he could provide for a wife and a son..."

"You had a child?"

"It was quite a coincidence then, a fat little boy, ai, he only lived two years..." Her eyes reddened, and she pulled at her jacket.

He looked blankly at the unfortunate woman who had just told him all the troubles in her heart. He did not know what to say. There were no words to console such an unfortunate and sorrowful person.

Just then Jingad returned home. When he saw his daughter's mournful expression, he rebuked her, "Are you telling the guest that same old story? Aren't you sick of talking about it?"

Aim quietly rubbed her eyes and then carried the basin out of the room. Ahm was not fast enough to stop her. He felt extremely awkward and uncomfortable.

"Don't pay any attention to her idle talk. It's past history. She's a little unbalanced." The old man then asked Ahm, "So young man, what crazy thing really made you come all this way to look for me?"

"Well sir, there is something the younger generation respectfully requests of you," Ahm said quite reverently.

The old man silently chewed on his pipe. He waited for Ahm to continue.

Ahm summoned up his courage and went on. "A friend of mine in the provincial archaeological brigade told me about you. You were his guide when he came to excavate a tomb deep in the desert. He said that only you could go that far into the desert and not get lost. Please help me. Lead me into the desert to look for the Holy Land of Bomb that I told you about!"

The old man still remained silent. His one good eye was lightly closed, almost as if he were sleeping. He savagely tapped the bowl of his long-stemmed pipe and then said quietly, "I am old and of no use anymore. Look for someone else! Or else rest for a couple of days and then go back. Don't sit around and go looking for things that don't exist. Believing that nonsense will drive you crazy."

Ahm was startled. He was about to implore him again, but the old man waved his hand. "Don't say anything. There's nothing to discuss. Go to bed!"

The old man said nothing else. He sat on the edge of the *kang* and rubbed his two bare feet together to wipe off the dried mud and ox manure. Then he slid backwards on to the *kang*, lay down, pulled up an old cotton blanket over his stomach, and very quickly began to snore with the rhythmic sound of a buzzsaw.

Ahm could only lie down and sleep, too. He was very disappointed. He could not understand the old man, and in his bewilderment he eventually drifted off to sleep. After sleeping for how long he did not know, Ahm was jerked out of the struggles of a nightmare by the sound of the old man yelling and screaming out the window, "Aim! Are you out of your mind?

What're you doing walking in the yard in the dead of night? Aren't you afraid that a wolf will carry you off? Go back to your room and go to sleep!''

Through the unpapered window lattice, Ahm could see that Aim was standing in the yard looking up at the heavens. Her wraith-like body was bathed in silver moonlight. She was trembling, as if she were unable to stand the weight of the moonbeams.

She turned slowly and stared at her father. Under the moonlight, her gaze appeared dim and distant, as if waves of uncontrollable emotion were surging through it. Sorrow? Hate? He saw her gaze and said nothing more. He just coughed drily and sighed.

Aim walked slowly back to her room. As she walked she hummed a plaintive, ancient song. The sound drifted faintly through the tranquil night, increasing the feeling of desolation.

Endlessly flowing, endlessly flowing,
The waters of the old Black River,
Endlessly pouring, endlessly pouring,
The tears of my two eyes.

Jingad's one good eye blinked.

The sky was not yet completely light. A shaft of light reached in through the square window. This was already enough. Even if the old man shut his eye tightly, his sensitive eyeball could still catch the stealthy light of dawn through his eyelid.

He inclined his head and looked at the far end of the *kang*. In the darkness, he could hear the young man breathing. The old man rose slightly, slipped off the *kang*, and stole out of the room. Two camels, one with brown humps, one with white humps, were lying at the base of the hitching post in the southeast corner of the yard. The old man walked over and patted their necks. He pulled out a lump of salt from a hemp bag and put it in a wicker basket by the side of the camels' mouths. They perked up and eagerly opened their mouths and extended their tongues to lick the salt. As they were eating they occasionally looked gratefully at their kind master. He massaged the necks of the beasts and chuckled, "All right, all right, don't look at the old man like that. From today on you'll be working your tails off. Feeding you a little salt is nothing. Here, have a little more!"

The old man put the saddle between the two humps. He carried out two plastic barrels from a room and filled them with water. Each could hold almost a hundred kilograms of water. He packed some stores, bowls and pots, and other necessities onto the back of the camel. Clearly, all these things had been prepared well in advance and then placed in the storeroom. Aim came out silently and helped the old man arrange everything. The two of them went about their work silently. From the storeroom he brought out the hunting rifle and a knife and cleaned them.

"Aim, go to my room and bring me the wine jar. Don't wake up the man." The old man packed the gunpowder and shot.

Aim looked at her father and then went in. In the west room the man from the city was still sleeping soundly. She hesitated for a moment, and then decided to go over to him.

"Wake up..." she said softly as she looked out of the window.

The man from the city did not stir.

"Wake up!" She pushed his shoulder gently.

Ahm awoke with a start. "What?" He raised his head and saw a pair of dejected eyes.

"Don't make a sound. Don't you want to go into the desert and look for something? Look!" She motioned with her mouth towards the window.

Ahm raised his head further and through the hazy heat saw the kneeling camels, all packed and waiting for Jingad to set off. His jaw dropped stupefied. He rubbed his blurry eyes. Where had those camels come from? They were obviously loaded for a long journey. Was he going into the desert? He did not have any time to think. He leapt out of bed and hurriedly dressed.

"Don't tell him I told you. Go out in a moment," she urged him softly.

"Thank you, you're really nice. Thank you."

"You don't need to thank me. I'm worried about the old man going into the desert alone ... but he doesn't let me say it." Aim pulled a large wine jug from the cabinet and walked softly out of the room.

He really should thank her. Otherwise he would have been an orphan abandoned in the desert. The ghost of the omnipotent Jiangar was everywhere. He hurriedly collected his belongings and, like a student, slid his backpack onto his back. He appeared at the door, but he did not immediately go out.

Old Jingad took the wine jug from his daughter's hands and put it into the basket on the camel's back. Everything was set. The two looked silently at each other for a moment. But in the split second that their eyes met it was implied that this was their final parting.

The old man's expression remained severe. He did not look again at his daughter's face. He mounted the white-humped camel.

"Whoa, rise!" he ordered the animal.

The white-humped camel first stood up on its forelegs and then on its hindlegs. The old man rocked as the camel rose. The brown-humped camel, attached by a rope to the saddle on the white-humped one, understood and rose with it. The old man urged the camel towards the southeast. He did not look back. Aim did not look either as her father set off on his expedition. The two seemed to be in some kind of tacit agreement. She lowered her head and walked back towards the doorway. She pulled down a hoe that was hanging under the eaves and headed off towards the fields. The whole time she kept her head lowered and looked at the ground. She also covered her mouth, as if she were trying to suppress the strong waves of emotion that were surging through her heart.

The narrow path skirted the southeast edge of a dune and then headed straight into the western desert. Old Jingad sat crookedly on the camel's stable back, his eye focussed ahead. When he turned past the dune he suddenly saw Ahm standing ahead, waving his hands.

The old man pulled in the reins and looked silently at him with his one good eye.

"Old man, don't go off alone like this. Ha, ha, ha. Take me with you, won't you?" Ahm looked up and smiled imploringly.

The old man still did not say a word. His one good eye again stared at him with its needle-like gaze.

"Sir, won't you get bored all alone? Another

person means another pair of eyes and another pair of hands. Please, sir, show a little mercy and take me with you." Ahm said with a smile as he tried desperately to escape the cold stare emanating from the one good eye.

"Where are you headed?" the old man finally asked.

"I'm going into the desert, just like you. Sir, I know that you are also looking for something."

"I'm taking a different route from you. I'm looking for something other than what you're looking for."

"Who cares, we're both looking for something. Perhaps we can search together? Strange things can happen in this world."

"Don't jabber with me! Get away from me!" the old man ordered.

"No, no, sir, I won't be any burden to you. Please, I'm begging you," Ahm said, now quite agitated.

"Pain in the ass!" The old man jerked the reins.

The white-humped camel obeyed its master's command and started to walk slowly as if there were no one in front. The camel's hooves left gigantic, round impressions in the soft sand. Its outstretched neck was about to knock over Ahm, who was still standing in front of the beast.

Ahm jumped to one side.

The white-humped camel quickened its pace as it passed him. Ahm was dumbstruck for a moment, and then he ran ahead and tried to stand in front of the camel.

"Sir, listen. I'll lead the camel. I'll cook. I won't cause you any trouble. I'll be as good as a cat!"

The old man ignored him, his one good eye searching the great desert ahead. He pressed the camel to move faster. Ahm walked backward in front of the camel and pleaded with him. In the end there was nothing he could do so he moved to the side and let them pass.

The camel gradually moved further and further away. Ahm stamped his feet, ground his teeth and followed along behind the camels. But he was unable to catch up. He resolved to keep up his pursuit. He wanted to see where that stubborn old man, that one-eyed ghost was going. He said to himself, even if he goes to the ends of the earth I'll follow him. He yelled, "Sir, wait for me!" and quickened his steps. He walked at a good pace, not too fast and not too slow, so as to avoid expending all his energy at the beginning. He must not collapse from exhaustion when he reached the old man's first camp site. After he had gone four or five *li*, the camels had already long disappeared from sight. He was alone in the vast desert, but he did not lose heart. He dauntlessly and resolutely followed the clear tracks in the sand.

He climbed up a sand bridge. Suddenly he saw the two camels in a depression at its base. The old man was sprawled across the back of one and looked as if he were asleep. His eyes flashed, and a smile spread across his sweaty and grimy face. He slid down the slope on his rear end.

"You bastard! You are really a pain in the ass!" the old man said from the back of the camel.

"Sir, you really know how to make a person run around!"

"Climb aboard!" The old man extended a hand to

him.

His vice-like hand grasped Ahm's and pulled him onto the camel as if he were lifting a bundle of straw. Ahm sat behind the old man.

"If you are going to accompany me, you have to listen to me. First, you are not allowed to ask me my business. What I am looking for has nothing to do with you. Second, you are not allowed to mention that holy city. I'm not at all interested. Third, you're not allowed to go wandering off on your own. If you do and something happens, I'm not responsible."

"Fine, I'd agree to a hundred conditions!" Ahm answered happily from behind.

They climbed the dune ahead of them. Old Jingad scanned the surrounding desert. He narrowed his one good eye and meticulously examined the floating dunes around them. He spotted something and then jerked the reins to proceed.

"Sir, tell me a story, otherwise all this rocking back and forth is going to put me to sleep."

The old man hesitated for a moment, and then said, "That's not a bad idea. An old story would help to break the monotony."

"Once upon a time there was a village in the desert. The villagers lived off meagre harvests from crops planted in the dunes. Their lives were very difficult. One spring those evil beasts, wolves, started causing trouble. They killed several oxen, leaving the village in uproar. The villagers chose six well-known and experienced hunters to hunt down and kill the wolves. They hunted for about a month and in the end they had killed all of the pack except for one mother wolf. This mother wolf hid in a distant cave and gave birth to cubs. There was a brash young man in the hunting party and, not satisfied that the evil mother wolf had escaped, wanted to hunt it down and kill it. The old man who was leading the hunting party thought it was all right to leave one wolf. It was too cruel to wipe out the whole pack. He tried to dissuade the young man. Who would have thought that in the middle of the night the young man would ride out alone on his horse. He returned the next day at noon with five wolf cubs skewered on an iron stake. There is no need to say how satisfied he was with himself. When he found the mother wolf's lair, she was out searching for food. The little bastard took advantage of the mother wolf's absence to slaughter the cubs, but then he grew scared that she would return. He knew that a mother wolf that has lost her cubs is the most vicious beast. The little bastard stirred up a nest of trouble and then slunk home. From then on the village faced disaster.

"Every night the mother wolf approached the village and howled mournfully, so sorrowful it was terrifying. And each time she came the village lost another animal, no matter how diligently folks kept watch. She was an extremely cunning and vicious wolf. She just ripped out the innards of the animals, but did not eat any of them. The villagers tried their best but could not find a way to get rid of the wolf. This torment went on for almost two months. The whole village was exhausted and on tenterhooks. The old head of the hunting party had a two-year-old grandson whom he treasured. One day, the child's mother returned from fetching water to find that her child who had been playing indoors was nowhere to be seen. None of the neighbours had seen him. It was as if the child had sprouted wings and flown off. He had disappeared so suddenly. The old hunter looked everywhere but could find no trace of him. He looked for two years but still found nothing. The mother cried herself almost to death, and the old hunter was on the verge of madness. One day the old man grabbed his gun and walked into the dunes. He had a mysterious premonition that he was going to search for the mother wolf. Ever since the disappearance of his grandson, the wolf had not been seen. He had a strange idea, but he did not mention it to anybody. About a hundred *li* away in a clump of bushes on a dune, he finally discovered the mother wolf, He crept up close and from very near pulled the trigger. There was the thud of an explosion, but the powder had blown up in the bore, and from then on the old man was blind in one eye. And from then on neither hide nor hair of that mother wolf was seen…"

The old man grew silent. His dark, tawny face was dignified and imposing.

Ahm felt his heart beating rapidly. That pair of despairing eyes, that shadow wandering under the moon, that gravely wounded face, that one good eye, all these images floated before his eyes.

"The story you told me is very sad. I'm sure that sooner or later the old hunter will find his grandson," Ahm said.

The old man's thick eyebrows twitched, but he did not respond.

They proceeded silently to a dune the shape of a half-moon. The old man ordered the camel to stop and then slid off its back. Ahead there was the stump of a willow tree. He walked over to examine it. There were some faint tracks that looked as if they had been made by blowing tumbleweed. But they also looked as if they could have been made by a broom. It was hard to know which without careful examination. The old man's eye followed the track as it stretched to the west. After a moment he muttered something and then climbed back onto the camel.

They followed the trail of the rolling tumbleweed. Ahm was puzzled but he did not dare to ask. He cocked his head and looked forward. What were the tracks? Could they be…?

The tracks stretched on with no beginning and no end, like a magic rope trying to bind the enormous beast of the desert. Ahm thought it was the track of some living creature. It occasionally disappeared, probably erased by the wind, but then it would reappear in the distance, straight and unbending as it stretched into the horizon. Apart from this one track, the surrounding desert bore no trace of any other living creature. Everything was the same colour, the same texture, dry, dull and endless. The sky was grey and hazy. Everything here was dead; nothing breathed. In this enormous, boundless, yellow world, humans were too insignificant and weak. They were like pathetic strains of algae. Ahm could not help but wonder if the Holy Land of Bomb had really been swallowed up by the "evil ghosts" of the Manges Desert. When he was three years old Jiangar had conquered the seventy-two evil ghosts of the Manges Desert and then built his holy city, but had it in the end been smothered by this evil yellow demon? He was perplexed.

They set up camp.

The next day they continued following the tracks. Old Jingad was worried that he had packed only enough water and stores for one person, so they now travelled both during the day and night. They napped on the back of the camel. Luckily, the desert moon illuminated the sands.

At dawn on the fifth day, the mysterious tracks led them into a bizarre place. Ahm was amazed to discover that this was the ruins of an ancient city! On a stretch of smooth and stable sand, the ruins of city walls were scattered over a large area. Only the brown foundations remained of the crumbling and weather-beaten old walls. There were half-buried, tottering stone sculptures of rams, camels and legendary beasts. Dried bones and shards of tiles and pottery were scattered everywhere. Ahm was overjoyed. A surge of wild happiness swept through him. He wanted to scream but he was sharply restrained by Old Jingad. The tracks that they had been following had disappeared in this hardened sand.

The old man silently slid off the camel and handed the reins to Ahm, who dismounted after him. Then he pulled out his gun and loaded it. A cold glare shot out from his good eye. Ahm grew tense. The old man motioned for him to lead the camels along behind. His gun at the ready, he walked stealthily in front and acted as guide. He crossed to the east of the disappearing tracks, curled around to the south and then walked in face of the wind into the ruins. The old man's expression was severe, but unfathomable anxiety and deep hatred were visible through his cool exterior.

No sound came from the dark ruins ahead. There

were no birds circling overhead, no dust swirling, no wind blowing. There was nothing alive in this place. They entered the mysterious ruins. The old man chose a concealed spot that was protected on three sides by crumbling walls and ordered the camels to lie down. He pulled out a knife and handed it to Ahm to use to protect himself. Then the two walked out of the enclosure and quietly worked their way north. The old man's one eye alertly scanned every structure, every piece of ground and every wall. They searched as they moved forward. They had walked about a hundred metres when suddenly the old man grabbed Ahm and pulled him to the ground behind a mound. Ahm was trembling with fright. He did not dare breathe. He raised his eyes and looked ahead. He did not see anything. He only felt the gloomy, oppressive silence that enveloped this place. It seemed to conceal some terrifying will to kill. The old man's one good eye was staring at some spot ahead. Ahm finally saw what he was watching. Thirty or forty metres away, at the base of a mud wall, there was the dark opening of a hole.

"That hole is..." Ahm asked in a whisper.

"A wolf's lair!"

Old Jingad hatefully spat out those two words. His teeth were clenched tightly together, and there was a fire in his eyes.

3

The two lay there motionless, pressed against the wall like geckos. The sun in the southeast beat down on their backs.

Inside, the lair was pitch-black. There were only two green points of light flashing in the deepest recess of the cave.

The hairless cub struggled to raise his head. He painfully raised his two front legs and then, shakily, straightened his rear legs. Finally he stood up. He tried to take steps, but his body trembled and his two front paws collapsed with a "plump!" He was still very weak.

The two points of fire extinguished. The hairless cub closed his eyes. His breathing was laboured.

The old mother wolf had been gone for two days searching for food. The hairless cub was anxiously awaiting her return. She should have been back long ago. What had happened? His stomach was rumbling with hunger. The hairless cub restlessly turned his neck, and in the darkness his two green eyes flashed again. He rested for a while. When he had regained enough strength, he again struggled to stand. He could not just wait to starve to death. He had to move. His legs trembled as he started to lift his body. At the same time, he pushed his blunt nose against the ground and licked his dried, meaty smelling blood from the sand. He snorted and then let out a mournful wail.

There were some chicken feathers with bits of skin attached. He gulped them down ravenously. He continued to crawl shakily as he looked for food. Now that his stomach had something in it, he had a little strength. He slowly crawled towards the opening. The lair was stuffy and gloomy. He desperately wanted to walk out into the vast desert, to feel the sunlight on his body, and, most importantly, to go hunting for food.

Rays from the scorching noonday sun slanted into the lair. The entrance was dazzlingly bright. The strong light forced the hairless cub to squeeze his eyes shut and lean unsteadily against the wall for a moment. As he gradually adjusted, he opened his eyes and began to sniff around. He sniffed at the fresh prints the mother wolf had made when she left the lair. He squinted his eyes and looked out into the splendidly bright desert. He silently put half his head out of the entrance and listened alertly for any noises in the surrounding desert. The ruins of the ancient city were silent. The desert itself was like a gigantic, slumbering beast. There was no wind, no rain, no sounds of any animals. There was only the blistering sun. The whole place felt like the inside of a steam cooker.

The hairless cub grew brave and walked right out of the cave. Ah, the sun was so comfortable, the air was so fresh. The field of vision was so wide! He happily let out two howls of freedom. This was his announcement to the ancient ruins and to the endless desert that he had returned to life! He had beaten death. He had endured the pain from the vulture attack and was alive again. He could again follow his mother out on her forays. This broad desert would forever belong to them. By right of the fierce battles they had fought, they were the only masters of this place.

The hairless cub stood at the entrance of the cave. The warm sun was soothing to his body. Occasionally a whiff of moisture from the world outside the desert floated by through the air. He lifted his head back and tried to capture the moisture and pull it into his lungs. He stuck out his red tongue and licked his mouth. His stomach once again began to rumble. The radiant sun and the fresh air had stimulated his appetite. He lowered his head and began searching the sides of the entrance of the cave. He picked a bone, bleached white by the sun. He chewed on it a little, but it had no flavour so he tossed it aside. He sniffed at a pottery shard. It has a meaty smell to it, so he picked it up and licked it but then quickly dropped it. At the base of a wall was a colony of black ants. They were wriggling in a dense, tight black mass. This was their group army. The hairless cub squatted off to the side and watched their singular battle formation. He bent down and sniffed at them, and they had a strange smell. He extended his tongue to try a few, and they tasted all right. Thereupon he licked the whole army clean. And then he licked the anthill. Very quickly he had licked away any traces of the ants or their home.

His tongue made a clicking sucking sound as he lazily cleaned his mouth. A group army was now in his stomach, but it had not reduced his hunger. Once again he began to sniff around searching for food. He killed a bug with one swipe of his paw and swallowed it. A golden beetle flew past his mouth. He lunged at it, snapped open his mouth, and in a split second the sounds of the beetle's body and wings crunching in his sharp teeth emerged from his mouth.

He savoured its flavour as he chewed.

It seemed that he remembered or felt something in the back of his mind and suddenly stopped chewing and gazed attentively off to the east. He looked confused and puzzled, as if dimly recollecting something. In that instant, what ideas were passing through his simple mind? Was he remembering the distant traces of his birth? Was he thinking about his travails as he followed the mother wolf around? Or was he thinking about the enchanting green plains in the east? His chapped, narrow face looked sad and disappointed.

He raised his head and suddenly let off a long howl towards the east. It was a sorrowful, miserable, haunting sound. His voice trembled slightly. It sounded like the wails of a baby. Two tears rolled down his coarse, narrow, hairless face...

The rifle began to tremble in Jingad's hands.

He rubbed his eye with the back of his hand and stared intently at the strange beast. It was like a wolf but it wasn't, it was like a monkey but it wasn't. It did not have hair covering its body, nor did it have a tail. Its front limbs resembled legs and hands. They could grab, swipe and run. My god, what kind of creature was this? Couldn't possibly be?... The idea that had long ago lingered in his head once again flashed through his mind. His chest tightened, and drops of sweat appeared on his forehead.

"That's it! Old man, that's the creature I ran into on the dunes. Ah, no, it's a wolf!" Ahm said in a low voice.

The old man trembled violently. His mouth twisted to one side, and he clenched his teeth audibly. He silently lowered his head. He did not want to look any longer at that strange creature. With his trembling hands he quietly pulled back the gun.

"Old man, what are you doing putting away the gun? Aren't you going to shoot it?" Ahm asked anxiously.

"If you don't shut your god-damned mouth, I'll feed you to that wolf!" The old man rushed over and grabbed Ahm's throat and shook him violently and crazily, growling like an angry lion.

"Old man, let me go! Please, let me go...." Ahm's face had turned white and his pupils bulged. He was like a struggling, cackling chicken caught in the grip of a pair of vice-like hands.

The old man tossed him to the ground as if he were a bundle of hay. He knelt on the ground, his breathing coming in gasps, his hands covering his face. He groaned like a wounded animal. After a while he opened his good eye. He calmed down and fell silent. Ahm looked at him in terror and moved several metres away. He was afraid that the old man would again charge at him and strangle him. He did not even dare breathe deeply. His body was still shaking.

After a time the old man stood up.

"Go back to the camels!" the old man ordered him feebly.

Ahm followed fearfully. They crouched down and silently wound their way back to the dark, secluded niche where the camels were kneeling peacefully as they ruminated the food in their stomachs. Their peaceful characters were in harmony with the desert. Perhaps the ancient tranquillity of the desert had forged their dispositions. Perhaps it had even created the camels themselves.

The old man began to work furiously.

He pulled the basket off the back of the brown-humped camel. From the basket he removed the jug of wine, which so far he had not touched. The jug was crudely made and had a wide round bottom. It was sealed tightly by a soft, leather rag jammed into its mouth. The old man used a knife to cut the string binding the stopper and pulled out the leather cover. At once a strange and pungent fragrance emerged from the jug. Very soon the whole niche was enveloped in this thick, strange, liquor smell. Ahm was startled. What kind of smell was this? It smelled like liquor, but it was thicker and more enticing. It smelled as if it contained some strange Chinese medicinal herbs. It was slightly pungent. It was the combination of the medicinal herb smell and the thick alcohol smell that made it so heavy, allowing it to permeate the surrounding air and not disperse. The more he inhaled the more Ahm wanted to go on inhaling. As soon as the smell was absorbed into the lungs, it flowed through one's whole body, making one feel incredibly comfortable and relaxed. Gradually you would want to yell and dance, then it would make you complacent, then your limbs would go slightly numb, and your head would slowly begin to feel comfortably dizzy, and then in your enjoyment you would finally lose all strength, wishing only to drift off into sleep.

"Cover your nose! You fool, don't smell it!" the old man yelled at Ahm.

"Old man, that ... that ... " Ahm stubbornly asked another question.

"It's drunken weed, Chinese Ephedra, and dried apricot root ... concocted to make a poisonous brew! Do you want to sleep for several days and several nights?"

Only then was Ahm scared, and he hurriedly averted his head, covering his nose, and retreated several paces. He looked in fear at the devil's jug in the old man's hand. It was poisonous liquor, but why didn't the old man seem to care? He looked carefully, and he saw that the old man had stuck something hard and black into his mouth. He did not know what it was, but it must have been something that counteracted the effects of the liquor.

Gradually Ahm realised what the old man was planning to do.

He saw the old man grab an iron hook and use it to pull out two chickens from inside the jar. He used his knife to chop up the chickens, now soaked through with the liquor. He wrapped the pieces of chicken in cloth and then buried the jug in the sand. The old man took the bundle of chicken, and tossing another bundle to Ahm, told him, "Follow me!"

Ahm felt at the bag. There seemed to be a rope of some kind inside. Without saying a word, he followed the crazy old man out of the enclosure.

They returned stealthily to the spot behind the wall from where they had observed the wolf's lair. That strange creature had gone, perhaps back into the lair. The old man stood up, scanned the area around the opening and the surrounding desert, and then again examined the sounds from the ruined city. He was worried lest some other animal or wolf would suddenly appear.

"Wait for me here. Lie down, and don't give yourself away." The old man leapt over the mud wall and ran over to the dark hole with the agility of a man half his age. His feet were nimble and silent, and in the blink of an eye he was beside the hole. He listened for sounds from within the lair, and then pulled out a piece of the chicken which he quietly tossed into the entrance. Then he retreated, dropping pieces of chicken behind him as he went. He walked about one hundred metres and then stopped at the base of a ruined wall. He dropped the rest of the chicken here. He signalled to Ahm to come over. Then the two concealed themselves near the wall.

They waited anxiously. Ahm was so nervous he could hear his heart thumping.

In a short time, the strange creature bounded out of the lair and started gulping down the fragrant slices of chicken. His eyes were wide with greed as he continued to search along the ground for the chicken pieces, sniffing this way and that as he followed the old man's trail. He walked a few paces, stopped, and then moved along. When he discovered the last pile of meat, he leapt on it with a "whoosh" and ate it without even raising his head. His hard sharp teeth crunched the bones which he swallowed along with the meat. In the blink of an eye the chicken had settled in his stomach. Suddenly, he became weak, his body began to tremble all over, his head dropped, his eyes closed slightly, and he collapsed motionless to the ground like an old drunk.

The old man leapt up and rushed over. Ahm followed closely behind.

While they were running over the old man grabbed the bundle from Ahm's hands. He quickly pulled out the thin hemp rope and the iron wire. They ran over to the side of the creature, which by then had totally lost consciousness. Without another word, the old man bound him tightly with the rope. After he regained consciousness, the creature would have a very difficult time breaking free, regardless of how much savage strength he possessed. The old man stuffed a handkerchief into the creature's mouth. Only at this point did Ahm carefully examine the thing that they had captured. His body was more than a metre long. He was hairless, stark naked. His thick, bark-like skin was covered with scabs and scars. In some places a kind of bright, oily substance had congealed on his skin. His arms were long, his mouth was slightly convex, and, although the rest of his body was hairless, his face did have some very fine hairs on it. His black, shoulder-length hair was dirty and dishevelled. He looked like some species of monkey. Ahm's gaze dropped to a spot between his legs, and he was startled. What dangled there was the penis of a man.

Thereupon Ahm cried out, "It's a human! It's a man!"

"You're right! It is a human. It was once a man." The old man said quietly.

"Who is it? What kind of person is it?" Ahm looked at the old man and asked.

"He is my grandson!" The old man's face was twisted in agony. He reached and lightly caressed the coarse skin. A tear glistened in his eye.

"Uh? This is a wolf-child? And he is your grandson!" Ahm cried out in amazement. He thought of the story that the old man had told while they were riding on the back of the camel. Evidently the old man's lost grandson had been carried off by the mother wolf and had turned into a wolf-child. Filled with apprehension and a strange feeling, Ahm bent down to look at the wolf-child. He seemed to be seeing the "origin of mankind" for which he was searching.

"Come on and help me. We need to get him out of here quickly!" the old man said. The two of them picked up the wolf-child and hurriedly returned to the camels. The old man pulled out a large hemp bag from inside the basket and used it to cover the wolf child. Then he stuffed him into the basket and secured it tightly to the back of the brown-humped camel.

"Old man, are we going to leave now?" Ahm asked.

"Uh-huh."

"Let me examine these ruins!" Ahm requested. His desire was very strong now that he had seen the mysterious ruins for which he had so arduously searched.

"There is no time. The water and food are almost gone, and if the mother wolf returns there will be trouble," the old man said coldly and firmly.

"Old man..." Ahm still wanted to plead.

"There will be another chance, but now it's absolutely impossible. Move!" The old man speedily packed up his things and climbed onto the white-humped camel. He yelled again at Ahm, who was staring enthralled at the ruins, "Are you waiting to die? Get on the camel!"

Ahm sighed, silently picked up a shard of pottery, examined it carefully, and then said with infinite sadness, "Ah, the holy land has become a wolves' nest, and there is no trace of humans ... goodbye, Bomb!"

The sound of a dog barking echoed through the night.

It was the bark of a lazy dog awoken from his dreams. He let out a couple of groggy yelps and then drifted back to sleep. Silence returned to the small village. The darkness added an even thicker and heavier cover to the normally tranquil village and it seemed to conceal in here everything that lived and died in the world.

There was some movement at the mouth of the village. There were the heavy slow sounds of hooves tramping through the sand as they returned from a long journey. This was the sound of camels' hooves. The brown-humped camel snorted nervously. His short tail flicked back and forth continuously. He was carrying some strange creature, half-man, half-beast, and was agitated by its wild, animal smell. But the sleeping village remained silent. Its inhabitants were totally unaware of the returning travellers.

Jingad had deliberately chosen to return in the dead of night.

There was no moonlight, no starlight; there were no lamps burning in people's houses. Darkness covered everything and made them invisible. The old man was leading the camels. He wound his way from the western edge of the village to the northwestern part. He arrived at his own door and made the camels lie down.

Aim's room was dark and silent. The old man pulled out a key and groped in the dark until he opened the door to the storeroom. He lit the small lantern in a niche in the wall. There were two rooms, and they were filled with odds and ends. In one corner stood a singular object: a large, iron cage. It was made of thick, iron wire, and was big enough to hold a person either standing or lying down. It also had a door. The old man went over and opened the door to the cage. Ahm and the old man carried in the wolf-child, pulled off the hemp bag, and lifted him into the cage. Then they bolted the door.

The wolf-child lay paralysed on the floor of the

cage. He was still tightly bound, and he had not recovered from the effects of the liquor. He had no strength to resist. Only his cold, dark eyes flashed as they looked apprehensively around the room. His gaze suddenly fixed on the lantern. The dancing flame terrified him. He wanted to cry out, but the towel was still stuffed into his mouth. He could only turn his body and shrink into a ball in a corner of the cage.

Old man Jingad looked silently at the wolf-child as he squatted and smoked.

"Old man, you had this cage ready for a long time. Did you know that your grandson was still alive?" Ahm asked quietly.

"No, I made the cage for the mother wolf."

"What? Do you mean that you had no idea that your grandson was still alive?"

"It's strange, but I had several dreams in which a little wolf cub kept biting me. I believe in dreams. If a nursing mother wolf has no cubs, she will carry off children and nurse them. I always believed that my little grandson had been carried off by that mother wolf, but I did not think he would still be alive today. I made this cage for the mother wolf. Who would have thought...? We must have sinned greatly for my family to be subject to such a fate. We have produced a wolf-child!"

The old man's expression was sorrowful. Ahm felt deep sympathy for this family in their misfortune. The two were silent for a time. In fact, a pair of eyes had been watching them ever since they had entered the yard. The eyes belonged to Aim. She had tossed and turned in her sleep and was plagued by nightmares. As soon as the heavy hooves trampled the sand by their gate she awoke. But she did not have the courage to run outside immediately. In the darkness she saw them carry something into the storeroom and could no longer restrain herself. She leapt off her *kang* and rushed out.

A dim shaft of light escaped through the narrow crack in the door. She pressed her eye against the crack and looked inside. Then she quietly opened the door and walked in, her eyes fixed on the iron cage. Suddenly, she cried "Ahhh" and tried to rush over. But Jingad grabbed her arm and held her back.

"Child, don't be anxious, your father has something he wants to say to you."

Aim twisted her body as she tried to break free of her father's grasp.

"You're right, child, this is our Gouwa. He has grown up. He grew up on wolf's milk. He's a little wild. We have to take things slowly. He will get better, but don't be hasty…"

"Let me go! Let me go!" Aim cried as she struggled. "My son, little Gouwa, my son…"

"Child, listen to me. Right now Gouwa is a wolf-child."

"Let me go! I blame you for everything! You drove off the child's father, you led the wolf hunt. You are the one who turned little Gouwa into a wolf-child. I hate you! Let me go!" Aim screamed crazily.

The old man fell backwards, either because of her hate-filled words or some crazed rush of strength.

Aim raced over and pressed against the cage. She stared with wide eyes at the wolf-child curled in the corner. She was trembling slightly. That dirty, shoulder-length hair, those thick, leg-like arms, that coarse-skinned, strong, naked body, those cold, wild eyes... Could this be the Gouwa for whom she had pined for seven years? Could this be the child she had carried for nine months and for whom she had endured shame and insults? In the wake of these thoughts, a warm surge of maternal love rushed through her body and asserted control. She tore back the bolt, yanked open the door, ran into the cage and threw herself on the wolf-child. At the same time she uttered a heart-rending cry, "My son!... My son!..." Tears poured forth and dropped onto the wolf-child's cold, hard skin. She removed her jacket and placed it over the wolf-child. Then she pulled out the towel that had been jammed in his mouth.

The wolf-child was startled. His nostrils flared and he let a deep growl, "Grrr, grrr." A frigid gaze shot from those cold and unintelligent eyes. As soon as Aim removed the towel from his mouth, he growled fiercely and bit her wrist.

Aim let the wolf-child bite her. Although his sharp teeth tore deeply into her flesh and dark red blood poured out, she still did not pull back her hand or cry out. She actually extended her other hand and gently caressed his head and neck. She said soothingly, "Child, go ahead and bite, it makes your mother's heart feel a little better..." Broken-hearted, she began to cry.

She gently rubbed her hot face against the wolf-child's head.

A stream of clear spring water. A breath of warm spring wind. It was the call of a mother's boundless sacred love, lost soul, return!

The two rows of dagger-like teeth gradually loosened their grip and eventually released the soft and tender wrist. Perhaps, her motherly caresses as she rubbed her face against his head reminded him of the prodding of the mother wolf's sharp snout. Perhaps this maternal appeal aroused some distant and dormant humanity within him. This was how the miracle occurred. He raised his half-man, half-breast face, his wild gaze became puzzled, his nostrils flared, and he stuck out his tongue and licked away the salty tears from his lips. His unlifted, unintelligent, blank, angular face resembled a question mark: Who am I? Where am I from? Who are you? Why are you caressing me with your face? Are you another mother wolf who rubs her face against me to express her love? And why is that salty water flowing from your eyes? Since the salty water started to drip from his own eyes, he had sucked up every drop and obtained a kind of pleasure. His anxious, unsettled heart was consoled, and from somewhere he had the urge to lick away the blood oozing from the wound on Aim's wrist.

Aim gently hugged his coarse neck. Her face caressed his dry hair.

Jingad and Ahm watched this scene and were stunned. When Aim ran into the cage their hearts were in their mouths. And as soon as she pulled the towel out of his mouth, they expected the wolf-child to leap on her and rip out her throat. The old man had stood at the door of the cage, ready to rush in in case anything happened. But he was unable to believe the events that unfolded before his eyes. How could a wolf-child who had been suckled on wolf's milk since the age of two and had grown up in a pack of savage, bloodthirsty wolves suddenly become so docile. This was a good omen. He prayed to God. Perhaps his grandson would really recover his humanity and return to the world of men. His heart suddenly grew warm and he forgot the pain caused by his daughter's anger. His seven years of arduous searching as he tried to repent for his sins had finally borne fruit. God had opened his eyes and taken pity on this lonely, guilty old man. He stood up and handed his daughter a piece of cooked meat. He said, "Little Gouwa needs to eat something. Feed him this!"

Aim looked at her father and silently took the piece of meat and placed it by the side of the wolf-child's mouth. He sniffed at it and was immediately aroused by the meaty smell. He snatched at it and began chewing.

When he saw that, Jingad called softly to his daughter, "Aim, come on out now. Little Gouwa has had a few hard days tied up on the back of the camel. He's tired and needs to rest."

"No, I'll sleep with him in here."

"Child, don't be foolish. It could cause trouble. If he goes wild and escapes, we'll never catch him again."

Aim said nothing. She was afraid of losing her son again. She looked at her son as he chewed ravenously on the piece of meat. She patted him lovingly and then walked out of the cage.

That night, the father and daughter laid out some straw by the side of the cage and slept there. Ahm obeyed the old man and went inside to sleep. It was his most comfortable, peaceful night in more than ten days.

At dawn the next morning, Ahm returned to the

storeroom as soon as he awoke. He bumped into the old man as he was returning from putting the camels out to pasture. He noticed that the old man was carefully carrying a wooden bowl in his hands. The bowl was filled with clear water. Ahm was puzzled and asked, "Old man, what kind of water is that that it is so precious?"

"Holy water. Half is dew from the top of the grass, and half is today's first bowl of well water. That is why it is so precious."

"What's it for?"

"To summon back little Gouwa's soul."

"Summon back his soul?" Ahm was puzzled by this. He followed the old man into the storeroom.

The wolf-child was sleeping soundly, lying in a corner of the cage like a dog. His legs were curled up under his body and his arms were stretched out in front of him. His head rested on his arms. Although he was sleeping soundly, his eyes were not completely closed. He seemed to be furtively watching, and the gaze that escaped through his half-shut eyelids was cold and bone-chilling. Aim was sitting very properly by the door of the cage. A strange and bitter odour permeated the room. Wisps of white smoke floated in the air. Ahm saw that the smoke was rising from an iron bowl placed in front of the cage door. The bowl was filled with chaff. Two sticks of incense were stuck in it. The chaff also smouldered slowly. There were no flames, just threads of smoke slowly rising and filling the room.

The old man passed the wooden bowl of water to

Aim and from the side picked up another wooden bowl that was covered by a layer of yellow window paper. He had Aim place a few drops of the "holy water" into the concavity in the centre of the yellow window paper. Then the old man began to slowly turn the wooden bowl in his hands. As he turned it he walked around the cage. At the same time he sang in a low voice the "soul summoning song". The melody was lingering and sorrowful:

Lost soul
Come home,
Aah hah heh yi, aah hah heh yi.
From the endless desert,
From the shadowy forest.
Come home, come home
You masterless soul!

There are ghosts above
And goblins below;
Return with haste to the world of love
Helpless and lonely soul!
If a python restrains you,
I'll cut him in two;
If dragons block you,
I'll banish them too;
Your mother is calling to you,
Your father is calling to you.
Come home, soul of our son!
Come home, soul of our son!
Aah hah heh yi, aah hah heh yi...

The old man sang solemnly and plaintively. He continued turning the bowl in his hand and walking around the cage. Each time he finished a revolution he stopped by Aim and asked gravely, "Has Gouwa's soul returned?"

Aim then answered, "It has returned!"

After he had circled the cage three times, he turned the wooden bowl more slowly. The drops of "holy water" on the yellow window paper gradually collected in the depression in the middle and formed one large, resplendent drop. This sparkling pearl of water was the "soul" being summoned home. If such a large and crystal clear drop of water did not form, then that meant that the soul was still floating in the other world. The summoner had to continue to sing and turn the bowl at the same time. This was an ancient custom that everyone in these parts believed in. According to legend, it only worked if you had faith. Ahm stood off to the side and almost cried as he listened to the mournful song. He felt as if something were tugging at his heart.

Old Jingad kept his gaze fixed on that pearl of water. He was so moved that tears welled up in his once good eye. Aim clasped her hands over her heart and bit her lower lip. She was trying hard to keep her composure and avoid ruining the solemn ceremony. But pearl-like streams of tears had already soaked her shirt. Ahm was also affected and tears fell from his eyes as well. He sincerely prayed that this drop of water was indeed Gouwa's soul and that it would return as quickly as possible and put an end to the sufferings of the old man and his daughter.

The old man grabbed a pinch of ask from the smouldering chaff and sprinkled it on top of the wooden bowl. Then he dropped the pearl of water on the wolf-child's lips.

Three times they summoned the soul in this way. The mournful tune resounded through the small room. The slow, sorrowful melody was really soul-stirring. It was a song suffused with human feeling, and one that had resonated through man's heart since time immemorial. Ahm believed that this ancient song could conquer wayward souls. If a lost soul still did not listen to the summons of this song, then that soul did not belong to a human being.

It might have been the effect of the soul summoning ceremony, or it might have been the lingering effects of the poisonous liquor, but whatever it was, the wolf-child was very quiet for the first two days following the ceremony. At the urgings of Aim, and in light of Gouwa's good behaviour, Jingad untied the wolf-child. But the wolf-child seemed to have been waiting for just such an opportunity. He leapt forward towards the open door. Fortunately, he was still chained by the leg. He collapsed with a "thud" outside the cage door.

Jingad was shocked for a moment, but he recovered his wits and rushed over and grabbed the wolf-child from behind. The wolf-child agilely turned his body and swiped viciously at the old man's face. The wolf-child's sharp nails ripped through his clothes and tore into his flesh, leaving several long, bloody scratches. The old man, gasping for breath, jumped out of the way. The wolf-child leapt back and forth in the cage, baring his fangs and growling ferociously. His ugly, animal-like face had turned savage and terrifying. He would have torn the throat of anyone who dared to get near him.

Aim's face had turned white.

"My son, calm down! Listen to me, don't be this way..." she said as she slowly approached him. She was still trying to use her maternal love and gentleness to appeal to him.

"Grrr!" he growled viciously as she walked towards him. Ahm pulled her back at the last moment, just as the two rows of sharp teeth were about to clamp down on her throat. Aim was terrified as she watched her son transform into a wild beast. In her sorrow she bit through her lip and trembled uncontrollably.

With a "crack", the old man pulled out a whip from behind him and snapped it in the air.

"Crack", the leather whip came down on the wolf-child's back. He squealed in pain.

"Get back in your cage!" The old man yelled as he pointed towards the cage. The black leather whip whistled above as it danced through the air like a snake.

"Don't whip him! Don't whip him!" Aim rushed over and grabbed her father wanting to wrest the whip from his grip.

Jingad pushed her away.

"If I don't use the whip, we can't control him, and he'll be a wild animal forever!"

The old man yelled angrily and snapped the whip above the wolf-child's head. The wolf-child stared in terror at the whip and retreated step-by-step. Just as the whip was about to strike again, he leapt panic-stricken back into the cage. The old man took two steps forward, closed the cage door, slid the bolt into place, and then put on the lock.

Imprisoned in the cage, the wolf-child paced back and forth and howled. He was really a caged beast now. With his sharp teeth he gnawed at the iron chain attached to his leg. He squatted on his back legs and angrily tore off the clothes on his body. Aim had spent ages trying to put them on him. In an instant, the floor of the cage was covered with shreds of cotton.

The blood had drained from Aim's face. The old man motioned to Ahm to help her leave the room.

As Ahm went to support her, her thin, weak body was already trembling uncontrollably. Her gentle maternal love had been crushed, and the blow was too great for her to bear. She was overcome with despair. Tears poured from her eyes, and she began to sway back and forth. Ahm tried softly to console her, "Aim, don't be too impatient. Right now he is still half-beast and half-human, and the beast half is still stronger. Don't give up hope, it'll take time."

Aim's head drooped. She went back to her room to rest.

Jingad silently examined everything, and then he too left the storeroom. After everyone had left, the wolf-child howled for a while longer and then gradually calmed down. Eventually he lay down in a corner of the cage.

Ahm accepted the old man's invitation to continue staying with them. He kept thinking about the ancient ruins that he had not had enough time to investigate. He did not want to leave right away. Also, he had been deeply moved by the misfortune of this family, and it had spurred him to consider from another perspective the meaning of life. He was vaguely aware of some deeper significance contained in the saga of this wolf-child. Apart from the surface struggle between man and beast, there was also a deeper meaning. Somehow, the "Holy Land" and the "cradle of mankind" that he had been searching for seemed to be inherently connected with this affair. He did not yet understand, but he considered the outcome of the affair to be of the utmost importance to him.

Jingad asked Ahm not to talk about the wolf-child with any of the other villagers. The old man felt quite ashamed, and he was worried that if word got out people would be drawn to the spectacle, and that would only cause more trouble. Ahm naturally agreed. He dived back into his ancient book, and he also helped Aim and the old man deal with the wolf-child. Aim had let it be known that she hoped Ahm would pay the wolf-child a lot of attention. Of course he understood what she meant. A small child needs a mother's love, but he also needs a father's love. That was especially true of this very special wolf-child. Ahm saw those deep and wounded eyes and was very moved by her faith in him. At the same time, he thought of the child's real father, now less an arm and back in the city. What was he doing these days? Bored and frustrated, he had looked for some momentary pleasure, which had produced this bitter fruit. He probably had no idea that the seed he had sown had sprouted into such a frightening creature. He should feel grateful to the mother wolf. He did not have to teach the child the rules of the world, the mother wolf had done it for him. Her rules? To bite. The world belonged to them, to those evil forces that attacked people with their teeth.

Seven days passed, and the wolf-child calmed down considerably. He had more or less accustomed himself to life in the cage. Maybe he thought that the cage was no worse than that ancient hole in the desert. Here, food was both plentiful and guaranteed. He no longer suffered from hunger. He began to live by the rules of people, except when he was led out to urinate. He would run over to a tree or wall, lift up his leg at an angle and then spurt out a stream of urine. Seeing this, the old man could only pull out his thing and demonstrate the method a civilised male used to relieve himself — one hand on the organ, one hand holding up the trousers by the belt, and a solid arc of pee directed in front of the body. When he did use the proper form, he squeezed his organ so tightly that he wanted to cry out in pain. The old man also demonstrated other forms of etiquette, like how to hold a bowl and use chopsticks, how to dress, how to walk on two legs. He tried to show him the proper way to use his arms and hands. After a month he had made great progress. After another month, he had begun to learn to speak. When he saw something round he said "egg-egg", and when he saw a chicken he said "chicken-chicken" but then he immediately took off after it, his eyes savage and fierce. If his grandfather were just a little tardy in catching him, he would have already caught one, bitten its head off, and stuffed it into his mouth, feathers and all.

He was closest to his mother, Aim. He let her scratch him, comb his hair, wash his face and feed him. He became her constant shadow. By now, they had already removed the chain attached to his leg. His disposition became more and more gentle, but he was still quite naughty. He would put his pants over his head and yell and scream, or he would grab his mother's ponytail and rub it over his now bald head. Once, when his grandfather was not looking, he grabbed the wine jug and took a big gulp. It was so harsh that he rolled around the ground clutching his mouth. Aim and the old man laughed so hard tears rolled down their cheeks. He was generally limited to the space of the storeroom, although occasionally they would take him outside to walk around. However, at those times he was always chained to the old man.

Aim had also returned to life. Her eyes sparkled, her face became ruddy and youthful. The weight and depression of the last few years had been swept away, and she was again filled with enthusiasm and excitement about life. A song was never far from her lips, nor did a smile ever leave her face. She had become a completely new person. She gave her body and soul to her son, hoping desperately that one day he would once again be a normal person.

Hypothetically, if things had continued progressing in this manner, and if what happened later had not happened, it is quite possible that the wolf-child could have recovered his humanity and returned to the world of men. Both Ahm and Aim did not seem to be aware of what was going to happen. But Old Jingad had never relaxed his vigilance. His dagger-like eye was always looking, watching for her to appear. In fact, somewhere in the back of his mind the old man had a sense of foreboding that a shadow was constantly following him. This vague sense kept him constantly on guard. Every night he grabbed his gun and patrolled the yard. Every dawn he went out to the outskirts of the village and examined the surrounding dunes. He knew that this sense of foreboding came from the mother wolf. But doubt continually tugged at his heart: where was that cunning old wolf? Where was she hiding when they caught Gouwa? Why had she not yet appeared? She should have come ... had she been killed by a hunter? Had she been attacked by a panther or a wild pig? He never became complacent. He waited with his good eye peeled.

And come she did; like a ghost.

It was one bright dawn. A wild animal stole along the base of a dune at the western edge of the village. The animal was extremely stealthy. There was a clump of tumbleweed on her head, and her whole body was pulled in under the plant. She silently approached two sleeping camels. Seen from a distance, it appeared that a clump of tumbleweed was slowly moving across the sand. There was a fresh scar on the back of her neck. The fur had not yet grown back. Part of her bushy tail was also gone. She looked fiercer than ever, this old mother wolf. A hunter had chopped off part of her tail, a brown bear had swiped a chunk of flesh out of her neck, but she had survived. She was the immortal embodiment of the wolf family.

The two camels lay there quite peacefully, their breakfast of grass ruminating in their stomachs. The time after breakfast was their most comfortable time of the day. They were completely unaware of the wolf. When they discovered her, the wolf shook her neck and wagged her tail like a family dog. They believed that she really was just a dog, so they paid her no more attention. They slightly closed their watery eyes and continued to chew over their breakfast. At this moment the old mother wolf really did not have any evil intent. She walked back and forth, sniffing here and there, stopping occasionally to listen, then lifting her snout to the sky breathing deeply. Finally, she fixed her gaze on the nearby village.

She camouflaged herself in tumbleweed once again and crawled silently towards the hamlet. When she reached a stand of trees at the western mouth of the village, the brave wolf tossed off the tumbleweed, dashed onto a small dune and let out a long, blood-curdling howl which seemed to carry across the whole expanse of the desert. But in an instant a rifle shot erupted from a clump of bushes in front of her where a hunter was concealed who had waited a long time for her arrival. The bullet whizzed past her head. Cunning though she was, she had not anticipated that a hunter would be lying in wait for her. Scared out of her wits, she tucked in her tail, lowered her head, and ran off in a blur towards the western desert. From behind her, there was no second rifle shot.

When the mother wolf howled, the wolf-child was inside playing with Ahm. As soon as he heard the distant sound, his body grew rigid and motionless. He listened attentively for a second call. But the familiar howl did not repeat itself. Instead came the shocking sound of a rifle blast. He was dazed. Ahm, sensing something was amiss, immediately began to play with the child. He tried to recapture the wolf-child's attention, but was unable to distract him. Only after Aim had fed him his breakfast did he return to normal.

Dusk on the second day.

From a clump of trees on the western edge of the village, the mother wolf once again filled the desert air with her frightful howl. By the time Jingad got close enough to shoot she had howled again. The wolf-child was in the yard, sitting in Aim's lap looking at the stars in the sky. As soon as he heard the first howl, his whole body began to tremble. When he heard the second, he became agitated, his eyes flared strangely, and he struggled desperately to free himself from Aim's embrace. Scared, Aim hugged him tighter and ran back inside. Ahm hurriedly closed the door and bolted it. Fortunately the old mother wolf did not howl a third time. With Aim's soothing words and Ahm's caresses, the wolf-child gradually calmed down and the howls seemed to fade from his mind. But every so often he glanced at the door, his eyes filled with both anticipation and fear.

The middle of the night on the third day.

That night the darkness was heavy and oppressive. Black clouds floated in from the desert, covering the stars, swallowing the moon, and quickly weaving a dense, still mantle over the sky. The weather was so hot and stifling, and the clouds were so thick and solid that the villagers expected a violent storm. But by the middle of the night, not a drop of rain had fallen from the dark clouds overhead and there was no lightning or thunder either. There was only silence weighing down on the world, the desert, and the village.

A lantern burned in Jingad's storeroom. The dim flickering rays of light hazily illuminated the peacefully sleeping Gouwa and Aim as she slept by his side. At the other end of the room Ahm lay on the floor with his clothes still on. His eyes were open and gazing up at the ceiling. He lay there motionless, lost in some deep thought. Old man Jingad was not around. He was probably outside somewhere, patrolling and standing guard.

The world around was deathly quiet. This silence seemed to conceal impending disaster.

Then, in the deep of the night, the soul-stirring event finally occurred. The night's messenger, that vicious, wild representative of the animal world — the mother wolf — appeared for the third time. She first let out a howl on the western edge of the village. This terrifying cry slashed through the night like a sharp knife through a man's throat, seeming especially terrifying in the gloomy, silent desert night. The sound carried a tremendous distance and the whole village was woken by it. The village dogs let out a couple of barks and then, intimidated by the wolf's howl, quickly sunk back into a deep sleep. Once awakened, the villagers listened attentively to the terrifying sound, but none were rash enough to go outside and face the darkness and the vicious beast. They silently curled up deeper into their quilts.

Only Jingad, the brave and solitary hunter, left his yard and headed towards the clump of trees at the western edge of the village. He stooped as he walked, his gun at the ready. Silently and cautiously he approached the spot from where the howl came. "Boom" went his rifle as he fired a shot. But the wolf's call suddenly came from the northern edge of the village. It was her second howl. The old man was startled and rushed towards the northern edge. But suddenly the mother wolf let out a third howl, and this time it came from the southern edge. The old man was surprised. He decided that the crafty old mother wolf was deliberately playing hide-and-seek with him.

Using the cover of darkness, she would exhaust him as she ran around in circles.

The old man's heart began to beat faster. He suddenly realised what the old mother wolf was planning to do! He could no longer just blindly follow her around in circles. He thought for a moment, his one good eye seemed to laugh coldly, and he bent down and silently hurried back to the main gate of his home. He selected a spot not far from the gate and concealed himself there. His hunting rifle was levelled at the gate.

There were no more gunshots and no more howls. The thick darkness returned to its silence. But this was even more terrifying. Danger was everywhere. A pair of deep green eyes flashed somewhere in the night, looking with hatred at the house made of earth. She was waiting for the next rifle shot so that she could judge the position of the hunter. She waited for a long time, but still it did not come. She was puzzled. She grew bolder and continued to slink towards the compound. Avoiding the main gate, she hid in the darkness behind the house, then lifted her head, opened her mouth, and let out a long howl. This was a different sound. It was not so wild or frightening. Her voice had become thin and long, as if she were complaining or crying, as if a silver needle had pierced her nose and entered first her brain and then the deepest recesses of her soul. It was a trembling, plaintive whine, full of the lingering sorrow of a bereaved mother. You could say that this was a call from beast to beast, a call from a mother to her offspring.

The old mother howled in grief and paced back and forth behind the house, never standing in one place. She was guarding against the hunting rifle and so kept moving from spot to spot in the darkness like a black ghost.

The wolf-child was startled awake by the first cry. Although the accompanying gunshot left him trembling with fear, her continuous calls made it impossible for him to keep calm. He looked around in agitation, his eyes constantly moving. Suddenly, he leapt up violently and bounded back and forth across the room. Aim awoke suddenly, and when she saw the state her son was in she was scared out of her wits. She jumped up and rushed over to him. She called out to him, "My son, calm down, listen to your mother, don't run wild ... my darling, listen to me..." She spoke softly and gently. It was as if a stream of clear, sweet spring water flowed into his tumultuous soul. Something seemed to stir within him and he suppressed the darkness in his soul, and controlled the wild blood flowing through his veins.

Aim went over and hugged his thin body and gently caressed his trembling shoulders.

For a long time it was silent outside. A strange call came from somewhere quite near the house. The wolf-child shivered, his mouth opened slightly, his nostrils flared, his face took on a feral expression, and his eyes flashed. He looked as if he were about to rush back into the wild. Aim was terrified. She pressed her lips close to his ears and urgently but gently tried to call to him, to call back his lost and confused soul with her maternal love, and with her love to contend with that horrible, soul-piercing call from the wild. With the goodness of her maternal love she wanted to defeat that evil call of the wild, to protect her once lost love that had now returned to her.

She kept turning her son's face back towards her as he struggled to look outside. She wanted him to face her, to listen to her words of consolation. But she saw that his eyes had become strange. Though he was looking at her, his gaze had become vague and distant. His enlarged pupils were straining to capture the wild call from outside.

The hellish howl came again, from behind the house, from the west, from the east, from everywhere... Each howl grew fiercer.

Aim's gentle, motherly appeals grew ever more gentle as she whispered in little Gouwa's ear.

The wolf-child's — little Gouwa's — face began to contort painfully. It was caused by desperate internal struggle. His body grew hot all over, his nostrils flared red, and the whites of his eyes became bloodshot. The wild blood within him had started to surge again. His body shook violently.

"My son, don't be scared, your mother is here, your mother will protect you, calm down, everything will pass..." Aim began to sob, and in her sorrow she held tighter and tighter his hot and trembling head. A strange feeling of terror filled her body. Her heart went cold.

The mother wolf once more let out a mournful howl. The wolf-child could no longer stand it. He opened his mouth and answered the mother wolf's call with a sharp bark. What else could he do? He had grown up drinking her milk, he had walked with her on the journey of life. He was closer to the mother wolf than to his human mother. The walls of humanity that Aim, Jingad and Ahm had struggled so hard to construct around his soul totally collapsed. He leapt up, escaped from the grasp of his human mother, and rushed violently towards the door.

"Son! Gouwa! Come back..." Aim cried out with all her strength as she ran over and grabbed her son round the waist. Tears streaming down her face, she called out again in a heart-broken sob, "Son, you can't cast aside your mother like this..."

The wolf-child turned his head back viciously, and for a split second seemed confused. But he had already forgotten who he was or this woman who was embracing him. He bit at her left shoulder as if trying to catch an enemy. His eyes were blood red, and his teeth and claws were bared. He looked fierce. He bit viciously into her shoulder and then pushed at her with his head. She crumpled to the ground as if she were made of straw. A hunk of flesh had been torn from her shoulder, and the blood spurted out as if from a spring. He rushed to the door.

Ahm had been watching this horrible scene and he was stunned. He quickly grabbed a wooden pole and rushed over. He swung the pole in the air as he tried to get the wolf-child away from the door. With incredible step, the wolf-child flew through the air as he leapt at Ahm and bit into his arm. Ahm cried out in pain and dropped the pole. Just as the wolf-child was about to rip into his throat, the mother wolf howled again. He immediately left Ahm, rushed to the door, burst through it, and in a flash had dashed into the infinite darkness.

Jingad, his gun levelled, lay behind a sand dune near the gate of his yard and waited nervously. He had no idea about what had happened in the storeroom. He guessed wrong. He thought that once the old mother wolf had lured him away she would rush inside and carry the wolf-child off. So he waited motionless by the gate with his gun at the ready. The old mother wolf did not storm into the yard but howled continuously in the darkness as she circled the yard, approaching and retreating. She drifted from place to place as if she really were a ghost of the night. First, the old man heard faint sounds from within the room, and then the wolf-child answering her calls. His heart skipped a beat and he prayed silently. Apart from praying, or listening to the dispositions of heaven, or things working out as ordained, what else could he do? Man was too insignificant when compared to the forces of nature. He had already used all his strength, and his life was almost drained away. He had no more strength to fight off the old mother wolf. If he did not do everything meticulously, it would be very difficult for him to kill the mother wolf, even in broad daylight. She was an evil messenger sent from heaven. The old man was suddenly aware of his own isolation and the isolation of all people. Man is so weak and powerless! Whether the wolf-child could withstand this final test and save himself in the struggle between man and beast depended on the will of heaven and on the forces of humanity accumulated within his own body.

"Wham!" The door to the storeroom suddenly burst open. A dark shadow flashed out as if an arrow had been shot out through the courtyard. The old man's hand trembled so violently that he almost dropped the gun. His heart felt as if it had been sliced in two by a blunt knife. His body went cold. What he had always feared had finally occurred. He saw that black shadow rush through the gate and letting out several wolf-like howls. Jingad's one good eye bulged. His mouth twisted to one side, he again raised the gun in his hands, and he tremblingly took aim at his escaping grandson Gouwa. Suddenly, the mother wolf, who had been hiding in the dark, emerged from one side and went to greet the wolf-child. The wolf-child let out a wild cry of happiness, jumped up and down, and ran in the direction of the mother wolf. At that moment, the old man's gun went off.

"Boom!" It was a murky, muffled explosion, as if someone had used a club to beat a bag filled with sand. But the sound tore through the black night sky and shook the sleeping village, shook the vast, wild desert, and shook the numbed souls of mankind.

The bullet hit the wolf-child.

His body shuddered. He made another couple of steps towards the mother wolf, then crashed to the ground like a wounded deer. His limbs twitched and convulsed, gurgling sounds emerged from his throat, and in his pain he breathed his last. The bullet had entered through the ribs on his left side. It had passed through his heart and lungs and out through his right shoulder. The old man had fired at very close range and had shot upwards as the wolf-child was jumping into the air. Warm, dark blood flowed from the wound like a red spring, covering his chest and his head, covering his strange, part-wolf, part-human body. There was still a wild glare in his eyes, which he had not had time to close. They looked off into the darkness towards the nascent rays of dawn. Of course, the dawn no longer belonged to him. His slightly twisted mouth looked as if it were straining after something it had thirsted for for a long time. His long face resembled a large question mark: Who am I? Where am I from? Where am I heading?

The mother wolf rushed over to the wolf-child's side. She sniffed and pushed at the bloodied body. She licked at his questioning face and then suddenly let out a long, sobbing howl. She raised her head, turned, and gazed for a long time in the direction from which the gunshot had come. The two deep green points of light burned coldly in the night. They were capable of piercing a man's soul. She howled twice in the direction of the dark spot and then left the wolf-child and headed unhurriedly into the darkness. She disappeared like a ghost. The symbol of civilisation, that evil weapon — the gun — for some unknown reason remained silent.

"My son!" A heartbroken cry rang out from the courtyard. Aim hobbled out, her hair dishevelled, her feet bare, her shoulder dripping blood. She threw herself onto the body of the wolf-child, embraced the stiffening body and tried to shake life back into it. Sobbing uncontrollably, she kept calling to him. She kissed the cold body, covering her mouth and face with his blood. Suddenly, she turned and looked in hate at Jingad, who was walking over to the body. She cursed him, "You killed him! You killed him! Kill me too! Shoot me!"

"Gouwa is dead? He ... he had turned back into a wolf. Child, he was no longer our Gouwa ... what else could I do?" The old man wept and covered his face and fell to the ground, tears streaming down his face. He dared not look at the body. After a moment he stood up and walked forlornly and unsteadily into the night, his gun trailing along in the sand.

"Hah hah hah!..." Aim suddenly began to laugh crazily, a laugh that was hoarse and sharp and terrifying. She circled the body several times and then ran off.

"Hah hah hah!..."

She had become crazed. In the dark night, the sound of that terrifying laugh reverberated into the distance.

Ahm picked up the wolf-child. He did not understand why the old man had fired. Had he believed that Gouwa's betrayal of mankind was unforgivable, so in his grief and outrage had pulled the trigger? In the end, who was right? Was mankind so sacred? Who should be punished for the sin?

Three days passed. Old man Jingad bought a coffin. In it he placed Gouwa's body, now dressed in new clothes. He carried it off and buried it. Everything was in accordance with the rites of human kind. He invited the neighbours to eat and drink. And he asked a Lama to read from the Sutras to expiate the sins of the dead.

Aim had been found and brought back, but she hid in her room and dared not come out. She kept repeating in terror, "The wolves have come, the wolves have come! The wolves have come into the village! Wolves are all over the village and the dunes!...." Every once in a while she would run onto a dune and call out plaintively, "My son, hurry home! The wolves have come, hurry home!" Then the vast ancient desert would grow silent.

Ahm wanted to leave. The episode of the wolfchild had shaken him to his very soul. His whole system of beliefs, all his spiritual supports, had twisted and collapsed. He needed to sort out his defeated beliefs and supports. He needed time to reflect deeply on the events so that he could gain a better understanding of life and mankind.

He seemed to have become aware of some greater truth. The walls of defence that the mother had struggled to build with her blood and tears could not withstand the three calls of the mother wolf. He was suddenly aware of the strength and horror of the evil forces of barbarism. Evil existed, and like night it was impossible to dispel. He did not want to think about it too deeply. Some things only confused people whilst others made them insane. There were some things which, if you understood them fully, would incur disaster. Mankind understands nothing, and in its ignorance it gains peace and propagates down the generations.

He parted with the desert. His only regret was that in the past he had fooled himself. That holy land for which he had searched so long, that Utopia, had never actually existed! It was simply an illusion. It was because it did not exist that mankind searched for it, and so the illusions went on in an endless stream. Mankind needed something at which it could direct its faith and its hope.

He went to say goodbye to Aim, but she no longer recognised him. Her two eyes were bright with terror, and she kept repeating her crazy warning, "The wolves have come! The wolves have come! The wolves have come into the village! The village and the dunes are filled with wolves!..." But who would believe the warnings of a lunatic?

After he had buried the wolf-child, Jingad disappeared. Several months later, so they said, the villagers discovered his body in the desert. He was locked in a deadly embrace with the lame mother wolf. His hands were wrapped around her throat, in an iron-like grip. The mother wolf's sharp teeth were buried deep in his neck. His blood had been dried by the wind.

Ahm departed.

Translated by Bill Bishop

The Sand Fox

Manges Manha — The Demon's Desert — is what the local people called the boundless stretch of barren land in the southwest of the well-known Horqin Grassland.

In the distant past, this had been a rich, fertile land with rolling, verdant grass. The land began to show signs of sand in the Sui and Tang dynasties over a thousand years ago. Even in the *History of the Qing Dynasty* and *Nomadic Life in Mongolia* it was recorded that the place had "good pasture, plenty of water and a lot of game" and had been the Qing emperor Nurhachi's hunting ground. Later, people began to farm the grassland, perhaps feeling that they ought to reap such fertile land, finally bringing calamity on themselves. The sand buried under the grass was exposed and began to loosen in the sun and shift in the wind. Helped by the wind, sand from the Mongolian Desert in the west crept eastward to be cradled in the Manges. In a mere few hundred years, forty million *mu* of fertile land became a dead, deserted world of rolling sand.

The area west of the Manges was a barren waste, while in the east, where sand dunes rippled, desert plants like sandwort and wormwood grew sparsely. Homesteads sprawled here and there on the dunes, still farming the sand, which yielded very little. In the days of wild enthusiasm in the late fifties, an army of labourers arrived carrying a banner inscribed: "Wrest grain from the desert!" They dug three feet deep, doing devastating damage to the dunes, where vegetation was already deteriorating. They had not stayed there long before a sandstorm buried their tents, forcing them to take to their heels, yet even this did not dampen their blind enthusiasm.

The homesteads on the dunes had retreated twenty kilometres east to Green Sand Town when a forestry centre was set up to tackle the sand. A man was needed to stay behind to look after the surviving desert plants.

But who would do it?

Behind a group of farmers with bowed heads, now employees of the new forestry centre, a slow, hoarse voice spoke up:

"Let me."

The eyes of the bearded centre chief lit up: Of course! Who would be more suitable than this ex-convict, who had been sent there from the interior? A man with no wife, no children and no belongings except two chopsticks, he had no one to worry about. The chief slapped him on the shoulder. "You're a damn good fellow. I'll wipe your slate clean for this. You're the master of the Manges now. You belong to the desert."

He stayed there twenty years. Perhaps his life had been too unstable up till then, and he was attracted by the tranquillity of the place. He often murmured softly to the yellow sand, "You are a demon. Who let you out of the bottle? How am I to get you in again? It's

Heaven's punishment." He repeated it every day while putting in willow saplings beside his house and sowing shrubs, camel grass and other plants on the dunes to hold down the sand. Beardy came sometimes and urged him, "Don't do that. It's no use. These dunes are hopeless. Sooner or later you'll have to leave here too." He protested inwardly. Leave here? Where am I to go? Can I leave the world? He went on planting. Unsure of his real name, people began to call him Old Sandy Man from his long tenure in the sand dunes. Later the story leaked out that he had been born in a village on the dunes, and that one night during a sandstorm bandits had plundered the house and killed his parents. When the house was finally buried by the shifting sand, he had joined a group of bandits to avenge his parents but had been sent to prison for it. Nobody believed that an honest and docile man like him could have been a bandit. Anyway, no one cared much about his past. All they knew about him was that he was a capable man and down to earth.

Later, Beardy brought along a woman deserted by her husband because he and his mother had condemned her for being barren. "Try to make a living together," he said. This "barren" woman bore him a daughter and died giving birth to a second child. He named their daughter Willow.

From that time on, tiny footprints appeared on the soft sand, trotting along like a lion cub beside the mother lion.

"What is that running over there, daddy?" asked the daughter. She was always asking about the sand dunes.

"A hare. A small animal that lives in the dunes."

"Catch it, daddy. I want it."

"No. We mustn't do that, child. We mustn't hurt a single blade of grass or insect here."

"Why?"

"Because we have so few living things here, and life depends on other life. You'll understand when you grow up."

She grew into a girl of eighteen, ruddy and well-proportioned and as pretty as a willow. In the last two years people had begun to contract land and be responsible for its output. Old Sandy and his daughter applied to contract the sand dunes the forestry centre was giving up. "Do you want to live by selling sand, Old Sandy?"

"If you live on a mountain, you live off the mountain; if you live by the water, you live off the water. I live on the sand, and I'll live off the sand."

"Live off the sand? Ha ha ha!"

2

A rare "yellow quiet" ruled the dunes. The air seemed to stand still, as if all the wind had played itself out. The desert rested quietly like a slumbering animal. In the southeast, the sun hung on the edge of the desert behind a white pall, as yellow and lustreless as a burnt corn cake.

Sandy squinted at the weird and extraordinary sun in the southeast, schook his head and bent down to resume his examination of the footprints. Beside a bush of grey wormwood, the footprints of an animal were clearly visible. He coughed again, his face red with the effort as he tried to dislodge the phlegm in his throat.

He panted hoarsely.

"Just gone by, my beauty, just gone by." He swung the rats in his hand excitedly.

"Dad!" his daughter called, weeding a plot of medicinal shrubs she had planted.

"Your droppings are green and thin. You can't have eaten any rats for days, poor thing." He was obvious to his daughter's voice as he whispered to himself, spreading out the rats along the path of the animal.

"Look at you, dad, all taken up with that sand fox again." She pouted as she approached. "We haven't set eyes on a man for over six months. I've almost forgotten what one looks like. Let's go to the centre, dad."

"A man? Well, you silly girl, just look at your dad if you want to know what one looks like."

"You? No, dad, you and I don't count. Men might have sprouted wings and an extra head nowadays, for all we know." Her eyes gazed into the distant east with longing, and she sighed softly. "The dunes are stuffy and hemmed in. I'd love to go to the centre and watch the people going in and out of the cinema and see a film."

"Silly girl!" Sandy shook his head helplessly and bent to his work again, unable to satisfy his daughter's longings. "The smell will lead you here, sweetie. I haven't seen you for months, old lady. Have you dropped your litter yet? I'm worried about you." After he had placed the rats on the track he squinted long at the line of footprints.

A few years before, the dunes had been plagued by rats that made holes everywhere and darted around under your feet. The stretches of carefully cultivated plants withered as their roots were eaten by the rats, which, like the desert, did their part to bring calamity to man. The old man had been mad with rage. He had laid traps, dug up rat holes and put down poison. Yet instead of killing the rats he had poisoned his hens. Later he had discovered to his surprise that the rats were decreasing and disappearing. He had been bewildered. One day, when he was walking around with a gun, he had spotted animal footprints jumbled together with traces of rats. Following the footprints, he had soon discovered a roan animal under a bush, a young, limping sand fox that must have been hurt by a big animal and come to the deserted dunes to nurse its wound. When the fox yelped at him, he had instinctively raised his gun, when his heart had leapt at a new discovery. That little fox had a rat in its mouth, and there were rat legs and tails scattered outside its den. As the fact came home to him, he had slowly put down his gun and retreated. The arrival of this stranger who could tackle the rats and protect the desert plants better than he could had pleased him. His respect for an animal he had not liked up till then had risen mightily when a technician at the centre had told him that a sand fox ate three thousand rats a year. He had built a den in a bush for the fox, which had made its home there. After its wound had healed, it had sometimes gone away for a few months but always returned to the place, a retreat perhaps from two-legged and four-legged hunters. It liked the dunes as well as the old man did, and between them had grown a mutual understanding that neither would hurt the other but live peacefully together deep in the desert and keep each other company.

Now both were old. Pregnant again, the sand fox was giving birth in some secret retreat. He mustn't search for her, as a female animal was so very protective of her young. All he could do was catch rats and leave them on her track.

The old man sighed and coughed again. The hot days and cold nights of the desert hurt his windpipe and lungs and gave him bad asthma. His back and legs were failing too.

"If only that vixen could turn into a person, dad," said his daughter melancholically. "They used to say that foxes turned into beautiful girls. Do you think they turn into young men too?"

Sandy threw a silent glance at his daughter as the hard wrinkles on his face deepened, suddenly realising that she had grown up. He couldn't tie her young heart down any more. He would ask Beardy to have her transferred to the centre. This was what he had been dreading. He was aware that only the desert and the old vixen would stay with him all his life. Fate had brought him here, and he would never leave this demon of a place. He had an inkling that his misfortunes — his miserable life and the early death of his parents — had something to do with this demon. He had manipulated it. For half a life time he had tried to make a living on both sides of the Great Wall, and ending up in this place was the work of this demon too. He had no fear, but rather icy hatred. He looked up again at the strange sun. The white sand clouds beneath it were thickening, moving slowly and heavily. The old man pummelled his back and mumbled, "Who let you out of the bottle, demon? Are you going wild again?"

"Hey! Sandy!"

Two men on horseback called outside his home. A man took off his hat and waved at them.

"Ah! Someone has come, dad! We have visitors!" his daughter cried with joy.

"Yes. Who are they?" The old man rubbed his eyes and looked hard. "Beardy? Who's with him?"

"Little Yang, the secretary. Hurry up, dad. We mustn't keep them waiting." She dragged him in the direction of their home.

"How have you been getting along, old chap?" The centre chief still had a bushy beard and was just as straightforward as ever.

"'So-so."

"Only so-so? With all the land you've contracted and all you've grown? Why, the seeds alone will fetch five yuan sixty a kilo. You'll be rolling in money." He spoke as if the land would yield gold and crops shoot up like bamboo after rain. Beardy joked happily and slapped the old man on the shoulder.

Sandy laughed. He was fond of the man, although aware that he had drawn twenty years' pay as the head of the forestry centre for doing less in the way of sand prevention and afforestation than in that of making himself a name for drinking and hunting. "What brings you here, boss?"

"Well, I'm off to be advisor to the county forestry bureau. I've come to pay you and the dunes a visit before I go," said Beardy with feeling. "I'm sorry to have left you here in the dunes for all of twenty years. How about having you transferred to the centre before I leave for good?"

"Oh, no, I like it here. I don't want to leave. This is home to me, ha, ha!"

"You're a stubborn old man. I want to do something for you before I leave. You may make one request."

"Well — I do have a small request." The old man threw a glance at his daughter, then hesitated. "Well, no, I suppose I don't. Not really."

The daughter chimed in, "Ask the visitors in, dad. What are you standing there for? I'll make you something to eat." She was buoyant, stealing glances at the fair-complexioned young secretary.

"Ah, yes, come inside. I have some good wine too." Perking up, the old man briskly invited the visitors in.

"There's no rush. We have all day." Beardy looked at the sky and then around at the dunes. "We'll just take a turn round the dunes and see your plants."

"Well —" Sandy looked at him, pondering what he had said — his heart had missed a beat at that "just take a turn" — and his glance fell on Beardy's shotgun. The secretary had a gun too. "Okay, you can look around. But why are you carrying guns?"

"Just a precaution. What if we should come across some wolf in the dunes?" Beardy joked.

"Hm." Sandy thought for a while. "How about this, boss?" he blurted out. "Don't bother walking round. Just shoot at my chickens. I don't fancy keeping them and I don't know what to do with them."

Beardy was stunned. Then he shook his head and laughed. "You're a strange old man. I'm telling you, we'll just take a turn."

He could say nothing, despite his apprehension. He spoke gruffly to his daughter, "Take them round the dunes, child."

"No, no, there's no need. We're on horseback. She can't keep up with us."

"She can take the donkey. We have a donkey. It's only right for her to show the boss around." The old man insisted stubbornly that his daughter should go with them on the donkey, and she seemed happy to do so.

Beardy had to comply with his host's wishes.

So the three of them, two on horseback, one on a donkey, set out along a twisting path into the dunes.

Full of misgivings, the old man gazed after the departing party and then moved his stiff legs towards the chickens in his yard. Here in the desert, he usually let them roam the dunes, so they were quite wild. He chased them and couldn't catch a feather. Panting and angry, he collected the eggs, went in for a handful of rice and called them. The chickens quickly followed him in. He closed the door behind them.

The room was instantly in a commotion as the chickens cackled and fluttered among the pots and rice bowls.

3

A shot rang out from way down the dunes as the old man was happily slaughtering his chickens. He did it in a strange way, breaking the chicken's spine first, twisting its head round to tuck under a wing, then dashing it to the ground so that its legs stretched and went stiff. In this way he killed six, one for each person to eat and two for the men to take away. He did not grudge them, for chickens, growing mainly on their own in the dunes, were nothing precious. The sound of the gunshot stunned him. He gaped and dashed outside, cocking his ear towards the dunes, but they had fallen silent again.

"Perhaps it went off accidentally, or they were shooting for fun," he consoled himself. He returned indoors, where the six plucked chickens lay in a row on the chopping board waiting to be cooked.

"Bang! Bang!" More shots rang out.

Jumping up as if scalded, he dashed out and looked towards the dunes, his heart contracting. What he had dreaded was happening: they were hunting.

He knew on his finger tips how many hares and pheasants there were in the dunes. After he had contracted and planted the dunes, animals and birds had begun to appear in the last few years. It was now breeding time. It wouldn't do to slaughter them like this. He could have kicked himself.

The thought of the fox made him shudder. She had cubs. Let her stay clear of them. His anxiety carried him flying towards the dunes. But where were they? His chest heaved as he panted along. He stopped to take a breath and looked around at the world he was so familiar with. He knew every mound, every plant and that everything was governed by heat and drought, evaporation being twenty times precipitation. The plants, in order to survive, grew abnormally. Tamarisks cut down the size of their leaves to decrease evaporation. The leaves of others had entirely degenerated, so that photosynthesis was carried out by their trunks and branches. Some had turned grey to reflect and survive in the strong light and oppressive ultraviolet rays. To survive in the adverse environment, all lives in the desert struggled every moment against death. He admired the plants and animals in the desert and looked upon them as his model and companions, heroes defying the demon. To fight the demon desert, men, animals and plants had formed a harmonious, natural liaison.

He pulled himself together and proceeded.

A rider approached. It was his daughter. He looked silently at her face, from which all signs of joy were gone. Head bowed, she dared not meet her father's eyes.

"They are hunting."

He gazed at her silently.

"They're shooting our hares and pheasants."

The old man's gaze was still fixed on his daughter's exhausted face.

"And they're good shots too, damn them. Is everyone outside these dunes as wicked?"

Only then did he speak, coldly, "Didn't I send you just to show them around?"

"I tried to stop them. I shouted. I tried to take their guns," she quickly explained. "Beardy ignored me. Little Yang said, 'Hares and pheasants are wild. They're not your old man's chickens and rabbits. You've contracted the dunes, not the hares and pheasants.'"

The old man's jaw dropped.

"Did they get ... a lot?" he muttered after a time.

"Three pheasants, five hares, and..."

"And what? Out with it."

"The fox."

"What about her?"

"They found her den and they're chasing her."

"Why the hell did you come back then, you idiot? Why didn't you stop them and save her?" The enraged old man raised a fist. Veins throbbed on his forehead, and blood rushed to his face.

"They followed her into the desert; my donkey couldn't keep up." She stood before her father, braving his wrath with a sad smile on the corners of her mouth. "She was brave. She ran out of her den with two cubs in her mouth and one on her back straight into the desert."

"The desert?" His fist dropped, his sunken cheeks twitched, and his eyes turned to the deep desert in the west. "They've gone into the desert?"

A wind rose in the southeast, all the plants on the dunes swayed, and the white sand clouds that had gathered under the sun moved into the Manges. A bad storm was on its way.

"Dad." She swept a scared glance at the southeast where she could see nothing now except a long, hazy wave rolling rapidly nearer. "Let's hurry home, dad. The well isn't covered."

Still he stood and looked towards the west. "The desert. They went into the desert." She dragged him after her as she ran towards home. The ominous wave, bowling along just above the ground, caught up with them as they reached home. The sand rustled in the wind, which carried fallen leaves and broken grasses up to the darkening sky. The sun, shielded by a wall of yellow sand, hung listlessly over the desert like a yellow-painted balloon, devoid of its usual menace.

But the wind was scorching, licking at their backs

through their clothing as it rolled in from the desert. Sand made its way into their ears and mouths and eyes. As the wind reached a climax, it shook the desert.

"The wicked sandstorm! The cursed demon!" She spat as she ran to cover the well, shoo in the chickens and close the door and windows.

His brows tightly knit, the old man gazed speechlessly towards the west.

"Dad?"

"They won't get in from the desert in a storm as bad as this."

"It serves them right."

"It'll cover every footprint and landmark." The old man's face hardened. "They'll be lost out there."

"Forget about them. We didn't ask them to go."

"Listen, child. Fill a bucket with water and pack some rations."

"Dad?"

"Get moving."

"No, dad. You're too weak. You're ill."

Unheeding, he went to the outer room, filled a bucket and put all their corn buns and parched flour into a bag. Then he fetched some clothing from the inner room and began to tie up his waist and trouser-legs.

"You mustn't go, dad, please," she begged, throwing herself at his feet and hugging his legs.

"They will die with no water or food, child. The demon is after them. And the fox too."

"But you're not well. You won't be able to breathe in the storm. You'll kill yourself instead of saving them."

"I can stick it out. This will keep my asthma under

control." He pulled out a bottle of wine and took a swig.

"No. Let me go. You stay here, dad. Let me go."

"You'll get lost out there. You don't know it well enough. I know this demon. I can find them. Get up, child, and let me set out. Now!" An unswerving, steely resolution showed on the old man's solemn face.

"No. I won't let you go. No!" She clutched his legs tighter.

He shoved her away and plunged into the raging sandstorm carrying the water, rations and clothes.

"Dad!"

She scrambled to her feet, took her father's stick from behind the door and plunged into the storm too while the door slapped and banged behind her.

4

Father and daughter trudged along in the blazing desert.

For a day and a night they found nothing. The storm never let up, continuing to swallow everything with smothering force. The willow leaves shrivelled, drooping like hanging rags. Dark sand gathered like black flour under the sandwort bushes. All the leaves of the plants that had grown sparsely and with difficulty in the desert withered and became so dry that they crumbled between one's fingers, and the wind stripped the leaves off their branches in no time. It was a cruel world.

Sandy trudged like an old camel. He shielded his eyes with his left hand and held his stick in his right, stopping every few steps to cough. Sometimes, when the wind was too strong for him to breathe, his face turned purple as he fought for breath, and he would turn around and take a sip of his wine. His daughter, who tagged behind him with the bucket of water and the rations, sometimes helped him to pull his feet out of the soft sand.

When the wind let up in the afternoon of the second day, the desert plunged suddenly into silence. The hopping, moving, wild sands were now as docile and quiet as a child who had misbehaved and was now waiting for punishment. Only after a night and two days' wildness was the demon tired out.

The old man's eyes searched the rolling, yellow sand that stretched all around him endlessly, monotonously and dizzyingly. Was all the world made up of sand? You couldn't see a thread of green or hear a single chirp of insect or bird. At times like this one might be consoled even by the buzzing of a fly; the existence of precious life would drive away the dreadful shadow that gripped one's heart. But no. There was no sign of life except one's own scorching breath. The frightened daughter gripped her father's clothes. The old man's lips were cracked and bleeding, but he shook his head when she handed him the water bottle. They had used up a lot of water without finding the two men. Who knew how long they would have to stay in the desert?

Beneath a sloping sand bank, she saw a dark spot and ran to it. It was the tip of a saddle protruding from beneath a sand drift. Unable to pull it out, she dug away the sand and was alarmed to find a dead horse beneath the saddle. She screamed.

"Come here, dad."

The old man realised that the horse must have been frightened, left its rider in the storm and been buried by the sand.

"Where's the rider?" asked the daughter.

The old man silently looked around at the sandhills.

"How did you know they came this way, dad?"

"I guessed it. The fact that the fox escaped into the desert with her cubs was proof that she had a den here. But where would she dig a hole in this drifting sand? Then I remembered that there was a ruined city here that I had taken some archaeologists to a few years back. She could only have made a hole here. So I headed straight for this place."

"But where is the ruined city? I can't see it."

"The storm has changed the lie of the land. We'll walk on and see."

They proceeded.

By dusk they finally found the two men on top of a high dune. Half of Beardy's body was buried, his thick bushy beard filled with sand. His eyes closed tight, his head turned to one side, he must have stuck out his tongue and licked the sand, for his tongue was sand-covered. The secretary was crouched face down as if lost deep into a long-awaited dream. His hand clutched at his chest, which must have been burning inside him.

Sandy licked his dry lips and heaved a long sigh.

"Look what you get, all for a sand fox. At least you've chosen a good spot. If you'd collapsed beneath the slope you'd have ended up like your horse."

The old man flung his stick away, crouched down

and with his daughter helped the two men up. He carefully gave them water, and they gradually came to. Then he fed them parched flour mixed with water.

They revived.

"Oh, it's you, old fellow. Thank you." Beardy smiled wryly.

The secretary showed his sincere gratitude too.

What's the use of your gratitude? The old man thought as he rose silently and tossed them the clothes he had brought. "Put them on. It's freezing at night. You hunters will be frost-bitten."

He moved away to look around. The sun had set. He saw nothing in the dusk. Sure enough, the sand emitted a cold which floated up, spread and chilled the air. The old man coughed painfully while his daughter pounded his back gently. Beardy and the secretary looked at him.

"Where is the fox you were after?" the old man suddenly demanded.

The two men looked at each other speechlessly.

"Well, where is it?" the old man boomed. They became startled as he looked at them with eyes like cold knives.

"We didn't get it. Honestly. It ran faster than a horse in the desert. And then we got lost in the storm," Beardy explained awkwardly.

The old man turned away, not wanting to look at their faces any longer. He moved a few steps further and gazed for a long time into the hazy, mysterious distance, his swarthy face expressionless.

"Let's go home, dad. It's scary here." She walked up and touched his elbow softly. He nodded, took the bucket, filled his water bottle and returned the bucket to her, saying, "You get them out of the desert. Go straight east to where the moon rises. You'll be out by dawn."

"What about you, dad?" Her heart pounded with fear.

"I'll look for her. She has cubs and no water. They'll die of thirst." He never took his eyes off the gloomy desert.

She shuddered silently. After a long pause she asked, "Is the ruined city very far?"

"I don't know. Probably not. Maybe just ahead."

"Well then, Sandy, after that fox?" said Beardy, picking up bits and pieces of their conversation. "Good for you! The damned beast almost killed us." He patted his gun, which he still had. The secretary had lost his.

The old man shook his head with a wry smile. he didn't want to explain anything at a time like this. Would Beardy, who had always enjoyed hunting, understand his feelings for the fox? He turned to his daughter. "Off you go now. When you pass that dead horse, be sure to cut a large chunk of meat. Your rations won't last long."

She nodded quietly, looking tearfully at him. She bit hard at a corner of her scarf to keep from breaking down. She knew he would never turn back once the decision was made, which made her put all the blame on the two men before her. They had come to this place and disturbed its quiet, its peace and its ecological balance and brought the few lives in the desert to the brink of death.

"Don't go, sir. You can't just leave us to her!"

said the wretched young secretary.

"Hah! I can guarantee your lives, you coward," shouted the girl at the man from the centre, her feelings hurt. She hardened instantly and told her father, "Off you go, dad. I'll get them out of this place and then come back for you."

"Trust her. She's reliable," the old man said calmly. She picked up his stick for him and took off her coat to wrap around his shoulders.

The desert at night was like a black sea stretching out silently before them, profound, mysterious and unfathomable, as if waiting to swallow all life that dared to challenge it.

Sandy straightened up and made his way into this black sea. "I'll be back for you, dad. Take care." The daughter followed him a few steps, her eyes moist. He soon disappeared into the darkness of the sandy sea. From time to time a few laborious coughs could be heard in the distance.

5

Willow was startled from her sleep by a shout. The night before, when she had taken the two men to the dead horse, they had been so tired out they had had to make camp in the open.

"What's that? Look!" shouted Beardy.

She looked. Forty metres to the east, on a sand hill, stood the fox, her fur like a flickering ball of fire, extremely attractive in the morning rays as she suckled a cub, her maternal posture revealing no inclination to interrupt the feeding and run for her life.

"That damned beast! So it's here." The sight of

the fox worked Beardy up so much that he grabbed his gun.

The fox must have been attracted by the smell of the dead horse. Her hunger had led her here. Where were her other two cubs? The one with her must be the weakest, which often gets the most protection, with animals as with human beings. The fox gazed at the group of three, opening her mouth and licking her dry lips. Then unexpectedly she stood up on her hind legs, showing her beautiful white chest, and waved her forelegs at the people; perhaps this was how foxes greeted. The cub rose between her two legs along with its mother and held on to the nipple, hanging there like a gourd. Then the fox seemed to sense the danger. But instead of running away, she looked with pleading, pitiful red eyes at the human beings who were masters of the world.

The girl was stunned by what she saw.

"Its fur is damn pretty. I've never got such a beautiful fox in all my life. I haven't suffered for nothing." Beardy was flustered with excitement.

He took aim with a quivering finger.

"Don't shoot. Please. You mustn't." Startled, Willow threw herself madly at Beardy.

Too late.

A sharp shot shook the quiet morning of the desert. Its terrible echo reverberated there for a long time.

The fox fell, blood gushing from where the bullet had pierced her chest and seeping into the loose sand, which instantly turned dark brown. Her eyes were still open, gazing at the blue sky with helpless sadness, while two tears stood at the corners of her eyes. The poor cub still clutched at her teat, sucking greedily at the blood-stained nipple that yielded no milk.

Beardy was dazed and frightened. "Heaven," he said, putting his head in his hands. "What have I done?"

He flopped down on the sand, looking first at the dead fox and her wailing cub and then at the gun in his listless hand. All his life he had thought hunting justified, but today he was bewildered, suddenly wondering if he had done right. He felt the desert expanding, squeezing and pressing down on him. Men were so insignificant here, so lonely and helpless.

A man came walking towards them over the desert. He was coughing as he walked, and in a single night he had become much older: sand filled the wrinkles on his face; he had lost his hat and his grey hair was all dishevelled; his bent body seemed about to fall with the next gust of wind. But he proceeded with firm steps, following the track of the fox. Suddenly he stopped and stood, not believing what he saw, rooted to the ground, rubbing his old eyes with his sleeves. After a while, he advanced slowly, knelt down beside the fox and caressed her head with shuddering hands. With trembling fingers he closed her tearful eyes while two bitter tears rolled from the sand-filled corners of his own over the dark, protruding cheekbones on to the dry sand, which instantly absorbed them He knelt there quietly, his head bowed. Remembering something, he fumbled in his bag and produced two fox cubs, which he placed beside the one on the sand, then began to give the three motherless cubs water.

None of them drank. All crawled laboriously towards their mother, the weakest falling flat in the struggle, unable to right itself for a long time. Each took a blood-stained nipple.

Sandy's face twitched. He rose abruptly and went towards Beardy, who stood there woodenly awaiting punishment. Sandy halted in front of him with a stern face and cold, boring eyes, then grabbed Beardy's gun, broke it on his knee and tossed it away, howling like a beast, "Damn you, you desert demon! It's all your fault. I hate you. Who let you out of the bottle? Who was it?"

His hoarse voice bellowed over the quiet, boundless desert, which felt nothing and breathed death. To the desert, men were insignificant.

"I'm scared, dad." Willow came up and took his arm. "Let's go home. I miss it. That's the best place, at home on our sand dunes. I'll never leave them." She picked up the three cubs and clutched the warm little lives close to her body.

They started out eastwards, to their green home, leaving firm footprints in the barren waste. The wind rose again, chasing after them and covering up their footprints, pushing them along, trying to swallow and overtake them as it swooped into the east.

Translated by Yu Fanqin

Sand Rites

Hark! That frenzied melody, Song of Andai.
Release! Your languishing tight-bound hair,
Fling off! Your oppressing strains and cares,
Seize! The freedom of lion and tiger — dance, oh
*   dance, Andai!*

— Lyrics from the Song of Andai

Several hundred pairs of unshod feet stomp in surging frenzy upon a patch of scorching sand.

Underneath the fiercely beating sun, the loose crystalline earth glints and shimmers, yet the barefoot men and women tred heedlessly upon this torrid shifting sand, senses devoted solely to the curious instrumental cacophony spurring on their prancing gyrations.

Before them, the desert stretches to the horizon like a vast herd of hideously snarling beasts. Behind them the landscape humps and shrugs and enshrouds itself and its groaning impoverished villages in a blanket of rising dust.

Round and round a lofty dome of sand the tattered peasants twirl to their peculiar orchestra of lustily vying ox horns, handbells, *henggerge* drums,* ukuleles, reed flutes, gongs, cymbals and other instruments blaring and pounding and strumming and crashing out a shapeless sonority that congeals into a forceful throbbing beat. From within the midst of the furiously dancing mass a lone voice sweeps upward and soars into a long luridly rushing wail:

> When Mount Sumbur was still a hillock,
> And the Sundalai Sea a frog pond,
> Our forebears worshipped Heaven and Earth,
> And sacrificed milk and meat upon the Oboga,
> And drove off evil and summoned sweet rain when they
> danced the dance of Andai!**

A motley sound issues forth from several hundred throats, the hoarse, the reedy, the bellowing, the piercing, all colliding in choric refrain:

> *In the sand! We pay our homage in the sand. Hoo-hey! Andai!*
> *We leap, we jump, we let our feet fly! Hoo-hey! Andai!*

---

*Henggerge drum: an oblate wooden drum about eight inches high and fifteen to thirty inches in diameter, each end covered with sheep-, cow-, or horsehide and played with curved drumsticks. The body is painted vermillion, blue, or green and further adorned with pairs of golden dragons or other decorative patterns. It is also known as the Mongolian drum.

**Mount Sumbur: a mythic mountain of prodigious height, the Buddhist Mount Sumeru. Sundalai Sea: as the Buddhist's Sea of Fragrance surrounding Mount Sumeru. Oboga: a mound upon which sacrifices to the local deity are made. Andai: an ancient form of eastern song and dance in Inner Mongolia, traditionally practised to combat evil spirits, worship Heaven and the gods, cure diseases, and dispel the makings of disaster.

The powerful howling nimbus of song surges upon the ether and slams ceaselessly like an angry ocean's unrepentant breakers against the sterile plain in front, the carbuncular expanse behind and the imperious aridity that imprisons earth and sky.

An altar and a bonfire crown the rounded apex of the dune. Offerings of fruit, figures shaped of dough, incense, and whole sheep lie before the fire. Blood flows from the slashed throat of an ox onto the altar then drips and splatters to the ground where it clots and crusts like a blood-black scab over the surface of the sand. Swarming flies zoom and buzz. Hardened knots of dry almond wood crackle and pop in the fire. Smoke rises like a column, solid and straight into the sky, then billows and floats tenuously until the high-riding drought-driven wind sweeps it away.

Here the *böge* — or the *udugan* in the case of a woman — reigns in Shamanistic supremacy, carrying the congregants into delirium with a garish slicing wail that hovers like a vapour over the frenzy of noise. The ceremony harks back to the days before Lamaism spread its influence over grassland and desert, and Shamanism expressed the essence of people's spiritual concepts and ruled as the unchallenged dispenser of religious authority. In his right hand the *böge* wields a black leather whip, lashing into retreat the evil drought-spreading spirit. A bell in his left hand incessantly jangles as he dances, leaps and rushes about before the fire gesturing in wild contortions and shrilling an endless maniacal stream of incantations. His spine-tingling ululations gradually roughen and thicken into barbarous shrieks and bellows as he frequents the altar and hacks off chunks of meat which he flings into the fire. In stark contrast a presiding *udugan*, hair streaming past her shoulders, face aflame with rouge and paint, initiates the dance of Andai with nimble dreamy steps, flourishing colourful fluttering streamers as she pirouettes and capers about with ravishing terpsichorean grace.

That the *böge* and the *udugan* should appear here upon the same ritual "stage" signifies a drastic shift from accepted practice; for the religious affinity and identical spiritual functions of male and female conjurers notwithstanding, the Shamanistic "mass," as its were, is deemed the domain of either the one or the other, but not both. The drought, however, with it unprecedented, mind-muddling severity, has trashed this taboo. It is in desperation that the inhabitants of these precincts have cracked open their coffers to offer handsome sums to both *böge* and *udugan* to combine their necromantic powers in this last-ditch appeal for spiritual intercession.

Two *xabinar*, or disciples of the shamans, are kneeling off to the side observing respectively their Master and Mistress display of prowess. The *udugan's xabi*, a girl of fifteen or sixteen, frequently casts her glances upon the *böge's xabi**. The boy maintains a wooden expression, though set into his sallow and emaciated face are two very prominent and compelling coal-black eyes. A well-roasted chunk of lamb rolls out of the fire to the knees of the girl *xabi*. Surreptitiously she reaches out her hand, snatches it up, and tosses it before the kneeling boy *xabi*. His stomach rumbling in its

---

*Xabi is singular, *xabinar* plural. This term is more commonly associated with Mongolian Buddhism rather than Shamanism.

perpetual hunger, he gulps painfully a mouthful of saliva. He looks at her. A flicker of something intangible passes through his eyes.

The ritual enters into crescendo and arches inevitably toward its climax.

The *böge* and the *udugan* each manifest a deity. Both sing with ever intensifying passion and dance with ever greater fury until they are shrieking and bounding and whirling, lifting their knees and bending their backs in riotous contortions like demented raving lunatics run amok. The separate invisible entities to which each pays homage take possession of their bodies. The thudding of the drums quickens and amplifies until the air throbs with a rumbling pandemonium like the raging of a hurricane, the roar of a tidal bore. The multitudes surrounding the dune vault with them into insanity. Ragged clothing flaps about their bodies, clumsy naked feet stomp and drive into the sand, hundreds of wailing voices cry out to the sky, sand-dust rises in roiling plumes until the dune is cloaked in a heavy yellow-grey mantle. This is Chaos, a seething churning ferment, desert sand and human beings impacted and shapeless in a great hazy tangle of commotion, endlessly whirling and rushing. And from the midst of this furious maelstrom come blasts of cries and howling lamentations like a violent disgorgement of turbid waters long pent up behind the sluice gate, complaining to Heaven, ranting indignantly at the spirits, raging against Fate. The monstrosity of motion overwhelms a number of frail elders, who collapse to the ground. They struggle to escape the dark and terrifying vortex, to crawl out from the dense, entangled forest of wantonly pumping, herky-jerky legs. But the feverish turbulent throng is as insentient as the boundless sea of sorrow, its cresting delirium dimming all other considerations. Here and there an upper limb fragile as a hempstalk appears, a hand reaching desperately out between the cracks of hammering heels and shanks, groping frantically, scratching at the sand, and then back it shrinks and disappears once again into the heart of the tumult.

Night descends. For the moment the fever of an extremity of fatigue has replaced religious ecstasy. Bodies in narcotic-like slumber litter the dune, higgledy-piggledy, lying where they succumb to exhaustion. Now and then a dark shadow leaps up and cries out in the throes of a dream, and rushes helter-skelter before tumbling back to the earth in turbid unconsciousness.

In the translucent darkness, the *udugan* drags her *xabi* out from a clump of bushes. She jabs an awl at her little shivering body. "Little bitch!" she scolds. "Time to let some of your overheated blood! A *udugan* may lie with a hundred different men, but never, NEVER with the *böge*'s disciple!" Each prick of the awl elicits a piteous cry, and the sharp tip comes away brilliantly red.

In a grove of trees, the old *böge* fixes his coal-eyed *xabi* with an angry glare as the boy bites down upon the blade of a knife and swears, "I, Shuangyang, swear to Heaven that I will obey for life the *böge*'s directive and never touch an *udugan*. May I be shot with ten thousand arrows if I break this rule!"

In the twenty-ninth year of the Republic, or 1940, a rain-making ritual took place in Black Sand Village of gigantic proportions, staged by a people who owed their existence to a complicated web of intermarriage between Mongolians, Khitans, Mohes, Manchus, and Han Chinese. Fully believing in the efficacy of seven days and seven nights of feverish dancing and sacrificial worship, they were convinced that the evil spirit inflicting drought could be driven off, that Heaven would unfailingly deliver rain, and that the desert could be contained. Nonetheless, the unprecedentedly severe drought of that year was not alleviated. Fifty-one villagers starved to death, over two hundred others fled to more amenable climes, while the fifteen who remained ended up buried in the sand along with what had been Black Sand. The entire willage was wiped off the face of the map.

The following year those who had left returned to find only a vast white sandy expanse where their village once stood. Imbued with the tragedy of this event, they trudged ten miles east to a patch of earth characterized by a humped and mounded topography and there re-established Black Sand Village. Among these was Shuangyang, the coal-eyed *xabi*. Later the *udugan'* s disciple, Heye, also appeared upon the scene.

1

He'd been twining rope for three days and three nights now, and his palms were cracked and bleeding. He sat astride a mighty tree stump, pinning the rope he was fashioning underneath him with the weight of his body. With both hands working at crotch level, he twisted two strands of hemp into one. Upon completing a length, he would raise himself slightly and shove it beneath him such that he looked from behind to be growing a tail. Eventually he would fasten three such tails into a triple-edged wooden frame vaguely shaped like a dog's head. As he operated a wooden pulley, this dog-head contraption would twist the lengths into a plough rope as thick as a hoe handle and capable of withstanding a pull-weight of over a thousand pounds. A lesser rope would fail against the strain the ox would exert upon it when pulling the plough through the earth of the sandland.

He had his head lowered, intent on his task. His naked back, gleaming and black, and traversed with a long purple scar of recent origin, humped upward like the curve of a plough frame. Several flies revelled in the camouflage offered by this swarthy expanse. Now and again he would glance upward, and these flies would lift into the air in alarm, circle once and re-alight, regaining their invisibility.

It was the mounding sand to the west that kept drawing his glance.

Mute it sat, an arid tumulous enigma, unfathomable in its vast and shimmering taciturnity. Rising and falling like the humps of a camel, it sprawled, fanned out and rushed off to the western horizon, straight into the Great Manges Desert*. Under the radiation of

---

*This is the Horqin Desert of eastern Inner Mongolia. It is referred to here by the name of Manges, in Mongolian mythology and folk literature a malevolent spirit dedicated solely to wreaking havoc and destruction upon the human race. A hideous, self-transmogrifying monster which eats people and is full of cunning tricks. Its most salient characteristic is its multiple heads, which range in number from twelve, fifteen, twenty-five, ninety-five; the more its heads, the greater its strength and savagery.

the sun it produced an extravagant glare that dazzled and stabbed the eyes. "It's never been so bad" he muttered. Sweat beaded across his forehead, threatening to roll down into his eyes. "The dogs've really gone crazy this time. Dry as a bone and all shrivelled up, everything is... If it keeps this up, then it'll be another 1940..." He sighed. The sharp creases of his forehead deepened, his squinting, perennially inflamed trachomitous eyes darkened in contemplation.

He bent his head back to his work. His knotty finger-joints recalled wind-sere tree roots. He could no longer straighten them. His finger-tips had lost their nails long ago — they had virtually rotted away — so his fingers were stubby and bald like little drumsticks. This was the result of years of furiously scratching out a living among the sand dunes, where any living thing was doomed to become warped and deformed. He stood erect and beat the stiffness out of his back. Affixing his completed rope onto the yoke, he set it on the ground and stretched it out. Then he lifted down from the wall a curved-shaft plough and attached to it the iron ploughshare. The plough had been idle ever since he'd hung it up after spring planting. And now... He sighed once more and shook his head.

Noon was upon him.

Diabolically, the sun sent down its fires. Katydids perching upon stray green bristlegrass at the base of the courtyard wall were chirping up a clamour that seemed to intensify the heat and aridity to the point of unbearability. He picked up the sweat-soaked shirt beside him and mopped his face and neck. Squatting restfully on his heels, he gazed in silence at that sand-domain. He'd planted over half an acre of corn there, and it had all shrivelled up and died. Not a drop of rain had fallen since he'd planted the seeds. For the entire spring, the heavens had been as spotless as a toddler's bottom licked clean by a dog. Not even a slap-sized cloud had floated by. The corn, the millet, the sorghum — all had sprouted only to wither into dry dead stalks before achieving a handspan of height. This year, Black Sand Village, which depended for survival on extensive cultivation of the sandland, wouldn't harvest a grain. The villagers had no last trick up their sleeves to sidestep the whims of Heaven. And that irrepressible conquering spirit of the old days was gone. In the old days it was, "Bring on the drought, we'll go all out; the tougher the drought, the bigger the harvest." Now all anyone did was fold their arms and wait for rain. Day after day, the villagers would get up mornings and eye the southeastern sky for crimson sunrise clouds. Evenings they would search the western horizon for waterbearing cumulations. And they would sigh and moan and bellyache, and lock their brows into perpetual gloom. As the drought dragged on, they fell into despair, succumbed to fear and turned to the exploitation of their own individual resources. Those who had the contacts went off to the cities and towns to hire themselves out for odd jobs. Those who had some brains went traipsing around the countryside peddling whatever ingenious commodity they could come up with from village to village. Those destitute of contacts and brains stayed home and fought with their wives and stared at the bottoms of hens waiting for the eggs to drop. Those with neither contacts nor brains nor chicken butts upon which to pin their hopes simply closed their eyes and said, "Socialism never starves you — the country would never ignore its own people!" But in fact, back in 1960, this village had carried over ten starved corpses out to their final resting places — many were children and the mothers simply couldn't cope. That's what they said, anyway. Otherwise there would've been nothing with which to console themselves nor anything to live for.

Three days earlier, there'd been a sudden rain. But people had just curled their lips in contempt and cursed Heaven. What good's it to pour a ginseng infusion down a dead man's gullet! It's too late! You think those withered plants are gonna grow new sprouts? No way! And forget about replanting, because there's not enough time before Frost's Descent.

"Shit! Just look at this rain — just like an old widow who doesn't come 'til dawn!"

"Like a stallion trying to mount an ass — keeps missing the right spot!"

Several old farmers had been standing in the rain showering themselves and chatting. He's been squatting aloof off to the side contemplating that demesne of scrub-scrabbling sandland. The silken threads of rain trickled into the trenches of his neck and flowed on downwards. His cotton jacket cleaved damply to his skin, so sensuously, wetly soothing after a hundred or so demonically dehydrating days. And then it came to him — there was one crop perfectly amenable to the present conditions! Yes! If he planted it now, it would ripen before the first frost. Red broom corn millet. He'd learned of it in his youth when he'd followed his master *böge* to the Eastern Wasteland for a conjuration ceremony. Red broom corn millet seeds were not to be had around here, so the day following the rain, he set out in his little rubber-wheeled cart for the market fair in Oxbow, about forty miles off in the Eastern Wasteland. He'd returned just yesterday with a bag of seed for which he'd traded a two-year-old pig.

"Bitchbrat!" he shouted toward the hollow next to the front door.

Momentarily there popped up from the edge of the hollow a moppet-head, the owner of which was leading a black bullock. An old dog shambled along beside him. This was a little mud monkey of a boy, about eleven or twelve, black as a newly distilled chunk of charcoal. Ochre pants adapted from an old pair of adult undershorts hung from his skinny little behind and flapped around his legs with every step. He was naked from the waist up, and you could count his every rib. That's all he was, black skin stuck onto a diminutive skeleton with no flesh sandwiched in-between. Strangely enough, his little sandy belly bulged rotundly, audaciously preceding him with pride, just like the swollen gut of a katydid filled with grassjuice. His most noticable aspect, however, had to be the long shiny keloid on the crown of his head, looking for all it was worth like somebody'd run a vicious fingernail across the surface of a watermelon. He said when he was little he'd had a boil and the local doctor had branded it right off with a branding iron.

"Dad, you called?"

"What do you mean dad? I never said I was adopting you! Hitch up the cart, we're going!"

"What're you so crabby about! I thought we were

going tomorrow."

"Don't talk so much! I changed my mind."

He took the bullock's lead rope from him and fastened it to the post at the base of the wall. Yesterday on the way home he'd run across a young hitch-hiker in tight pants with bun-hugging pockets and a brass plate riveted right atop his butt. His hair was so long it covered the nape of his neck. It was only his eyes constantly blinking behind his glasses that prevented him taking the hitchhiker for a highwayman. Since he had business in their village, he ignored the brass plate — it could've been a steel plate for all he cared — and gave him a lift. But wouldn't you know it, after he boarded the cart and started talking, he learned his business was researching the "Andai". He said he wanted to save this valuable piece of national cultural heritage and that he'd come to interview the "Andai King". His forehead had knotted at once into a black frown, and he fictionalised about having to go to a neighbouring village to take care of some business, thus right smartly evicting Mr Brass-Plate-Pants from his cart.

He pushed the rubber-wheeled cart out, hollered at the black bullock to back its butt up between the shafts, fitted the yoke upon its shoulder, put on the back pad, tightened the girth, and coiled the lead rope around its horns. After that he loaded the plough into the cart as well as a seeder-gourd, the bag of seeds, a supply of food, and the wattles and wood for building a temporary shelter. Little Bitchbrat carried out two old rolled-up carpets and some pickled radishes.

"We didn't forget anything?" he asked.

Bitchbrat ran back, his feet thudding on the ground,

and returned with a one-and-a-half-gallon plastic basket of sweet potato hootch.

"Let's go," he said.

"Wait a minute!" Bitchbrat cried out in alarm. All in a fluster he rushed back, urgently yanked down his pants, and squatted at the base of the wall. An explosive, sputtering accompanied his production of a spreading liquid. "I caught me a few fat locusts a little while ago — they're very rich," he explained with an apologetic laugh.

"You — you're full of shit!" Helplessly he looked at that shiny runny pile. "What happened to that biscuit I gave you?"

"I'm saving it for tonight. You don't have all that big a supply of food."

He's got a good heart, the little feller, thought the old man.

"Go ahead and eat it. We've got a lot of hard work ahead of us come tomorrow, and you have to keep your energy up. You won't like it if I make you stay behind."

Bitchbrat rose to his feet and pulled up his pants. Glancing at the old man, he pulled a corn biscuit about the size of a fist out from his inside pocket and swallowed it with one great bite.

The old man's heart ached as he watched him eat. How on earth did this little whelp survive before I found him?

"Let's get going," he said.

Just as the cart got underway, they heard someone shouting outside the courtyard wall.

"Lao Shuangyang — "

It was Meng Ke, the village headman. Following

him was none other than the stranger with the brass-plate pants. And trailing behind him was that contingent of idle buttinskies that no village could do without. Whenever something was up, they were sure to be there, putting in their two cents' worth. He brought the cart to a stop and waited for the headman to say his piece.

"Let me introduce you — *what a bitch*!" The interruptive exclamation flew out of his mouth, followed by a noisy sucking of air. The fortyish-year-old headman had a toothache, and his cheek was swollen up the size of a yam. With every sentence he would suck in a breath of cooling air. "This is Comrade Yushi, from the County Cultural Centre." Air sucking. "This here is the 'Andai King' you're looking for, Mr Lao Shuangyang." Another swig of air. "Well, you old coop — *bitch, anyway*! — it looks like they want the dog-piss-fungus growing back in the palace again!"

Yushi was stunned. Disconcertion suffused his face. "It's ... *you* ... So you're..."

He didn't respond. His impulse was to leave, but that would hardly be appropriate. He brought out his pipe and dropped to a restful squatting position.

"So, sir, *you're* the 'Andai King'!" Yushi exclaimed admiringly.

"Hey, you forgot a word," one among the idle cronies piped up. "'Eight' comes after 'king', you know!"*

A burst of hearty laughter from his buddies.

---

*King-eight" or *wangba*, a word of disparagement meaning "cuckold".

Still he said nothing. He sucked noisily upon his pipe. After an interval he said pointedly and evenly to Yushi, "You're mistaken. That's ancient history."

"*Hai!*" the headman cried in gutteral exasperation. "What kind of a way is that to talk, all gruff and stubborn — *Sssffftt*" — sibilant intake of air — "the gentleman's come a long way just to see you! *Such a bitch, sssffftt* —" Buttressing himself against the toothache, Headman Meng Ke rattled on feverishly, "The gentleman here, Comrade Yushi, says our village is the home of the Andai, a wellspring of tradition, and he wants to gather it all up and put it in order and take pictures and make recordings and write articles! *Sssffftt*. And he wants to organise the whole village to dance the Andai and pay us for the loss of our working time that all this will entail. And after he returns to the county seat, Comrade Yushi is going to arrange for our village to receive expenses for its cultural undertaking! *Sssffftt* —"

Lao Shuangyang eyed the headman blandly. He wasn't moved in the slightest. He just kept puffing on his pipe and gazing at the western sand dunes.

"Fercrissake, say something!" the headman burst out. "What a bitch!"

"I got no time,"

"What?" The headman was taken by surprise. "You don't have time?"

"Ha — he's busy embroidering posies and stitching shoes and piercing his ears, getting ready for his marriage to the prince!" The idle kibitzers burst into another round of laughter.

The headman bent down and peered into Lao Shuangyang's impassive face. "You don't have time?" he pursued.

"That's what I said, I don't have time."

"See here now, you'd better think on that again." The headman adamantly enunciated each word, leaving no room for ambiguity. "This is a big thing involving the whole village. The whole village stands to profit from it. So you better think on it." He ended with a great siffling breath.

"I'm going into the sandland."

A great gasp exited everyone's open mouth. Laughter followed.

"Into the sandland? What — you looking for a wife or looking to hang yourself?" someone asked.

"To plant red broom corn millet."

The headman and the group of cronies let out another gasp.

"Lao Shuangyang, what's the matter with you anyway? You've been out in the sun too long — Look how late it is — *what a bitch* — you think you're gonna get grain? You'll be lucky to get grass!" Meng Ke ridiculed.

"Red broom corn millet takes sixty days to mature from the day the seed is put into the ground. It's still seventy-two days to Frost's Descent."

"Listen to me," Headman Meng Ke softened his tone considerably. "Forget that. Just let it go. At your age, what do you want to be going into the dunes for, making yourself all exhausted. There's no need to suffer like that. When the remunerations are dishanded, yours certainly won't be less than what you can get out of red broom corn millet! *Sssffftt* —"

"I don't need money. I need grain."

"If you have money, you think you won't be able

to buy grain? What's to worry about! Use your fucking brain, man!"

"It wouldn't be my own grain I grew myself." Lao Shuangyang gave his pipe several knocks against his shoe and rose slowly to his feet, the picture of phlegmatic deliberation. He turned his head for a look at the sun. "I gotta get going. I need to get there before sunset to put up the shelter." As he spoke he walked past him and picked up his bullwhack.

"*Jia*!" he shouted to the bullock, cracking the lash. "Bitchbrat, get into the cart!"

"So, you're really leaving? Just like that?" Headman Meng Ke approached the cart and grabbed its shaft. His voice was shaking with repressed anger.

"Watch you don't get goared." He walked over and gently pried the headman's fingers off the shaft. "*Jia*!" he hollered. The black bullock leaned into the yoke, and the number-three rubber-wheeled cart nimbly began to roll. Bitchbrat made a dash for the cart.

"Little bastard, just stop right there! What are you doing here anyway! Get out of Black Sand!" The headman, overcome with pain from his abscessed tooth, took it out on little Bitchbrat. He knew this orphan had wandered in from some other village about a fortnight ago and had been staying with Lao Shuangyang. People were saying Lao Shuangyang was getting ready to adopt him.

Lao Shuangyang stopped dead in his tracks and fixed Headman Meng Ke with a silent withering stare.

"The sky's my blanket, the earth's my bed, in

Nature's arms there's naught to dread! It's — none — of — your — biz — ness!" Bitchbrat chanted tauntingly, placing significance upon each syllable. With his fingers he pulled down the skin beneath his eyes, showing the headman red-rimmed eyeballs. Then like a little black demon he flashed over to the cart and climbed aboard. The old dog, Dragon Master, shadowed him from behind.

"The vengeful ghosts of the Great Manges Desert are waiting for you! Mark my words — two fucking days, tops, and you'll be hightailing it back here! Asshole!" Headman Meng Ke held his swollen cheek and angrily shouted at the cart as it departed into the distance. As village head, he'd been losing sleep over how to scare up the cash to buy back the grain the village needed to get through the famine. Yushi's appearance was a godsend, and if everything worked out and they really got ahold of this wad of cash, their problems would be solved. But now this bastard Lao Shuangyang had spoiled everything, so he had every right to blow his stack!

"Headman Meng, what's to be done?" Yushi asked anxiously. "How can we accomplish anything without the Andai King?" He gazed flabbergasted after Lao Shuangyang's disappearing figure.

"Humph! Nobody's indispensable! Let's go and see the Andai Queen! Yes, we'll go see Aunt Heye! *What a bitch*! Yessir, we've also got in our village here an Andai Queen!"

2

The older men of the village all said that Aunt Heye had been a very pretty girl in her youth. The younger men believed every word of it. For though she was well over fifty, she still brushed her hair with "essence of dore". This essence of dore was a viscous liquid obtained by soaking elmroot bark in water which when brushed on the hair imparted to it a smooth and glossy sheen. This was the one and only luxury product that accrued to the women of Black Sand. Aunt Heye's hair was truly beautiful. Not a single white strand was to be found, despite her age, and it was still thick and fluffy. She would coil it up into a bun, fasten it with a black silk hairnet and apply essence of dore to the rest of it so that it gleamed like obsidian.

"Men love women who are clean and neat and make themselves up nicely," she would say with a sigh.

People bandied it about that she had loved quite a few men in her life — and had been loved by quite a few as well. Going about from village to village in her *udugan* days, she had attracted the admiration of untold numbers of amorous men. Then during the era of Land Reform, *udugan*-ism had been declared superstition, naught but the flim-flammery of witchcraft, and was banned, effectively depriving her of her livelihood. To make things worse, her mistress, with whom she'd formed a close survival alliance, up and died. Having nowhere to go and no one to turn to, she thought of that pair of coal-black eyes and came to Black Sand Village looking for *him*. It hadn't occurred to her that Coal Eyes might already be married, and this being the case, she found herself totally adrift without the foggiest notion of what to do. The branch secretary of the village at the time took her plight to heart and married her to his own younger brother, who was a cripple. This arrangement far from satisfied her inclinations, but in her desperation she submitted to fate and slept with the cripple for five years before he died — of the *udugan*'s "prowess" as the villagers would have it. From that time on, she was thought of as a jinx who brought evil down upon the heads of men. That's what people said, but that didn't keep any man who set eyes on her from drooling. Strangely enough, after the cripple died, she turned down every suitor, no matter how persistent he was, and never married again. And as she was childless — the result of a potion her *udugan* mistress had given her — she was to this very day all alone in the world.

But she had never been lonely. With the advent of her widowhood, her two adobe rooms became the village "hotspot", so to speak, a kind of village activity centre.

Those who were on the marriage market, those who were married but discontented, mature and elderly widows and widowers with no other family ties, those bored out of their skulls with home life, and children who had nowhere to play after dark — such were the people who converged upon her two adobe rooms every evening after supper. Here they could get up games of poker and Chinese chess, play upon the various lap violins and bamboo flutes and the three-stringed plucked mandolin that she kept on hand, or snack upon tea and "Russki-cracks"* and crabapples and sometimes even candies that she would dole out to everyone. Of course, this was an inevitable breeding ground for rumours and malicious gossip concerning,

---

* Melon seeds.

for instance, which young maiden had exchanged handkerchiefs with which young buck; or which married lady was making it with which married man; or which kid stole fried millet or muskmelon from his own home and brought it here to give away ... stuff like that. Inevitably, in the eyes of upstanding citizens, all sorts of evil activities occurred in these two adobe rooms. During the "four clean-ups" movement the place was targeted as a "brigands inn", the meeting place of unsavoury reactionaries. During the "cultural revolution", it was violently attacked as a "bunker" harbouring class enemies and the forces of evil. Nowadays it had acquired a number of new monikers: matchmaking salon, gambling den, teahouse, venue for incitement ... etc. etc. It had been outlawed, banned, and regulated throughout the years according to the ideology and demeanour of each particular era. And time after time Aunt Heye submitted to various forms of investigation and demands for abject apologies and confessional explanations. But then, each time once the ill wind had swept on by, her place would rebound like an irrepressible natural phenomenon and recover its former flourishing state. And Aunt Heye would just as naturally retrieve her identity as the warm and welcoming hostess, mistress of amiable recreation and good cheer.

When Headman Meng Ke brought Yushi to meet her, she had just arisen and was combing her hair.

The previous evening, there had been card games on the northern *kang*: six young ladies and men playing "rooting pig" and "go fish". Some old guys had been playing chess on the southern *kang*. Off to the side several musicians were playing and singing the

Song of Andai and some other old songs like *Eighth Rhyme* and *Immortal Blossom*. On the floor and in the outer room a bunch of children were playing hide-and-seek. She had persuaded someone who was unoccupied with games or music-making and just hanging around to make tea for everyone while she herself sat at the head of the southern *kang* telling the fortunes of two lovelorn demoiselles, attempting to divine lovers for them with the Eight Trigrams. She kept looking toward the door, and everyone knew whom she was looking for. Tiezhu, the son of the former landlord Baoshan, was an old bachelor well over forty. He'd never been able to get himself a bride because of his class status, though he had cravings and desires just like any other normal man, and so he was a frequent visitor at Aunt Heye's home, helping out with this and that and placing himself at her beck and call. Their relationship was quite intimate. Now the landlord was no longer a landlord as everyone was regarded as a citizen of the nation, and Tiezhu had become engaged and would marry into his bride's family.

The door opened. He was here. He was holding a greasy package of soft deep-fried dough sticks.

Aunt Heye gave him an oblique glance, shifted her position on the *kang*, and continued to lay down the cards. Tiezhu, leaning his hip on the edge of the *kang*, set the package on the tea tray next to her.

"Today's the day for giving betrothal gift," he said, not daring to look Aunt Heye in the face.

Aunt Heye didn't respond. With her hand she restrained the two young ladies, who had risen to take their leave.

"Today I saw her face for the first time. It's all pock-marked."

"Humpf! The landlord's spawn is worried about looks! You're *lucky* to get a pock-marked one to give your father a clutch of grandsons — your ancestors must've burned a *ton* of incense to Heaven!"

"So, then, you agree with this arrangement?"

She said nothing. An interminable time dragged by before she opened her mouth. "What good would it do to disagree? Can I hold on to you forever? You are your father's son…"

"I have three younger brothers waiting. If I don't get married, then they can't either, and Father's afraid our family line will die out…"

Suddenly Aunt Heye felt the utter meaninglessness of life. She'd come here for Coal Eyes, but circumstances had denied her desire. Now this long-standing relationship forged out of mutual desperation was coming to an end. He was tossing her aside, leaving her alone — again. If an enemy were manipulating her life, he or she couldn't be any more effective than this. She gathered in the cards spread out upon the table. Her eyes were red. She yawned.

"Just go. Go on, *go*," she said to him.

Tiezhu looked at her timidly. In the days when he was treated like a dog — as worse than nothing — it was this woman who had gathered him into her delicious bosom and let him have a taste of life as it should be. It mattered not that she had more than a decade on him — he would have done anything for her back then — he would have died for her, he would have killed for her. Now he had to leave her. There was simply nothing to be done about it.

After the last of the pleasure-seekers had left, she'd

fallen into a nightmarish coma, which didn't release her back to consciousness until this noon. Her eyes were puffy, her head wooden, her heart leaden. Those nightmares — she'd struggled and struggled but couldn't drag herself out of them.

And now here was Headman Meng Ke — no small reason for surprise. This person had never lightly crossed her threshold.

She offered him a basket-tray of cigarettes and poured two cups of tea and pressed into service a small plate of dried-out tea-cakes as well. Then she brought out her long-stemmed pipe and, holding it rifle-style, began puffing billowing clouds of smoke.

Meng Ke introduced Yushi and launched into a glowing account of his project.

"Andai?" Aunt Heye's eyes lit up the moment she heard the word.

"That's right, Andai. We're going to do it again, several days of excitement!"

"Andai..." A tinge of red flew to her cheeks. Her pipe hand began to tremble. Meng Ke hadn't anticipated that she would get so excited. The prospects looked good.

"Andai. Gee, Andai... But it's been more than ten years. The Andai's been dead for more than ten years. And I died along with it..." Her voice was approaching inaudibility.

"Well, we're having a resurrection! Hot-damn! Comrade Yushi says it's a valuable cultural legacy. Get all your light-footed graces out of mothballs and put on a stunning performance, just like before! And at the end of the year you'll even have money for the grain buy-back."

"The Andai ... you dance it for its own sake. What's grain buy-back got to do with it?"

Meng Ke explained the deal, but he could have saved his breath. Only the Andai itself in its intrinsic being held any interest for her. The Andai, indeed, was her soul — the soul that her *udugan* mistress had injected into her body. It had happened when she was about thirteen. She'd developed a mysterious condition marked by listlessness and exhaustion and general neurasthenia that left her as thin and weak as an attenuated blade of grass. Her parents sought the curative powers of the famous "White Sparrow Hawk *udugan*". This *udugan* kicked her parents out of her room, covered the door and windows with blankets, and proceeded with the cure. She started by humming a compelling tune that surged into the veins and set off feverish palpitations of the heart. Then with langorous, dilatory grace the *udugan* climbed to her feet and set to fluttering around her, adopting by and by a series of provocative manoeuvres designed to stimulate the ailing one. And she would approach her dancingly and reach out and place her hands upon her in one or another vital spot and chafe, manipulate and massage. Those hands of hers were hot — scorching — and sent shooting through her a powerful bolt of ... *something* ... that would cause her blood to rush and roil and her entire person to shiver and vibrate. Afterwards — she didn't know how this came about — she found herself upon her feet and she began to emulate the *udugan*'s sweeping rhapsody of motion, for enchantment had enwrapped her and she was possessed of an unrestrainable urge to dance. At least six hours, possibly more, passed as she danced and sang and vented a tremendous energy. Throughout the sweat rained down from her, poured off in sheets as if she'd just stepped from a bath. She entered into a state of bliss, of utter floating relaxation, as if her inner substance had transformed into the elusive chimerical energy of fire and electricity. At last she collapsed. Her fatigue was absolute — and absolutely liberating. All earthbound inhibitions had fled: she was freedom incarnate.

The lower part of her body was drenched in red, the blood of her menarche. This first blood of puberty had been dammed up inside her and was the provenance of her long debilitation. Her rapture with the Andai dated from this time. The Andai's powerfully evocative melody would pierce her to the core, seize her very essence and command her entire body to shake and tremble with an agitation next to impossible to control. She deserted her parents and ran off with the "White Sparrow Hawk *udugan*".

The Andai had been with her all her life and had in fact been the master of her entire fate. Just as it had been banned during the period of land reform, so she'd been forbidden from roaming about like a gypsy offering her services as a witch. At the end of the 1950s, someone had dug up the Andai as a treasure, casting her into the limelight of celebrity before misfortune struck again during the "cultural revolution". Now someone else was knocking upon the door of the Andai. But whether it was banned or promoted, condemned or exalted, the commotion was nothing but pious rantings and flagrant manipulations by people with nothing better to do. Their agendas were irrelevant to her. For in her universe, life and the

Andai were one and the same, unified and inseparable. In the Andai she found intoxication and detachment from the material world, and in the Andai she sought...

"So, what do you say, Great Aunt?" Meng Ke prodded, dragging her back to the present. "You have no problem with this, I presume? We've decided to ask you to take charge as the commander-in-chief of the performance this time!"

"Me? You want *me* to be in charge?" She hesitated. "What about the Andai King? Shouldn't Lao Shuangyang be doing this? What, he's kicked the bucket?"

"He's not at home." Meng Ke didn't divulge the truth, that Lao Shuangyang had turned him down.

"I saw him driving his donkey cart back from the market last evening. How can he not be at home?"

"We went looking for him. He's gone into the sandland."

"The desert?" She clucked in amazement and disapproval. There it lay, the sandland, in the distance beyond her window. Misgivings filled her heart. The old thing, what was the matter with him anyway, going off into the sandland at this time of the year? What in the heck was he doing? This heap of sand's had him bewitched all his life. He's poured his whole soul into it. The fiery glow in her eyes faded and, steeped in regret, she shook her head. Without the Andai King, it just wouldn't be the same.

"Great Aunt," Meng Ke appealed unctuously, "you can do it without him. Besides, I must be honest and tell you that this may be the last chance you'll ever have to dance the Andai again!" How cunning he was, like the seasoned hunter siezing the heart of his prey. How softly and subtly did he release his spear.

"The last time ... the last time..." She spoke in a near whisper as she gazed transfixed out the window. Her features took on the lineaments of grief.

"Okay, then," she assented, "I'll dance the Andai this once last time..."

Meng Ke and Yushi released long sighs of relief. But even in their sense of accomplishment, they could not help but notice in her utterance a chilling tone of tragedy, like an evil wind from the grave pouring into their ears and filling them with bonechilling desolation.

3

The sandland byway was soft and yielding beneath his feet and calming to his heart. The rolling dunes greeted him, welcomed him like an affectionate woman who'd been waiting for ages to gather him into her arms. He strode along in a soaring spirit of confidence, leading his ox cart, his child, his old dog. He would subjugate this violent, cunning woman.

"You really pulled that one off, you wily old fox," he exulted to himself. "You flung them all off — the headman, Brass Plate, the Andai and *her*..." Here he experienced a stab of misgiving.

His face was angular and lean, as if hewn by a knife, and overlayed with coarse armour of stubble and a rampant web of wrinkles: an ancient artefact in sturdy black copper. All his life he'd been setting his curved-shaft plough to the sandland while the fierce and unrelenting sun and the sand-laden wind ploughed his face and body in turn. Several decades of this had forged him into a form reminiscent of an old elm tree hacked by knives, chopped by axes and smothered with countless scars.

He drew to a standstill. Here the road curved. He cast one last look at the village.

His gaze fell immediately upon that two-room adobe house. The stove-pipe growing crookedly out of its pitched roof was emitting a thin white column of smoke that was marching straight into the heart of the firmament. Was it breakfast or lunch? Had she had another bad night? Why she was always torturing herself, this crazy woman? She was old now, but her heart still wouldn't give up. Sometimes he couldn't understand her anymore than he could understand the mysterious desert. She would accede to Meng Ke's wishes, even if it meant endangering her very life. Anything to dance the Andai. It really was too bad that he'd miss seeing her dance. If it weren't for this sandland and his having to plant his red broom corn millet, he wouldn't have left. Maybe he would even have succumbed to the temptation. Maybe he wouldn't have been able to resist the seductive power of the old crazy woman, and he too would have danced the Andai. After all, he'd been quite famous there for a while as the Andai King.

Well, he couldn't do that now. He had to do something about this sandland, make her know who was boss, this fascinating woman who unrelentingly lured men in pursuit of her. This time he would step upon her broad bosom, grab her by the neck, rip open her back with his sharp iron ploughshare, and scatter his red broom corn millet seeds into her body. He couldn't miss this opportunity, the last chance this year to get a harvest. Hers was a fierce and violent temper, fickle and maliciously capricious. Countless times she'd punished him and beaten him down — him and all the other planters in the village. Now she was worse than ever — now she wasn't willing to yield up a single grain. He refused to accept this. He would carry out one last subjugation. You couldn't be too indulgent with this woman.

He commanded the bullock to resume the course. Awaiting him was a great combat, a great clashing of wills, a knock-down drag-out fight, and he would wrench his livelihood and his reward from her with his blood and sweat. It had always been like this for the peoples of sandy precincts, ever since ancient times. No matter how stingy Heaven and the sandland proved, generation after generation, they had carried on indomitably, ploughing and planting and harvesting, harvesting and ploughing and planting, building up a life for themselves imbued with a distinctively regional purpose and meaning.

In an undertone he hummed an old tune. There were no words, it was just a tune to be hummed, simple, vigorous, primitive. He hummed it slowly, drew it out to match the rhythm of the bullock's stride.

"What's the Manges Desert really like?" Bitchbrat, who'd never ventured into the sandland, was full of childish wonder.

"Climb up to the top of that sand ridge up ahead and you can see it.

"Wow! Look how high!" Bitchbrat cried in awe. The ridge jutted from the surface of the ground at an acute angle and stretched itself out. Lofty and alarmingly steep, it lay there like a giant sleeping dragon imperiously blocking the way into the sandland. Up the sharp incline the little byway crawled, ever more timorous and cowering, growing fainter by the yard as if fearful of inflicting a scar, finally vanishing completely once it crossed over the top. The little sand tumuli and stubby humps on this side were all bowing in deference before the looming colossus, a crowd of loyal, obedient subjects protesting their homage to the haughty liege lord. Scion of temporality, the mighty monarch was the handiwork of the savage southeastern wind, deposited here only this spring.

"This is the threshold of the Manges Sandland," the old desert hand said. Bitchbrat stuck out a gleeful, marvelling tongue.

The black bullock set himself to the slope, leaning all his weight into the yolk as he strained to haul the cart to the top.

Lao Shuangyang waved his bullwhack in gentle intimidation over the bullock's head, urging him along with a chiffling of the tongue. Bitchbrat lent a hand by pushing the cart from behind. The old dog, Dragon Master, dashed on ahead to the top of the ridge, where he proceeded to bark in majesty at the Great Manges Desert and its dunes ranging out to the northwest infinity. Two barks was all he could manage before the scorching heat silenced him. Tongue lolling out, he panted for air.

The Great Manges Desert lay spread out before them. A torrid breeze brushed across their faces and arms, the stifling heat diminished by its soft touch. The vast illimitable expanse of untamed wilderness filled Bitchbrat with a sense of awe and dread as he gazed upon it, the dazzling glare glancing off its surfaces forcing his eyes into narrow slits.

"It's so bright it hurts to look!" he exclaimed.

This *femme fatale* of a desert was fully armed with the maximum measures of luminosity and heat conferred so eagerly by the sun. She weltered voluptuously in this shimmering sadistic radiation. In the foreground massive dignified dunes emitted white blazes to char the skin and smelt the eyes. The dunes further in the distance were chromatically less intense, though thermally just as potent, sending out undiminished waves of sultriness. An aureolic glow seemed to be pulsing from within them, an incandescence, transparently white and amorphously remote. Beyond this area of sun-blanched effulgence and to the horizon all topographical distinctions dissolved into a hazed white obscurity akin to the tenuous clouds above. Like a massive flock of clustering sheep, those dunes rolled onward, transforming into a pearly hallucination, a foaming tidal bore that stretched on to infinity, melding earth and sky into one vast alabaster expanse.

They were on the edge of the sandland, a scrubby sandbound wilderness some fifteen miles in circumference perched on the periphery of the Great Manges Desert. Only a few acres of this sparsely vegetated area was amenable to cultivation. In the last two years, the arable plots in close proximity to Black Sand Village had all been distributed among the citizens for private cultivation. As no one had coveted the sandland, it had been left unallocated, free to be worked by anyone so inclined.

Lao Shuangyang pushed his frayed and broken straw hat back on his head and swept his squinting eyes over the tumuli in the distance. Where are you, you red broom corn millet patch? he thought. I must find you! A hawk was circling in the sky, the sun glinting off its wings. That patch of sacred land he sought was surely hidden among those dunes. Success or failure depended upon his finding it. After decades of battling the dunes for a living, he knew well that finding the sacred earth was the crux of the matter, that to plant your seed anywhere else meant all your backbreaking work and everything you had put into it could be wiped out in a minute by a whirlwind, a front of hail, a swarm of sand grouse. It was steeped in enigma, this sandland. There was something inexplicable about it, something unknowable and beyond the ken of humans, a mysterious quality impervious to the tentacles of intellect and insight. Time and again he'd come back to it, unfailingly over the years, to wrench from it the substance of life, and to probe it and explore it, to pursue and discover the secret, the essence of that mysterious quality. And this had become the reason for his existence, a lifelong quest fueled by the seductive dream of controlling and mastering that mysterious quality: for if he could do that, then he could subjugate the sandland. An obsession, it was, abnormal really, a spectacularly tenacious reminder of childhood. Knowing that, however, did not diminish its vexatious hold upon him. It had started with a whirlwind.

He'd been only eleven at the time, a cowherd for Scarface Guan. One day he drove the herd into the Manges Sandland where the other cowherds didn't dare to set foot. Around noon a small black whirlwind popped out from behind a dune. Swirling and whirling it gradually moved toward him. Now whirlwinds were rampant in the sandland. They swept up sand, leaves, dry grass and whatever else happened to be in the way and flung this debris about as they roared and wailed along, charging piles of sand and groves of trees and low-lying depressions. The children used to say with gnomic wisdom that every whirlwind harboured a bunch of mischievous ghosts. Every time they saw one, they would spit — because evil spirits were repelled by spit — and run off and hide as far away as they could. This time, though, he stood his ground. He fixed the whirlwind in his sights and told himself, a living person can not step aside for a dead ghost! This time I'm going to see just what those ghosts they're always talking about are really like. Onward came the whirlwind. His spine went numb with fear and in his horror his hair stood on end, but he still refused to budge. Water flows along its destined path, the wind blows wherever it will. Rasping and scraping along, that whirlwind hugged the ground, turning and twirling, not caring a fig that a boy was standing in this path. It just crashed and sped along the route it had chosen for itself. He raised his herding whip and brandished it at the whirlwind, and just as it was about to sweep him up into its vortex, he shouted, "Okay, ghosts, where are you! I'm not afraid of you! Come out of there, I dare you!"

Suddenly it was pitch black and cold, and he was being sandblasted and pelted with grass and leaves. Then the whirlwind moved on. The dust and sand of the momentary chaos settled back to earth, and peace reigned once more. The boy fell unconscious to the ground, foaming at the mouth. The calves he'd been herding surrounded him and mooed. As luck would have it, just at that time a soccerer — a *böge* — happened to be passing by and discovered the presumptuous if pitiful little urchin. The *böge* watched the departing whirlwind and fulminated, "Is that you, you arrogant Headless Ghost? You can't even let a little kid that happens to be standing in the way alone, can you! Evil! You're nothing but evil! Poor little kid who dares to challenge ghosts, I'll save you!" Then the *böge* began moving his hands over the child and pinching him as he chanted incantations and circled him, leaping and singing. He kept this up for quite some time until the child finally came round.

That was when he'd thrown away his herding whip and started following the *böge*, high on the hope that he could learn how to subjugate the sand demons and the wind goblins and master that mysterious quality of the sandland. Even now the very thought of the "Headless Ghost" driving the whirlwind still set his heart palpitating, for he could never figure out why he had swooned. He'd taken to standing off to the side after that and scrutinising whirlwinds that came his way, but all he'd ever seen was a turbid yellow mass of swirling sand. "An evil wind bewitched me, that's what happened," he finally concluded. But his master, the *böge*, said, "You're wrong, child. That was the Headless Drought Spirit — the commander of the fifteen hundred vengeful ghosts of the Manges Sandland. Just look what you did — you invaded his territory, didn't burn any money for him, and you blocked his path and whipped him to boot. So of course he would wreak revenge on you." Lao Shuangyang sort of half believed this, but what he really believed in was the omnipresence of that mysterious quality.

In the year of land reform, the old *böge* was executed because he'd performed an exorcism upon someone who'd died in the process. He himself had been sent back to his home village. Those sad and anxious days still burned vividly in his memory. He'd returned to the village of his birth to find only a vast swath of sand. His parents, he learned, had fled. But his grandmother couldn't bear to be separated from her native earth and had come back. She, along with the entire house and courtyard, had been swallowed up by the drifting sand.

Crazy with grief he searched for her remains, for she'd been the one closest to him. The kindness, warmth and love she'd showered upon him was the best shield he could have had to protect him from the chill he felt from his fellow man. He never did find his grandmother's remains, so he appointed her a proxy grave, a certain sand tumulus he found that was always green with grass. There he burned paper money and made sacrifices for her. After that he threw himself into the work of refounding Black Sand Village. With the advent of the New Society he married but his tubercular wife died attempting to give birth to their first child, which also died. Thus to this very day he'd been living alone in this vast and boundless world.

"Bitchbrat! Hurry up!" He settled upon Raptor's Hump, the proxy grave of his grandmother. In the vicinity was a depression amenable to cultivation. He drove the cart down the sand ridge.

"Here I come!" Bitchbrat ran barefoot down the slope, creating a cloud of sand-dust in his wake.

Lao Shuangyang watched the joyfully bounding boy

with crinkling affectionate eyes.

He had literally picked Bitchbrat up off the street. That day he was coming back from the sandland when he discovered lying by the side of the road a feral child. A wandering beggar-child, the curiosity-seekers clustering round had said, one that had eaten some poisonous viper-nest mushrooms. Lao Shuangyang picked him up like a bundle of straw, took him home, and poured some swill down his throat. The child started vomiting at once, and when there was nothing else left to come up, he retched on convulsively, as if he would expel all his insides. Then Lao Shuangyang butchered his only laying hen and poured the fresh chicken blood into the boy's stomach.

"Who told you to bring me back!" the kid began cursing upon regaining consciousness.

"By my grandmother's twat," he cursed back, "what a big mistake that was, saving your lousy little life!"

"Do you have any more poisonous mushrooms?"

"What for?"

"So I can eat them again."

"Ah ha! So you ate them on purpose! By my grandmother's twat, you've got guts! What mystical skill are you cultivating?"

"Suicide! What else!"

"So you know about suicide already, at your age. What's wrong? Tell me about it."

"I don't wanna talk about it. Wait 'til I'm done dying, then I'll talk about it."

After that, though, he did talk about it, on the condition that he wouldn't get sent back home and could stay with the old man. Bitchbrat was the fifth of seven children. Of his four elder brothers, only the eldest had found himself a wife. The family had spent several thousand yuan on getting him married and was virtually bankrupt. When Bitchbrat was born his parents had been hoping for a girl they could exchange later for wives for his other brothers. They hadn't counted on yet another baldy-brat. From day one he'd been subjected to dirty looks, slaps and punches, and the more he grew, the more he really did look like a literal son of a bitch. "There's no reason whatsoever for living," he said.

"Did they get any girls after you?"

"They got zilch! Two more bald-brats. They gave them away. People said my mum's like alkaline earth that'll grow sorghum but not millet."

"Ha, ha, ha! You naughty little monkey! Forget about the snake-coil mushrooms. You just come with me and we'll grow some red broom corn millet!"

The sandland approach stretched before them like a snake on the move. Bitchbrat's naked footsteps dug deep in the sand like the lumbering paces of Blindy Bear*, as he stamped hard through the scorching surface sand to the soothing damp layer underneath. Ahead of him the bullock pulling the cart began to empty its bladder. Inspired, Bitchbrat pulled his little pecker out from the folds of his giant pants and shot out spurts of urine as he walked along. Ox and boy left behind them in the sand two winding trails of dampdots, which quickly dried and hardened.

"You know what, sir? People're saying Tiezhu's

---

*Blindy Bear — a black bear whose black eyes merge with the colour of its fur, giving the impression it has no eyes.

gettingmarried..." "Yeah, what about it?" Lao Shuangyang asked.

"That'll free up Aunt Heye!" Bitchbrat said.

"Yeah, what about it?" Lao Shuangyang asked again.

"Why, then I'll have a stepmother!" Bitchbrat laughed gleefully.

Whomp! Lao Shuangyang walloped Bitchbrat on the back of the neck, sending him into a flying "dog eats shit" tumble, flat on his face in the sand. Agilely he sprang back to his feet. "Ptui!" he expelled the sand from his mouth in grainy disgust. "Ptui!" Indignant with injury, he shouted, "Who told you to get drunk and bawl and blubber all over the place! Heye this and Heye that! You should of heard yourself!"

"What? Is that true?" Lao Shuangyang came to a dead halt. "Did I really go on like that?" He looked at Bitchbrat with stunned bewilder-filled eyes.

"Yes, you *really*, really, REALLY went on like that! You were shouting it out like it was your most favourite thing in the world!" Bitchbrat became more and more adamant, and he pouted his little lips.

"I see." Lao Shuangyang's embarrassment was surpassed by a tangle of emotions that came welling to the surface. "You don't understand, little monkey!" he said.

"Whaddaya mean I don't understand!" Bitchbrat cried. "I understand everything! You think about her every day, I know it! And every night she's over there wishing and wishing for you." He'd become very bold, enunciating this latter in a voice clear and distinct.

'I used to be a *böge*, you know that? And she used to be a *udugań*. In those days, *böge*s were not allowed to get married. But in particular they were absolutely forbidden to touch *udugan*s, and that's something the masters really pounded into our heads." Lao Shuangyang looked toward the sky and breathed a sigh glazed with desolation.

"Yeah but your masters' re all dead, right?"

"Yeah ... but their words didn't die."

"Riiight! Their words are *living* — get it? Living things change. They adapt!"

Lao Shuangyang was speechless. This clever observation had slammed elegantly smack into the centre of his chest. His face furrows twisted into anguish.

"It's too late. We're old. Both of us've got one foot in the grave — not a stinking iota of nothing is left for us..." He took a dirgeful pause. "Well, anyway," he continued, "the only thing I'm interested in right now is getting this red broom corn millet planted..."

Bitchbrat looked away. A sand dune had sprouted a crewcut of swallows ranged across the top. Just what he needed: something to count. The old man, the boy, each maintained a silence, each brooding upon his own separate sorrows.

4

Yushi was struck by her peculiar gaze. There lurked in it the hollow look of devastating loss and immense irretrievable distance. There was something else as well, something hidden that he couldn't quite put his finger on. Mystery was her name, this Andai Queen, defining her as much as it did the Andai King. Mystery, indeed, enshrouded the entire village and penetrated it down to its every nook and cranny. He plumbed the depths of all possible explanations for this impression. Perhaps it was the desert's ancient isolating silence casting itself like a dark perverted shadow upon this outpost of human habitation. Or maybe it was an atmosphere of despair born of a ruinous drought such as few had seen before. Or — and this he found most intriguing — could it be an aura emanating from the mysterious Andai, rooted in the nebulous mystical antiquity of tribal culture? Yushi mulled over these things. Such a strange old fellow, the Andai King, throwing over the chance to dance the Andai for that practically hopeless red broom corn millet. And here the Andai Queen was all but ready to lay down her very life for the sake of that same Andai. What was going on here, anyway? It occurred to him in a rather inchoate way that he would have to trace the very origins of this ancient rite if he were ever going to solve these mysteries.

Headman Meng Ke arranged for his meals to be supplied by different families. From one end of the village he would eat his way across to the other. He would live in the headman's house. The buildings of the old production team had been privatised two years earlier during the property distribution, so official visitors were put up in the headman's house, for which the headman could draw hosting expenses from the public treasury. He had a five-room house built of costly polished brick, and an eminently classy abode for this sandy back water.

"Every family will take turns bringing you good things to eat. Are you familiar with this arranged meal system?" Meng Ke asked.

"When I went for my tour in the countryside, that's how we ate — by the cooking-pool method. I'm not particular at all — just so I'm not a burden to anybody." Yushi was packing up his travel bag.

"Say, what are you doing there?"

"I won't be staying here. There's a place that's much more suitable."

"Where?"

"The Andai Queen — Aunt Heye — she's got her northern *kang*."

"You're going to stay at her house?" Meng Ke's voice drew out in a long question mark.

"Is there a problem with that?"

"Um, there are some things that you should maybe know about. This Aunt Heye, um, well, it's like this. She was a *udugan*, and all her life she's been very ... loose, let us say. Her life-style is ... you know ... not exactly saintly. There's always something questionable going on there, and I'm afraid you'd be setting yourself up as a target for gossip."

"Huh, is that all? I don't care about stuff like that. I look at it from the modern standpoint and do what I have to do without worrying about what people might say. I have my own moral standards, and they're not subject to the control of public opinion." Yushi laughed as he spoke, and he picked up his travel bag.

Meng Ke at first took this for willfulness. But then he considered that Aunt Heye's being over fifty would preclude any hanky-panky. This young fellow, after all, couldn't be any more than twenty-seven or -eight. So he chuckled and helped Yushi with his bag. "Well, in that case, it might be a good idea. You can get a lot more done in such close proximity to the Andai Queen." With his thoughts fixed on that sum of money that Yushi could bring in, he didn't really care about the hosting expenses that he would otherwise be able to get.

Aunt Heye was quite surprised. Meticulously she swept off the mat of the northern *kang* with a stiff broom and spread some plastic sheeting on top. In the corners of the *kang* she sprinkled a layer of white "six-six powder"* to keep down the fleas. Human habitations in this desert domain provided a most favourable breeding ground for this shrewd little parasite. Her own toughened skin and sinewy flesh didn't yield much blood, so she wasn't subject to the painful burning itching their bites could cause. But she didn't want this tender city youth to get all bitten up.

Yushi discovered that Aunt Heye's house was as decrepit as an old crow's nest. He had visions of it collapsing in the middle of the night, burying him and Aunt Heye alive. But he needn't have worried really, because the building's structure and the materials that went into it were exceedingly simple. The walls were constructed of reed matting plastered with several layers of mud. The roof consisted of interwoven osiers topped with pressed sorghum stalks and cattail leaves further coated with a layer of solonetz (alkaline earth). The roof beam and purlins weren't even as thick as the diameter of a rice bowl. Thus, even if these materials did fall on top of their heads, it couldn't be fatal. Crude housing like this was quite common in Black Sand. Of course, big powerful families like that of Headman

---

*Benzene hexachloride.

Meng Ke, who'd somehow managed to get rich while everyone else was left behind, provided higher class accommodations for themselves.

Aunt Heye's house had no convenient access to water. The creek that once ran past her door had dried up, obliging her, along with a lot of other villagers bereft of wells, to fetch water in from the Black Sand River nearly two miles to the south. This was a river of turbid astringent water that flowed hesitantly along in its dry brown-yellow bed after having had its greater part siphoned off by the arid desert that formed its banks. On several occasions Yushi had arisen early to fetch water for Aunt Heye, only to discover her water jars already filled. Someone had beaten him to it.

Who? One day when he awoke, the rays of the sun had not yet alighted upon his paper windowpane. In the outer room he heard the sound of banging water buckets, Stealthily he arose and followed the deed-doer all the way to the Black Sand River.

His quarry walked with an agile step, his body bent forward, his feet moving like the wind. Once he'd filled the buckets Yushi appeared before him.

"So, it's you — you're Tiezhu, aren't you?" Yushi had heard of this person.

Tiezhu made a non-committal grunt. There was something unfavourable in his countenance, a look of reptilian wretchedness.

"What's all this water business so early in the morning? Can't you at least wait for daylight before you start banging the buckets around?"

"Daylight?... Heh heh heh, with all the gossip-mongers around, I'd be a fool."

"Sit down a bit. Here, have a smoke." Extending

him a cigarette, Yushi sat on the river bank. Tiezhu hesitated. Then he took the cigarette and squatted on a little dirt ridge a short distance away.

"How long have you been making it with Aunt Heye?" Yushi plunged right in.

Tiezhu started.

"It's okay, I'm cool — Aunt Heye's already told me all about it."

"Not so long — ten years maybe." Tiezhu licked his lips and stole a glance at Yushi.

"Then why don't you marry her?"

"Marry her? Heh heh heh…" Tiezhu rolled his eyes toward the sky and gulped back his words.

"What's the matter?"

"Nothing's the matter, heh heh heh," Tiezhu demured. Then he said, "Who would dare marry her? Even if you discount that she's a lot older, she used to be a *udugan*! Heh heh heh…"

"Yeah? So she used to be a *udugan* — so what?"

"That's not something you people who spent all your time in school would know about." Tiezhu lowered his voice. "In those days, *udugan*s were not much different from good-time-gals shacked up in brothels…" He laughed like a cat yowling in the night.

Yushi leaped to his feet. If a wasp had stung him, he couldn't have been more swift. His interlocutor had spoken so frankly — so nakedly — that words utterly failed him. His impulse was to slap that sallow, wretched-looking face of his, but he forced himself to be civil.

"So, you've been sleeping with her for over ten years like a prostitute!" Yushi said coldly, staring daggers at him. "But you shouldn't forget that this *udugan* made you, a half-dead corpse, know that you were still a man with a prick! If I were Aunt Heye, I'd have cut off that treasure in your crotch long ago and fed it to the dog!"

Tiezhu blanched. "Please, I beg you, don't tell her I said that! I just lost my head, I didn't mean it..." He'd pasted an ingratiating smile on his face, just like the first time he'd tried to elicit Aunt Heye's forgiveness!

Yushi of course would not repeat these words to Aunt Heye and get her all upset but he felt very sad for her.

Tiezhu left with his buckets of water sloshing and swaying on his shoulder pole.

Yushi remained sitting on the river bank, staring at the Black Sand River. It really was an exaggeration to call it a river. It looked like a narrow silver-grey ribbon vaguely glimmering in the dawn's early light, still and silent. Its headwater lay about twenty miles off, at the base of a hill, and as it proceeded along, it fed on waters that the desert wrung out of itself and poured into numberless, tiny dryland creeks. But this was the source and course of that eminent river known as the Western Liao. Its fame went all the way back to the ancient Khitans of the Liao Dynasty, who left their writings for later generations to peruse. To look at this toad-piss water was to marvel that it should have acquired for itself such a grand reputation. And yet, there had been not only the Khitans. Meticulous research had revealed that before them there were the Donghu, or the "barbarians of the east" and the Sienpi; and these were followed by the Mongolians, the Mohe, the Nuchen, the Manchus, and the Hans, who came in through the Shanhai Pass. It was the intermingling of all these peoples that endowed the region with its colourful history and its distinctive cultural properties. The very antiquity of the Andai, he surmised, its tenacity as an established rite and the wealth of implications it evoked, probably had something to do with this river — the river squeezed out of the desert.

A keen blade of light slit ruthlessly through the sombrous sky and brought the outlines of the Black Sand River into sharp relief. Yushi marvelled to find that this slim ribbon-river had virtually slashed and hacked its way through the sandland, carving out a broad channel through which to carry forth its scarce waters of life. Subject to constant attack and invasion by the shifting sands on either side, violated by its own thirsty bed unceasingly sucking away, it had nonetheless made the trek across the vast, boundless domain of dunes. What persistence it possessed, what dauntless devotion! This was a stubborn river, a passionate river, a river determined to beat the odds. It made a daring investment to achieve its goal, applying part of its waters to soaking the sand of either bank and the rest to barging across the desert wasteland that would stand in its way and stop it. Naturally all that remained was but a thread, but it was an invincible thread, the silver shaft of a long sure-shot arrow. Herein lay the spirit — the soul — of the river. And what about the Andai? Was the Andai the spirit — the soul — that invested the traditional culture of the region? Yes, Yushi thought, the Andai was just like this river. And the Andai Queen was the incarnation of this spirit.

He stood up. Reluctant to leave, he cast a parting glance upon the river, then turned and walked back.

He still hadn't thoroughly figured out this river and the Andai. He would have to dig his heels in here for a long time before he could do that. To really know this swath of sand beneath his feet, this river, and the Andai was not something to be accomplished in a day or two, nor even a year or two. It was something that required decades, nay, several generations. Fortunately, he himself was a son of the sand, and the desert flowed in his veins.

He quickened his steps. This morning he was slated to meet with the village elders for a group discussion. He arrived back at Aunt Heye's just in time to see Tiezhu making a hasty escape from the courtyard. Aunt Heye had slopped both his buckets of water onto the courtyard ground. Tiezhu looked thoroughly crushed. She was roundly cursing him out: "Mangy dog! You really take the cake! Get out! I never want to see you again!" She tearfully watched Tiezhu's wretched-looking figure growing small in the distance. It was hard to tell whether she was crying for him or crying for herself.

Yushi said nothing. Indeed, there was nothing to say. He greeted her, then went on to Headman Meng Ke's house for the meeting.

He found the place, to his eminent surprise, teeming with the very old. At least fifteen of the attendees were over seventy, and five of these were octogenarians. He couldn't get over it; one wouldn't expect that an impoverished backward place like this with its infertile sandland soil could sustain human life to such an extent. One by one Yushi brought out bottles of clear liquor, cartons of cigarettes, and packages of cakes with which to ply the conferees. Things immediately livened on. Instead of a dreary forum of prim, stiff-backed participants pulling long bored faces, he had a party-like atmosphere with everyone sipping, snacking and getting all rosy-faced as they chattered away. Meng Ke, who'd initially raised an eyebrow at Yushi's procedure soon decided it was a brilliant move. There was a lot more to this young fellow that met the eye, he thought. So easily had he gotten these old timers, total strangers as they were, to open their hearts to him.

"This here Andai, it started way back when Gheghis Khan, the Mongol emperor, gave the Horqin Grassland to his younger brother as a fife," one of the octogenarians initiated through his broken buck teeth. "I heard my grandfather say so when I was little."

"In actuality," one of the others injected, "'Andai' refers to a certain spirit." The speaker, literate in the classics, continued at a learned leisurely pace. "Acording to legend, it involved Maitreya, the Living Buddha. Centuries ago, in Big Hure* in Northland, Maitreya's mother came down with a strange lingering illness. Maitreya gathered up a whole crowd of lamas to recite the sutras, but it didn't do any good. So he turned to a Shaman, a *böge*, to perform an exorcism; and for good measure he called in people from all around to sing and dance. Finally the offending spirit relented, but his was only temporary. The *böge* told Maitreya that to effect a total cure he would have to take her to convalesce in Little Hure

---

*Big Hure: ancient Ulan Bator; Northland (Mobei): today's Outer Mongolia; Southland (Monan): modern Inner Mongolia; Little Hure: present day Hure Qi, in eastern Inner Mongolia, near the Liaoning border; Darhanqi, in central Inner Mongolia, today combined with Muminggqanqi to form Darhan Muminggqanqi.

and Mongoltown in Southland. Thus the Buddha's mother took a cart and headed south. When she arrived in Darhanqi, a split in the cart's planks occurred, and a portion of the Andai spirit escaped through the crack. When she got to Little Hure, one of the cart's wheels fell apart, and another portion of the Andai spirit scattered. After the cart was repaired and it got to Mongoltown, they ran into a gang of robbers. These robbers hijacked the cart, leaving behind in Mongoltown the entire remaining portion of the Andai spirit. From this time forward, the Andai has been handed down in that swathe of territory encompassing Darhanqi, Little Hure and Mongoltown."

"Aw, that's just a lotta malarky!" another old cadger munching cakes begged to differ. "Actually there are two kinds of Andai. One is the 'Orge Andai' and has to do with marital unhappiness. The other one is the 'Ada Andai*', which is for exorcism. Basically, the 'Orge Andai' is for curing illness in women, and everybody gathers together to sing and dance. The 'Ada Andai' is when the *böge* and the *udugan* lead all the people in a dance to drive out demons and repel evil and remove impending ill fortune. Several villages get together to perform the Andai over seven seven-day periods, or forty-nine days. There are shorter ones too, only three to five days. Whether short or long, though, it's really crazy!"

---

*A malevolent spirit, enemy to both humans and to Tegri (top benevolent spirit in the Mongolian Shamanistic belief system), Ada flies about spreading alarm and disease. It is the author of unspecific debilitating ailments, which it causes by taking up residence in the victim's body.

Yushi could barely contain his excitement. He seized upon every word the old men uttered, filling page after page of his notebook, ravenously capturing every detail. And still he urged them on.

Aunt Heye, who had maintained silence up to now, slowly sipped her black tea concentrate and said, "There are all kinds of stories about how the Andai came to be. The one with the widest currency, though, is the one I heard from my mistress when I was still a girl. She said that in the ancient times there was an old man in Gorlos Qi* whose beloved only daughter came down with an illness that wouldn't go away. At the urgings of his relatives and friends, he put her into an ox cart and took her to distant Mongoltown to a special doctor. The day he got to Bayan Hua Prairie of Little Hure, the axletree of the cart suddenly broke, and they were stuck there. Meanwhile, the daughter's condition was worsening and there was nothing the father could do about it. So he began singing a tragic song railing against Fate. The sound of this singing moved the local people, who gathered round the ox cart and joined the old man in his singing. And they started to dance, too, as a means of comforting his suffering soul. Little did they know that their singing and the general warmth and passion they generated would touch the patient to her very heart. She got down out of the cart and joined the crowd in the singing and dancing. The sweat was pouring off her, and her condition improved with each passing day. That's where the name 'Andai' came from: it's also known as

---

*Gorlos Qi, in northwest Jilin, now known as Qian Gorlos Qi, also called Qian Gorlos Mongolzu Zizhixian.

'Ōndei' and it means 'lift up your head and rise from your bed'."

"Lift up your head and rise from your bed! So that's it. What an interesting story — it explains everything!" Yushi exclaimed, enraptured by the revelation. What it meant was that in the face of a difficult life and under the control of an unjust fate, the working people had created the Andai, and the Andai was closely linked with their fate. In the midst of black days and in the clutches of injustice, they had "raised their heads and got up from their beds". This was a compelling call to action through the form of song and dance!

Suddenly Yushi had an idea: this place was in the grip of a big drought, so why not organise a giant Andai performance? He could bring in his old classmate at the television station to film it! Yes! This was extremely valuable material, and once old people like Aunt Heye passed on, the wealth of songs and all the dance steps of the Andai would be lost. Yes, this should be done. It was a project well worth doing. And besides that, the television station was well endowed, so its involvement would benefit Black Sand Village tremendously.

He sent off a long letter to his former classmate who now worked in the Literature and Art Department of the television station.

5

Raptor's Hump was self-possessed, imbued with a vital energy, like a hawk on the verge of lifting off into the sky in a great flap of its wings. Thrusting a bald top high into the air, it looked around superciliously upon the empty sky, the vast wilderness, the desert sand.

Already dusk was upon them.

They chose a low-lying area covered with cock-claw reeds to unload their cart. The cock-claw reeds meant they could sink a well and be sure to get water. The first order of business, though, was constructing the shelter, a major operation. Siting it at the base of the dune, they sank the posts, topped them with crossbeams, and covered those with willow wattles. They couldn't afford to be sloppy with any of these tasks. The shelter had to withstand the "patronage" of the wild pigs that would come rubbing up against it in the night, and take the brunt of constant sand storms as well. Within no time, the ageless, empty sand flat boasted a triangular-shaped shelter imbued with primeval creative ingenuity. Lao Shuangyang and Bitchbrat occupied one end of the shelter and allocated the other end to the bullock and Dragon Master, according them treatment worthy of humans out of fear they would otherwise fall victim to wolves in the night.

"Bitchbrat, go fetch some dry roots and kindling!" Lao Shuangyang was off to one side surveying the lay of the land in preparation for digging a well.

Bitchbrat bounded over, whistling happily. This was his chance to explore. He'd been harbouring visions of a place lush with milk berries, sweet-and-sour wild bamboo shots, ambrosia-laden sheep-tit vines, and studded with sand pits chock-full of quail and wild pigeon eggs, and surely there was wild honey to be found as well.

"Don't go wandering off. Watch out for Zhang the Third!"

"Zhang the Third?"

"The wolf!" Uttering the actual name of this beast was bad luck in the desert, but there it was; it had slipped right out. "You stinkin' little bastard," he swore, "you talk too much! Go and do as I say!"

Bitchbrat was used to living in the wild. The thought of this particular beast didn't phase him a bit. He hitched up his sagging pants and ran off.

He climbed to the top of Raptor's Hump. As he surmounted the dune's bald pate, a sunset panorama spread itself out. It was a rapacious scene, a drama of the desert swallowing the sun. He stood there mesmerised, black belly sticking out, watching the ingestion in silence. He could feel the suffering of the sun. It was trembling as if in the throes of a struggle, its illumination growing pitifully dimmer, transmitting an anguished cry of pain. Stripped of its solar dignity, it appeared exceedingly round and vaguely fuzzy, like the de-shelled, de-whited yolk of an egg. A lurid orange hummed at its centre, while a glowing golden aureole luminesced around it. Treacherously, the silhouetted desert below caressed its prey even while absorbing it in its greedy maw. Soon there remained only a little half-circle. Bitchbrat swallowed. Then the anterior sandland caught his eye, for it was bathed in the rosy luminosity spilling over from the edge of the west. And the white sandy slope of the dune scintillated with a sprinkling of gold dust, No! Not gold dust, it was phosphorescent eggyolk dust! He stood there transfixed, imprisoned by a resplendence he could not bear to set a clumsy foot upon. The rosy sunlight enfolded the half-naked child in its softening embrace. Soon the glittering auric yolk-dust blushed to a saffron-yellow, then deepened to dusky goldenrod. Gradually it contracted, as if its edges were rolling up, and took on a tinge of plum-red that faded into purple-black... Astonished, Bitchbrat lifted his eyes and saw that the semicircle of eggyolk was no more; completely swallowed by the desert, it was, its legacy a fitful smear of purple cloud, a dolorous veil of tears.

"Bitchbrat! What are you doing standing there like a dummy! Have you lost your soul, or what?"

Reluctantly he turned away. Then he remembered his task. With a burst of zeal, he scrambled to descend the dune. His legs slipped out from under him and down he went into a rolling tumble, no more able to stop himself than a helplessly rolling log. He wrapped his arms around his head and and abandoned all resistance, turning and tumbling and gathering the detritus of the dune, until all there was to see was a trundling ball of sand. A living study in terracotta, he picked himself up at the bottom. "Ptui!" he cleared his granular mouth. "Ptui!" None the worse for wear, he sprang to his task. Naked, brittle roots stuck out from the side of the dune, where the slope was subject to the onslaught of the wind, testifying to a land once draped in green. Kicking at them and scrabbling them out, he soon had himself a large bundle.

With the efficiency of a burrowing marmot, Lao Shuangyang had dug a well in the cock-claw reed patch. A metre or so in depth, it had around three of its sides piles of excavation dirt that he'd tamped with the back of his spade. The fourth side he'd left open for entry and exit, forming three or four steps for this purpose. On the bottom was a round bottomless basket set in to prevent the collapse of the sides. Bitchbrat looked in and discovered — a limpid azure pool! It reflected along with the sky his own bobbing, dishevelled, sand-covered head.

"Wow, sir! Look what you did!" Bitchbrat walked down into the hole. He knelt, placing his hands on the ground, and extended his head into the well for a long cool refreshing draught. He'd never tasted better, it seemed, even if it did have a tinge of the typical astringent earthen flavour of the desert. He stood up and wiped the wet sand off his mouth with the back of his hand. "Ah, that's so good!" he exclaimed. "Just what I needed!"

As dry as the sandland is, it yields water to those who know where to look. For the water table is high, and once it rains, almost any well dug in a low-lying area will be a wet one. Lao Shuangyang took a bucketful to the black bullock. "Quite a bit of water has collected in the low-lying areas since it rained several days ago. We have to hurry and take advantage of this to get the seeds planted. Time is of the essence." Lao Shuangyang took off his shirt and squatted down. He sank both hands into the damp, cool sandy mud he'd just dug up and smeared it all over his front and back. "Ah —, ah —," he groaned in delight, as if its soothing coolness were penetrating his very bones. When he'd finished slathering his upper body, he smeared his legs as well, from his ankles to his calves and on up to his thigh. His black skin, heretofore tight and parched and encrusted with a white efflorescence of dried sweat, began to take on a healthful ruddy glow and to retrieve its suppleness and elasticity. To Bitchbrat's amazement, the old man's scrawny shrunken torso assumed an aspect of rock-like solidity, strong, hard and substantial. Wet sand therapy, obviously, was a dynamite defence against the effects of the insidious desert heat. Emulating this peerlessly ingenious procedure, he shrieked in delight with the salubrious pleasures of a wet-sand bath.

They ate supper and turned in early.

An urgent bladder woke Bitchbrat in the middle of the night. The old man's straw pallet was empty. Rubbing his eyes, he went out and found him sitting on the flat of sand before the door, his arms wrapped around his knees. He was gazing intently upon that low-lying plot that he would plant. At his feet rested a pile of pipe ashes. Silvery was the slope of the dune, as was that latent piece cropland, in the flooding light of the moon. He walked over and silently took up a seat beside him.

"How come you're awake?" the old man asked after a lengthy interval.

"The bullock's stinky piss woke me up; and the dog's smelly farts. What about you?"

"I'm wide awake. I've slept for sixty years and don't have any more sleep left in me."

"Well, then, it's really neat sitting like this."

"Yes... Listen — the sandland's chattering."

"Chattering? What's it saying?"

"It's all sighs. Listen."

Bitchbrat held his breath and cocked his ears, but could hear nothing resembling a sigh. There was only the swooshing of the tireless nocturnal wind blowing across the sandy slope. Washed in the dense luminosity of the moon, the sandland seemed supremely serene, sunk into the depths of slumberous oblivion.

"It's been sighing for decades, for centuries. Humanity's a hopeless case." The old fellow fell to mumbling to himself. After awhile he said, "Tomorrow we'll plant the seeds. Ah, yes, red broom corn millet..." He had some of the seeds in his palm and he was stroking them. Bitchbrat took a few grains and examined them closely in the moonlight. So, he thought, you're what's keeping the old man awake. Smaller than sorghum seeds, bigger than millet seeds, they were smooth, round, hefty, and glitteringly translucent.

"Can these stop the desert from sighing?" Bitchbrat asked.

"Yes. This is a crop that loves to strike its roots in sandy soil."

And so, Bitchbrat, too, became a believer.

Just when the eastern crossbeam was turning white, Lao Shuangyang hitched up the plough. The day offered only these few hours from early dawn to around noon for planting. Once the sun reached its zenith, the sandland turned into a steamer, radiating heat that neither humans nor draft animals could withstand. They began their ploughing at the southern end of that lowlying tract.

Labouring on their patch of land, they became a work of art, a beautiful pastoral composition of tilling and seeding.

In the first rays of the morning sun, the black bullock was leaning into the yoke, the thick plough rope pulled taut. Lao Shuangyang trod barefoot behind, guiding the plough. On either side of the steel ploughshare, the soft, loose sandy earth was opening up like two waves rushing to opposite shores. Behind him, a seeder-gourd slung diagonally across his shoulder, little Bitchbrat was making a clack-clack-clacking noise by striking with a stick a hollow wooden tube sticking out of the seeder-gourd's top. The vibration of each blow urged out a few brown-yellow grains, which were then separated by grass tassels inserted into the open end of the tube. Thus they fell evenly by twos and threes into the wet earth of the newly opened furrows. Dragon Master took up the rear. A rope was looped around his neck the other end of which was attached to an ovoid wooden roller that he was pulling over the length of the furrow, tamping the newly sown seeds into the earth. Here was primitive agrarianism re-enacted, the cooperation of human and animal in the most ancient of quests for basic subsistence. The rapping upon the seeder-gourd carried clearly and rhythmically on the air, accompanied at irregular intervals by a couple of cracks of the whip, the continuous dampened rustle of the ploughshare turning up the earth, and the raspy turning of the wooden roller tamping it down. An elegant pastoral concerto this was, a solemn, harmonious elegy of primitive simplicity.

Three days later found them steeped in crisis. The frightful evaporation rate of the sandland was rapidly obliterating the salutary effects of the rain that had fallen several days previously. Less and less water was to be had from the well, until it could ooze out a mere five or six bowls a day, far from enough to supply the needs of both animals and people. Lao Shuangyang dug the well a few feet deeper, but this brought no appreciable improvement, leaving them with the only alternative of restricting their intake. Bitchbrat took over

Dragon Master's job, while Lao Shuangyang, cracking his bullwhack, drove the dog off to return to the village. But the dog circled round several dunes and came back, plopping himself down at the door of the shelter. They didn't give him any water. But while they were occupied in the field, he sneaked into the well and drank it dry.

Lao Shuangyang hardened his heart. He caught the dog and hanged him from a wooden piling. They were getting sick of eating only corn meal mush anyway.

His eyes brimming with tears, Bitchbrat embraced the old dog about the neck and wouldn't let go.

The dog, though, didn't seem in the least upset by his impending fate. He just sat there contentedly, not a flicker of distress in his unblinking eyes, as if he simply deemed his sacrifice a most appropriate means of paying his master back for the years of care and kindness he had given him.

When Lao Shuangyang pulled the rope taut, Bitchbrat screamed and fled into the shelter. Lao Shuangyang fixed his eyes upon that piece of land waiting for them to come and plant it, and upon the sandland beyond rolling on infernally toward the south. He grit his teeth, tightening his cheeks, and his hands shook violently. Dragon Master wimpered once, like one relieved of a great burden, then went limp.

Bitchbrat had withdrawn to a corner in the shelter, where he sat immobile, blindly staring before him. Despite earnest threats and cajolery, he refused to look at the dog meat dished up steaming and savoury, so Lao Shuangyang let him be.

Two days later, the bullock collapsed in the field. He'd been underwatered, underfed, and overworked until he just couldn't pull that heavy plough any more. A wrought-up Lao Shuangyang whipped him furiously, tearing away clumps of fur and raising long bloody welts. The bullock only closed his eyes and suffered the beating, for he had no strength to pick himself up.

There was nothing Lao Shuangyang could do. He flung his bullwhack to the ground and threw his arms about the animal's neck. Two turbid tears dropped from his eyes. Contritely, he rubbed the bloody marks he'd inflicted and murmured, "Old Matey, I've been cruel to you…"

Silently he removed the bullock's yoke and released the girth. He stood up and slung the yoke across his right shoulder, turned his head and hollered at Bitchbrat, "You walk the plough!"

Bitchbrat looked at his scrawny withered figure, not budging from where he stood.

"Are you deaf? Hurry up and start walking the plough! Did you hear me!"

"No! I'm not going to do it," Bitchbrat said coldly.

"You'" He picked up his bullwhack.

Bitchbrat looked at him unmoved.

"Are you going to walk it or not?"

"No." Bitchbrat stuck his belly out and straightened his neck.

Lao Shuangyang brandished the bullwhack overhead, where it remained poised upon the hairline between violence and retreat. He threw it away. Then he lurched several steps toward Bitchbrat and dropped heavily to his knees before him. "Little Ancestor, I'm begging you! There's only a couple of pounds of seeds left. This broom corn millet will be our food for all of next year! You understand, Little Ancestor?"

"You mean for us both? You mean I'm still going to be with you next year?"

"You'll be with me forever. You'll not be my adopted son. No, you'll be my adoptive father!"

"Oh! You're going to take me as your adopted son?" Bitchbrat eyed the old guy incredulously. Then, aloofly, he walked over to the plough. Placing his diminutive hands upon it, he righted it, pausing to give his eyes a vigorous rub with the dirt-encrusted back of his hand.

Lao Shuangyang stood up and put the yoke back on his shoulder.

"I hate you, Dad," Bitchbrat said calmly behind him.

"I hate this desert, sonny," Lao Shuangyang replied, darkness occluding his face.

The ploughshare stabbed into the sandy soil. Lao Shuangyang bent forward, tensed his leg muscles, and pulled with all of his might. Back he rebounded, as if the rope were a spring. The plough hadn't moved an inch. Bitchbrat set the ploughshare slightly higher.

"Set it back down to where it was! We're planting broom corn millet, not radishes!"

"Okay, okay, you crazy old coot. Go ahead and pull. See if you can outpull the bullock!"

Lao Shuangyang leaned forward until his shoulder paralleled the ground. Grimacing, he fixed his bulging eyes ahead of him. Blue veins bulged upon his forehead, like earthworms. Pea-sized beads of sweat dripped down from his temples. "Heh!" he roared, feeding his task with a dose of wrath. The ploughshare shivered, and the ploughshare shook, and finally it began to eat its way through the earth. One step, two steps, three steps ... ten steps ... fifty steps... Bitchbrat couldn't believe that scrawny body of his harboured such great strength.

The bullock-sized yoke weighed heavy and hard upon his shoulder blade. Soon fine black-red streaks of blood were oozing out from under it.

Bitchbrat drew himself to a halt. He said nothing as he removed his only piece of clothing, those flapping adult undershorts that hung off his butt. He walked over to the old man, who was still pulling earnestly, and stuffed the pants between his shoulder and the yoke. Now he was totally naked, his skinny black buttocks flexing and relaxing with his every step. The right one had a shiny scar, legacy of a dogbite. His little pecker stood out a mite from between his stalk-thin legs, the noon-day sun glancing shinily off the tip; for he had just relieved himself and a pearl of pee still quivered there.

Lao Shuangyang looked back at him and couldn't help laughing. "Sonny, like that you are the handsomest of them all, even handsomer than Luo Cheng!"*

Bitchbrat ignored him and took up the plough again. They slogged on for twenty or thirty metres, then retraced their steps, one operating the seeder-gourd, the other pulling the roller.

---

*Luo Cheng — a comely young warrior in traditional popular fiction and opera who died tragically.

6

Let your black hair down, ah, Andai!
Don't be sitting glum, ah, Andai!

Humming the "Andai", Aunt Heye stepped softly toward the "oboga", a mound of sacred sand. The delicate light of the moon enveloped her. Her song flowing forth like a crystal source filled the stillness of the night.

Fickle is the wind, you know, ah, Andai!
So you should don your long, warm gown, ah, Andai!
Endless are our cares, you know, ah, Andai!
So you should excise those childish worries, ah, Andai!
....

Plaintive was her murmured song. Only at such times of solitude, caressing thus the notes of the Andai, could she commune with that ubiquitous spirit and truly feel it was there for her. And it would reach in and seize her loneliness and give her in its place a sense of serenity and release. Here in the obscurity of darkness, the spirit of Andai was palpable. She'd been seeking that mysterious spirit for ages, and now here it was, hovering in its astral plane, charisma shining forth in a resplendent aureole of light.

She'd become a VIP virtually overnight. Yushi had invited in the people from the television station, while the County Cultural Bureau had sent in a contingent of their own based upon his report. And so tiny little Black Sand Village was once again back on the map. An air of excitement and festivity was beginning to set in. The villagers had done an about-face and were now smothering this queen in sincere smiles and generous gestures of support. They were wrapped up in the revival of the Andai and the rituals of paying due respect to the spirits of the sand and the rain, for they deeply feared the drought and had a healthy reverence for the desert.

Only she was seized with depression. Their infectious enthusiasm had failed to penetrate her profound loneliness or her heavy knowledge that they were, at the base of it, looking at the bottom line: the Andai for them meant money, cold hard cash with which to buy grain. Even Yushi had an ulterior motive, to make a splash in socio-cultural circles with his inquiry into an ancient tribal legacy that would promote his own welfare. Nobody truly cared about her nor had any concept, let alone understanding, of her bleak friendless existence, the hell of her private apartheid, the turbulent wrenching emptiness of her utterly forsaken heart. For that matter, nobody really cared about the Andai or considered its future. They shared not her fascination with the mysterious unknowable spirit of Andai. It was hers to swallow the bitter pill of this fact alone, with astringent water, no less.

This time it was strictly based upon a sense of mission that she had decided to dance the Andai. Through this last opportunity she hoped to enjoy the happiness of roaming about the magical, mystical world of Andai to seek that spirit and capture it and meld her own forlorn soul into that realm of detached, aloof existence. Fate this one last time would surely recompense her when it was time for her to go.

The oboga was a natural sand hill, its rounded top levelled to form a broad sacrificial altar. Long streamers in four colours had been stuck into the sand at each of the four corners. They fluttered slightly in the night breeze. A pile of firewood sat in the centre along with an altar table. A live trussed-up sheep lay atop the table, ready for the morrow's sacrifice.

Slowly she climbed to the top. As she surveyed the arena prepared so meticulously by the villagers, her youthful *udugan* days and the richly varigated sacrificial scene she'd had a part in resonated in her memory. And there rematerialised a certain day and a certain venue, the recollection of which turned her eyes toward the deep hazy distance of the desert. She sighed. Where was he? Why had fate not ordained this one last time for them? What kind of a spirit was this red broom corn millet that it had besotted him so?

An opportunity irretrievably lost. Sorrow penetrated to the depths of her soul.

The first time the two of them had jointly performed was in the heady latter part of the flourishing fifties. That morning, several grass-green jeeps came roaring into Black Sand Village in a cloud of dust. This was an unprecedented event. Several gusty bare-bottomed boys chased along after the jeeps on their willow-stick horses, barely visible in their dusty wake.

That same evening she was summoned to the Production Brigade Office and introduced to an elegant woman in her forties, dressed with impeccable taste. A woman of substance, she was, someone you couldn't ignore. Later she learned that this was the daughter of some big official and that she herself held an office of no small import.

"Don't be afraid. Let's have a little chat." Her glasses reflected sheets of light, but this did not obscure her gentle friendly eyes. "You were a *udugan*?"

"Mmmm ... huh...," she mumbled affirmatively.

"You danced the Andai?"

"Uh-huh... Yes."

"Can you teach me?"

"Teach you? Teach you to dance the Andai?"

"Uh-huh," the woman adopted her style of reply. "And also him, them, the whole village." With a casual sweep of her hands, she indicated her entourage and the various brigade, team, and commune cadres.

"Chief, that's superstition, trickery to fool the people. I wouldn't dare to dance it. I haven't danced it since I went through education during Land Reform... " She'd stammered this out, not knowing what to say.

The woman laughed good-naturedly. "You don't have to worry about that," she said. "We're not doing superstition — no attempts to drive off evil or work cures or anything like that. We just want to sing and dance and adapt it to new content." The woman beamed as she looked at her uncomprehending face. "Now we want to sing the praises of the Three Red Banners and the Communist Party, and the peasants should do this in their own style. That means making use of the Andai, which is a form of mass participation singing. Of course we'll create new content for it — new words."

Aunt Heye didn't know what to say to that. She simply mumbled, "I don't know how to make up new words..."

"Someone will do it for you."

She was silent. This was something new, something

different. After all this time, the reviled Andai stamped out during Land Reform was suddenly wanted back. What was going on here? Possibilities began to unfurl in her heart. Fulfillment was to be found after all in this irresistible woman's irresistible proposition: she couldn't turn her down even if she wanted to.

"There's also a *böge* in the village," she offered helpfully. "He dances better than I do."

"I've seen him already. He refused. He didn't make any bones about it — real blunt he was." There was a light in the woman's eyes that bespoke faith in her. "I was hoping you could help," she continued. "You could go and ask him for me. What do you think?" It was as if this woman knew the details of their relationship and had something in mind.

"Me?" she queried, abashed. She shifted awkwardly and the colour flew to her cheeks. She wasn't used to face-to-face interviews with persons of prestige. And here that gruff old Shuangyang had actually had the audacity to turn her down!

"I hope you don't mind my imposing on you like this. My concern is for your Andai as an art form. If you update it and give it some innovative content, it can continue to be passed down to future generations, and your identities as *böge* and *udugan* will not have been in vain. The Andai will not be buried with you. I think that if any kind of folk art is constantly refurbished with new social content and takes on a new form which gives expression to this social content, then, and only then, can it shine with a radiance that will never be extinguished."

Her powers of persuasion were truly admirable. Aunt

Heye felt herself drawn to her, this woman of warmth and embracing amiability. So for the sake of the Andai, and for the sake of this woman who regarded her so highly, she really did go looking for Shuangyang.

"You better just go. I'm not going to do it." He slammed the door on her proposal.

"But listen, this is a chance to rescue the Andai from oblivion, an undreamed of, golden opportunity. If we let it pass us by, we may never get another!"

"I'm not doing it. That's not the Andai a *böge* dances!"

"So what kind of Andai does a *böge* dance? If we miss this opportunity, it'll go with us to the grave! Don't be an idiot. The important thing is that the Andai lives on, understand? It has to be handed down, otherwise it will end with us!" Suddenly she gave him a deep, emotion-laden look. An extraordinary splendour shone forth from her beautiful eyes. She said in a low voice, "If you can see your way to getting into the action, I'll marry you…"

He looked at her in astonishment. Slowly, he answered, "But I have a wife."

"Your wife?" She clucked her tongue. "She's but a tubercular ghost!"

"But she's alive."

"She won't last long."

He had nothing to say to this. She knew that ever since she'd come to Black Sand, he'd been repressing the feelings aroused in his youth and keeping clear of her. Circumstances, it seemed, always came between them, as if an invisible icy cold hand were separating their destinies. But she could not forget the dream of her youth, and though this dream had been washed in the sands of time until it was torn and tattered and seemed utterly hopeless, she'd never given it up. Stubbornly she fantasised its realisation.

"You cheated me out of the first half of my life. Are you aiming to cheat me out of the second half too? Why do you think I came here to Black Sand in the first place — for that crippled ghost? You blockhead, how brutal you can be — worse than a wolf —"

Shuangyang was silent. His heart was a cauldron of crashing waves. He understood her, but his experience of life and society's moral imperatives had woven themselves into a net he could not escape. He was no longer the man he'd once been. He thought of his sick wife, and he thought of the teachings of his dead master, and he thought of what she had been through and of her status as the widow of the brother of the old Party Branch Secretary. But locked deep in his heart was a burning, abiding love for her.

"Okay, I'll do it," he said. He couldn't hurt her again.

Their dancing made them famous. Their perfect coordination was poetry in motion as they led the entire village in the singing and dancing for seven days and seven nights. The Andai made Black Sand famous, and the commune, the whole county, the entire prefecture, in fact, became all the rage. In the evening and throughout the day the peasants waved their axes and sickles as they danced and sang all over the fields. An old lady who heard the Andai song over the loudspeakers began waving her long-stemmed pipe and dancing to the music, and she danced and danced until her adobe *kang* caved in. This ancient folk dance did indeed prove worthy of its name, "Öndei", lift up your head and rise from your bed, for it too had resurrected itself. The dance movements of the Andai had been adapted and modified with the help of the cultural troupe. The lyrics were written by the scholars and thematically dedicated to the Three Red Banners of the Great Leap Forward, the People's Communes, and the General Line of Socialist Construction, they sang the praises of the Party and the Party leaders with lines like: "Revolving around the Sun, we are not cold; Following the Party, we are not hungry," and "The Three Red Banners are a beacon, the People's Communes a golden bridge." And sometimes lines such as these would pop out as well: "Lama, what are you doing sitting horny on my *kang*? Watch out my hunter husband doesn't come back and skin you alive!"

They performed themselves into Communistic Red. That woman of prestige conferred upon them the titles of "Andai King" and "Andai Queen".

That night, only after the rooster crowed three times did they bring the Andai to an end. The peasants tramped out from the club with pickaxes on their shoulders and went directly to the fields to launch the Great Leap Forward and plough their furrows deep. Exhausted to the point of collapse, the two of them had been ordered to go home and rest. He walked her to her house and went in for a drink before going on his way. But then he fell into a coma-like sleep on her *kang*.

Stupefied, face still flushed, she looked at this man sleeping like the dead. The Andai had turned her soul upside down, she felt wild and crazy, and here this guy was, *sleeping*, of all things.

She loosened his clothes for him with trembling

hands.

Right away she discovered he was wearing a pair of tight deerskin underpants! Both sides had been lashed up with ten or so leather thongs knotted so tight that they would have to be cut to get them loose. Startled, she snatched her hands back as if they'd been burned by fire, but it was an icy rock she'd touched, not a body of living flesh and blood.

He spoke dazedly from the depths of his sleep, "I'm afraid, afraid I won't be able to stand it..."

"Why do you think that?" She lowered her head, broken-hearted, and stammered, "Do you really dislike me that much?"

"No, it's not like that. Listen, I tell you, in actually in all my life the woman I like the best is you..."

"Is that true?"

"Yes, it's true."

"Very well, then." She picked up a pair of scissors from the head of the *kang*.

"What are you doing..." His hands flew to his crotch.

"If you don't move your hands, I'll plunge these scissors right into your belly!" she said violently.

He was astounded. He believed she was fully capable of doing just that.

Her hand rested gently upon his abdomen as she cut the knotted leather thongs one by one. He dared not move an inch, and as he lay there his body began to burn. From his heart the blood rushed up to his throat and onwards to his cheeks and straight to his forehead. When the last thong fell away, the scissors clattered to the *kang*. Her heart was beating wildly. Before her eyes was a strong, healthy, naked male, lying there like a huge fallen tree. Black-brown skin, bulging pectorals, straight legs, and that mysterious male weapon... This was the dream she'd cherished since youth, the dream snatched by fate and drowned in the bittersweetness of life. She gave a gentle sigh and calmly disrobed. She lay down next to this fallen tree. That body next to her was as hot as if it were on fire. Wave after wave of heat swept over and enveloped her. She shook uncontrollably. After getting over their initial anxiety, she and he tentatively explored each other and embraced. Both were amazed to discover that after having not slept for several days and nights, their exhausted bodies now possessed such enormous energy.

Afterwards, she saw him off. She said, "Don't think badly of me..." She knew that this was the first time and the last time. Crying as if her heart would break, she watched his faltering, swaying figure as he walked away. She was crying for herself, and for him.

In the years that followed, he and she lived as strangers in the same village. In such close proximity they were, and yet they may as well have been on opposite ends of the earth. In the wink of an eye, several decades had passed, and time had changed both of their hearts to wood. Now the Andai, on the eve of its rare performance, resurrected him in her mind. Mournfully, like the cry of the wild goose seeking a mate, she thought of the man carrying on his bitter struggle alone in the sandland. Only the Andai could bring them together. They each had their own pursuits, she knew, their own homes they struggled to maintain, their own tragic attempts to obtain what they could never get. There was simply nothing to be done for it.

When she thought of this, she became much more peaceful in her heart.

The next day. Before dawn. Several hundred Black Sand villagers of every age and description were gathered around the sacred sand mound — the oboga. The television cameramen were positioning themselves for the best angles and shots, the sound mixers were setting their levels, and a little distance off, their diesel generator was roaring.

Headman Meng Ke addressed the villagers from atop the oboga. "Yes, everyone, you heard me right. Our revered leaders can be nothing but candid with us here in Black Sand. Black Sand Village is the home of the Andai. The history of this is as long as you care to think back. Shit, in the fifties, this was the cultural centre of the whole district. So today we have to put on a good show for our revered leaders — we can't disappoint them! This year we've suffered a big drought, and not a grain will be harvested, so our revered leaders couldn't have chosen a better time to come and investigate how the Andai was traditionally performed. Today we've set up this sacrificial altar on which we'll sacrifice to the spirits of the sky and the sand, and we'll drive away evil and pray for rain. So in dancing the Andai, we kill two birds with one stone! Every participant will be compensated for every day of work missed. As soon as the money is received by us, it will be distributed evenly among everybody. So let's everybody dance 'til we drop! Our ability to buy grain depends upon it!"

The headman's pep talk was sincere and forceful and entirely seductive. Several hundred people watched his big mouth working, eyes full of anxious expectation, as if coins were going to start pouring out of that black cavern any minute now. All held their breath and quietly tensed for the great explosion of energy that they would expend so their bowls could be filled with moldy buy-back corn!

After Meng Ke finished speaking, he motioned to a white-haired, silver-bearded presiding elder off to one side.

This old man, who had once been a *Gebhui** Lama in the temple, was holding in both hands a snow-white *hada***. He bowed thrice toward the oboga and in a sonorous voice began to recite:

When Mount Sumbur was still a mudball,
And the Sundalai Sea a frog pond,
Our forebears worshipped Heaven and Earth,
And sacrificed milk and meat upon the Oboga,
And drove off evil and summoned sweet rain when they
*   danced the dance of Andai!*
Like the lark, raise your voices in song!
Like the lion, leap into the dance!

The peasants around the oboga responded:

Ah, Andai!
Ah, Andai!

Now the lead singer, Aunt Heye, dressed in a black silk gown and supporting a young woman gowned in white and crowned with a green scarf that completely

---

*Gebhui — a mid-rank Lama in charge of monastic discipline.

**Hada — a piece of silk often used as a greeting gift among the Tibetan and Mongol nationalities.

covered her head, stepped slowly into the circle formed by the crowd. She led the young woman to a block of wood in the centre and had her sit down on it. Then she straightened up and flung the coloured scarves in her hands up into the air. From one side of the dune there sounded a note from a long ox horn, followed by a surging, momentous thunder of drums. The overture to the Andai, "Powerful Leaping Waves" had begun. It rose and fell melodiously with a slow and languorous rhythm, like a gentle spring breeze, filling people's hearts with the lapping of waves. And they saw Aunt Heye move her famous "youthful fluid shoulders" and she began to dance, easily, lightly, like a leaf fluttering in the wind. Waving her two colourful scarves up and down and around, she flitted and fluttered about like a bright butterfly in its graceful erratic dance upon the air currents.

She moved toward the woman in white, singing:

Loosen your black hair, ah, Andai!
Don't sit there brooding, ah, Andai!
The people have all devotedly gathered here, ah, Andai!
It's time to dance the frenzied dance and sing the manic song, ah, Andai!

The peasants, too, began to step to the rhythm, following the dance movements of the *udugan* and responding sonorously in refrain, "Ah, Andai!" over and over again. As the dancing proceeded, there gradually formed a gigantic circle with the *udugan*, Aunt Heye, and the young woman in white suffering the "Andai disease" in the centre. Aunt Heye's long jet-black hair cascaded down her back, like a waterfall.

Two glittering earrings dangled above her shoulders. Her silver bracelet glinted in the sun as she waved her coloured scarves about, the little bells upon it tinkling sweetly. Her beautiful black gown clung to her body, and its hem brushed lightly against the sand, revealing now and then her unshod feet like two golden lotuses peeking shyly out from underneath the lotus leaves. Her eyes glittered with blazing, mind-altered passion as she cast them upon the desert and at the sky.

The drums surged into a thunderous roar. Aunt Heye flung up her arms and knelt with her left knee toward the sacrificial altar. She remained there, motionless, head bowed slightly, face imbued with solemn respect, as if she were engaged in a lengthy prayer. A complete hush fell upon the crowd. All seemed to be holding their breath waiting for something. Then a four-stringed lap violin entered this moment of serenity with its haunting sound as gentle and delicate as a babbling brook. Slowly, it played another Andai song, "Ah-Ha-Ho". Aunt Heye slowly raised her head, and her black hair covering her face fell back. She began stomping out the rhythm of the music, and she resumed her impassioned singing, directing her song toward the woman in white still sitting motionless with her head covered.

> *Hard as iron and steel be,*
> *Raging fire melts them;*
> *Critical as your distress may be,*
> *Dance the Andai and you'll forget!*
> *Ah, Andai!*
> *Come! Come! Ah, Andai!*
> ....

The afflicted woman in white finally seemed unable to resist. Languidly she stretched her arms and worked her waist, slowly she reached for the green scarf and pulled it off. Tremblingly, she rose to her feet. She was very young and very beautiful. Once she had arisen, the accompanying music shifted to another lyrical tune, "Hejiya".

Udugan Aunt Heye led the crowd in dancing around the woman in white and in taking turns to ask her the source of her troubles and to inspire her to speak of them and disburden herself:

Do you have grievances towards your parents?
Do you hate your husband?
Are you suffering lingering mother-love?
Are you hung up on your old-time lover?
....

Under the guidance of the *udugan* and the encouragement of the mellow Andai song, the woman in white began to respond. A blushing glow came to her face, an amorous light to her eyes. She began to match the *udugan* in the slow rhythmic movements of her hands and feet. With a sharp contrast of black and white, the two women danced around each other, like two butterflies fluttering about in a floating chiaroscuro. The soft, melodious Andai song rose and fell, now fast, now slow. Now it was like a valley wind, now like a forest brook, and it made the fervent dancers more and more intoxicated with that intensely touching melody.

Like the tides, like the wind, like fire, the song and the dance were the essence of raw inspiration.

The woman in white finally unleashed her inner

thoughts and sang out the source of her torment:

> *I sewed for him in the light of the moon*
> *An apricot yellow vest,*
> *And if I had known he would go away,*
> *I should rather have burned it.*
> *Oh, my love, too late to regret!*
> *Ah, Andai!*
> *It was of silk, that vest of red,*
> *Sewn with the blood of my heart,*
> *And had I known he would change his mind,*
> *I should rather have ripped it to shreds!*
> *Oh, my love, too late to regret!*
> *Ah, Andai!*
> ....

The *udugan* sang to her a song of persuasion:

> *If a kite string breaks, the Trigrams say,*
> *It's useless to get another,*
> *Oh, my poor little sister!*
> *Your heartless lover, he's changed his mind.*
> *You wring out your tears, but you will find*
> *It will get you*
> *Nothing.*
> *Oh, my poor little sister!*
> *The more your mind turns and churns*
> *And hangs perilous in the air,*
> *The more your body must endure, sicker and sicker,*
> *And sicker.*
> *Throw off the torment in your heart,*
> *Join us in the dancing art,*

And praise the spirit of the Heavens,
And coddle the spirit of the sand,
And pray for sweet, sweet rain!
Oh, my poor little sister!
....

Through this amalgam of chanting and persuasion by both the *udugan* and the crowd, the woman in white finally came to realise the truth of what they were saying, and she threw herself into the Andai sacrificial dance.

The musicians broke into a fanatically throbbing Andai melody.

Udugan Aunt Heye's dance style transformed, and she led the woman in white along with her. In consonance with the driving music, the two of them swayed their shoulders, twisted their hips, stamped their bare feet into the sand, and zealously threw themselves into wild, crazed, untrammelled dancing. At this moment, she was nothing like a woman over fifty. The lissome flow of her gait, the agile movements of her body, the graceful beauty and utter ease of her dance steps could hardly be matched even by an eighteen-year-old. This portion of the Andai dance, wonderfully executed and unrestrained, symbolised in all its aspects enthusiasm, joy, fury, and desire. Her seductive black gown floated and swirled like a black oceanic wave, like a black whirlwind, as she fluttered about over the entire dance arena. Meanwhile, the white gown followed her closely in an exquisite harmony of motion evocative of whitecaps rushing toward the shore. Then the black whirlwind and the white froth bit each other and reflected off each other, now dancing in tandem in a particular spot, now separating and whirling and rushing off with lifted skirts to opposite ends of the arena in scene after soul-stirring scene.

This was no longer the swaying, graceful rhythmic beauty of dance performed to soft sweet music. This was the wail of distress, agitation and incitement, pursuit, prayer, and unrestrained wrath! This was mankind's solemn yet mysterious, violent yet plaintive, denunciation of Nature — the desert, the gods of Heaven, the evil drought spirit, and unknowable fate! That resounding clapping, that rapid stomping, those violently twisting and swaying bodies, those bold and unrestrained movements, that swishing and flapping of skirts all expressed this denunciation. And especially that proud head, frequently raised up high was even more completely expressive of the Andai—"Öndei" — and its meaning of "raise your head and get out of your bed", that is, stand tall before it all. And what this means is that only the songs and dances of the Andai, unique in the world, so intensely express the spirit of the working man and woman — human pride, human dignity, the human aversion to surrender, and the human condemnation of and protest against the gods and spirits of heaven and earth and indeed humans themselves!

Yushi and the television reporters watched this profoundly moving performance and were shaken to the roots of their soul. Especially Yushi, who was intensely moved. Its multifarious dance moves and rich lyrics, its combination of intensely stimulating rhythm and graceful, gentle languorous moves, and its simple, vigorous, popular style all recalled the dance form that originated among the common folk of Latin American and is now all the rage the world over — disco. Yushi thought, the reason why the Andai is so durable and has such popular appeal is probably because it came from the common people and was perfected over time and passed on by talented folk artists like Aunt Heye, the woman in white and the Andai King, Lao Shuangyang, whom he had yet to get to know. It was clear that this is the singing and dancing of rustic worker-artists, created out of the need to express a wide range of emotions.

The lenses of the video cameras ceaselessly tracked the black whirl-wind and the white froth as well as the wave-like masses who supported their demented dancing and wailing. This was one reel of invaluable artistic material.

At this time, the presiding elder atop the sacrificial altar began an ululating chant in a voice loud enough to top all the other sounds:

Lead the rain dragon from the north sea,
Scoop up sweet moisture from the east sea,
Summon the river goddess from the west ocean,
Entice the clouds from the south ocean,
Drive off, yes, drive off! The evil drought spirit!
Sacrifice, yes, sacrifice! To the spirit of the Sand!
Ah, Andai!

The villagers gave a thunderous reply:

Draw down the water from the mountain heights,
Sing, oh sing! A hundred days!
Draw up the water from the grasslands,
Sing, oh sing! For fifty days!

Drive off, yes, drive off! The evil drought spirit!
Sacrifice, yes, sacrifice! To the spirit of the sand!
Ah, Andai!
....

Through its special enticing beauty, the Andai had conquered these peasants. All seemed bewitched, and they sang wildly and danced dementedly as if possessed by spirits.

On the sacrificial altar atop the oboga, the sacred fire was lit. The old priest folded his hands and began to chant the sacred texts, and as he muttered these prayers, he frequently poured oblations of wine into the fire and threw in sacrificial items.

Aunt Heye's cheeks were glowing as brightly as rosy evening clouds. An unusual and frightening light beamed from her eyes, as if she were whirling and swirling in the clutches of an inescapable maelstrom...

The completely demented peasants clustered round the two women like torrent after torrent of surging turbid water. Aunt Heye was like a top spinning within the maelstrom of turbid water, whipped on by the loud pumping Andai tune and the throngs of peasants surrounding her, spinning and spinning to eternity...

Suddenly, there was a long sigh released toward heaven and a burst of insane laugher that cut through to the very bone, and Aunt Heye fainted dead away, falling flat on her back in the turbid dust. Her lower body was awash in viscous red blood...

7

The seeding was completed.

Lao Shuangyang beat the kinks out of his back and

lopped upon his pallet of dry grass. As he lay there he polished off a bottle of clear sorghum liquor. Then he slept deeply and dreamlessly for a day and a night. His adoptive son, Bitchbrat, sat next to him with a couple of wormwood stalks in hand, chasing away the flies that were wont to settle upon his injured shoulder. It had been rubbed raw from the pressure of the plough rope, and now the blood and the pus were forming a lustrous scab. Bitchbrat frequently reached out and tested the old man's breath with the back of his hand. He was afraid his dad would pass away silently in his sleep.

Lao Shuangyang finally moaned and opened his eyes.

"Dad, are you still alive?" Bitchbrat asked.

"I walked right up to Yama's front gate, but he wouldn't have me."*

Bitchbrat poked around in the fire and turned out a piece of roasted dog meat, which he handed to him.

"Where did you get the dog meat?"

"It's the piece you gave me. I buried it in the sand behind the shelter, and when I dug it back up, it was still good. The sand's really a good place to keep things fresh."

"You eat it, it's yours."

"I can't eat it now, I can't get it down. Go ahead, you eat it. It'll give you strength for when we go back home tomorrow."

"Tomorrow? Sonny, we have to stay here for several more days."

"What — are we waiting to die?"

---

*Yama — King of Hell.

"We're waiting for the red broom corn millet to sprout. It'll take three or four days for it to sprout, and we have to keep the birds away while the seedlings are young. We didn't go through all this trouble just to feed the birds, did we now?"

Bitchbrat remained silent.

"What's the matter? Have you reached the end of your rope?"

"No. But we don't have water. How can we survive? Even ground beetles need moisture, so what about us big humans — do you think we can make it on that little bit of frog-piss?"

"We'll go out after a bit and look for another vein. We'll dig several wells and see. Perhaps one of the other depressions has a stash for us!"

Lao Shuangyang gobbled up the dog meat and immediately felt more energetic. As he ate, Bitchbrat sat with his back to him. Lao Shuangyang let his eyes linger upon his skinny little body. There was nothing left of him but bones. His naked black-brown skin was coated with a layer of fine, light yellow sand-dust. Sweat rolled down in rivulets across this little desert expanse, flowing toward the cleavage of his buttocks. Suddenly he wondered whether this little whelp had really not wanted the dog meat, or whether he had deliberately saved it for him. His heart swelled warmly.

"Bitchbrat, come here."

"What?"

"Did you..." He wanted to ask him whether he really didn't want the dog meat or... But then he felt this was really an unnecessary question. He knew already his adoptive son's temperament. Within that fleshless frame of skin and bone beat a warm and sympathetic heart. He felt that though there were only the two of them here deep in the wilderness, an old codger and a young whelp, the place was overbrimming the warmth and generosity of the human spirit. He gave a cough and said with a voice barely audible, because there seemed to be something stuck in there, "You need find some meat to eat, too. Here in the sandland there is a kind of little animal whose meat is even more tasty than dog meat. Okay, I'm going out to catch some for you."

"What kind of critter is that?"

"The jumping hare.* It's a kind of wild rodent with short front legs and long hind legs. It's greyish-yellow with a soft white belly. And its meat is clean. Normally I don't like to kill the creatures of the sandland, but today for my adoptive son I will make an exception."

Shouldering spades, Lao Shuangyang and Bitchbrat went out onto the dune.

It was just as he had said. On the slope of the dune they found a lot of damp sand that had been flung and scattered here and there into lines about a yard long. At one end there was a little hole that had been plugged with dug up sand. This was the entryway to a burrow. Lao Shuangyang dug several spadefuls out from this entryway, exposing a little round burrow that was pitch black inside. There was no telling how far deep it ran.

"It's such a deep burrow. You think we can dig them out?" Bitchbrat was squatting off to the side,

---

*Jumping hare — the popular local name for the Mongolian five-toed jerboa, a burrowing desert rodent very similar to the North American kangaroo rat.

his head cocked inquisitively.

"Ha, that's just what a greenhorn would do, try to dig them out. Just watch your dad."

Lao Shuangyang put down his spade. At a spot one or two yards above the entryway, he began tramping in the sand with his heel. Soon he uncovered another aperture that had been camouflaged under a thin layer of sand. "You see? That's the jumping hare's window. It's his escape-hatch. Smart little bugger, isn't he! If anyone tries to dig in through the main entryway, he just breaks his way through the dirt covering his escape-hatch and runs away. You see, every creature has its strategy." As Lao Shuangyang spoke, he took off his shirt and fitted the arm-hole over the window entryway. Then he anchored the rest of the garment in place with tamped down dirt. Then he tied the end of the sleeve shut with a piece of rope. After that he sharpened a long willow stick and thrust it into the main entryway, shaking it vigorously around in there and hollering into the hole.

"Sonny, keep an eye on that window-way!"

Just as he said this, there was a sudden rushing sound, and a panicked jumping hare bounded out of the window-way. Bitchbrat leaped over in a flash and grabbed the end of the sleeve and held it tight. With great elation, he shouted, "We got it! We got it!"

"Ha ha ha! Your first catch! Once we skin it and clean it, we'll have a good three ounces of meat!" Lao Shuangyang picked the jumping hare up by its long tail and hefted it to estimate its weight.

Following suit, they quickly caught more than ten jumping hares, which they impaled upon a willow branch, shishkebab style. When they returned to the shelter, they skinned and cleaned them, filled the chest cavities with damp sand, sprinkled on some salt and threw them into the fire to roast. A savoury odour began to fill the whole shelter. His mouth watering, little Bitchbrat plucked one of the jumping hares out of the fire and began to gnaw at it noisily, even though it was still half raw. Bitchbrat could catch jumping hares all by himself, and one day on a slope of black sand he caught an unusual one that had black and grey fur and was much bigger than the average jumping hare.

"Ah ha, sonny! You've caught "Mr Brass Buttons" himself. What a coup! He's the king of the jumping hares, the finest specimen of the animal. Oh, excuse me, he's a she, and she's pregnant!" Lao Shuangyang couldn't praise him enough.

Bitchbrat didn't have the heart to kill this "Mr Brass Buttons" that was about to become a mother. He leashed her with a piece of rope and kept her as a pet.

Lao Shuangyang went looking for water. He investigated numerous depressions and finally chose one that looked like the bottom of a wok. The well he dug yielded enough water to get them through several more days. Three days later, just as he predicted, the little sprouts of red broom corn millet began poking their heads through the ground. They were tender green with two little leaves charmingly sticking up. Lao Shuangyang was overjoyed. He set up a scarecrow fashioned out of dry grass and tree branches.

After several days, they went sauntering out to the field one morning and discovered several sand grouse. They ran over to take a look. Several of the little sprouts had been pecked up by their roots. Lao

Shuangyang's heart ached, and he screamed as he picked up some clods of earth and threw them at those loathsome birds to chase them off. Who could have known that that very afternoon there a black nimbus would fly out from the depths of the western desert that was actually a swarm of sand grouse. These birds were not afraid of people simply ignoring their shouts and all other attempts to chase them away. They set down over the entire field. Lao Shuangyang was in a fury. He cursed them angrily and hollered and shouted, raised a clamour and chased after them with a club. Bitchbrat too took up some willow branches and ran back and forth trying to chase them off. But the ravenous desert birds would rise up from one spot and fearlessly re-alight somewhere else. The two of them ran back and forth, back and forth, tiring themselves out, but it did no good. Lao Shuangyang waved his club about, striking down several of the sand grouse. Suddenly those cursed birds rose up with an awful clamour and rushed en masse at him, attacking him about the head and face in vengeance for their fallen comrades. The old fellow was in an awful fix. He wrapped his head in his hands and arms and tried to dodge the birds. Soon his face, neck, shoulders and arms were coloured with blood.

In despair, Lao Shuangyang cried out, "God! You have ruined me! My red broom corn millet —"

He flung himself on the ground and beat the earth, crying. His pipe and his pack of matches fell to the ground as well. Bitchbrat stood watching, stupefied. When he saw the matches, he suddenly came to life. He shouted, "Fire! Burn them with fire! Burn them with fire!"

Lao Shuangyang suddenly came to his senses. He leapt up and took off his shirt and touched a lighted match to it. When it was burning roaringly, he raised it high and waved it around, rushing toward those rapacious birds. Meanwhile, Bitchbrat ignited a bunch of firewood and joined the offensive. Sand grouse are also called "stupid half-pints" because they are by nature mindlessly fierce and weigh in at just about eight ounces. When these stupid birds saw the fire, instead of fleeing, they rushed at the old guy and his waving torch. The result was that their wing feathers caught fire, and the fire spread in a flash, engulfing their whole bodies. The flaming birds passed their blight to other birds, and whipped by the air currents of their own flight, the fire burned all the more vigorously, and soon the sky was filled with scurrying fire birds. In no time at all, their wings were burnt black, they could no longer fly, and "plop plop" they fell to the ground. Flapping their charred wings, they ran aimlessly around. Soon the ground was covered with burning birds leaping about, like lots of fire-balls rolling around. In their terror they squawked and shrieked, struggling and twitching as the smoke poured off their bodies, and then they dropped dead. The air was filled with the stench of burned feathers and flesh.

"Ah ha ha ha! Now that's what I call a real coup! That's really just too perfect! Stupid birds, they got what they deserved. Teach them to mess around with men! Sonny, you're really something — you could be a military strategist. A joint fire-storm operation! Ha ha ha, come on, let's pick up our roast — we won't have to worry about meat for awhile!"

Lao Shuangyang laughed heartily. Waving his burning shirt, he chased after the remaining unscathed sand grouse. These finally flew up high to get away from the fire and in a great panic fled.

They gathered up the dead and injured sand grouse and took them back to the shelter. There was enough to keep them well-fed for five or six days. They stuffed themselves and burped and belched in postprandial contentment, and their lips shone with oil and boasted flecks of ash and remnants of feathers. And their emaciated frames began to fill out with flesh that gave tone to their tight, dry black skin. Since they had the sand grouse, Bitchbrat's "Mr Brass Buttons" was spared. And to top it off, she whelped a naked squirming litter right under Bitchbrat's quilt.

Lao Shuangyang packed up everything for the return trip, but that night there occurred a life-threatening event that even he, old desert hand that he was, hadn't anticipated. Toward evening, when the slanting rays of the sun manifested a tinge of yellow, he had become suspicious. By dusk, when the western sky was a swathe of crimson, he was certain there would be a wind storm by midnight. The saying goes: "Morning sun veiled in red, flying sand and scudding stones; solar halo in the afternoon, watch out for the wind." However, he was not bothered by this. The little sprouts had already grown tall enough not to be harmed by the average wind storm, especially since they were growing in a low-lying area, which meant they couldn't be buried in drifting sand. He and Bitchbrat went to sleep free of any apprehensions.

After midnight, the wind started up, and it was indeed a strong one, a sandy, pebbly wind that dimmed the stars and shifted entire dunes. When it had first kicked up, Lao Shuangyang went to check on the field. After walking around it he decided that it was in no great danger. A wind that rises in the middle of the night necessarily dies with the light of day. So he went back to the shelter and went to sleep.

Having raised their shelter smack against the base of the dune, it was surrounded on three sides by sand. They had done it this way out of convenience. Now the wind that could bring no harm to the seedlings drove the sand so that the shelter was completely surrounded. While its inmates were sunk deep in sleep, the wind deposited upon it sheet after sheet of sand so that by daybreak the only evidence of its existence were two roof beams sticking out of a dune.

Lao Shuangyang had a dream that he couldn't breathe. In the nightmare clutches of suffocation, he fought to drag himself to consciousness, but his efforts failed against the phantom ropes that had him pinned to his pallet. Finally at the pinnacle of asphyxiation, he gave a shout and thus woke up. Pitch blackness greeted his eyes. He could discern nothing, not even his own fingers. The air was dead-still and intolerably close, the atmosphere oppressive and thick with isolation. Something was crushing his chest, something heavy and implacable and intent upon bursting his lungs.

Suddenly it hit him, a cold slash of mortal dread: this is the end! The shelter's been buried in the shifting sand!

Groping for Bitchbrat beside him, he felt his inert form. The child's breath was weak, a barely-there whisper of warmth. His heart contracted into ice. Stirring himself to struggle, he put his enfeebled body to a crawl toward the door, a task that stretched toilsome minutes to agonising centuries. Finally he reached the door. Waveringly he climbed to his feet. Summoning every ounce of his strength, he pushed, but the door wouldn't budge. Sand that had sifted in through its cracks was piled high against it. What to do? No air, no way out, and he was extremely weak. It would be harder to get out of here alive, he thought, than it would be to ascend into heaven.

Lao Shuangyang sighed mournfully. He reached out and caressed the unconscious Bitchbrat, his heart filling with sorrow and regret. He shouldn't have brought him here. Already made to depart from the world, and at such a tender age. It wasn't fair. It was all his fault. And then there was Heye... Now why should he think of *her* all of a sudden? At this time. At his last gasp. But how he wished he could see her one last time... How was she doing now? Did she achieve the insanity of the Andai? Those two adobe rooms so fascinating to all the men of the village!

She was another one brought to trouble because of him. He owed her. There were only two people in the whole world he owed, and it was only these two who elicited his anxieties for their welfare.

The red broom corn millet, though — now that was something he regretted to his very bones. Never again could he nurse and protect those fragile little sprouts. He couldn't weed them or cultivate them, he couldn't take in the harvest, he couldn't thresh the grain. Never would he feel those hefty round grains in the palm of his hand. Ah, how temperamental, fate, just like they say: man proposes, God disposes. All his efforts had been for nothing. His entire being rebelled against this trick. His only consolation was that he'd been able to grow his crop at all, that miraculous red broom corn millet! At least his little sprouts would continue to grow and come to fruition. He took some comfort in knowing that. In the dense airless dark, his steely mouth curled into a bleak smudge of a smile. There was nothing to do now but wait for that final moment when he would step into the beyond for his eternal rest. He'd been a hard-living man and he was tired now.

All thoughts, all aspirations dissolved into nothingness; his soul achieved tranquillity.

As Lao Shuangyang was fading out, Mr Brass Buttons, in the corner where Bitchbrat had tied her, began to squeak and strain wildly against her tether. She set to gnawing her restraining rope desperately. Soon the rope was sliced in two, and she leaped from her nest and clambered up to the ceiling, where with all alacrity she began burrowing further upwards. She disappeared deep into the lengthening hole and then bounded back to take up one of her babies in her mouth and carry it up. Back and forth, back and forth she tirelessly, instinctively, shuttled, carrying swooning babies and feverishly digging, until finally she broke through to the light and freedom of the outside world.

8

Aunt Heye was bleeding profusely from her uterus.

Thanks to Yushi, she'd been dragged out from under the feet of the insentient crowd that would have obliviously trampled her to death. She did not thank him for this. He'd saved her, it seemed, from the fate she sought; thwarted her plan to die in the Andai arena. Yushi lobbied her to go to the hospital, but she refused, saying she was living on stolen time anyway, as her condition dated from early youth. When it's time to go, one ought to be graceful and go. Her condition was rooted in her dancing, she said. If she hadn't engaged in the Andai's intense physically and gotten overexcited, then it would not have manifested itself. This time, it was manifesting itself severely.

She was lying upon her adobe *kang*, atop a thick layer of dry, soft, fine sandy earth. The men and the women who used to frequent her place were now avoiding the filthy adobe house and very rarely showed their faces. The task of caring for the patient thus fell to her boarding guest. Still, there wasn't much to do, since she wasn't taking any medicinal decoctions nor eating much (indeed she essentially ate nothing). The only thing that needed doing was the changing of the layer of sand that was her underbedding whenever necessary. Fortunately, dry sand was abundant in these parts, so this was not difficult.

The patient was surprisingly serene and felt no discomfort or pain. "When the blood flows its course, the bleeding will stop, and everything will be all right," she would say to Yushi with a consoling smile. How much blood did she have in her anyway? Her face was as white as the paper windowpanes, as if just about all her blood really had flowed out. Her breathing was weak, as thin and tenuous as a fine hair. Yushi's heart constricted within him, clamped by an iron claw.

His own affairs served to worry him as well. The television people had all gone home, as well as everyone from the Cultural Bureau. His former classmate had already taken the recorded materials back to be edited and dubbed. He should go back, too, to put his Andai materials in order and write a publishable paper. His dream was to "burst upon the scene" with this thing. But he didn't have the heart to abandon Aunt Heye.

One day Aunt Heye said to him, "You go ahead and leave. You have important work to do, and I'm not going to die for awhile. I have to wait until he comes back. I have to see him one more time before I depart."

He knew now whom she was referring to.

"I only ask one thing of you." She fixed her eyes on him.

"What's that? Just give the word."

"Go see Headman Meng Ke. Tell him to send someone out to look for that old goat. He's been gone for over two weeks, and who knows if he's dead or alive? Everybody's just forgotten about him, and I'll just bet something's happened." She sighed.

"Okay, I'll go see the headman now." Yushi stood up.

"Hold it, not so fast. The headman's got grudges against him. He won't send someone just because you say so. You have to hold that subsidy money over his head. At the moment he's still beholden to you."

"I understand."

Yushi found Meng Ke at the pig butcher's house. He'd drunk his fill and was stuffed to the gills and his head and neck were crimson. As soon as he learned why Yushi had come, he gravely wiped his greasy mouth and said it was none of his affair.

"You'd better make it your affair, because you as village headman will be responsible if something happens to him!"

"Responsible my foot! Fuck, man, being the headman doesn't make me everybody's grandson! I can't be following everybody's butt around all day! There are several hundred people in Black Sand, and they've all got two legs — you think I can keep up with them all?" The hadman's language as much coarser than usual when he was drunk, and he'd forgotten for the moment that there was still something he wanted from his interlocutor.

He left Yushi no choice but to haul out the mace that Aunt Heye had told him to use.

"Look here, Comrade Headman. Lao Shuangyang is the famous Andai King. I still have to talk with him to supplement my materials. If you don't find him, then it won't be very easy for me to get that subsidy money of yours — or the cultural work expenses either."

These were the magic words. Meng Ke blinked his bleary eyes and took a long steady look at him. Finally it came back to him. His creased, liquor-flushed face broke into a wreath of smiles. He placed a staying hand on Yushi and said, "Don't get excited. That was just the liquor talking. Don't take it seriously. Fuck, I'll send someone to look for the old bastard right now..."

Riding upon the wave of his victory, Yushi decided to go after another foot of rope to add to the inch he'd already gotten. "And another thing, I have to get back to the county seat to write my article and to do the running around necessary to get the money for you. So you have to send a couple of ladies over to take care of Aunt Heye. She's sick and all alone in the world, so according to the commune's policy, you have to look after her. Not to mention that she got sick doing a public service for you."

Headman Meng Ke smiled bitterly and agreed to abide by his wishes.

9

A thread of cool fresh air penetrated Lao Shuangyang's suffocated lungs. Gradually, he regained consciousness. Beside him, Bitchbrat was stretching his arms and legs. A continuous stream of fresh air was flowing into the shelter.

"Dad, I had a nightmare, a real long bad dream, and I couldn't wake up no matter what. How come it's so dark in here? It's not morning yet?" Bitchbrat was shouting in the darkness.

"Little dummy, our shelter has been buried under drifting sand! You actually fuckin' died and came back! Now I don't know what's happening — there's actually a breeze blowing in here!" Lao Shuangyang rolled to his feet. He felt around in the dark for the oil lamp and struck a match to it.

"Well, by my grandmother's grave, we are under the ground! Good! That'll save on coffins!" Bitchbrat was terrified.

"There's no need to be afraid. King Yama's not going to get us yet. Somehow, I don't know how, you and I have been saved. Truly it is that Heaven does not cut off the road to the living." Lao Shuangyang raised the lamp and inspected the place where the wind was coming into the shelter. He quickly discovered the little round hole through which the wind was puffing its way in.

"Dad! My Mr Brass Buttons! Mr Brass Buttons and her babies are gone!" Bitchbrat was off to one side of the shelter.

Lao Shuangyang slapped his leg as he suddenly realised what had happened. "Praise be to Buddha! Thanks to your Mr Brass Buttons, you and I are not done playing in this world yet! After this our sacrifices won't be to the Buddha but to your Mr Brass Buttons!"

Having regained his strength, Lao Shuangyang began calculating how to get out of this tomb. The only way was to break down the door and dig a path through the sand with the spade. He set to work. As soon as the door was broken, the accumulation of sand outside collapsed and poured in. Lao Shuangyang spaded it out of the way. After an hour of strenuous digging, the doorway was finally cleared, and they climbed out of the shelter into the brilliant light of the world.

It took a long time for their eyes to adjust. Under the glare of the sun, they were like two dumb doggies blinking in stupefaction and gulping the fresh desert air with wide open mouths. Covered with sand-dirt from head to toe, they looked like terra-cotta figures unearthed from a tomb. Lao Shuangyang flew off to his red broom corn millet field. As luck would have it, no serious damage had been done. The seedlings at the higher end of the field had had their roots partially uncovered, while those situated lower had been partially buried. Lao Shuangyang smacked his forehead and breathed a sigh of relief.

"Sonny-boy, we can't go home yet. We still have work to do. We have to add some dirt to cover up those roots, and we have to uncover those plants that have been partly buried. We'll be mighty busy for several days!"

"That's okay, however long it takes. Home is where the heart is. Anyway, I like it here. Dad, why don't we just stay here 'til after the harvest!"

"My boy, what a brilliant idea! We'll stay here and protect the crop right up to the last! At most, that'll be forty days or so. But we'll have to make a trip back to the village to stock up." Lao Shuangyang was excited too, and he reached out and pulled his adopted son into his embrace. With his broad palm, he rubbed his scarred little yellow head. This was the adoptive father's first demonstration of affection toward his adopted son.

Their decision to stay, though, presented them with the problem of where to live. They had nothing with which to erect another shelter. Lao Shuangyang pondered this and quickly came up an idea. They would clear away the sand blocking the entrance to the existing shelter, making a two-yard wide entryway, the walls of which they would reinforce. This way, the buried shelter would become a solid, cool cellar. Once the door was closed, there would be no need to worry about wolves getting in.

"Sonny, we'll live in a cave just like Zhang the Third."

"Hey, cool! I'm sick of being a human anyway. I was just wishing to be something else." With his bare buttocks and his belly sticking out, Bitchbrat delighted in the idea of this cave-like cellar that would never see the rays of the sun. He'd been going naked ever since he'd padded his dad's shoulder with his pants and they'd been thoroughly ruined. Lao Shuangyang had no more undershorts with which to fashion him another pair, so he'd tied his cotton shirt around him to cover up his behind. But Bitchbrat was reluctant to wear it out of fear of ruining it. Fortunately there were no other people in the desert and besides, even in dirt-poor Black Sand Village, it was considered normal for eleven-and-twelve-year-old boys to run around with naked backsides.

They continued their work in the field. Adding dirt here and clearing it away there was a tedious task that fully took four or five days to complete.

One day, the young lady who'd been sent to take care of Aunt Heye said to Headman Meng Ke, "Aunt Heye's not doing very well. I'm afraid she's close to the end." Suddenly Headman Meng Ke remembered he hadn't sent anyone to go looking for Lao Shuangyang. This he remedied in haste, sending two peasants into the sandland with a message.

The news of Aunt Heye's impending death threw Lao Shuangyang into a fever, and he shouted, "Bitchbrat, hitch up the bullock!"

"What for?"

"We're going back!"

When Lao Shuangyang rushed into Aunt Heye's adobe house with Bitchbrat, that unfortunate woman was at her last gasp. But she recognised Lao Shuangyang. A smile appeared on her face, and she nodded at him.

"I've come back, you crazy old lady. How are

you? Nothing serious I trust? I've come to take you to live at my house!" Lao Shuangyang bent over and spoke into her ear.

"Ah, ah, that's ... good. I've waited for forty years..." With great difficulty she moved her lips.

"It's a bit late, but there's still time..." Lao Shuangyang clutched at his chest anxiously.

"It's not too late yet, I haven't kicked the bucket. Anyway, it's all the same..." Something was rattling in Aunt Heye's throat, a piece of phlegm in there rolling around.

"Okay, let's go then. To my place. I'll take care of you. And we also have an adopted son. Bitchbrat, come and greet your mum!" Lao Shuangyang hollered toward the door.

Clad in his dad's cotton shirt, Bitchbrat came in and cried respectfully to her, "Mum!"

A spark came into Aunt Heye's eyes. She'd never had a child of her own. Grasping Bitchbrat's hand, she made as if to speak, but then gave only a slight sigh that seemed to say that all of this had come too late. Her expression was mournful. She turned to Lao Shuangyang and said feebly, "I ... I'll not go to your place. I want to see your red broom corn millet, that red broom corn millet that's got you so fascinated... I was dancing, and that's all I'd see, red broom corn millet... And the Andai and the red broom corn millet got all mixed up and entangled with each other. So I really want to see that red broom corn millet... Take me there instead..." She broke into a debilitating cough, a reflex against that piece of phlegm, but she had not the strength to cough it up.

"Okay," Lao Shuangyang agreed solicitously, voice

imbued with heavy sorrow. "Let's go right now. I'll take you to see the red broom corn millet..."

He gathered her up from the *kang*, feeling her pitiful slightness. How aggrieved he was to think of the blooming, beautiful, robust woman she had been, reduced like this to a bag of bones. She wasn't even as heavy as a bundle of straw. Time and life had ravaged her, eroded her body, sucked her dry until all that remained was this fistful of straw.

He settled her into his cart, making her as comfortable as possible. Then he loaded in some dry rations, water, and various useful articles. Little Bitchbrat led the black bullock while Lao Shuangyang stayed by Aunt Heye's side to support her.

The three of them with their cart went deep into the sandland.

Lingering purple-blue pigeon flowers and red *saralung* lilies* greeted them gladsomely. Diminutive lizards, scarab beetles, and little white mice frolicked along either side of the road. The sun slanted gentle rays upon the western sand ridge, smiling benignly upon this special ox cart.

The nearer they drew to their destination, the more excited Aunt Heye seemed to grow and the pinker became her cheeks. Lao Shuangyang mirrored the opposite, becoming more dispirited and agitated the closer they got. A shadow hung over him, a shadow of secret mournful sighs.

When they got to Raptor's Hump, the sun was setting.

Lao Shuangyang pulled the cart to a stop at the shel-

---

* *Saralung* lilies: morning star lilies.

ter's entryway, intending to carry Aunt Heye in for a rest. She said "No" and pursed her lips toward the field. Without a word, Lao Shuangyang gently picked her up and carried her south to the red broom corn millet field.

He set her down amidst the growing crop.

Her eyes began to shine, as if life had returned to her body. With an obvious mustering of effort, she cast her gaze all about her, surveying for lengthening moments the flourishing seedlings, her mouth moving wordlessly, as if she were being deeply drawn to this miraculous crop in the desert, these tender, fragile seedlings contradicting the vast desert wasteland with their greenness, bursting with the power and might of life, eulogising the glorious achievement of creative human labour.

"Well ... Old Man ... I gotta ... hand it to you... Such beautiful gleaming red broom corn millet... I've been seeking the soul of Andai all my life ... and here it was the whole time ... a green spirit ... a green soul. What can ever stop the green?... The desert?... The...?" Aunt Heye was gasping for breath. She gathered up every ounce of energy in her and blurted, "Very good — now come here and kiss me..."

Heart bursting, Lao Shuangyang bent down and lightly pressed his dusty, stubble cheek to Aunt Heye's pale white one. Her face was burning. His eyes blurred.

Aunt Heye let out a long sigh and closed her eyes. On her face there appeared a peaceful smile. Gradually, the lineaments of this smile froze. The pink of her cheeks drained away, replaced by a lifeless waxy yellow. She stopped breathing.

A brisk desert wind began to blow, swirling grains

of sand into little eddies. Above the sand ridge in the distance, wild swallows were circling, looking for a home. The setting sun was flaming in the west, spreading its conflagration to the floating clouds and the desert below. The whole world was fire red. Those flaming wild swallows looked like brilliant red spirits, circling, ever circling until they mounted high into the sky and melded invisibly into the fiery red vault of Heaven.

Lao Shuangyang moved his face away from that cheek already grown cold, dropping two big ponderous tears upon it. He held her tight to him and sat there woodenly, stiffly, like a boulder. After some indeterminate time, he remembered something. He stood up and carried her back to their cellar and laid her on the pallet. He told Bitchbrat to go gather some firewood, as much as possible. According to custom, a woman who dies of illness such as Aunt Heye had just done had to be cremated immediately. The body couldn't be left lying in state overnight. This was to show respect for the deceased and to allow her to achieve an early detachment from pain and suffering and enter Paradise.

He went to get all the water that had collected in his several wells. Than he removed her clothes and cleansed her body.

Bitchbrat brought load after load of dry tree roots and timber.

Lao Shuangyang selected a flat piece of land and stacked the firewood high. He gathered up Aunt Heye and gently placed her upon this pyre. His shoulders were trembling. He had Bitchbrat stand with him silently before her remains. They bowed and muttered some words. Afterwards, he hunched over to strike the match. His hand was shaking violently, and after several tries, he still had not succeeded in getting the match lit. Bitchbrat helped him.

A little blue flame took tenuous hold, then gradually turned apricot pink. Whispy white smoke began to rise from the top of the apricot pink flame. The flame spread and grew into a crackling blaze. Nimble tongues jumped and leaped and began to touch a corner of Aunt Heye's clothing. Further on the fire explored until it was licking at her reposing body. It rushed upon her, then, that ardent, blood-red fire, engulfing her from all sides like a firestorm, swallowing her completely in an instant and transforming her into a part of itself. Together the body and the firewood burned in harmony, turning the pitch of the night and the sky and the desert into the red of the ages. Between Heaven and the black desert, there was only this body and the firewood burning together in an eternal flame.

Lao Shuangyang raised up his two hands a bowl of spirits and poured it into the flame in oblation. At the same time, there flowed from his throat that ancient eternal melody.

Fickle is that wind above, ah, Andai!
Bumpy is that road below, ah, Andai!
Clear as spring water this wine I pour for you,
So you may walk that bumpy road and brave that
    fickle wind!
Ah, Andai!

Human sorrows never end, ah, Andai!
Affliction is Woman's fate, ah, Andai!
The Andai filling my heart I sing for you,

*So you may banish those sorrows and afflictions!
Ah, Andai!*
....

That bleak and bitter Andai melody reverberated richly in deep turning layers of sound.

His upper body swaying gently, his feet stomping rhythmically, Lao Shuangyang began to circle the blazing sacred fire of red, dancing slowly, deliberately, so that he looked like a rushing, leaping camel burdened with a heavy load. His hands and feet moved in harmony, his head swayed slightly. He used his body fluidly, intentionally, imbuing each gesture and posture with meaning, moving along like a mountain of ice afloat in the sea, travelling with the endless waves toward the shore. In his left hand he held a wine bowl, while his right dipped into it with the rhythm of his dance. He would sing a line, then with a gentle, fluid motion sprinkle the wine into the fire. Thus dancing and singing and sprinkling wine, he paid tribute to the deceased. Lao Shuangyang's interpretation of the Andai invoked a powerful sense of dignity, a boundless, unforgettable, historical kind of dignity that only the performer who'd crammed in all his indomitability against and intense love and hate for all of Nature and the desert and Fate could produce.

At this moment, a youth was silently standing just outside the roaring fire's circle of light, taking notes swiftly, ardently, as one anxious to slack thrist and fill a starving stomach. Every once in awhile he would stop to imitate the novel dance postures. And finally he realised the essence of the Andai, its soul and its legacy transcending space and time. Only in its connection with this desert wilderness, the green seedlings, the intense fire, life and death, love and hate, labour and the fruits of labour can it manifest completely its intrinsicality, significance and glory. Only then does the spirit of the Andai come into being.

This youth was Yushi. He'd returned to the county seat, written up his report, secured the subsidy money, and then come back. Tenaciously, he'd continued to look for something, a search that had led him here to witness this solemn scene.

He thanked God for creating such an Andai, for creating such an Andai King and such an Andai Queen.

10

On the sixtieth day, they cracked out their sickles and took in the harvest.

One would think that red broom corn millet was magic, always maturing on exactly the sixtieth day, not a day earlier, not a day later. And once it matures, the harvest has to be completed within three days, for at the end of the third day, the thoroughly ripened grains scatter noisily to the ground with the slightest touch, inflicting incalculable losses.

At the head of the field, Lao Shuangyang put two sickles to the whetstone until they were shiny and hairsplittingly sharp. Then he spat upon his palms, flung out his arms, and moved down a furrow flashing both sickles, mowing down the plants on either side. Bitchbrat followed behind, pulling up what he missed.

Among all the inhabitants of Black Sand Village, the only ones to wrest a harvest out of the desert that year were Lao Shuangyang and his adopted son.

Translated by Josephine A. Matthews

SAND BURIAL

Prologue

A white wolf wobbled out from behind the death's-head sand dune.

Clearly, it had been chewing on the brittle sun-bleached ephedra* that dotted the surface of the sandland, for its eyes were tinged red, and it was reeling on its feet like a drunk intoxicated with white sorghum spirits. Its gaunt frame could barely contain the last of its energy, drained to exhaustion by hunger. The infant had made its debut in a dry and lifeless world that offered nothing more to fill the stomach than those tough and sere ephedra tufts, forlorn remnants of the previous year's grudging accession to life. In the afternoons, the seasonal wind would sweep down from Tengger Han Mountain to whip up the yellow sand and blot out the sky. Where better to be during this vicious blinding assault than curled up, eyes closed tight, at the base of the dune?

The wolf shook its head vigorously, an attempt to loosen the grip of its drugged lethargy. In its current state of fatigue and under the effect of the ephedra in its stomach, the wolf would be unable to contend

---

Ephedra sinica, known in Chinese as *mahuang*, a herb used in Chinese medicine.

intelligently with the coming sandstorm — this it knew with perfect and painful clarity. To be muddled in the mind now could well find the wolf buried under the all-smothering cloak of the shifting sand.

It climbed to the top of the death's-head dune. The desolation of the summit was complete, its dome as smooth and clean as the baldest pate. But the wolf had not scaled this height in search of food. It sought a perch from which to give voice to its soul. To stand upon the dune's high promontory and howl into the wind was the epitome of pleasure.

And so the white wolf stood, facing the wind, atop the bald death's-head dune, a pale, ghostly figure surveying its domain. The wind was but a gentle breeze carrying on its currents the lingering chill of retreating winter incongruously pricked with the scent and warmth of spring. A shudder passed through the wolf's white-furred body, that reached the depths of its belly, a shudder of incomprehensible anticipation. It's tail, which up to now had been brushing the ground, lifted itself into the air, revealing the spot that had been so securely hidden beneath its grand graceful bushiness. Yes, this was a she-wolf, and that spot had begun to swell.

"Ow-wooooo..." she lifted her voice, freed at last from the benumbing effects of the ephedra, and sent a sharp, mournful wail out across the wilderness, piercing its deathly silence with her instinct for life. The reply was bleak stillness, a drowning hush that was emphasised by its contrast to her life-affirming howl. Slowly she turned round and sat upon her haunches. She gazed pensively eastward, out into the endless distance spreading before her. Her eyes showed an ab-

abstract gaze, the look of reminiscing over a long lost past. Yet her bearing, the tilt of her head, the set of her ears, indicated attentiveness, an intense listening, as if she were straining to hear a voice that summoned her from an ancient time now faded to a vague memory.

An indeterminate amount of time passed. The lone white she-wolf abandoned her perch with an air of disappointment. She descended the dune, knowing that not much time remained. Soon the unbridled fury of the sandstorm would be upon her, and she must fortify herself with real food before it struck. Wolf, after all, does not live on wind alone.

She came to a tract of land overspread with loose soft sand. Here she discovered a number of small, recently dug burrows, the tell-tale sign of newly excavated earth at their entrance. She was seized with excitement. Her nostrils flared as she analysed the scent around each entrance, sniffing carefully until at last she settled upon a burrow where the recent portal diggings were among the most copious. Quietly she took up vigil next to it, a great white hunter whose instinctive strategy depended on exquisite patience. Her tense jaws split opened from time to time, freeing her tongue to lick her stern, parched lips. The blood repast, long overdue, was tantalisingly close to realisation. This was the ultimate of tests, not only of her fortitude her staying-power at the point of physical collapse but also of how well experience had honed her wisdom and judgement. With time at a premium, she'd placed all her stakes on this one burrow. The scent was unmistakable. The little creature who'd left it could not fool her. She knew precisely what she was doing.

Something stirred.

Moving with the stealth of a thief, a marmot emerged, paused on the sand, and began to scan the environs. With a cunning sense of timing, White Wolf slapped one paw over the burrow entrance while cuffing at the marmot with the other. The marmot reflexively launched into its own ingenious advance plan. Having sensed danger as it emerged, it had already ruled out a double-back retreat. Now making a lightning-fast decision it scampered toward a neighbouring hole, which was in fact connected to all the other holes by a complex of underground tunnels designed to assure clean escapes — and sending the likes of White Wolf into paroxysms of vexation.

But White Wolf was no amateur. As the marmot slipped through her paws, she ascertained instantly which direction it would take. With a "whoosh" and a "flump", she leapt upon the fleeing prey, pinned it down with her forepaws, and introduced it forthwith to the merciless trap of her jaws. Poor marmot. Its native intelligence did not serve it well enough. As White Wolf munched, crunching bones amid the yielding gristle, she savoured the long since tasted flavour of blood-bathed meat and emitted low gutteral growls of deep satisfaction. Her rarefied enjoyment was doubled by her discovery that this sandy tract was a marmot breeding ground.

Just as she was pouncing upon her fifth marmot, out from behind a bushy clump of sandpuff* sprang a black whirlwind which bore down upon her, seized the

---

Agriophyllum arenarium, (*shapeng* in Chinese); also known as *A. squarrosum*, or "sand rice" (*shami*) in Chinese.

rodent she'd already bitten into, and dispatched it to its stomach with mind-boggling alacrity. White Wolf was stunned.

The interloper was a powerful, majestically proportioned black wolf.

Thunder rolled from White Wolf's throat as she flew upon him, fangs and claws fully deployed for vengeance.

The black wolf dodged her first attack and stood aside with a studied air of contempt. Counter-offensive was the furthest thing from his mind. He looked at her curiously. She was like him, only her fur was white... and yet... there was something indefinably different about her. She was ... yes ... she had a slighter build than the average wolf — positively gaunt, she was — almost like a dog. And intelligence oozed from her — he was quite sure she was shrewder, more cunning, much more nimble of mind than the average wolf. But... she couldn't be a dog... could she? She was so thoroughly wild, a creature obviously born free and possessed of the ruthless ferocity to defend her integrity, as she'd just so unhesitatingly demonstrated. That was not the way dogs behaved. Dogs were bootlickers contaminated with the human odour of subjugation. So — just what kind of a wolf was she? Black Wolf remained poised upon the brink of indecision.

White Wolf rushed at him again like a streak of white lightning, teeth bared in fearless snarling assault. With split-second decision, Black Wolf opened his throat to a shrieking growl, thrust out his razor-sharp fangs, and launched himself into a wrathful countercharge. But to his own surprise, he dodged the clash at the last moment and wheeled round to White Wolf's hindquarters. Abruptly, he suppressed his welling savagery and advanced his nose toward the precincts of her undertail. He was stirred. He now knew what kind of a wolf this was: a female coming on heat.

The low growls rumbling in Black Wolf's throat gradually changed in timbre until they were suffused with tenderness. He nipped at her flirtatiously, suddenly a besotted lover.

An arresting shiver passed through White Wolf's body. She spun about and fled with Black Wolf in hot pursuit. Two bolts of lightning streaked across the desert sand, one white, one black, one preceding the other in a stark and stirring enactment of the eternal rage to live. Upon the sea of death that was the desert, a trail of swirling dust arose in frenzied celebration of this furious love-chase.

It was early spring, the time of mating and sowing of seed in the cyclical world of wolfdom.

Out of the remote depths of the dim far-flung east seemed to come a voice raised in that elusive summons of a bygone age: "Whitsey —. Ooohhh Whiiii-tseeyy —."

1

The donkey-drawn *lele** cart creaked and groaned as it

---

*Lele cart — a light weight, all-purpose cart that may be hitched to an ox, a donkey, or a horse. Its two over-sized wheels allow it move swiftly over grassland (and thus it is often called a "grass flyer") as well as to negotiate various types of inhospitable terrain from shifting-sand deserts to swamps.

ascended the sand-slope. This was the portal to the Manges Desert and its vast, parched inhospitality. As the cart triumphantly crested the summit, Yuanhui breathed a long sigh of relief.

"At last!" she cried, not without a note of exasperation. "We've finally reached the desert." With this observation, her heart skipped a beat: this was surely the very spot from which Whitesea had entered this demonic domain ... this *Manges* — this *monstrosity* — of a desert: What an appropriate name! Her lids lowered with the pain at the thought. *Don't dwell on it, it's just too terrible...* It was that storm of human unreason — another kind of monstrosity — that had torn her family apart, obliterated timeless sentiments, destroyed her home. Whitesea sallied forth into the desert, their son flew off overseas never to reclaim his homeland, while she was left to languish in lonely isolation in the capital. A desolate sigh unconsciously escaped her.

The cart driver twisted his head in her direction. "What's the matter — is it gettin' to you?" he inquired. "We've got a long way to go, you know. I told you it was a hairy trip, remember? Don't be comin' to this god-forsaken place is what I said. Yessir, I said so right from the start." His weathered face wasn't old, but it bespoke the age beyond innocence.

Yuanhui gave a rueful smile and shook her head. "No, it's not gettin' to me. Just ... keep on going." She eyed the hunting rifle slung across his back. His unusual and excessively developed powers of observation were frightening. That's what was getting to her.

She'd arrived yesterday in New Black Sand Gulch,

the last outpost of civilisation bravely perched upon the equivocal border of the Manges Sandland. After the cadre from the county forestry department who'd escorted her there had made all the necessary arrangements, she'd released her from further obligation so she could go back to the county seat whence they'd come. First thing this morning, the village headman, Elder Bao, assigned a people's militia company commander, a man named Tieba*, to take her into the sandland to look for the lama who called himself Yondon. The headman claimed that only this Commander Tieba could possibly find him because he was his nephew. And this Lama Yondon was the one and only person in the world her husband had associated with — indeed, lived with — before his death. It was essential to find him if she were to understand the circumstances of the final years of her husband's life, and to discover how he met his death.

"Commander Tie," she addressed the driver, the appellation endowed him by the villagers still awkward on her tongue **, "how long has it been since you saw your uncle?"

"Hmmm? A year maybe," he replied preoccupied. His eyes were sweeping the sandland, on the lookout for something. "No, no, must be longer than that — closer to two, I'd say."

---

*Tieba's name means 'fifty years old", a tribute to his father's age when he was born.

**In keeping with Mongolian practice, Tieba has only one name. It is very common, though, for people to be addressed by the first syllable of their names, as Tieba is here, when an honorific is used. What Yuanhui feels uncomfortable with here is having to address him as "Commander".

"Two years! I thought he lived with you in the village."

"Him? Har-de-har!" he laughed cynically. "That guy doesn't know the meaning of staying put. For the last few years, there's been hardly a day when he set foot in the village." Tieba hacked up a piece of phlegm and spat it out upon the sand. He swiped his mouth with the back of his fist. "He's what they call a *badirqin*," he added, "a wandering monk. There's *no* place he calls home."

A feeling of disappointment overswept Yuanhui. She lifted her eyes and gazed out across the vast scene of desolation that was the sandland. "So, then," she inquired, "just where are you taking me on this quest for the wandering monk?"

Tieba blinked his sly little eyes and laughed. "Even migrating birds have their stop-over points. That uncle of mine ... after he's been traipsing around heaven knows where for awhile, he's got his cosy little nest he always comes back to."

"Where's that?"

"The Temple of Viridity."

"The Temple of Viridity?" The name was familiar to her. Whitesea had written of such a place in the accounts he'd sent to the provincial office. Viridity, she she vaguely recollected, meant "green" — the Green Temple. She'd had the impression he'd been referring to an old temple that had been buried in the drifting sand. He'd noted that there he'd discovered a new way to check the advance of the desert. He'd been so excited about it, apparently, that he'd even forgotten he was supposed to be an *exile* (though of course his superiors would never admit it), and he'd actually had the audacity to make a most outlandish recommendation to the head of the Desert Research Institute: that the whole institute, lock, stock and barrel, be moved to the Temple of Viridity. Boy, was he ever out of it! His collegues at the institute had a field day with that one. There they were ensconced in the capital doing their research on the desert and coming up with all kinds of brilliant results that got them prizes and honours right and left — that would be the day when they moved out to the middle of the desert! So some of the people began looking at her with mockery in their eyes, just to see what her reaction would be. Well, what kind of a reaction could she possibly have? She was numb, she had no feeling left, her heart had turned to a chunk of wood the day Whitesea had gone off to the desert. It was dry, dead, had no blood in it left to bleed. Five years — she hadn't seen him for five years. When it finally came to her that perhaps she herself had been at fault, that she'd been living a lie all this time, it was already too late. The institute received a brief telegramme from the Manges Sandland: Whitesea dead. Sand burial. Yondon.

She'd fallen into a bitter sea of self-recrimination and remorse. The pain was so unbearable she'd wanted to die.

But she was no ordinary woman. She vowed to go herself into the Manges Sandland and clear up the mystery of her husband's life and death. And while she was at it, she would apprise herself of that "Viridity Model" of desert control he'd found so worthy of exaltation. Of course there was as well that person who'd sent the telegramme, the one called Yondon. She wrote to her son in Australia, expressing the wish that he join her on the quest for any traces his father might have left behind. His return missive put it to her bluntly: he wanted her to come to Australia, he would handle all the formalities. She could only smile bitterly at this turn of affairs. They had once been a family of three, the proverbial firmly-standing tripod, yet there'd been no harmony. Now that only the two of them remained, there was no reason to assume they'd have common ground on which to stand. Besides, she'd already decided to throw her lot in with her husband, dead though he was, and she couldn't turn back now. The research proposal she'd presented to the newly appointed administrators of the Desert Research Institute had been approved with promises of full support, and the first thing on the agenda was an investigation of the Viridity Model. She was as convinced as Whitesea had been of the feasibility of the Desert Research Institute setting up a research and experimentation station for sand control out here.

"How much further is it to the Temple of Viridity?" Yuanhui asked Commander Tie.

"Fourteen-fifteen miles."

"How's the road — good all the way?"

"Road? Lady, there is no road!"

"Well, then how do we get there?"

"We just feel ourselves along blind." Commander Tie's eyes flitted about, taking in the wild environs on all sides, as if he didn't have his mind on the task at hand.

"You seem to have something else on the agenda, is that so?" Yuanhui inquired.

"Nothing of any consequence. I'm just looking for a wolf."

"A wolf!" Yuanhui was startled.

"That's right. A white wolf. Last night it made off with another one of my sheep. It comes round here once a year and steals my fuckin' livestock, god-damn wolf! The filthy motherfucker!" He unleashed his curses with impunity.

Yuanhui was repelled as she recognised with an aching heart the ugly face of obsession. In this world, she thought, everyone has his own affliction, his own torment that he can't for the life of him get rid of. There's always something to make life miserable, somebody to give us the shaft and plunge our minds into turmoil, incidents that eat at our hearts and arouse black thoughts in the middle of the night; busy, busy, busy, we are, running here and running there, never a moment's rest; the whole human race caught in a meaningless cycle of life and death. So exhausting, this business of life! Well, maybe the ancients were right when they preached the doctrine of inaction — just sit there and let it all roll by, like water off the duck's back, don't say anything, just be silent and serene. Everything goes its own way anyway, so just ignore it and save yourself a lot of grief. You hear, Yuanhui? This means you!

The *lele* cart proceeded in silence, leaving on the roadless sandland two wheel tracks writhing across the surface like a pair of surrealistic, elongated snakes.

Tieba's small round eyes were operating on overload. He had a hunch that the sly white wolf was concealing itself somewhere on the sandland waiting for the most opportune moment to attack. They'd been enemies for ages now; the contest between them had a long history. Cold daggers of light glinted from his eyes narrowly slitted against the sun as they surveyed every tumulus, dune and clump of sandpuff.

They'd been travelling along for some time when the donkey stopped and planted its feet widely in the sand and relieved itself of a gushing stream. From the parched sand arose the pungent odour of fresh urine.

"Let's rest a spell. The donkey needs a break too," said Tieba.

Yuanhui got down from the cart. She wandered over to inspect a high dune, one side of which had been scoured away by the seasonal wind so that it resembled a precipice. The top of the dune and its sloping lee side were sparsely covered with felon herb*, wild jujube**, and some kind of a tussocky plant she didn't recognise. She noted that the clumps of this latter were particularly hardy and rooted so tenaciously and broadly that the sand had stayed put despite the wind, giving rise to the peculiar precipice-conformation which the dune had taken on. The side of the dune facing the wind had been blown away precisely because those clumps of sand-grabbing plant had not taken root there. She scrutinised this plant with wonder and amazement. Suddenly she remembered that in her husband's letters, he had trumpeted his discovery of a miraculous plant in the Manges Sandland that the locals called *xibag* artemisia***. This must be it, she thought. This plant has to be that miraculous *xibag* artemisia.

Artemisia argyi.
**Ziziphus jujuba*.
****Artemisia ordosica*, or "black sand artemisia". The Chinese name is *youhao*, "oil artemisia".

"Come on, let's go! We gotta move!" Commander Tieba shouted and waved his hat at her from where he was inspecting a line of tracks in the sand. His voice rang with excitement and urgency. He was holding a freshly killed sand grouse.

"What'd you find there? Your uncle's footprints?"

"Better than that! It's the white wolf, I've found the white wolf's tracks! See, look, they're fresh!"

This is getting ridiculous! Yuanhui thought, grimly amused. As they once more got underway, however, she discovered to her dismay that Tieba's route was paralleling the animal tracks. "Are we looking for your uncle," she asked tartly, "or are we looking for that wolf?"

"Don't get excited, it's all the same thing. If you'd open your eyes a bit, you'd see these tracks are heading right in the direction of the Temple of Viridity."

After about half an hour, they came to a gentle sand ridge which took them to a modest height but which afforded an expansive view. Tieba pointed to a patch of green off to the west. "That's the Temple of Viridity," he said. Yuanhui's spirits perked up. Then she saw a man on a donkey approaching them from the north by way of a path cutting across the sandland. He was intoning the words to an old traditional song:

> *Fickle* — *is that wind above,*
> *Bumpy* — *is that road below,*
> *Ahh* — *haa* — *heii* —

With its long-spun wailing notes, the song imbued the listener with sense of bleakness and melancholy.

"Ehh? Who's singing 'The Fickle Wind'?" Tieba, who'd been scrutinising the tracks they'd been following, raised his head in surprised curiosity and discovered the donkey-rider was but forty or fifty yards off. "Hey, you there!" he called out to him, trying to catch his attention.

The rider leaned in their direction and strained to see the source of the shouting.

"It's him! I knew it, it's my uncle! Let's go!" Tieba flicked the reins and they lurched forward. Yuanhui could hardly contain herself for joy. The old fellow had a broken straw hat crammed on his head and wore a deep chocolate-brown robe that was frayed and tattered. His gaunt sun-blackened face was as hardened and furrowed as the bark of the sandland's Siberian elms.

"What're you doing here?" he asked his nephew with obvious displeasure. The coldness in his voice could have dropped the desert temperature a few degrees.

"I, ah we, are looking for you," Tieba hastened to explain. "This here lady's from the provincial capital and she's come to visit Viridity. The headman's approved it all — arranged everything."

The old fellow eyed Yuanhui cursorily, then his gaze drifted on to the slain sand grouse that had been tossed into the cart. He exploded in anger.

"You've been killing things again! Haven't you sinned enough as it is? Except for jerboas, there's nothing left in the sandland — you and your kind have killed off everything else!"

"Come, now, Uncle," Tieba sniggered, "you're exaggerating — what about the wolves! Last night one made off with another one of my sheep, and guess who it was — that white wolf!"

"White wolf?" the old man started. The expression on his face turned to one of keen interest, and his eyes began to gleam. "Are you sure you haven't been imagining things?"

"If you don't believe me, its tracks are right over there to prove it. I followed them all the way here. The damned critter — I'll bet it's right around here somewhere."

"Tracks? The white wolf's tracks? Where? I have to see this!" the old man exclaimed. His eyes glittered and his features became suffused with impatience and urgency. He turned and dashed off toward the sand ridge.

"That's your uncle, Lama Yondon?" Yuanhui asked, incredulous.

"None other!" Tieba returned, making not the least effort to conceal his contempt. "The nuttiest of the nut cases from here to kingdom come!" he added with emphasis, though he was not distracted from his vigilant inspection of the environs. He seemed to sense a presence, for he pulled back his rifle bolt with a smart, heart-rapping "click-clack".

But all there was to be seen was Lama Yondon mounting the sand ridge and making a beeline for those tracks. He looked at them with intensity, mumbling to himself, "Look at that print! There's no doubt about it! Look at that print!" Then he straightened up and raised his hand to shield his eyes from the sun as he looked all about for the one who'd left its signature in the sand. He called out in a drawn-out wail, "Whiiii-tseeyy—, Whiiii-tseeyy—"

Only absolute silence came back at him out of the desert desolation.

Out in the distance, a certain clump of artemisia bent down and sprang back several times, as if something were concealing itself there. Then absolute stillness reigned once more.

"*Ai!*" Lama Yondon sighed. "Gone again. I'm still not forgiven. The villagers still stand accused." His sighs filled the atmosphere with regret as he descended the ridge, climbed back upon his donkey, and rode off, his figure slumped on his mount.

Seeing his uncle heading for the Temple of Viridity, Tieba urged Yuanhui to retake her seat on the cart. "Quick!" he shouted. "Get in, we gotta catch up!"

"He doesn't seem to be too appreciative of our presence," Yuanhui said doubtfully.

"He doesn't like to have *anybody* around. And if a non-believer sets foot in the Temple of Viridity, he thinks a great sacrilege has been committed ... except for that other half-cracked character who showed up here a number of years ago — what's-his-name ... Whitesea."

"Oh, yeah? How did this Whitesea person manage to get on your uncle's good side?"

"I have no idea. When we get to Viridity, you can ask him yourself. I think, though, he won't let you stay there."

With a flick of the reins, Tieba set the *lele* cart in motion, and once again the squeaking protest of unoiled wheels invaded the silence of the sandland.

Yuanhui said nothing else. She gazed upon the fig-

ahead on his donkey, the man with a hint of a geriatric hunch. She was convinced that whatever her husband had achieved, she could replicate — for she was now crazier than he had ever been.

A vast white expanse of drifting sand in the southeast corner of the Horqin Sandy Land was where the Temple of Viridity was located. The locals have dubbed this expanse of drifting sand Manges Mangha, which means Demon Desert. The area, though, was not always a lifeless heap of sand where not even a blade of grass could grow. It used to be humped and bumpy sandland hospitable to hardy vegetation, whose fixed dunes permitted grazing on their summits while the slopes and lowlands could be coaxed into productivity. With a sparse array of natural villages scattered throughout, it used to support quite an impressive number of Mongolian herdsmen as well as farm families who'd immigrated from other areas. Furthermore, the Temple of Viridity was at one time a place of considerable note, with thirty or forty lamas of various ranks housed in the temple and offerings constantly set before a trio of golden statues representing the Buddhas of the past, present and future: Kasyapa, Sakyamuni, and Maitreya. Here in those idyllic times, incense smoke ever curling into the air signified devotion undiminished by ease. Devout men and women flowed through the temple halls in an endless stream. The Temple of Viridity was an important centre of Lamaism on the Horqin Grassland. And Black Sand Gulch was situated but a stone's throw away. Then the desert began to take over, and stinging air-borne sand swallowed the entire area, sometimes with mind-boggling speed. Almost every house in Black Sand Gulch was completely buried in one big obliterating gulp one night when the sandstorm of the ages struck. This was the last straw for the villagers, who finally admitted defeat and moved their community to a new site about twenty miles away, founding the current-day New Black Sand Gulch. How did it happen that in a mere hundred years the area declined into this wasteland too terrible to look upon, this limitless white desert of death? People muddled along in total ignorance. Some cursed Heaven for sending drought nine years out of ten. Some cursed the infertility of the land and its refusal to yield to cultivation. And some cursed people themselves as a self-destructive Blindy Bear, who in the face of hunger and cold knows only to lick the pads of his paws and roll himself up in a deathtrap of a cubbyhole — unsalvageable degenerates, that's what people were.

Lama Yondon, however, had his own explanation for what ailed the land. The spread of the desert, he avowed, was directly related to the Temple of Viridity being torn down. With its destruction, people lost their reverence for the deities and the Buddha. This loss of faith in turn deprived them of the protection of these spirit guardians, who were nothing less than the life-force of the universe, who signified the universe and resided, ubiquitous if unseen, in every stitch of its fabric. He paid a price for this belief for those were the days of political type-casting, and the village powers-that-were branded him a reactionary lama perversely recalcitrant in the face of reform, one of the reviled "twenty-one unsavoury types" to be ostracised and punished. Every day he was sent into the sandland to pull the harrow as a means of purging himself of his crimes — and, by the way, to gather firewood for the politically pristine leaders, who were too busy with the purification movement to resolve their own heating problems. Two birds with one stone.

Then one frigid early-winter day, he dragged his abused, labour-swollen legs back from the sandland and discovered a stranger in his tumbledown packed-mud house, seated on a tightly furled bedroll in the middle of the floor. A thin, white, bespectacled face tilted up at him as he entered, flaunting a broad shiny forehead that seemed hardly contained beneath his indigo cloth cap. A net bag crammed with books, toiletries, a wash basin, and a pair of shoes sat fatly at his feet.

Lama Yondon froze and stared. The stranger, too, indicated a complex of profound discomfort, but he managed to squeeze an apologetic smile out of his lips. He rose to his feet.

"Be you deity or be you demon?"

"I ... I'm not ... er, well yes, I *am* a demon, a 'demon of reactionary society'..." He rubbed his hands with an air of humble courtesy and made a rather incoherent attempt to explain his presence. "They ... ah ... the village government ... uh ... they sent me here to learn from you how to pull the harrow ... yes ... that's what it's all about ... I'm to learn how to pull the harrow."

"Ha, ha, ha..." responded Lama Yondon mirthfully in spite of himself. "So you're to learn how to pull the harrow, eh?" These days, learning-campaigns covered just about everything under the sun, and everybody was busy with "Learning Editorials"* and "Learning Quotations"**, "Learning the Loyalty Dance"***, "Learning from Dazhai" and "Learning from Daqing"****... But this was the first time he'd ever heard of *Learning the Harrow* — boy, did that sound weird! Back in the days when he'd been a *Gebhui* Lama in the Temple of Viridity, he'd taught the little novices their sutras. Now he would teach someone how to pull the harrow. Well, it was something different, all right.

"Just who are you, anyway? And where do you come from?"

"I'm Whitesea, and I've been sent down to shape up... er ... from the Provincial Desert Research Institute. I just got here today. They sent me here to you — you're supposed to teach me how to pull the harrow so I can be reformed." Whitesea spoke earnestly and with a sincere display of respect.

Lama Yondon received this information in a cloud of perplexity. Why did people have to be banished to the edge of a desert in order to be reformed? What was the matter with reforming them in the city? And what about people who lived on the edge of the desert — where were they supposed to go to be

---

*...i.e., studying the editorials published in the *People's Daily*.

**...i.e., the quotations of Chairman Mao.

***A dance of set choreography expressing loyalty to Mao Zedong, performed to such loyalist songs as "Red Sun in Our Hearts", "Long Live Our Leader", etc., circa 1967-69. Its performance was required of everyone, including the elderly.

****The Dazhai Production Brigade and the Daqing Oilfield, both held up in their heyday as models of achievement and self-sufficiency, and both later discredited as having received government aid.

reformed? It's always been like this — all those venerable years of history, and they still haven't figured out a better way to reform people. He was on the verge of asking his interlocutor what he'd done to get himself sent here, but then he thought better of it.

The next day, they went into the sandland together: To pull the harrow.

Now, the harrow is an implement designed especially for gathering sandland fuel — vegetation suitable for feeding cooking and heating stoves. It consists of a thick wooden shaft about six feet long connected to a sturdy frame affixed with forty or fifty six-inch curved iron teeth about the thickness of a chopstick. The end of the shaft is placed upon the shoulder, and a short bar fits across the upper chest from shoulder to shoulder. When the harrow is pulled across the land, its teeth pierce the surface layer of the soil and tear up all the vegetation lying in its path by the roots. Leaning deeply into the crossbar, the puller drags the harrow until it is full of vegetation. Then he stops and frees what has been collected in the harrow's teeth and heaps it in a pile. Thus gathering the vegetation harrowfull by harrowfull, he creates a high gigantic pile of fuel, which he then transports back to the village by means of a cart or dray. The harrow itself weighs from thirty to forty pounds, and in the course of a day, the puller walks an equivalent of at least thirty to sixty miles, an exhausting proposition that even a man of steel can't take after awhile. This is labour reform truly worthy of the name.

Silently, Whitesea watched as Lama Yondon began his demonstration of the harrow.

With horror he saw the sandland plants so tenuously clinging to life — absinthium, Asiatic wormwood, sheep grass*, sandpuff, and many others all being indiscriminately ripped up by their roots by the remorseless teeth of the harrow. A heart-rending cry leaped from his throat: "Stop!"

Lama Yondon halted and blinked with surprise. How come this unassuming, obsequeous book-man had suddenly become so vehemently angry?

"What? What's the matter?"

Whitesea approached the lama with deliberate steps. "You mean that's the purpose of pulling the harrow — to gather up all this stuff?"

"Well, what else on earth for! You think we do it for our health?"

"Do you people here depend totally upon such harrowed-up vegetation for fuel?"

"That's correct — what do you think? We've been doing it this way for generations!"

"But this is madness! It's total, absolute destruction! If anything accelerates the spread of the desert, this is it! No wonder this place has become a barren waste! Oh, my God! Oh, my God, what a deplorable crime!" Whitesea stamped his foot in his growing tide of indignation. He squatted down and with an aching heart picked up an uprooted absinthium and inspected its roots. He wanted to determine whether any root fragments were left in the soil.

Lama Yondon cast an apathetic eye upon this

---

*Aeurolepidium chinense (Leymus chinensis). so named because sheep like to feed on it.

maudlin display of flora-sentimentalism. *Look at this idiot!* he laughed to himself. *Talk about the head in the clouds!*

"Stop acting a fool and let's get on with the harrow-pulling. You say it's destruction, and maybe you're right, but what else can the people stuck out here in the middle of nowhere burn for fuel — their own fingers?"

Pierced by this dolorous truth, Whitesea's heart bled in lamentation, long beyond tears. "I'm not doing it," he announced with finality.

"You're not doing it? Ho, I see. Well in that case, I suggest you go back where you came from."

Whitesea was struck dumb. In silence he took up the harrow's hefty shaft and placed it on his shoulder. His heart trembled with the unthinkable criminality of what he was about to do.

And across the sandland there appeared a parallel pair of lines, two feet apart, the scarifying marks of twin harrows combing ruthlessly through the sand. White dust arose in the wake of each harrow and hung starkly, and when it settled, the denuded land lay disconsolate and sere, like a living body brutally stripped naked and left exposed to the harsh glare of humiliation. Its piteous aspect, its heart-wringing disfigurement bespeaking the pain of a helpless, wounded spirit was too dreadful to behold. With startling swiftness, these swaths of nakedness marched across the land, crisscrossed and interlocked, expanding their domain until this section of the sandland appeared in its new and vulnerable nakedness swathed in an epic gargantuan net.

It seemed to Whitesea that he could hear behind him the weeping of the plants ensnared in the harrow's teeth and feel the freshly denuded land trembling with the trauma he was inflicting upon it. He was a scientist and he'd poured his life's energies into studying the desert, researching its subtleties, bringing its secrets to light. He'd always advocated the unification of such academic endeavours with pragmatic attempts to curb the desert. Subjugation of those forces that caused desert expansion — that had been his dream; he'd dedicated his life to ferreting out an effective means to do precisely this. The encroachment of the sand was one of the four great disasters facing humanity. Already a full thirty-seven percent of the earth's land surface had succumbed to the sand and was barren desert territory. And the growth of the desert was proceeding at a startlingly rapid rate. If a way were not devised to control it soon, this planet upon which humanity depended for its very existence could well be completely covered with sand in the not too distant future. There were those who shrugged off such predictions as gross exaggeration, the mere ranting of alarmists, but he was convinced of its truth. Now here he was at last, sent as he'd always desired, into the sandy precincts. This was an invaluable opportunity to pursue his research right on the spot, where he could observe up close and over an extended period of time, the behaviour of the desert. This would allow him to develop a concrete working model of desert control.

Lama Yondon seemed perfectly attuned to this lifestyle which was the invention and the mandate of previous generations. And he'd embellished it with a practice that contributed to the maintenance of his spirituality as well as ameliorating the fatiguing effects of his tremendous physical labour: as he pulled his harrow, he recited the sutras. He, too, hated the desert, because the sand had buried the vestiges of the Temple of Viridity upon which he'd relied for his spiritual sustenance. The desert was a great evil spirit in his system of belief, a demon of death and destruction and when the temple was torn down, it had been released upon the earth to wreak its havoc. This was retribution, Heaven's punishment for man's reckless misdeed.

At dusk, when the pale yellow sun was sucked down into the western desert, the two of them quit their labours and went home. Every muscle in Whitesea's exhausted body ached. Lama Yondon went out to relieve himself at the base of a dune. The silence in which he left Whitesea was soon broken with his excited shouts.

"Quick! Come and look — see what I found!"

Whitesea walked over to the scene of excitement.

Lying in a clump of sandpuff was a shivering puppy tiny as a newborn kitten. It was snow white, with its little legs erratically kneading the air. Its two piteous obsidian eyes wavered about uncontrolled. On its forehead was a little tuft of fur so fine and white as to be transparent. It couldn't have been more than several days old, and its little mouth, emitting little infantile groans, searched about for a teat to suck upon.

"That couldn't be a wolf pup, could it?" Whitesea asked as he glanced uneasily about the wild surroundings.

"Whoever heard of a snow-white wolf!" Lama Yondon scoffed. "This is an abandoned puppy. Yes, it's got to be — someone didn't want to be bothered with raising it and so tossed it here. Either that or its mother went looking for food and got killed by someone scared of rabies. Oohh, look at the poor little thing, isn't it pretty, yes such a pretty little creature, yes indeed!" Lama Yondon was uncharacteristically excited, and he displayed an uncommon affection as he took the little dog into his arms. He stroked its silky soft fur, cradled it gently against his bosom, and talked to it in a soft sentimental patter. "Oohh, oohh, such a nice little puppyyy —, let me take you home, I'll take care you, I'll be your mummy and your daddy, poor little thing, thrown out here in the big bad wilderness, you'll freeze to death, you'll starve to death, but I won't let that happen, nooo; the Buddha sent me to find you, I heard him and I came to save you, poor little thing!"

In fact, Whitesea had no objection to this adoption, and Lama Yondon didn't have to cite the will of the Buddha to convince him. After all, Whitesea himself was just like a helpless homeless dog who'd fallen upon the mercy of another to keep him in shelter.

Still, the lama prattled on in justification. "Anyway, it was Heaven who made sure I was in the right spot at the right time, which means this puppy and I have a special affinity. It was destined. The way things are these days, how often do you run across someone you've got affinity with? It's the will of Heaven, and Heaven's will can't be disobeyed!"

The way Whitesea saw it, the old lama had lived a solitary life for so many years that he'd drunk the cup of isolation, desolation and loneliness down to the dregs, and now that this lovable little puppy had appeared on the scene, it was for him like finding a kind of emotional bulwark, a kindred spirit with whom he could exchange comfort and affection.

And so the little menage of miscreants, that mini-reformatory for two, embraced a third party. Naming the tiny new member of the family, the old lama produced one of his rare smiles and said, "I've got just the name — Whitesy ... the snow-white child."

Whitesea smiled, moved by the old lama's selection of a name for the little dog homophonic with his own, a charming tribute, that he felt belied the aloofness the lama was wont to display. Inspired thus to bonhomie, he returned humorously, "I have an even better name — Little Lama."

Lama Yondon's face changed instantly and he gave a clap of glee. "Perfect!" he chortled. "Ingenious! We'll have different names. I'll call it Whitesy, and you call it Little Lama. And why not — people have more than one name, so why can't animals?"

Strangely enough, the little dog itself came to answer to both these names. But no one would have predicted it would do so selectively, ignoring the old lama's use of "Little Lama" and refusing to recognise Whitesea's use of "Whitesy". It granted separate patents to each and wouldn't permit either to encroach upon the other's exclusive domain.

The little puppy's helpless whimpering brought fuzzy-warm vitality into the dark dank atmosphere of the earthen room. The two men became rivals for its affection and nearly came to blows at times over whose bed it would occupy at night. Such occasions obliged them to revert to such childhood contests as "guess-fingers" and "rock, scissors, paper" to resolve the dispute.

2

Whitesy, Whitesy, Whitesy... Three years? Five? Seven? Just how long had it been, anyway? This summons from a two-leg reverberated in her ears like thunder and sent tremors through her soul.

White Wolf ran, she ran with the blood-rushing intensity of the adamantly untamed.

It was as if she'd thrown herself upon the mercy of the wilderness as a progenitor of freedom, where wild flight could soar unrestrained to the heights of insanity, where she could escape that summons simultaneously familiar and strange. It had been a very long time, now, and all that should be forgotten she'd relegated to the dustbins of memory. Yet her experience of coexistence with the two-legs was permanently engraved on her bones and heart. She didn't know why over all these years she harboured an unabiding enmity for the two-legs, including that one particular old man, but especially that one who carried the rifle — the hunter: he aroused in her a horror that sent her hackles bristling and drove her blood burning through her veins with righteous indignation. The enmity she bore for mankind vastly surpassed any vestige of attachment that lingered within her being.

It was fear that had precipitated her flight across the sand; not fear of that man whose evil was palpable, but of the firearm he held in his hand. They had to have their guns, the two-legs; without their guns, they wouldn't be able to accomplish anything.

At last White Wolf arrived at a cave situated deep within the desert. Located at the base of a towering sand crag, hidden behind a dense overhanging growth of artemisia, the cave's black mouth gaped. This was their — her and his — home. Ever vigilant Black Wolf leaped out from a clump of willows atop the sand crag and came down to greet her. No fresh kill dangled from her mouth, disappointing his expectation of dinner. He lobbed a couple of displeased growls at her then softening, nuzzled her in forgiveness. White Wolf had no interest in such intimacies and walked away from him. Languidly she stretched out upon the sand next to the mouth of the cave. Once again her eyes drifted into abstraction as she gazed off toward the east.

Black Wolf was unreconciled to her aloofness. Wrapping himself in a matter-of-fact air, he ambled leisurely over to her, stretched out his neck and nudged her already distended belly with his muzzle. He then moved on to sniff with the greatest of respect at her nether parts. He was in full grasp of the fact that in the not too distant future, he was going to be a father. However, his efforts to draw out her affection only succeeded in provoking her. With a furious snarl, she whipped her head about and seized his ear in her teeth, inflicting an instructive wound. Black Wolf leaped away from the assault and exhibited indifference. Following impregnation, the she-wolf is the undisputed dominator of the lair. She harbours such ferocity that her mate can almost never come out the winner in any dispute. Black Wolf thus stood off to the side with gentlemanly forbearance, maintaining a policy of equinimity in the face of her unpredictably shifting moods. He yawned widely, distracting his enormous blood-yearning mouth from its deprivation, and gave his body a deep, invigorating stretch. Then with a nimble bound, he regained the height of the sand crag, where he lay, his head upright, in his position of vigilance.

At dusk, the two wolves, their stomachs rumbling with hunger, set out for the east.

This time Black Wolf took the lead. Stretching his legs into a vigorous rhythmic stride, he fairly flew over the sand straight toward the eastern edge of the Manges Sandland and the Temple of Viridity. Leaving nothing to chance, he'd already selected a specific object of attack. It was not for nothing that he'd achieved his respectable age and was still flitting about the wilderness despite years of human endeavour to remove him.

They passed through the undulating dunes under which the old village lay buried and stole into the grounds of the Temple of Viridity.

They came upon a dilapidated two-room mud house. The target of their assault, an emaciated old cow, was tied to a stake behind it. They needed only to bury the kill in the sand, and they'd have meat enough for a month which they could enjoy at their leisure. It wouldn't spoil.

Light penetrated the window of the house and dazzled their eyes in the blackness of the night. For some reason which Black Wolf could not fathom, the mere sight of lamplight or a flame filled him with dread. Perhaps it was a genetic trait passed down from his forbears that caused the mischief. Probably back at the dawn of time, when the remote ancestors of today's wolves tangled with primitive men, they were brought to grisly defeat by means of the torches they bore in their hands. Otherwise, man's ancestors would not have been primitive men, but rather wolf-men.

White Wolf, it seemed, didn't share this phobia. Quite on the contrary, she had some kind of an affinity for the light and felt herself irresistibly drawn to it. Standing on her hind legs, she placed her paws upon the window-sill and looked in. And there it was, that familiar old face. It was the very same old man who'd made her heart pound and her flesh crawl when he shouted "Whitesy, Whitesy" over and over that afternoon. So, this was where he lived. Then she remembered something. Silently, she dropped down from the window-sill and swiftly rounded the house to the back. There she discovered Black Wolf already within striking distance of that unfortunate old cow. The cow, having perceived its danger, was circling the post to which it was tied, frantically trying to break free of its halter. Its nostrils were flaring with panic and a low bellow of dread rumbled from its throat.

White Wolf took a look at the cow, a flash of the past streaked out from her memory, and a shiver passed through her. It had been enormous, that teat, most inappropriately sized for her tiny mouth, and it had flowed with nourishment so copious — truly a river of milk — that she'd choked in getting it down.

When Black Wolf leaped up to seize the cow by the throat, White Wolf sprang over and hit him broadside in mid-air. Stunned by this unexpected attack, Black Wolf dodged to the side, and only then did he know that it was White Wolf who had intercepted his strike. He was enraged. Wrathfully he bared his teeth and snarled a dire warning: she'd better not interfere with his business, or there would be hell to pay. But White Wolf, far from being cowed by his threats, was ferocious as never before as she lunged for his throat. This was the end of the road for them, was her message; they were finished, no longer mates, and this time it was for real.

The two estranged wolves tore into each other in a pitched battle of growls and snarls and claws and snapping murderous teeth. The terrified, bewildered cow stared with wary popping eyes at the savagery playing out before her. Beasts they were, and none so beastly as lovers turned enemies. Nothing less than mutual slaughter would serve to quell their rage. They slammed into each other, brutal and insensate; fangs slashing, jaws grasping, claws impaling, fur flying, they tumbled and rolled in the dust, and still their frenzied virulence was unabated. But White Wolf's pregnancy put her at a disadvantage, and she began to flag. Just at this time, a clamour of hammering on tin pots or other metal implements burst out upon the rooftop of the hut, a cataclysm of percussion accompanied by a loud and raucous voice crying, "Wolves! Wolves—"

This was man's age-old way of scaring off wolves.

And indeed, it was effective. Black Wolf in his fright immediately released White Wolf, turned tail and ran for the great western desert. Dragging her exhausted and unwilling body, White Wolf fled in a different direction. She hadn't gone far, though, when she stopped, turned and looked back at the hut. The old man came down from the roof and led the cow inside. The light went out. White Wolf let out several low anguished moans. Then silently she left. From the distant western desert came the faint aggrieved strains of Black Wolf's ululating voice. At last it died away, and the mysterious peace of the black night was restored to the desert.

The site where the old village used to be.

The *lele* cart was passing by enroute to its destination. No one would ever know there used to be a village here, for all traces of it had been buried completely by the shifting sand. Occasionally some weathered bones or a few pottery shards might peek through the yellow sand, proving that people did once live here. The fine and soft yellow brown-drift sand had swept through the area and gently swallowed every living thing in its path. On this old village site where countless generations had lived and multiplied, there grew not even a blade of grass. There were no bird calls to be heard, no insects to be seen flying about; while overhead brooded a broad lifeless sky. The gloomy, dry atmosphere of death hung constantly above the boundless shifting sand.

Yuanhui was suddenly struck by an inauspicious thought: would all the habitable areas of the earth — the cities, the rural villages, the open country, the forests — all one day be just like this former village site? Is that what the distant future held for mankind — utter disaster? All living things on the planet would be like these weathered bones: the life sucked out of them beyond redemption. She shivered, though she wasn't cold. She dared not think of it. Fortunately, the *lele* cart soon began to leave this zone of death behind.

After another mile or so, they came to the Temple of Viridity, where Lama Yondon lived. Of course, the real Temple of Viridity no longer existed. When the temple was torn down, the bricks and tiles were carted to the new village site and used to build the village office buildings. Even if it hadn't been dismantled, it would have been completely covered by the blown sand. The temple in its present incarnation consisted of a two-room mud house which Lama Yondon had erected on the original site.

Yuanhui discovered that the several hundred *mu* of land surrounding the Temple of Viridity was completely different from that of the old village site a mile or two to the east. This slap-sized place surrounded by sand was covered with green vegetation! She cried out in amazement, "It's a real miracle! A miracle of life!"

In actual fact, the sight was equally unexpected for Commander Tie. He hadn't been back to the area since he left with the rest of the villagers. Indeed, none of the other villagers had been back. Only his Uncle Yondon, ever attached to his deities and buddhas, had returned and established himself here after he'd been declared a good person — that is, not one of the twenty-one unsavoury types. Everyone thought he'd been living the life of the alms-begging wandering monk. It had never entered people's minds that he was out here developing the Temple of Viridity's slap-sized piece of land into such an oasis of survival. Even Tieba found himself staring in surprise: could it be true that there really were guardian spirits protecting his uncle and this piece of land devoted to them?

Yuanhui scrambled down from the cart and started making a close examination of this miracle of life.

She discovered that the maker of this marvellous achievement was that miraculous plant, the *xibag* artemisia!

The shifting sand's domain stopped here, its rambling, swallowing destruction kept out by expanse after expanse and clump after clump of this bizarre-looking glossy-green plant that was multiplying and spreading over the land. This artemisia that was not quite three feet tall and bristled with luxurious collateral branches and grew in tussocks. It was tolerant of drought, loved sandy soil, and was very hardy. No wonder her husband said it was a precious plant that would change the desert. Intermingled with the *xibag* artemisia was yet another plant, the sand willow.* This woody plant also grew in clumps, putting out stems six to nine feet high, sending its roots deep into the earth, and covering itself in a thick profusion of light green leaves. Drift sand could bury it up to half its height, and still it would stand staunchly straight. The wild wind could bend it to the ground, yet afterwards it would defiantly spring erect, exhibiting in its graceful sway its tough, pliant tenacity. It was only because of these two plants that the slap-sized grounds of the Temple of Viridity continued to hang on at the very edge of desert's gaping mouth and hadn't been reduced to dead zone.

Yuanhui's heart filled with a tangle of emotions as she faced this place where her husband, Whitesea, had lived out his final years battling on behalf of life. This, then, was the "Viridity Model" he had talked about. She resolved to inspect conscientiously and research throughly this miraculous model. If it could really, as her husband had so glowingly said, be proved a feasible prototype for controlling the desert, then her next step would be to do her utmost to complete her husband's unfinished work. She would summarise and

---

**Salix psammophila.*

popularise this model as well as establish here an agency of the Desert Research Institute. The pressing matter of the moment, though, was to talk with Lama Yondon and gain an understanding of her husband's situation and to find the notes and materials he'd left behind.

Tieba stopped the *lele* cart before Lama Yondon's door. He unhitched the donkey and released it into the artemisia pasture in front of the door, where his uncle's donkey was grazing. The two animals raised their heads and eyed one another, gave out long glad brays of acknowledgement, then came together and nuzzled each other in an investigation of gender.

"Uncle!" Tieba called out as he pushed open the unlatched wattle door. "*Yi?*" he uttered in puzzled surprise. "Where is he?"

From the outside, the mud house looked frightfully deteriorated, but inside it was spic and span. A mud brick *kang* occupied the sunny window exposure. Spread out on top was a narrow cotton-padded mattress and blanket, and beside this was a low square *kang* table wiped shiny through the years. A neat stack of Buddhist scriptures sat upon the table, weighted down with an exquisitely wrought little brass bell and a delicately crafted string of ebony rosary beads. The back wall was hung with a Buddha-niche that contained a bronze statue of the Bodhisattva, Avalokitesvara Guanyin, and portraits of the Dalai Lama and the Panchen Lama. A burning *jula* lamp and smoking incense sat before the Buddha-niche. Yuanhui knew nothing about Lamaism, but the religious atmosphere of the environment inspired her with a sense of serene harmony, tranquillity, and solemn respect.

"My uncle was a lama at the Temple of Viridity for twenty or thirty years, and the only thing he learned was cleanliness. Look how clean this place is — it's cleaner than the township public health centrer. Sit down for a while. I'll go and look for him." Tieba went out. Yuanhui didn't dare stay there by herself and so followed him back outside.

Lama Yondon, weighed down with a bundle of stove fuel, was rounding the corner from the back of the house.

Tieba hastened over to relieve him of his load, but Lama Yondon side-stepped him. Though the old gentleman was a bit out of breath, he was loathe to give his nephew a chance to show off. It was obvious that the two of them held each other in mutual disregard.

"Uncle, I've escorted this lady here under the orders of Village Headman Bao. She's a big professor from the higher echelons of the Provincial Desert Research Institute and she's here to carry out research." All of Tieba's arrogance deserted him before his uncle, and he spoke in a hedging, non-committal tone.

"So? If she wants to do some research, let her do some research. What's that got to do with me?" Lama Yondon tossed his bundle of fuel near the door and slapped the dust off his clothes.

"She came here specifically to see you."

"To see me?"

"Yes."

"A lone lama out in the middle of the wilderness — what for?"

Tieba was stuck for words. How was he to know why Yuanhui wanted to see Lama Yondon?

"Venerable Master, Esteemed Big Brother," Yuanhui addressed both of them deferentially, "it's like this: Before Whitesea died, he wrote a letter to the Desert Research Institute that set forth the situation at the Temple of Viridity. The current head of the institute takes what Whitesea wrote very seriously and has sent me to look into it." Yuanhui searched Lama Yondon's face and added, "At the same time, I want to gain an understanding of Whitesea's life and work here before he died."

Lama Yondon shot a glance at her when she mentioned Whitesea's name, a look as sharp as a dagger. He washed his hands in the wash basin, then went into the house and sat down upon the edge of the *kang*. He didn't say anything.

Yuanhui began to feel ill at ease. She hadn't expected that the old man would be so cold and disagreeable.

"Esteemed Big Brother, how about you? Can you tell me about Whitesea? Or can you give me the things he left behind?" Yuanhui screwed up her courage and made this request with the utmost of sincerity.

"Give Whitesea's things to you?" Lama Yondon shot back in cold counter-inquiry. "On what basis? Who are you to him?"

"I... I... I'm his...wife." Yuanhui finally got it out.

"You're Whitesea's wi... wife?" Lama Yondon took a long steady look at her. "Whitesea never mentioned a wife."

"Well, I used to be his wife. Then afterwards we ... got divorced. Looking back on it ... well, I wasn't fair to him. I made some mistakes that I've come to regret..." Yuanhui really felt like bursting into tears before this man with whom Whitesea had shared adversity. She wanted to pour out the guilt in her heart.

"He never left any instructions with me to hand his things over to anyone. And I didn't know too much about what he was doing either. This Temple of Viridity 'grindstone*' that he told you about, I have no idea what that is. Here's the Temple of Viridity — you take a look and see for yourself if there's any 'grindstone'." Lama Yondon added some butter to the *jula* lamp in front of the statue of Buddha, saying as he did so, "It's getting late. If you want to take a look, I suggest you do it quickly. Otherwise you won't be able to make it back to the village before nightfall."

Yuanhui felt anger rising in her. It was bad enough that Lama Yondon refused to tell her about Whitesea or to hand over his things. Now he was ordering her off the premises. His cold unapproachability was hurtful and depressing. She could see that Whitesea had never forgiven her and that the old lama was taking revenge out on her on Whitesea's behalf. But she had no intention of being put off so easily.

"Venerable Master, my plan is to stay for several days here at the Temple of Viridity to carry out some research, and I'm looking forward to your ... hospitality."

---

*The words for "model" and "grindstone" are homophonic in Chinese (*moshi*), prompting a misunderstanding on the part of Lama Yondon, who is untutored in the concept of models or paradigms.

Lama Yondon scowled and said, "Madam *Danapati**, I am a *monk*, and for you to stay here would be most inconvenient. I am unable to help you. I strongly suggest that you return with haste to the village." He pivoted and with a wave of his hand rebuked his nephew, "Why are you still standing there? Get a move on! Hitch up the cart and take this visitor back to the village, otherwise tonight you'll be camping in the middle of nowhere!"

Tieba shook his head and said helplessly to Yuanhui, "Let's just go back. That's the way he is — he never listens to reason. I'll go hitch up the cart."

Tieba went out. Lama Yondon folded his hands and prayed before the Buddha-niche. Then he sat crosslegged before his table on the *kang* and read his scriptures, turning the pages one by one. He paid no attention to Yuanhui. It was as if there were no other living soul in the room.

Yuanhui had no choice. "Okay, then," she said, "I won't bother you anymore today. But I'll be back."

Lama Yondon did not react. His thin, haggard face was set into the lineaments of solemn detachment. And from it — or from his forehead — seemed to emanate an utterly transforming glow of pietistic mysticism.

It was after Yuanhui and her cart driver left that White Wolf and Black Wolf showed up.

Whitesy grew up with all the advantages any domestic dog could ever dream of.

In competing for her affections, her two masters both

---

*Danapati, "alms giver".

openly and surreptitiously showered her with all she could desire. They raised her with leniency and doting indulgence. Whitesy became the battlefront upon which the two of them deployed all the armaments of their wit and ingenuity. The ranking master of Lamaism and the scientist each brought wisdom from two widely divergent domains and unwittingly ended up subjecting Whitesy to a kind of experiment. The central concern of the Buddha-focussed lama was to impress on Whitesy fidelity to vegetarianism, and so he adamantly opposed feeding her anything of animal origin. At stake was Whitesy's *buddhatā*, or Buddha nature, for "every living thing possessed *buddhatā*," and Whitesy's had to be cultivated so that she could become a merciful, benevolent dog. But Whitesea advocated respect for dog morality — the canine standard of ethics to which dogs instinctively adhered — and so fed her according to the way dogs would naturally feed themselves. The feral ancestors of today's dogs had eaten meat in the wild, and this aspect of their nature had not changed with domestication. Thus, he opposed trying to make Whitesy vegetarian. And consistent with this point of view, he insisted on upholding the other aspects of canine tradition as well, saying that it was unnecessary for her to adhere to human standards of behaviour. In this regard, the old lama of course exercised his power of veto. He was the one who had discovered Whitesy, and he was the one who occupied the seat of head of the household in this *ménage à trois*. Whitesea was obliged to recognise his prerogative on this front, and could only watch how things developed in secret disagreement.

During the day, Whitesy went with her two masters

into the sandland to accompany them as they pulled their harrows. In the evenings she would tumble and frolic back and forth between the two men's beds. Lama Yondon fed her gruel and vegetable broth straight from his mouth. But the little dog was still at the suckling stage and would groan and moan to indicate that her stomach had not been satisfied. Even more salient was the fact that she was not growing or filling out. Especially in the evening when she would crawl into one or the other of their beds, her little wet mouth would always be rooting around at their chests. One night, the old lama jerked awake and found that Whitesy was frantically sucking upon one of his nipples. Her sucking was vigorous enough to cause him pain.

"We have to feed her milk. She's too young," Lama Yondon said, realising the truth.

"Yes, we have to feed her milk," Whitesea nodded in agreement. "And when she grows teeth, we'll have to feed her meat," he added, not losing his opportunity to expound his view.

"By what name do you call her?" Yondon asked.

"Little Lama," Whitesea answered.

"Lamas don't eat meat. They believe in Buddha and adhere to vegetarianism." Yondon gave him a supercilious look.

Whitesea stared at him. To himself he thought, okay, old lama, so you really want to raise her to be a little lama!

It was a still, moonless night.

Lama Yondon picked up scrawny little Whitesy and carried her outside. Whitesea followed along at his heels.

At the bend of the Yangxib River was a covered pen where the production brigade kept brood cows and their newborn calves. Lama Yondon stealthily slipped into the pen and squatted by the hind legs of a milk cow of mild nature and a greatly swollen udder. He held Whitesy up in both hands so that she could suck upon one of the cow's teats. At first, the cow and Whitesy were not used to each other. But after the exceedingly hungry little dog took a swallow of milk, she began sucking at the teat in earnest. The cow, whose udder was painfully full, felt a relief that put her at ease.

The little dog moaned in satisfaction as she suckled.

The cow lowed softly in contentment.

Lama Yondon watched with a loving fatherly smile. With overwhelming gratitude, he patted the cow's back and caressed her neck.

Whitesea stayed by the gate of the cow pen, acting as a lookout. The slightest noise would make him jump, but once he saw how well things were proceeding in the pen, his heart melted with tenderness.

They repeated this feeding mission for several nights running. Whitesy was obviously fattening up, and with her gain in weight, her needs increased and her appetite grew. She was more reluctant than ever to eat their gruel and broth.

"The little bugger, she's grown greedy."

"After a few days, we can wean her off milk and give her solid food..." He didn't dare mention the word meat, but simply let the unspoken notion hang turgidly in the air.

"Yes, but not meat. Not a morsel of flesh will pass her lips," Yondon bluntly countered.

"We don't have to feed it to her. She'll find it on her own."

"If she does that, then out she goes — I'll have nothing to do with her." The old lama said this very calmly, without a hint of outrage. But the resolution in his voice was unmistakeable. "I will absolutely not allow her to become entrenched in the evil practices in which men wallow. Men are cruel, arrogant carnivores. Just look at you non-believers — what *don't* you eat? Creatures that fly, creatures that run, creatures that swim, and you eat them with a vengeance so that nothing is left. Take chickens for example: chicken legs, chicken wings, chicken stomachs, chicken intestines, chicken combs, chicken heads, chicken skin, chicken feet, chicken liver, chicken blood, chicken necks, chicken gizzards — except for chicken feathers and chicken shit, there's not a single part of the chicken that's left! Even wolves in the wild are not so thorough. What a sorry lot humans are — pretty soon they'll have eaten the earth clean of everything that exists!" Lama Yondon stopped and sighed. "You tell me," he appealed in exasperation, "where does redemption lie for these creatures called men?"

Whitesea's hair was standing on end. Never in all his life had he heard such a strangely enlightening view, nor observed nor pondered upon mankind's eating of chickens and other animals from such a lofty angle. He didn't know what to say, nor did he know how to refute this view or what approach to take in the attempt. People ate all sorts of things, and Chinese in particular could be characterized as absolutely omniverous — there was nothing that they didn't eat. On this point, mankind really was the dominator of the earth. Suddenly he had an extraordinary idea, and he asked himself: was there on the earth or somewhere in the vast universe an animal that feeds on mankind, or some kind of material or immaterial thing that controls and governs the destiny of mankind?

"Yes, there is. There is something that resides above mankind and controls it." It was as if Lama Yondon had read Whitesea's mind and were setting forth his own thoughts on the matter. "This dominator is Nature in all its mystery, or what Taoists call the 'Tao' or 'Way': 'The Tao that can be told, is not the eternal Tao.' In Lamaism, it is the Buddha, the omnipresent Buddha. The Buddha is the final authority over mankind."

Whitesea knew that this old lama before him was no ordinary lama. In the past he had at the great Temple of Viridity risen to the high scholarly position known as *Gebhui*, which was equivalent to a current-day high academic position. But he was not in total agreement with the notion that the "Tao" and the "Buddha", which were religious doctrines, could be equated to the natural laws of the universe. Nor did Whitesea believe that little Whitesy could really obey the commandments of Lamaism and not touch meat her whole life — unless she eluded contact with this complicated world and lived out her entire lifespan in the sole company of Lama Yondon.

They continued to surreptiously feed Whitesy on the milk of the production brigade's cow, and she grew into a bouncing, rambunctious little dog.

One day, Lama Yondon was summoned to the village government offices by the People's Militia.

Whitesea went out to pull the harrow by himself. When he returned in the evening, Yondon hadn't yet come back. He was worried and slipped furtively down to the village headquarters to look for him. There in the village headquarters courtyard, that particular milk cow was tied to a stake and Lama Yondon was on his knees before her. A militiaman with a rifle across his shoulder was standing guard behind him.

Whitesea knew that their milk pilfering had been discovered. The old lama was in the act of begging forgiveness for his crime from the production brigade's revolutionary milk cow.

The old lama didn't come home until the middle of the night. Whitesea helped him to the *kang*, where he sat, and applied hot towels to his knees, which were swollen up to the size of steamed buns. He brought him some hot porrige and some steamed corncakes but the lama wouldn't eat. Instead, he reached out and drew Whitesy into his embrace, who had come rushing to greet him with ecstatic leaps and bounds. He held the little dog so tightly that she moaned in pain. Two streams of tears trickled silently from his eyes and dropped onto her head and mouth.

Whitesy looked up at her old master's face as if she could feel and comprehend what he was feeling. She licked the tears which had fallen on her mouth and tasted their saltiness, then extended her long red tongue and licked the tears from his face.

Whitesea's heart palpitated with excitement. Such a sensitive and intelligent dog!

With this, all of Lama Yondon's physical and psychological pain and all the indignity he'd suffered fell away, and he gave a comforting smile.

"Do you know what I was saying to myself as I was kneeling before the cow begging forgiveness?" Lama Yondon asked.

"It must have been, 'Revolutionary Grandmother Cow, I've been bad, I've been so bad that death wouldn't atone for my sins!'"

"Ha ha ha. Nope, that's not it. What I said was, Thank-you, Honourable Cow. In the next life, this old lama will certainly be reincarnated in your stomach. No human is more merciful, more tolerant, or more honourable than you."

"Ha ha ha..."

Lama Yondon went to the village headquarters for three days in a row. On the third day they simply kept him there — put into solitary confinement. Not long after that he was transferred to the commune. When Whitesea inquired, he learned that it wasn't just a matter of stealing milk. Those who held the reins of power were demanding that he turn over the three golden statues of the Buddhas of the past, present and future that had been enshrined in the original Temple of Viridity. When the land reforms were initiated, these statues had disappeared, and this disappearance had brought about terrible mistreatment of the living Buddha and the older and younger lamas housed in the temple. Several of them had died. Now this old case had been re-opened, and if the priceless golden Buddhas were not recovered, the voices of the "revolutionaries" would not be stilled.

Now there was only Whitesea to take care of Whitesy and every evening she would whimper as she looked for Lama Yondon sniffing and rooting around his bedroll and his mat on the *kang*. Sometimes she would curl up there and pass the lonely night by herself. She had perceived the disturbed and unharmonious atmosphere that existed in the world of humans, and she became vigilant and cautious. She lost her bouncing playfulness. Whitesea stopped pulling the harrow. Instead he arranged to go and help out at the Learn From Dazhai Scientific Farming Group, and he couldn't take Whitesy with him. She knew what to do, though. First thing every morning, she would disappear. Whitesea didn't know where she went but she would be gone the whole day and return late at night. And she didn't demand anything to eat or drink; now taking responsibility for herself and solving the problem when she was out. She conducted herself like a member of some "reactionary gang", laying low or moving about discreetly in the full knowledge of her status and the limits it imposed. Whatever she did, she didn't want to incur unnecessary trouble. This, of course, made things a lot easier for Whitesea. Upon returning in the evening, she would lie down in the spot where the old lama used to sleep and whimper and moan with the heart-breaking strains of an orphan in mourning. On these occasions, Whitesea would take her into his arms to comfort her, stroking her fur and telling her that the old lama would soon return if only they waited patiently. Thus in his embrace, she would gradually settle down and peace would come to her, and she would even deign to go to sleep in his bed. The next morning before Whitesea had awoken, she would already be gone.

In truth Whitesea knew very well how Whitesy spent her daylight hours: every day she was out there searching for Lama Yondon!

She searched around every house and outbuilding, here, there, and everywhere. When she'd done combing the village, she went to look for him in other villages. Every evening she'd return utterly exhausted, dragging herself in spiritlessly, sometimes with bloodied paws or torn fur, other times plastered with mud and sweat, her belly and legs soaking wet. It was clear she went through a lot out there, fighting with other dogs, being chased and beaten by people, wading through rivers and fording streams as she covered great distances. Finally, one day, she came to the commune, and there she found the lama confined in a little building that was a grain mill. From this time forward, she kept watch over this little mill, not at the door, of course, but in a little grove of trees nearby. She was very vigilant, and if anyone started to approach or tried to catch her, she would disappear in a flash, leaving no trace behind her, and her would-be assailant cursing in frustration.

What was truly amazing was that during this period she did not touch meat. One time Whitesea threw her a chicken bone, but after sniffing at it, she lowered her head and walked away. In the past, in order to prevent her from wanting meat, Lama Yondon once threw a piece of meat to her, and just as she was about to eat it, he snatched it away and gave her a thrashing. After that, Whitesy expressed no interest in meat, for she was long on memory and was a dog who acted in good faith.

One day, Lama Yondon was released and declared innocent. In those days, guilt and innocence often alternated and were transformed one into the other. Today's hero could well be tomorrow's convict, while today's convict might be tomorrow's hero.

Whitesy danced and leaped for joy when the old lama returned. She gamboled and frisked around the fragile bag of bones he'd become. The collapsed tripod of their menage once again stood tall, the only changes being that Whitesy had grown up, and the two men had grown much older. Then about this time, Whitesea received a letter from his original unit informing him he could return to the city. He tore it up, saying that the first steps in controlling the desert had to take place here and that his research also had to begin here. With unparalleled enthusiasm and a genuine concern for the cause of humanity, he threw himself into his work. Every day he collected materials and arranged and classified them as he studied the growth patterns of the desert plants in the area and the changes in weather over a period of a year and how those changes affected the plants. He took notes, wrote treatises, and pursued detailed fieldwork. For his part, the old lama looked after the plot of land that had been allocated to him.

Then that year of great drought began and so did Whitesy's misfortunes.

In the sandland, drought prevails nine years out of ten. Generations of farmers had inured themselves to this inevitable weather pattern. But this year was extraordinary in that the drought and the ravages it imposed started in the winter. For the whole winter no snow fell, and when the spring arrived, there was no rain either. Finally at the beginning of summer, a sprinkle begrudgingly fell. The farmers lost no time in getting their corn into the ground while there was still some moisture in it. Then with anxious eyes they waited for the little shoots to sprout. And when they did, the developing ranks of plants were cared for with a concern befitting a priceless crop of ginseng. Water was carted in by hand for individual irrigation, and the farmers weeded and cultivated though the fiery sun beat mercilessly down as they stooped in labour. And this exacting and exhausting toil was kept up throughout the summer until at the beginning of fall, the corn stood tall and green, and the kernals were juicy and fat. With the drought having extended like this over a two-year span, most of the sandland farmers were reduced to eating only one meal a day, and they tightened their belts and waited for the new grain to be ready.

Empty-bellied men staggered along the village street with equally empty-bellied and unsteady livestock; but they were nothing to the wobbly, empty-bellied dogs.

One night, the militiamen on crop-watch patrol heard a swishing noise coming from within the ripening corn. Someone was stealing the young corn! Cocking their rifles, the militiamen slipped silently into the towering crop-curtain and discovered not people, but a pack of starving village dogs gnawing on the immature corn. They had acquired it very ingeniously, by standing on their hind legs and pushing the stalks down with their chests, then using their front paws to brace the tender sweet ears of corn, they tore hungrily into them. The militiamen fired their rifles, but the acutely alert dogs were already gone, melted without a trace into the obliterating density of the night-enshrouded stand of corn. Anger churned in the farmers along with their heartache, but they could do nothing about it. What was worse, the pack of corn-eating dogs didn't confine themselves to just one or two villages, but went from village to village devouring crops and creating a daily-expanding circle of destruction.

Consequently, the township government pasted up this official notice: DOG EXTERMINATION. Every village and every family mobilised, and thus was launched a war on dogs. The village head and the party secretary led the campaign to rouse the people: Exterminate Dogs, Protect the Crops; Defend Our Grain, Defend Our Nation. Everywhere slogans resounded in the air.

In the sandland, the race of dogs met with catastrophe. Every village crackled with rifleshots; the fever of extermination reached into every corner of human habitation. From dawn to dusk the anguished cries of dogs mingled with the maddened shouts of men. Out in the wilds, wounded dogs could be seen in bloody frantic flight with club-swinging, gun-shooting death-squads in hot pursuit. Ever since dogs were first domesticated, they had been man's faithful friend and reliable servant. Through thick and thin they stuck by man, laying down their lives for him while asking little in return. The master would throw them a few gnawed bones, and they would be satisfied and eternally grateful with happily wagging tails. Although they could only bark and not speak, they possessed the intelligence, faithfulness, sensitivity, honesty, and loyalty that humans themselves could seldom hope to replicate. But now they had been cast aside by their own masters, rejected, betrayed, all because of a momentary insufficiency, a temporary destitution. Their masters ignored thousands of years of friendship and unstinting service and turned upon them in a perfidious attempt to wipe them off the face of the earth. In the dogs' anguished cries were the words: what false friends men are, what selfish, pugnacious creatures!

"Om mani padme hum!"* Lama Yondon folded his hands and murmured in prayer. "It's not their fault, it's not the dogs' fault, they are not to blame, they're not to blame ... " He sighed dolefully. "How can people put the blame on them, you are their masters, they are not the ones who should be killed!"

Whitesy was curled up listlessly at their feet, her eyes closed.

"What are we going to do about her? She already knows what is going on. You see that? Every time she hears a gunshot, she starts to shake. Oh, what are we going to do!" Whitesea broke his chaff biscuit in half and placed it before Whitesy's mouth. Whitesy didn't even touch it. She kept her eyes closed but her ears stood at alert, catching every little sound that came from outside. With every gunshot, her eyes would pop open and she would look at Lama Yondon's face and shift her legs restlessly. "She's scared to death. She hasn't eaten for two or three days." Whitesea gently patted Whitesy's neck and said, "Ours is the last dog left in the village. Old Lama, what shall we do? The head of the dog extermination squad is your nephew. Why don't you go talk to him, plead for mercy?"

"Huh! That beast! I've been praying to Buddha for several decades, and I never thought that such a

---

*The Six-syllable Charm, an incantation invoking the aid of Avalokitesvara Guanyin, the Bodhisattva of infinite compassion and mercy. It means literally, "Oh, Pearl on the Lotus Flower".

sinful degenerate would come from my own family!" Just as Lama Yondon was in the midst of this fulmination, Whitesy leaped up from her spot at his feet and bounded to the door in a stream of fierce barking.

"Uncle, are you at home?" Tieba's inquiring voice came from the courtyard. He had a gun in hand and two militiamen in tow. All three men were wearing red "Dog Extermination Squad" armbands.

Whitesy was barking violently, and she peeled her lips back from her teeth and rushed forward to prevent the death squad from entering the house. Although all three men had guns, when they saw Whitesy's ferocious leopard-like display, they backed off. One of the militiamen raised his rifle. Tieba reached out and pressed the barrel down. "Not so fast," he said. "This is my uncle's beloved pet. Let me go talk with him before we actually do it."

"Uncle, I have to talk with you. Let me come in," Tieba hollered from outside the door.

"Whitesy, come back here. Let them come in," Lama Yondon was afraid they would open fire right away and wanted to get Whitesy out of harm's way. Whitesy returned to Yondon's feet and sat down. She glared fiercely at the three executioners.

"So, what is it you have to say?"

"Uncle, we've killed all the dogs in the village. Only your Whitesy is left. We've left Whitesy 'til last out of deference to you — I am, after all, your nephew, and I couldn't do any less, even though the headman has been giving me flack. But now I can't put it off any longer. You must resign yourself to it and hand Whitesy over to us." He'd couched his words in the form of persuasion, but in reality it was an order.

"You'll have to shoot me first," Yondon said. "Me first, and then Whitesy."

Tieba was stunned.

"Great Uncle, everybody else in the village has had their dogs killed. What do you think everyone will think if we make an exception for you? It wouldn't be fair. People wouldn't like it. This is for the public good, and we can't let personal considerations interfere with duty — you just have to accept it like everyone else." This was one of the militiamen who spoke, and his voice was very threatening.

"Hah! Public good my foot! My dog didn't touch the corn, not a single kernal — so what would other people have against me?"

"It's no longer a question of whether or not the dog ate the corn. It's a question of equality. Everybody else had to give up their dogs. If you keep yours, things could get real ugly for you — and I wouldn't be able to guarantee your safety." Tieba kept up the pressure.

"Just cut the blather — kill me first, then you can take Whitesy." Yondon stood there grimly and said no more.

Disconcerted, Tieba blinked his beady little eyes. Then he stamped his foot and huffed out, taking his men with him.

The next day, Headman Elder Bao sent someone with a message that he wanted to see Yondon and Whitesea at village headquarters. Yondon tied Whitesy to the house pillar. She knew that he was leaving and barked in frenzied protest. There was great fear in her eyes.

"Don't worry, we'll be right back. We're just going to talk to the headman so he'll give you a reprieve." Yondon patted Whitesy's head and left, putting a padlock on the door.

It was not until the two unsuspecting men got to the village headquarters courtyard that they suddenly realised that they'd likely fallen into a trap. They turned around and ran back.

A rifleshot.

Their hearts leaped into their throats. It was too late!

They ran like a fire-driven wind and dashed into their courtyard just in time to find Tieba raising his rifle for a second shot. There was Whitesy tied in the corner of the courtyard, blood flowing from her leg. But seemingly unaware of her wound, she was rabidly flinging herself against her chain toward Tieba, snarling and snapping with untempered ferocity through her bared teeth. If it hadn't been for the chain, she would have leapt upon him and ripped him apart. Tieba laughed coldly through his gritted teeth, savouring the dog's maddened hopeless struggle against the deathblow he was about to deal her.

"Don't shoot! Stop!"

Yondon and Whitesea bolted toward Tieba and pushed his rifle just as he fired. The bullet whizzed past the dog's head, missing by a hair.

"You filthy beast!" Yondon cried dementedly as he flew upon Tieba. "Take that! And that!" He pounded upon him furiously with his fists, a man completely transformed. Tears streamed from his eyes, his literally foaming mouth twitched with fury. Eyes the colour of blood, he seized Tieba's gun, threw it on the ground and kicked at it savagely. And he kicked at it and kicked at it until, his anger at a fever pitch, he reached the corner of the courtyard, where he threw it into a pool of composting manure.

Tieba stared at him in utter consternation. It had not occurred to him that his uncle would return so soon. Nor did he foresee that his normally mild-mannered uncle who wouldn't hurt a flea would fly into such an insane rage. All his nerve left him. He wheeled about and fled.

Yondon and Whitesea ran over and embraced Whitesy. They unchained her and with all alacrity bound up her wound. Though the wound was not life-threatening, it was quite serious and would take time and much care to heal properly. Whitesy moaned, and her body shivered as if it would never stop. For several days running, she whimpered and cried day and night. Yondon had some understanding of traditional Tibetan-Mongolian medicine, and he found some herbal medicines, ground them up and applied them to her leg. Neither of the men dared to leave the house again and leave Whitesy alone. For her part, Whitesy lay inert upon the window-sill, her eyes filled with anxiety as she looked out into the distant desert wilderness.

"She's so strange — what's wrong with her?" Whitesea asked, puzzled.

"She wants to leave us," Yondon replied. He walked over and embraced her head and sighed. "She's afraid of people, now, deathly afraid. She's lost her faith in man and wants to get away. She wants to go into the wilderness where there are no people. Because that's where her ancestors came from."

"Yes, I see. Even the two of us together can't protect her. The dog extermination squad is out there watching this place, lying in wait ready to shoot her at the first opportunity. They're not going to just forget about it." Whitesea, too, was deeply worried.

"Yes, and she's a very intelligent dog. She understands perfectly well what's going on. And she doesn't want to be a source of trouble for us. *Oṁ maṇi padme huṁ*! We're her masters, but we can't protect her. So what are we to do? *Ai*! We'll have to let her go, back to the wilderness, back to Nature. And then everything will be up to Buddha."

It was a bright moonlit night.

The two men washed Whitesy's nearly healed wound for the last time. They crumbled up both of their chaff biscuit rations and made a porridge, which they fed to her. Then they led her surreptitiously out of the village. Whitesy seemed to know what was going on for without a whimper or a whine, she cooperated fully with whatever her masters wanted her to do, like an obedient child being sent alone on a long journey. She limped a little on her hind leg.

The three of them trod silently through the liquid moonlight that flooded the wild sandland.

About eight or ten miles out of the village, they came to a place of utter desolation where no men lived. Here they stopped.

Lama Yondon untied the rope around Whitesy's neck. Gently he patted her back. He pressed his face against her muzzle and stroked her fur for a long time. Whitesea stood to the side silently watching the heartbreaking farewell scene.

"Go, Whitesy, go. Go as far as you can so you'll never run into people again. The further you can get away from civilisation, the better. You have no way of understanding the human world, and you can't learn human ways. Go. From now on, you'll have to rely totally upon yourself. Be careful of your leg. Be cautious until you know this place. Yes, you will get to know it, and you will live. Live, Whitesy, live. This is where your ancestors came from. It's good to be a wild dog, very good. You won't have to be at the beck and call of humans any more, and you won't have to be bothered with their trials and tribulations. Go. Go live your life in the way of your ancestors. And from now on, eat and drink whatever you like — you don't have to keep the old lama's commandments any more ..."

Lama Yondon talked on with uncommon garrulity, just like a doting parent sedulously issuing instructions to a child going off to seek their fortune in the world. And Whitesy stayed there very still, with her eyes half-closed, listening. The old man's tears silently slid down his face and splashed upon her mouth. Just as before, Whitesy stuck out her wet tongue and licked these tears. And then she lifted her head and licked the tears on the old lama's face. Her soft wet tongue gently licked, conveying to him her limitless sincerity. Her tail wagged slightly, as if mourning the imminent separation. In the corners of her eyes were two crystal tears. After that, she walked over to Whitesea, lowered her head and pushed it against his shins. Whitesea felt like a dead piece of wood. He was crying in his heart but nothing made him tremble more than the fact that the old lama had released Whitesy from religious discipline. Whitesy went up on her hind legs and fell into Whitesea's embrace, her tail wagging contentedly. Then she dropped back to the ground and began to gambol around them, circling and circling, kicking up her heels and yipping joyfully. It was as if she were using this light-hearted display to dispel the heavy sorrow of departure. With her last encirclement, she dashed off into the wilderness.

She broke into a run, a limping run at first, but then she settled quickly into a smooth vigorous stride. In a twinkling, she disappeared like an illusion into the soft pale moonlight of the vast sandland.

How silent is the earth, how vast and recondite and mysterious. And it is at night that its detachment from all things — its aloof and uninvolved nature — becomes most apparent. For it contains all the living creatures who could not exist without it, and all things rational and irrational, perfect and imperfect, strong and weak, all of life and all of death transforming one into the other, all caught up in samsara, the eternal cycle of birth, suffering, death, and rebirth.

Lama Yondon stood motionless atop a dune, silently praying. He prayed for the dog now far away, for the sand beneath his feet, for the friend by his side, and for that bright moon-flooded night.

"*Oṁ maṇi padme huṁ*! May the light of Buddha shine upon all living things!"

3

Every time the curtain of night enveloped the Temple of Viridity, there appeared a white spirit that glided and hovered about the grounds. A smaller version of itself faltered along behind. These two snow-white figures circled the temple, once, twice, thrice ... and still they continued, deliberate and lingering, not daring to get too close, and yet unwilling to leave.

The ears of the larger one stood at alert, listening intently at every suspicious little sound. Her eyes glittered green as she scrutinised every nook and cranny obscured by the blackness of the night. And so it was that every night she unfailingly materialised with the dark to make her rounds, circling, ever circling, like a vigilant and faithful foot patrol. But the moment that fireball emerged from the eastern sand-horizon to fix the sandland in its scorching rays, this white spectre vanished silently into the depths of the boundless desert. It was as if she paid her liege to the moon and belonged to the lunar world, an envoy of the night and a guardian of the dark.

On several occasions, when a thick layer of midnight cloud blotted out the light of the last quarter moon, out from the bowels of the western desert leapt a shadowy denizen of the obscurity, shot, as true as an arrow, toward Viridity. This obsessive and cunning black spectre was determined to have his defining moment with that cow. And yet his attacks had been foiled every time, nipped on the verge of victory just outside the cowshed by a white spirit streaking out of the gloom to engage him in battle. Overwhelming was her aggression, remorseless her ferocity, and in just a few savage skirmishes, the black spectre would turn tail and flee. Even camouflage failed. He sneaked into the cowshed once disguised as a giant sandpuff but his scent gave him away and his exposed tail received the full brunt of the white spirit's very corporeal teeth. Infuriated, he threw himself into one last life-and-death struggle, matching the finest of fanged weaponry and two accumulated fortunes of wit, courage and fortitude. Blood-red fury glared in the combatants' green eyes, blood-soaked shreds of fur and skin hung from their mouths. In a storm of chases and leaps, howls and rolling grapples in the sand, they turned the ground into a violent expanse of blood and sweat, torn fur and severed pieces of tail. Still the battle raged on, until at last that little half-grown spirit threw itself into the fray and sank its teeth into Black Wolf's throat. Though its teeth had not yet acquired the razor sharpness of maturity, the accuracy and force of its bite, and the tenacity with which it held on, delivered terror into Black Wolf's heart. He felt himself suffocating, and was forced to realise the tragic, bitter truth of yet another defeat, and that he would never rise in triumph over this opponent — his nemesis — whom he could never challenge again. He shook off the little spirit, extricated himself from the deadly clutches of White Wolf, and fled back into the desert whence he came.

Every night from the roof of the old mud house an old man observed the nocturnal goings on. Issuing no shouts nor making any other noise, he sat cross-legged, hands pressed together devoutly before his chest. The night's combat proceeded before his watchful eyes, and in those eyes resided the light of comprehension, as if he'd discovered in the unfolding struggle the glimmering truth of in the worldly dichotomy of "yin and yang", life and death. There was prayer in his posture and expression, the look of communication with the spirits of heaven and earth.

When silence returned and night reclaimed all things and the white spirit again melted from sight, he fell into despondency. "Oh," he moaned with murmuring sadness, "she still doesn't want to come back. So many years in the wilderness and now it's in her blood — why should she come back? Alas, it's better for her not to. Oh, my Whitesy..."

After that, Black Wolf never showed up again, and White Wolf, in the wake of his disappearance, also vanished.

The old man refused to believe in her absence and continued his nightly vigil in anticipation of a reunion. Every night he mixed a bowl of tempting food and placed it near the gate of the cowshed. The following day invariably found it right where he had put it, surrounded by three-toed canine paw-prints in the sand. This proved that Whitesy was around, lurking somewhere beyond the prying eyes of men. She was, then, unable to slough off her childhood self, even though she declined to be dependent upon man for food. The old man, far from being daunted, felt encouraged. He kept on setting out his bowls of food hoping that one night she would eat.

This miracle did not occur. His offerings only succeeded in attracting an assortment of nocturnal hares, scavanging vermin, and one wily larcenous fox. Black Wolf and White Wolf, too, seemed to have left this stretch of sandy land. The Temple of Viridity returned to its former tranquillity. The old brown cow leisurely swung her tail and followed the master to the field to start the spring planting.

But all was not the same with the old man. He sank from sadness into despondency, and his leanness became emaciation.

Oh, Whitesy, where are you?

His old asthma flared up. Over the years, the dry, cold desert conditions had damaged his trachea and lungs. Gasping for air, his chest sounded like a bellows. He coughed all night long, night after night to clear his lungs of their thick yellow mucus. He knelt on the ground, his bottom pointing to the sky, and coughed with all his might. The veins of his forehead swelled, like earthworms. And there was only the cow to moo her sympathy.

He was waiting for the end. It was time to go.

Oh, Whitesy, where are you?

Sand swirled and eddied in the wind as the *lele* cart rolled again into Viridity, that isle of green in the turbulent sea of sand.

This time Yuanhui came accompanied by the head of the village Women's Federation, a woman named Aoya. She and Aoya removed bundle after bundle of things from the cart, while Tieba unloaded a tent. They chose a dry, flat patch of sand some forty or fifty yards from Lama Yondon's mud house, pounded stakes into the ground, and raised the tent in which they placed two army cots.

Yuanhui had gone through repeated negotiations with the County Bureau of Forestry and the township government before she'd finally persuaded them to send the head of Women's Federation with her and to arrange an extended stay at the Temple of Viridity. This mysterious green island in the middle of the desert, a jade stud set into the yellow sand, had beckoned irresistibly with its puzzling secrets. Here she would set up until she'd discovered the secret of its exuberant plant life and uncovered the tracks left by her husband.

The wind abated enough to allow the floating debris and dust to settle. The herbal scents of absinthium* and other wild plants infused the purified air. Sand willows straightened their long bent spines and unfolded their greyish-green leaves. The newly laid dusting of sand glistened in the sun. Lizards, beetles, chipmunks — the small creatures that had burrowed into the sand to escape the onslaught of the storm — re-emerged to cavort among the *xibag* artemisia and the Chinese peashrubs**.

The women trod across the soft shifting sand to call upon Lama Yondon. His old mud house appeared more tottering than ever, with sand blown into a tiny slope up against his door. The cow, Lama Yondon's life support, was lying on the ground just outside the hut chewing on corn leaves.

"Uncle, you have visitors!" Tieba announced.

"Great Uncle, I've come back..." There was something in the air that was not quite right.

Lama Yondon was lying on the *kang*, his breathing barely perceptible, his face a ghastly bluish mask. He was on the edge of complete physical collapse, like a lamp about to go out. Yuanhui, who had some knowledge of medicine, immediately took emergency steps to save him. It was plain to her that asthma had induced a crisis in his respiration, and being unable to feed himself, he'd grown progressively weaker until he'd slipped into this semi-comatose state. Feverishly, she ransacked her own cache of medicines for an anti-inflammatory and a phlegm-reducing preparation. These she administered to Lama Yondon along with some

---

Artemisia absinthium, also known as common wormwood.
**Caragana sinica*.

gruel which she'd had Aoya boil up.

After what seemed like the longest time, Lama Yondon came back to life.

"Is it you who saved me?" he asked upon opening his eyes.

"You saved yourself. I only helped a little," Yuanhui smiled.

"What do you want to help me for?"

"I couldn't very well stand by and watch you breathe your last when it could be prevented!" Yuanhui said, irked.

"And suppose I'd done it on purpose — deliberately to end it all?"

"Well, how was I supposed to know you were waiting to die?"

"*Ai*!" Lama Yondon sighed. "I've been here long enough. I can't go on. They both left me, so what's the point? I searched and searched, but to no avail. I'm useless, I suppose, of no value to one so self-sufficient, so I should just pass on ... call it quits... *Ai*... " His voice trailed off into abstracted silence.

"Who are you talking about?"

"Whitesy."

"My husband?"

"No, that dog... "

"Oh, you mean that white wolf... Why do you call it Whitesy?"

"That was her name when she was little."

"Whitesy's my husband's name. Why did you give her my husband's name?"

"To honour him, so there'd at least be a dog to think of him when everyone else had forsaken him."

Yuanhui felt she'd been stabbed in the heart. Her

forehead wrinkled up in agony.

"She had another name, too, back in those days: Little Lama. Whitesea gave it to her."

"My husband?"

"I don't know if he was your husband. He never mentioned it. All I know is that at the time our only companion was the little dog, Whitesy. She was the only living creature with whom we enjoyed a kind of sympathetic accord; indeed, the only one who was close to us and cared for us. But then both she and he tossed me aside and left, so I don't want to go on... I don't want to ... go on... " He let out a long sigh, as if relieved of a heavy burden, and closed his eyes.

Alarmed, Yuanhui nearly reached out and grabbed him. "Hey! Wait!" she cried. "Don't go yet. Tell me first how my Whitesea died ... and, ah, yes ... where are his things?"

"Don't worry, I'll not be dying just yet. I want to, but ... it's not working out. Just ... let me lie here for awhile, in peace — don't be asking this and that. I'll tell you what you want to know when the time comes."

"When will that be?"

"Soon. The time is near."

Yuanhui was so overwhelmed to hear this that she nearly cried. She looked at the old lama's meagre face with gratitude, gingerly got down from the *kang* and went out. "Thanks be to God," she breathed as she looked out over the boundless sandland. "He's promised to tell ... he's promised ... "

After sending off Commander Tieba, she and Aoya began to survey the green patch of land that was

Viridity. It was a little green island in a sea of sand, created by man and entirely dependent upon human management for its continued existence. First, *xibag* artemisia and sand willow had been strategically placed around a hub, to anchor the shifting sand and prevent further invasion from the surrounding area. Once this basic circle of stability had been established, it was treated to a comprehensive set of measures designed to increase its viability. The slopes of its sand mounds were planted with melilot*, a wind- and drought-resistant leguminous crop, as well as smatterings of purple-flowering alfalfa. The low-lying areas between the sand mounds were inset with patches of corn and sorghum, the apparent sources of the old lama's basic subsistence. On the edges of these diminutive fields grew wind-breaking trees — poplars and Mongolian calligonum — and a few white peashrubs. Yuanhui was struck by the felicitous design of this green isle — truly a *tour de force* of landscaping, she felt — that was unquestionably the product of a brilliant mind and years of careful, diligent planning and development. Obviously its architect was not only versed in the tactics of desert control, he was a botanist as well with a special knack for arranging desert plants to their most effective and mutually beneficial advantage. This person could not have been Lama Yondon, for Lama Yondon's sphere of expertise strictly encompassed the Tripitaka and Buddhist religiosity, and he wouldn't have any particularly compelling interest in natural science. No, this little oasis of green was most assuredly the masterwork of her husband, Whitesea.

**Melilotus suaveolens*, also known as sweet clover.

Yuanhui recorded her observations in her notebook, asking Aoya the names of the plants she didn't recognise.

"Eh? That's funny..." she remarked with a spark of realisation. "Aoya, what does Lama Yondon do for drinking water? Look around, there's no river here, there's no water hole, no lake, and I didn't see a well near his door."

"Oh, there's a well, all right. It's just not in front of his door. Come, I'll show you."

Aoya took Yuanhui along a little path beaten out over the years by human and animal feet. It led straight from Lama Yondon's door down to a low-lying area about a hundred and fifty or so yards off. Here, cock-claw reeds flourished and cattails grew thick and sand willows flared out in luxuriantly burgeoning clumps. For they had set their roots down in a basin, a depression that dropped off from the flat, surrounding land to a depth of sixty to ninety feet. As the two women descended to the bottom, they could immediately sense that the air had become fresh, moist and cool. Suddenly in a flutter of wings a host of birds large and small rose up out of the clumps of grasses and willow, and took to the air.

"It looks like we've disturbed the wildlife," Aoya commented.

"There wouldn't be any *wolves*, would there?" asked Yuanhui, suddenly alarmed.

"Wolves wouldn't come around in the daytime. In actuality, wolves are just as afraid of people as people are of them. If you don't bother them, they won't bother you. Only when they're cornered or starving do they attack." As she spoke, Aoya walked to the end of the path and parted the stand of reeds and grasses growing there and there was the well. About six feet in circumference, its water was crystal clear to its shallow bottom two feet below the surface. If Aoya hadn't parted the vegetation before it, Yuanhui would never have thought that such an exquisite draught of pure fresh water was hidden behind it.

"This is the well?"

"It's called a sand-well. Don't let the desert fool you. In good rainy years, you can dig a well in any depression and have it fill with water. But in drought years, now that's a different story — because the underground water gets drawn up very quickly to the surface and it evaporates. So, in the desert, you can get sudden windfalls of water; but the water table is very easily lowered dramatically — easy come, easy go."

"That's really interesting. I've been out to the capital of desertdom, Shapotou*, and the Tengger Desert there is completely different — its water table isn't nearly as high." Yuanhui spoke with a note of excitement in her voice.

"Well, you know, we're looking at a case of retrogression here — erosion. This didn't used to be a land of sand. It used to be the Horqin Grassland. It was a great lush green plain with lots of water and tall grass waving in the wind. Then it deteriorated into a sandland with all these sand humps all over the place. The whole process took only several hundred years," Aoya explained.

"Oh. That's really a pity. It's hard to believe that

---

*In western Ningxia, on the edge of the Tengger Desert, near the border of Inner Mongolia.

a great grassland should become a big desert like this, golden sand swallowing up verdant emerald waves. Really, it's as if a demon transformed it with some sort of magic. A horrifying magic."

The two of them left the sand-well. They'd walked back upon the path some thirty yards or so when Yuanhui casually cast a backward glance and caught sight of a miraculous scene. Around the sand-well an assortment of creatures had gathered, including a fox stretching its muzzle into the water for a drink, a pair of badgers and several marmots. Not far off were various birds like sand-grouse, bustards, sparrows, and pheasants. After a long hard day of searching for food, competing for mates and doing whatever else such creatures do, they were tired and thirsty, and with the approach of dusk they'd converged upon this only oasis within a radius of thirty-five miles to bathe, play and slake their thirst. Predators and prey, rivals and natural enemies all replenished themselves in perfect harmony, observing a truce of peace and mutual respect. Here was a glimpse of a truly different world, the Eden of our fantasies.

Yuanhui stood there transfixed. "Look at that," she said in awe. "They are so lovely, so interesting! Just like a bunch of well-mannered children — no fighting, no bullying, no pushing and shoving, those who came first stepping back quietly afater taking their drinks to make room for the late ones. Talk about amicability and peaceful coexistence... My, it's just as if there were a set of rules to be obeyed around the sand-well that no one would consider violating."

"Very true. The animals of the desert really do have

their own special rules — rules based upon their instinct for survival."

The two women chatted as they ascended the slope back toward the house. Some unusual sounds nearby attracted their attention. Yuanhui focussed her eyes on the rustling bushes. Sure enough, a few moments later, a man's head emerged, eyes looking left and right assessing the situation around the sand-well as he groped his way toward it. It was Commander Tieba, hunting rifle in hand.

"What!" exclaimed Yuanhui in astonishment. "What's he doing here? I thought he left. Aoya, we've got to stop him. We can't let him shoot the animals!" Yuanhui grabbed Aoya's hand, and the two rushed over to block Tieba. "Hey, what do you think you're doing!" they shouted at him.

"Shhh!" he returned in a savage whisper, waving them away. "Stay out of the way!"

"Old Tie," Aoya addressed him. "I thought you went back to the village, and now here you are again, popping up like a ghost or something — what's going on?"

"I found some fox tracks on the old grave mounds and followed them back here. Hot-damn! Look at all these animals — who'd have thought it!" Tieba, grinning broadly, couldn't hide his joy even if he had wanted to. "You know what a fox pelt brings these days? A hundred and fifty yuan! What a fucking godsend!"

"Oh, no you don't! These animals are off-limits!" Yuanhui gave vehement warning.

"Oh, come now, lady," Tieba laughed. "Foxes and badgers aren't on the national list of protected animals. What—you want to control the sky, the earth *and* my hunting? Well, I'll tell you, Madame Professor, you should just stick to your desert control and your green project — coming around interfering in other peoples' affairs and wasting their time is a no-no!" He gave a mirthful laugh and stepped around them. Paying them no further heed, he bent into a stealthy posture, rifle poised in both hands, and silently approached the sand-well. There he crouched behind a mound of dirt and aimed his gun.

Angry and upset by this man who wouldn't listen to reason, Yuanhui could only stare in helpless agitation at the carnage about to take place. She knew that in the desert the animals and the plants lived a symbiotic existence and formed a delicate food chain that shouldn't be tampered with lightly. Each individual plant and animal had its essential place. But all Aoya said was, "It's a hopeless case. Hunting is the be-all and end-all of Tieba's existence. He'll never listen to us." She did nothing to try to stop him. Yuanhui's eyes filled with tears.

Suddenly, the air was filled with a sharp metallic clamour — the sounds of banging iron instruments — and high-pitched shouts that cut right through the staccato noise: "Woo... Ooo... Wolves are coming! Woolvees...!"

The sudden pandemonium startled the creatures around the sand-well, and they immediately took flight. In the wink of an eye, all that remained was that tranquil patch of water, luminous and blue.

Tieba was stunned. Then his astonishment turned to wrath. "God-damn mother-fucker!" he cursed.

Deeply relieved Yuanhui spun around and looked up

at the crest of the slope from where the noise and shouting had originated.

There stood Lama Yondon, leaning on a cane. He was holding a rusty enamel washbowl and a small hammer. His pale ravaged face was solemn yet emitted a light of benevolence and detached serenity. The rays of the setting sun turned it bronze, a study in solidity and determination.

Only then did the two women discover the skyline to the west.

"Oh, my gosh!" Aoya exclaimed in astonishment. "Look at that. Everybody look — what's happening to the sky over there?"

The whole western sky was ablaze. Rising sand dust, floating clouds, and misty fog all burned red, blanketing the great western desert horizon like a huge thick curtain of flames. The knitted layer of cloud was being dispersed in all directions, spiraling higher and higher. Meanwhile, in the high altitude a violent change in the climatic conditions was rapidly erupting. Soon, the clouds were set aflame, turning the whole sky a deep blood-red hue. It was a bloody illumination; a floodtide of red to make people tremble with fear. At that moment, however, calm prevailed over the whole desert, a deathly, eerily soundless calm. The flocks of bustling birds had long vanished, and even the air froze. The calm was heavy, weightily suffocating. All beings trembled at the awesome scene, shaking like terrified little lambs.

"*Om maṇi padme hūm*! Heaven's signs are ominous. The day of reckoning is near. A great calamity will befall the people of the desert. A disaster is on the way. I have long been expecting this. Ah, alas ...

Merciful Buddha... " Lama Yondon folded his hands and devoutly prayed. "The drought lasted all winter and all spring, presaging this act of reckoning. The day has long been destined in Heaven, and there is no way to forestall it!"

Yuanhui, Aoya, and Tieba all gathered behind Lama Yondon. Frightened confusion filled their hearts.

The old lama glanced at Tieba and addressed him in an awesome voice of warning. "You, sinner, leave this place at once. Don't ever come again to this *Sukhavati*, this Pure Land, which is the land of Buddha. Don't ever use again your evil hands to spill the blood of living creatures. Heaven now bleeds the red blood of its wrath. Its punishment is coming. Ignore this admonition, and you will not be spared. Remember it ... remember it —"

With the departure of Whitesy, the days all lost their meaning.

Despite the elimination of the sandland dogs, the corn that had been saved still fell far short of the people's needs in that year of natural disaster. With hands outstretched to the government and to the outside world, they begged for relief grain, money, clothing. Death nonetheless stalked the sandland wilderness — the hollow-eyed, bloat-bellied death of starvation. People took to beggery in droves, putting the government and its leaders to shame. And Heaven remained relentless in its punishment. Great whirlwinds carried sand by the tons and dumped it on the already desperate and dying sandland villages.

One night, nearly all the natural villages in the vicinity of the Temple of Viridity were swallowed by the shifting sand. The government taxed its manpower and resources to the brink in the re-location of the newly homeless peasants, sending some to still existing villages, while building for the rest entire new villages in more habitable parts of the sandland.

For Black Sand Gulch next to the Temple of Viridity, there was no escape from its irrevocable doom. Yellow sand buried the houses, sealed the wells, and blanketed the fields, putting an end to all hope of survival. The government re-settled the villagers some twenty miles away, where New Black Sand Gulch was built. In fact, that particular stretch of sandland was already facing the onslaught of the desert, its delicate eco-system on the very brink of collapse. For people to move in and clear away its sparse cover of vegetation represented an open invitation to the shifting sands. The people and the land were caught in a vicious circle of survival and destruction.

"Humans are just like locusts in a drought year," commented Lama Yondon as he watched the villagers busily moving their belongings. "When they've devastated one field, they move on to the next, laying waste to one field after another until in the end they're reduced to chewing their own feet." He was perched on the chimney of his house. The sand had buried the entire structure leaving only the tip of the chimney exposed. A pile of his things salvaged from within lay at his feet, his bedroll, odds and ends of daily use, and those objects he treasured more than life itself: his scriptures and his statue of Buddha.

"I think of people more in terms of a colony of ants," Whitesea said. "They excavate one place to exhaustion and then move on to another, until they've laid waste to all places." He was sitting on his belongings, writing in the sand with a stick. He liked to write the character *zhong* ("centre"), a quadrangle with a vertical line cutting through the middle. He made the "square" though, like a little circle, and slashed that vertical line through extending an extraordinarily long way at either end. Some years ago, a glyphomancer had told his fortune by analysing the component parts of this character. He'd said that all his life he would be struggling inside the bounds of a certain restricted "circumference", the significance of this prediction lying in the fact that the concept of "circumference" is expressed as "square-circle" (*fangyuan*). Sometimes the "circumference" would seem square to him, at other times circular, but square or circle, circle or square, he would be trapped inside, never to escape the paradox of the circular square. But his abiding desire was to break free of this constraint, to crash through the dictate of the square-circle and establish his own independent way. But the line through the middle of the character meant that to slash through the square-circle would incite disapproval and turn him into a butt of criticism in other people's mouths (for the quadrangle was but a permutation of the character for "mouth", written as a square). All his life people would pour vitriol on him, dealing him one setback after another. The slash through the middle, furthermore, stood the character on an unstable tip, which indicated lack of the firm foundation necessary for significant accomplishment in life. He'd smiled wryly at this analysis and thought, so be it, if that's the way things are meant to be. He could not waste his energies pursuing accomplishment, the important thing was the process. The process, that is, of breaking out of the cage that was the square-circle. What was life, after all, but a few decades of journeying from birth to death. You emerge into the world, and it is called life; and you enter into the ground, and it is called death. And this journey, or process, Laozi called "emerge-life/enter-death". There was a logic in this, a "Tao", and whosoever should grasp it would have acquired the truth. He had but one aspiration, and that was to complete the emerge-life/enter-death odyssey without doing anything for which he would be ashamed. He wanted to live a life that was as full, as meaningful and as natural as possible given the circumstances, and of course, unobsessed with the fame and the fortune of the profane world.

"Aren't we moving out with the first batch of locusts — or ants?" Whitesea asked. He was still drawing his "*zhong*" in the sand. A tiny lizard blundered into his square-circle. With a quick shift of his stick, he pinned it down within its perimetres. The lizard squirmed as it tried to get free.

"You go on ahead," Lama Yondon said musingly He was gazing out in the direction of the Temple of Viridity. A moment crept by, then he said, "Let that creature go!"

"And what about you? Are you still determined to stay on here?" Whitesea lifted the stick and the lizard scurried away. Yondon gave him a grateful glance.

"That's right. I want to stay here," Yondon said.

"Stay here? In this old sand-buried village?" Whitesea looked at Yondon's earnest face in disbelief.

"No, no, not here in this particular spot. I'm

going to the old site of the Temple of Viridity. I'm going to build a little shed there for myself."

"You're going to live *there*? Why?"

"For me, that's where the Pure Land is, *Sukhavati*. When I was eight, that's where I took my vows to become a monk." Yondon spoke with deliberation. He'd obviously thought it over a long time. "I won't be a locust or an ant anymore."

"But ... *there* — how will you live?"

"I'll go out wandering everyday, begging alms, and come back to rest at night."

The notion struck Whitesea with great impact. Suddenly he had a brainstorm.

"Hey! I've got it! You don't have to go around begging like a parasite." Whitesea patted Yondon's shoulder in excitement. "I've been out there to that old site and checked it out. The land there is all mounded and humped — you know, with fixed dunes. Which means that all we'd have to do is control the indrifting of sand, and then we could add a layer of chernozem (black earth) and manure — organic fertiliser — to the fixed dunes, and presto! We've got arable land. If we succeed, we could live there for a long time, be self-sufficient, and put down roots. Then we could expand into the surrounding areas and create a green atoll in the ocean of sand. What do you say to that?"

"Who's this *we* you're talking about? It seems like you want to be my partner!" Lama Yondon was evidently impressed by the plan. He said smilingly, "You are a strange fellow. Instead of going back to the big comfortable city, you propose adopting the sandland and getting entangled with this old lama!"

"That's right. We were brought together over a long distance by fate. Nothing can break us apart. So, do you agree with my plan or not?"

"Well, let me think on it. This is not a simple matter."

"*Hai!*" Whitesea exclaimed in exasperation. "You old lama! You should change some of your rules of Lamaism a bit — get rid of the life-style that depends on begging and hand-outs. How do you suppose the Chan* Buddhists managed to survive and flourish in the face of untold vicissitudes over the centuries? Chan Buddhism came down from the eminent monks Huineng, Huairang, Mazu** and others to Master Baizhang. And this Master Baizhang laid down a monastic rule*** that stipulated that besides obeying the Five Commandments****, those who take their vows should raise and cultivate their own food, thus putting an end to the practice of relying on adherents for support and of the parasitic existence based on begging. They were to observe the rule that he who does not work one day does not eat that day. Therefore, after that, when the Tang emperor Wuzong***** repressed

---

*Also known as Dhyāna and Zen.

**Tang-dynasty Chan sect monks who lived between the seventh and eighth centuries.

***Whitesea is referring to the "Monastic Rules of Mount Baizhang", which was a Yuan-dynasty recompilation of the Tang-dynasty "Chan Monastic Rules" set forth by the monk Huaihai (AD 720 – 814).

****Pancasila: no killing, no stealing, no adultery, no lying, abstention from alcohol.

*****Reigned AD 840 – 846.

Buddhism throughout the country and temples were demolished and monks forced to return to secular life, only the Chan sect survived the disaster. Think about that. The main reason was that the monks of the Chan sect all engaged in farming. They were self-sufficient and not parasites on society. Also, even though their temples were destroyed, they could continue to meditate and worship even without scriptures and statues and temples. Putting oneself to cultivating the land and insisting on working with one's hands is to take hold of one's own destiny. Well, old lama, how about it? Why, we should learn from Master Baizhang and become self-reliant and make a living out of the desert!"

"How very wonderful, this Rule of Baizhang! Marvellous, marvellous, marvellous!" Lama Yondon clapped his hands and radiated smiles. "Lamaism really suffered during the campaigns of recent years. Around here, all the lamas were returned to civilian life, and all the temples were either demolished or transferred to other uses. Now, as I think about it, had our sect adopted the Rule of Baizhang a long time ago and become self-reliant through farming, we probably would not have turned out the way we did." Lama Yondon breathed a long soulful sigh.

"So, then, you agree! Let's waste no more time on words. We'll go and survey the place and pick a spot to raise our shed — right away!"

"Don't be in such a hurry. We should inform the village cadres first," Yondon said with calm deliberation, "and bring back our share of relief grain".

"Excellent idea. You, lama — you're learning fast. Careful calculation, making every cent count, that's the way to go. Now they're promoting contractual agreements, right? So let's just contract out that piece of old temple land. They'll be ecstatic to have two fewer people claiming a share of their grain."

It was just as Whitesea had said. The village government was very encouraging and supportive of their plan and even helped them erect a two-room mud house and dig a sand-well in the low-lying area ahead of the hut.

"This is great! Our own doghouse to sleep in," Whitesea chortled as he rolled gleefully on the *kang*, his feet in the air. "And our own well. This is it — we're home! Now we can see to the task of filling our stomachs. Starting tomorrow."

"How are we going to do that? Beat grain out of the sandland with our bare fists?" Lama Yondon, rag in hand, was meticulously polishing his little *kang* table. The table had been with him for thirty years, the only memento he had of the old destroyed temple.

"When I learned how to pull the harrow, I listened to you. This time you should listen to me. I guarantee you won't die of starvation." Whitesea pulled out from his pocket a wrinkled money order and handed it to him. "Tomorrow, you go into the county seat and cash this money order. Use the money to buy a cow and some corn and sorghum seeds."

"Wha—!? What's this? People are going to give me money for this wrinkled up old piece of paper? Very funny!" Yondon turned the paper about before his eyes, examining its green lined squares filled in with green characters. "Now you're making fun of the old lama!" he complained as he crumpled it into a ball and threw it back at Whitesea.

Only then did Whitesea realise that the old lama had never seen a postal money order. He explained to him in detail how money orders worked, then said solemnly, "This is my 'rehabilitation' money, my back pay for several years. You, you old lama, be careful with it. Don't lose it for me. The deadline for cashing it is almost up, and if we don't cash it right away it will be null and void and the post office will return it to the sender."

"So what have you been doing with it all this time? You go yourself. It's too much trouble. How should I know how to go about cashing money orders!" The old lama balked at the task.

"No, I have other, more important things to do. And besides, I know nothing about buying cows and seeds. You have to do it." At this point, Whitesea's voice had taken on the imperative tone of authority.

Thus prevailed upon, Yondon set out for the county seat the following morning.

He returned five days later with a cow and a donkey, the latter carrying a sack of seeds on its back. He discovered Whitesea bent under a load of black earth for spreading on the patch of sandland in front of the house.

"Ha, ha!" Whitesea laughed as he threw down his shoulder pole and baskets of dirt and ran toward Yondon. "You old lama, when you do things, you really do them right! Look at that —a donkey, too!" Joyously, he stroked and patted the animals and took a look at the seeds.

The sandland in front of the house had been transformed. Every inch of it had been turned over with a spade and then supplemented with black earth that had been thoroughly mixed in. The project was nearing completion. Yondon looked at it puzzled. There was nothing but sand tumuli in the vicinity — where in the world did he get the black earth?

"Ha, look at that, you bookworm!" he cried. "You didn't even wait for me — just did it all yourself. Where'd you get the black earth, anyway?"

"Over where the village used to be. It was just our luck — the wind uncovered a stretch of black earth that had been previously buried under the sand."

"You're kidding! All the way over *there*? That's practically two miles! You've been making four-mile round trips hauling this stuff in on your shoulder?!" The old lama walked over to Whitesea and peeled back his shirt collar. Both shoulders were covered with blood blisters, some crushed and clotted and angrily swollen. "What are you trying to do — kill yourself?" The old lama sighed.

"Come on, don't get all excited, it's perfectly normal — they'll heal over in two days." Whitesea brushed off Yondon's concern as he re-positioned his collar. "What's important," he continued, a note of anxiety creeping into his voice, "is that even with the black earth mixed in, this sandy soil won't grow crops. We have to add some organic fertiliser."

"Let's go to the village and get some sheep manure. Sheep manure is the most ideal fertiliser for sandland — it must be replete with that '*organ*'" — said with sly emphasis — "that you're talking about!" Yondon patted Whitesea's back, laughing to himself.

"Brilliant! Absolutely brilliant! Good, we'll go get some sheep manure," Whitesea agreed as he gave the

the donkey an enthusiastic slap on its rump. Startled, the donkey kicked up its hind legs, missing him by a hair.

"Ha, ha, ha! It's easy to flatter a horse, but not so easy to con a donkey! Ha, ha, ha..." The old lama roared heartily.

The next day they made the twenty-mile round trip to New Black Sand Gulch and returned with sheep manure balanced on shoulder poles, packed on the donkey's back, and loaded in the ox cart. They repeated this trip every day for a week. At last they had worked enough into the soil to have for themselves a good plot of arable land. And no sooner were their labours done than a timely spring rain fell. They rushed to get their corn and sorghum into the ground. When they'd finished the planting, they rested for two days. Then Whitesea said to Yondon, "Tomorrow, we'll go out and start gathering the seeds of *xibag* artemisia."

"What for?"

"To plant."

"To plant? Where?"

"All around the perimetre, outside the fixed dunes. That way, they'll keep the drifting sand out."

"Good idea. When *xibag* artemisia takes hold in an area and grows like crazy, there's no better way to check drifting sand. There's *xibag* artemisia growing on the sand humps near the new village. We should go over there right away and gather some seeds and plant them while the earth is still wet. They'll sprout quickly. That plant is as tough as a weed, and is easy to plant and to grow."

Soon, the two men could be seen on the sand tumuli around the new village, stripping seeds off artemisia plants, provoking the villagers to gossip about two starving nut cases driven to fill their bellies with artemisia seeds. Once these seeds were planted, they went to gather the seeds of the yellow willow*, which they planted inside the belt of artemisia. Their hard work yielded the results they had expected. Soon the plot of land before their door was studded with the green seedlings of corn and sorghum, while clumps of *xibag* artemisia and yellow willows grew thickly all along the periphery. Though wind and sand hit a few times, they persisted in hauling water from the sand-well to preserve these valuable green lives. Thus, in that first year they established themselves on the vast sandland, harvesting their own grain and stabilising the surrounding sand by keeping its drift to a minimum. The *xibag* artemisia and the sand willows grew exuberantly and spread, helping them thereby to maintain their claim upon their piece of land. At the beginning of the second year, Whitesea expanded the application of his area of expertise and made judicious, scientific choices of bushes and trees to add to their land's botanical variety. These included Siberian elms, white peashrub, narrow-leaved oleaster, melilot, and other woody perennials. Step by step, little by little he transformed this patch of sandy land, calling it "Viridity Biosphere". As the years passed, the "biosphere" grew like a rolling snowball until it became a most extraordinary spread of vegetation; a piece of green jade inset into the monotony of the sand, demonstrating human intelligence and creativity in the face of Nature's formidable strength.

*The sand willow mentioned earlier in the story refers in Mongolia to two similar plants, the northwest sand willow and the yellow willow (*Salix gordejevii*).

One evening, Lama Yondon looked out the window and said with a surge of emotion, "Ah, just look at that. Though it's no bigger than a man's fist, Viridity has truly become an island of green worthy of the name. And it's all thanks to Master Baizhang's monastic discipline."

"Hey, what about this Master Whitesea right here — he's the one you ought to thank."

"You and I — we are brothers in adversity, partners in affliction. Nothing can part us — except death. How can the words 'thank you' even come close to expressing the depths of feeling here?" Yondon's eyes deepened, then shifted toward the boundless distance of the sandland. "Where is she? Not a sound since she left, not a single sign. It's so hard not knowing whether she's alive or dead, or where she's drifted to." He sighed mournfully.

"She's a very unusual dog, a dog with human sensibilities. She's alive. If you feel lonesome, I can write to the people of the Provincial Desert Research Institute and invite them here on an inspection tour. Maybe we can even get them to establish a desert control station here with you as the head. What do you say to that?"

"Oh, please, have mercy on me. I don't want to have anybody here, except Whitesy. Let that Desert Institute of yours stay in the big city. Unless, of course, that woman whose name you're always shouting out in your sleep shows up. In this case this old lama will fold his hands in fervent prayer and recite the Peace and Benediction Sutra for three days to welcome both of you."

Whitesea's face flushed. He shook his head and

smiled sadly. He'd never mentioned to the old lama that he'd been married.

"She ... she's ... *Ai*! Let's not talk about her." He swallowed his words.

"Tell me — way back when they sent you down to get reformed, just what were you being reformed of? Some people said it was womanising, and others said foreigners were involved. I never asked you about it because I didn't want to open up old wounds."

"In truth, it was neither of those. It was only a matter that now seems insignificant — hugely laughable, really, to someone like you who's forsaken the world and has no quarrel with it. That year was an evaluation and promotion year at the institute, because two posts had opened up. And there was this obviously incompetent deputy chief in administration who wanted one of them. Now the first position had already been promised to the head of the institute; it was an internal decision made by the directors long before. That left the second position, and everyone was of the opinion that it ought to go to me, which I thought was reasonable — I mean, I knew I could handle it. But that deputy chief — he trained his sights on me." Whitesea descended into painful memories of the past. He took off his glasses and wiped them mechanically. "One night when I was working alone in the lab, a secretary came in to ask me about something. Somehow she got onto the subject of some personal problem she was having — I wasn't paying too much attention. She talked and I listened. But then the next day, the rumours were flying thick and fast that I'd had some liaison with her. On the heels of that incident was a lot of dark talk about the articles I had published in journals abroad, about how they said this and how they said that. The leadership called me in then to talk about going down to the grass roots for 'tempering' or whatever — so, I just decided to go with the flow and requested to be sent to your sandland here."

"Oh, so that's it — somebody had it in for you."

The two men fell into silence.

It grew dark. Yondon lit the oil lamp. Its dark red flame flickered in the tendrils of desert night wind slipping through the window cracks and turning the room's occupants and objects into dim brooding shadows. A quiet void was the night in the desert, steeped in mystery. After a time, the wind blew the flame out. Neither of the men moved to re-light it.

"Tomorrow," Whitesea mumbled after they'd lain down to sleep, "I'm going out into the sandland to excavate the roots of a Chinese peashrub for my *One Hundred Illustrated Plants and Their Root Systems*".

"I'll go weed the corn patch," Yondon replied, "and water it — the ground's a bit dry. When you go out, take something to protect yourself — the other day I saw a black wolf lurking about. And come back at noon. I'll make some pancakes and some wild onion and pigeon egg soup." He turned over on his side, but lay wide awake, plumbing the mystery of Whitesea. He was like an ascetic monk who'd come alone into the desert searching for some cause. With no wife, no family, no worldly desires, all he wanted to do was publish the treatise upon which he'd been working with such painstaking devotion. And, according to him, that's just the way humans were — pottering creatures who just had to fool around with something. It was in them to busy themselves with whatever they found fascinating and tinker with it — that indeed was their greatest source of happiness in life. He had said that this business of controlling the desert was of extremely urgent importance, a matter of life and death that was not just the concern of the great amorphous mass of humankind, but his own personal concern. Somebody, after all, had to do it. He was totally absorbed by deserts and desert vegetation, no less than the old lama was captivated by Lamaism and its holy scriptures. He'd gone several times with Whitesea to dig up plant roots and prepare drawings. He knew it was not an undertaking one would venture into lightly.

Meanwhile, Whitesea, too, was lying awake. Tomorrow he'd be working on the final root drawing for his *One Hundred Illustrated Plants and their Root Systems*. He was excited about it. He knew that when it came to desert plants, it was not enough to see just what was above the ground; one had to get to the roots, to take a careful look at what was hidden below. To dig up roots for drawing, he had to operate like a surgeon: with delicate hands and a sense of devotion. Only then could he avoid severing any of the lateral roots and thus compromising the accuracy and the reliability of the data. Even dwarf plants had large root systems, some extending as far as sixty to ninety feet in the soil. To render a complete drawing, he had to dig out a very large hole that extended as far and as deep as the system itself, tracking down every branch of the root to its ultimate end.

In the dim light of early dawn, Whitesea arose and set out. He'd stuffed his backpack with four or five cornmeal pancakes left over from the previous night, several water-rich radishes, and his drawing paper and instruments. Shouldering his steel spade, in high spirits he strode up toward the sandland.

On the surface of the sand, the dew had turned to a layer of frost. The dragonflies could not lift themselves off the willow branches on which they rested and were patiently waiting for the sun to come up and dry their moisture-laden wings. But the jumping hares who had been busy all night long searching for food, were boring holes in the sand slope to hide from the scorching of the rising sun. Each creature had its own methods of survival. Whitesea smiled knowingly, feeling how lovely they were. He tiptoed around a pair of wild quails sleeping together and continued on up the high sand slope.

Standing atop the slope, he looked around to get his bearings. That desert Chinese peashrub he'd planted three years ago was located on the top of a rather distant dune situated deep in the sandland. He pushed on towards it, covering probably seven miles of sandland before he found it.

This was a small enclave of profusely growing *xibag* artemisia. Here a Chinese peashrub, woody plant that it was, was lucky to survive. He'd planted it, casually, three years ago when he was sowing xibag artemisia seeds, just to see what would happen; and amazingly it survived, even flourished. Its foliage was luxuriant, a grey-green colour that was well-suited to the desert. Having already achieved a height of a little over two feet, it stood tall and graceful among the stunted *xibag* artemisia.

"Say, now, look at you! Such a vivacious lovely,

standing head and shoulders above all the rest! I really hate to have to dig you up." Whitesea took off his backpack and put it on the ground. He squatted next to the peashrub and examined it minutely for the biological secrets of its success. "Well, there's no getting out of it. I'm sorry to do this to you, but you'll have to be sacrificed to the greater propagation of your kind — and to do that I have to look at your roots. Forgive me."

He started to dig.

His digging was methodical and professional. Since it was over two feet tall, its root system had to extend at least nine feet deep. He applied his spade first to the layers of surface sand some distance from the base of the peashrub and commenced digging up an area of six square feet around it. He was afraid of damaging the root and dug very carefully. When he got close to the root, he cast aside his spade and set to digging with his hands, using a brush to clear away the sand. Whenever he separated a lateral root from the others, he measured and numbered it and then recorded the information in his notebook. This would enable him to make a complete, proportionately correct drawing after the whole root system was unearthed. He placed each lateral root in a thin plastic tube to prevent it from being broken.

In two hours' time, he'd uncovered only a dozen or so of the lateral roots and had reached a depth of about three feet. But the main taproot still remained hidden deep down, and it would be a long time before he would get to its tip.

"Well, you are really something! No wonder you're so tough and your trunk grows so solid and sturdy. *That's* why people love to use you to make rope. You're surely going to give me a hard time for the rest of the day!"

Whitesea climbed out of the pit to take a break. He chewed on pancakes and radishes and took a swallow of the water he'd brought with him from the sand-well to boost his energy. The sandland had heated up dramatically since the chilly early morning, having absorbed the venom of the sun's summer rays. With blinding brilliance, the noon-day sun beat down into the stifling torrid air. Whitesea finished eating and rushed back down into the pit to continue digging in the cool moist air that still lingered there.

Like a marmot making a burrow, he flung his spadefuls of sand to the top, stopping constantly to isolate with care each lateral root. Soon the taproot was hung all around with a cascading mesh of plastic tubing. Were it not for his patience and mastery, the lateral roots would have soon become entangled or broken. Even then, he inadvertently broke off the tip of one, for which he cursed himself roundly, though the broken piece was but an inch long and the thickness of a hair.

"You idiot! You clumsy oaf!" he cried in self-condemnation. He picked it up with a pair of tweezers and re-attached it with a piece of cellotape.

The further down he dug, the harder the task became, largely because it was increasingly difficult to fling the sand to the top. Already more than six feet deep, the room-sized pit was rimmed with small mountains of sand. Still, the end of the taproot was nowhere in sight. He began to grow disheartened as fatigue took its toll. He panted with his exertions and his stripped upper-body was plastered with sand-dust. Rivulets of sweat left muddy trails down his face. He sank to a sitting position, a mud-caked monkey paralysed at the bottom of the pit. He stared glumly at the taproot still staunchly thrusting deep into the ground. How far he didn't know. He began to hate it.

Damnation!

At that depth in the sand where the sun's rays did not reach, the air was damp and cool, penetratingly dank in fact, enough to make him shiver with a vague sense of horror. With a pounding heart, he scrambled out of the pit.

Outside, the sun was dazzling and the air oven-hot over the wide empty desert.

He lay down on the burning sand and gulped mouthfuls of water. Though he'd buried his flask in the damp sand, the water was already lukewarm. He threw down the flask and seized a pancake which he ate, staring at the drooping peashrub. Its woebegone leaves were wilting in the sun, now more grey than green. Let's just call it quits, he said to himself. Estimate the taproot's ultimate length and draw it according to that. His spirits lifted a little as he encouraged himself to follow this idea. But a few moments later he was excoriating himself. Whitesea! Shame on you, how could you stoop so low! Where's your staying power? Just a little more effort and the job will be done. How could you even think of cutting corners like that. Tricking yourself, — scientific skullduggery, that's what it is! You addlebrained dolt!

He scrambled to his feet and descended into the pit once again. Before disappearing below the surface, he tipped his face to look at the sun leaning off toward the western sky. Its glaring whiteness pierced his eyes, but he could still see its circular contour, a dazzling white disk floating in a halo of pure blinding brilliance. Pitch-blackness swiftly overlayed it, and for awhile he could see nothing. He continued his descent. At the bottom, he sat in the damp sand, eyes closed as he waited for the full restoration of his sight.

He didn't see the danger approaching. He only heard a loud crashing sound.

And with it he felt a great force slamming into his body and knocking him down. Then suffocation. That white sun — what's it done to me? Damn! He struggled. There was a great weight pressing down on him. He strained and heaved, trying to get out from under the unyielding sand. So this was what a sand avalanche was like. The walls of the pit had looked very strong, why did they cave in? Only then did the idea of death occur to him, and with this thought came terror. He renewed his struggle, but his exertions achieved nothing. His arms and legs were pinned fast, immovably encased. How could such soft sand that yields so easily to the tools of excavation be so firm and compact when it collapses on top of you? The blood surged and thrashed through his veins. His heart was being squeezed, tighter and tighter, until it would surely burst. A buzzing sound filled his head. His sand-clogged nose, mouth, ears swelled with the unbearable and mounting pressure. And he became aware that his face was pressed up against the peashrub's taproot. He didn't want to die. He couldn't die. It was not time to die.

But he died just the same.

In the last seconds, his consciousness contained but

one overwhelming image, that of the glaring white solar disk, dazzling and piercing the eye, expanding and filling his brain until there was only a blank white void.

That morning, Lama Yondon discovered that the sky was extraordinarily red, as if it had been smeared with blood. Garish incarnadine clouds drawn out to exceeding lengths streaked across like blood-laced rivers. And the vast sweeping desert lay beneath in unusual quiescence. Not a whisper of wind, not an unruly grain of sand, not a twitter from the birds. It was almost suffocatingly tranquil, despite the seductive sights and atmosphere typical of an early summer morning. As he hoed the weeds in the cornfield, Yondon felt a nameless unease. Suddenly a raucous crow swept by overhead, curdling his blood with its cry. For the rest of the morning, he was on tenterhooks. At noon, he ran back to the house, but Whitesea did not appear. It was this absence that brought it home to him that it was Whitesea who was at the heart of his inexplicable apprehension.

He forgot about making lunch and hurried out into the sandland. He searched high and low over its humps and dunes, shouting himself hoarse. The endlessly empty desert yielded no sign of Whitesea. Only his own gravelly voice echoed back at him from the high sky.

His sweat mixed with the dust clinging to his skin, turning it to mud. Still he searched on, until in the slanting rays of the setting sun he discovered a caved-in pit at the base of a rather distant dune. A bookbag, drawing papers, pens, rulers, and some outer garments sat by the edge. Dread seized his heart. He threw himself into the hole, feverishly digging and casting up sand with his bare hands until his fingers were torn and bleeding. Tears streamed forth in violent grief and his sob-racked throat ruptured and bled.

He cradled the lifeless Whitesea in his arms. Over and over he murmured in grief-stricken insensibility, "You, too, are gone. You, too, are gone. You, too, are gone... All for a root. All for drawing a peashrub root system, you are gone. You traded your life for a root. Oh, oh, oh..." he moaned. "Priceless was this root and thus stately was the interment ... a stately, dignified sand burial..." He burst into heart-rending wails and began to curse. "Damned root, damned root-system drawing, damned desert! I curse you all for eternity! You evil root, and you evil desert — give me back my brother, Whitesea!" And he fell into ululating wails.

Crazed with grief, Lama Yondon slid from lamentation into demented laughter and at last into benumbed stupefaction. Holding Whitesea's body, he sat motionless on the dune, silent, shedding no tears, stripped of passion and lost in oblivion. The evening passed, then the night, and still he sat. The morrow came and went, and there he remained. Only occasional mumbles issued from his throat: "Life traded for a root ... sand burial ... buried in the sand ... give me back my brother Whitesea..."

On the morning of the third day, he formally interred Whitesea. Following the custom, he washed the body with clean water and dressed it in a set of fresh clothing. Then he laid Whitesea gently down in the very pit he had dug himself. He placed a sheet of sacred abstract script on his chest and scattered the seeds of the five grains in his hair. Then with the care accorded fragile, precious things, he laid the peashrub bush including its plastic-tube-encased lateral roots next to his body. "With it as companion, you will not be lonely," the old lama murmured tearfully. With slow, lingering movements, he took his spade in hand and began shovelling sand down into the grave. Each melancholy spadeful wrenched from him a fresh round of tears, and he paused to let them fall as he recited a line from the scriptures. Three sticks of incense were burning by the graveside, their blue smoke curling upwards, vanishing into the clear sky. "You love the sand, you love the flora of the sand. Now they will always be with you, and you can continue to study them on the route to Heaven. This is a sand burial, my good brother, rare since ancient times — a sand burial for you..." His sobs choked off his words.

A fresh grave of yellow sand; a mound like a little hill.

The old lama planted before it three desert peashrubs. Around it he planted sand willows and *xibag* artemisia. The greening of this spot would await the passage of time. There he stayed by the grave for three more days before going home.

4

"Ow-wooooo..."

White Wolf lifted her muzzle westward, toward the blood-enflamed sky, and let out a long howl.

She stood atop a hatchet-hewn dune that seemed to rear up savagely from the desert floor.

These were the pneumatic sands of Naiman Qi in

the northern part of the Horqin Sandy Land. Here fixed and semi-fixed dunes were buffeted by seasonal winds into hundreds of ferocious forms until they resembled a horde of grotesquely postured stampeding beasts. Here a vast sweep of troughs and peaks undulates choppily to the horizon, and this wanton stretch of sand evokes a sense of treachery and danger in its every disposition. Dark roots and vines protrude grimly from the sand, unredeemed by a single blade of green. In the east stand scores of old elms that are, curiously, dead. Their sere branches spread out in ghoulish twists and turns, like bared fangs and brandished claws, each horribly contorted into its own unique pose of intimidation. It is as if Nature had suddenly frozen them in the prime of their lives, stripping them of their leaves and bark, and condemning them to an eternity of naked, dead exhibitionism. These are masterworks of the arid heat and violent sand storms of what has come to be known as the Great Yellow Demon Desert, home of the cataclysmic one-hundred-year storm. Occurring only once every century, or even longer, this climatic event instantaneously vaporises all moisture of all vegetation, leaving in its wake nothing but scorched leaves, dried branches and perished trunks so that even huge centenarian trees can not revive. It is the specter of Death for all living things, including man. Any man unfortunate enough to be caught in it meets his doom in swift, sure mummification. This is Nature's wrath, its fearsome, unforgiving punishment meted out to all, innocent and guilty alike. Ironically, people call these old dead trees the "Naimàn Immortal Trees". But where is this immortality? Was there immortality in their convoluted formation in life? Is there immortality in their grotesque configurations of death? Where was the immortality in their instant loss of the rich colours of life? There is no logic here, and yet people cling to this fanciful conceit.

White Wolf howled ceaselessly.

Her head held high, she gazed at the strange appearance of the western sky. There was fear in her eyes. Restlessly she moved about, her tail switching in apprehension. She dropped to the sand and crawled on her belly. She leapt up with agitation. She bared her teeth ferociously, howling and barking by turns. Her awareness of the coming terror — the inevitable holocaust — was ancestral, imbedded in that complex of animal instinct infallibly passed on through the ages and now concentrated in her blood. Right behind her stood that grove of desiccated "immortal trees". Her howling grew, with each passing moment, more steeped in horror and despair, a sound to make men's flesh creep. Yet anger, too, insinuated its note. Anger and the injured shriek of injustice.

White Wolf only knew to howl at the heavens. But her howling brought no change in its blazing, blood-drenched expanse. She leapt off the lofty dune and dashed into the grove of "immortal trees". The massive base of one of these trees harboured an inconspicuous cave where White Wolf had installed her offspring. Little White Wolf had fallen fast asleep while waiting for her mother to return with food. But White Wolf brought no food. She seized her pup by the ruff and re-emerged from the cave. Outside, she set her baby on the ground and proceeded with ruthless measures to drive her away toward the east. But though Little White Wolf had by now grown quite large, she was not yet ready to leave her mother. Back and forth, she dodged White Wolf's violent thrusts, unrepentently refusing to strike out for the east. She'd followed her mother there several times, and so she knew it was the land of the two-legs, of whom she was deathly afraid. Her mother herself had always been reluctant to go there, so why was she now chasing her off in that direction, *alone*? And why was there so much fear in her eyes? Why the sudden ferocity, this merciless refusal to indulge her child's rebellion? Where was her compassionate, *motherly* mother? The little wolf was confused and scared. White Wolf looked at her refractory pup and flew into a rage. With hideous snarls she pounced upon her and sank her teeth into her skin. Little White Wolf screeched in pain. But still she refused to leave. Her mother chased after her, snapping and biting with increasing savagery, striking terror into the little wolf's heart. Little White Wolf began to fear for her life. She now knew that if she didn't obey, her mother would bite her to death.

With plangent, anguished wails, Little White Wolf at last began to run. Toward the east, away from her beloved mother; into irrevocable separation. Unspeakable grief filled her heart.

White Wolf gave venomous chase, hurtling with growls and snapping jaws after her fleeing offspring to put an end to any notion she might have of turning back.

Two white wolves, one large, one small, streaked across the desert toward the east like two bolts of white lightning. At times, love is hatred, and loving entails denying love and driving the loved one away. It is a paradox the loved one may not understand, perhaps not to his or her dying day.

Once White Wolf had succeeded in driving her cub away, she unleashed a long howl of relief. Then she made for the Temple of Viridity, leaving a trail of white dust in her wake.

The moon was not like the moon. Dull, turbidly yellow, and spiritless, it seemed to be encased in a series of halos. The stars were not like the stars. Pale, lacklustre, barely visible, they seemed to be smeared over with a thin layer of frost that diminished their twinkle and blurred their form, as if the beholder were going blind. The night was not like the night. It had lost its usual soporific peace and tranquillity; unpredictable impulses, disquietude, chaos, and danger seemed to lurk everywhere .

It was a sultry, sleepless night for all creatures. All seemed to be waiting with bated breath for something dreadful to happen.

Yuanhui lay on her cot in the turbid daze of pre-sleep, her head vaguely aching. But as sleep would not come she gave up and opened her eyes. Aoya's bed was empty. At first she thought that the head of the Women's Federation had gone out to answer the call of nature, but the minutes ticked by and still she did not return.

Growing suspicious, she threw her wrap over her shoulders and headed for the opening of the tent. It was then she heard murmuring voices deep in conversation just outside.

"You'd better hurry up and decide. This weather is very volatile. It could change at any moment. So are you going, or not?" This was Commander Tieba, speaking in lowered tones.

"Let me think about it. You're absolutely positive the weather will change?" Aoya answered him with a question.

"You didn't see the sunset? There's no doubt about it, something big is going to happen. There's no time for hesitation. You should get out of here fast!"

"Well, I have to talk it over with Yuanhui."

"What the hell is there to talk about! She's bent on finding out how her husband died. Why do you have to hang around to the death?"

Aoya had nothing to say to this. After a moment, she said, "We can't leave until daylight, anyway. Let me explain the situation to Yuanhui, and if she decides to go, we'll go together, and if she decides to stay, I'll go with you."

"You're going to wait for daylight?"

"You're going out there in the dark? Not me, no way! If you want to go, you can go by yourself. Trying to find your way across the sandy wilds in the black of night is just plain crazy. It'll be amazing if you don't get lost and the wolves don't have your guts for dinner!"

Tieba obviously didn't dare to make the trip by himself in the dark. "Okay, then," he said with resignation, "first thing in the morning."

"Where are you sleeping? In the cart?"

"No, I'm going over to sit by the sand-well. I won't be able to close my eyes all night."

"What — are you still trying to shoot those creatures?"

"Naw, this time I'm not using the gun — save myself a lot of trouble with that old fart! This time I'm using exploding bait. I'll just scatter some of the savoury bait around the well, and by tomorrow morning, all I'll have to do is pick up the game." Tieba walked away, laughing gleefully.

Aoya was indignant. "You're a damned beast, Tieba!" she shouted after him. "One of these days you'll get what's coming to you!"

Yuanhui rushed back to her bed and lay down. Aoya's not a bad sort, she thought, just a little bit addlebrained, doesn't know right from wrong sometimes. She waited for Aoya to fall asleep, then she dressed quietly and sneaked out of the tent. She went to see Lama Yondon. By the moon's tenuous light, she made her way along the sand-path to the old lama's house. The night was truly strange. Birds flapped about in the trees, jerboas and lizards jumped and scurried restlessly along the path, as animals who sense an earthquake coming. It really looks as if we're going to have some unusual weather, she thought.

Approaching Lama Yondon's door, she witnessed yet another peculiarity.

Under the murky moonlight, the ailing, enfeebled lama emerged from the house, went around to the back, and, upon reaching the high sand dune by the cowshed, suddenly evaporated. Not believing her own eyes, Yuanhui trod softly over to the side of the cowshed and looked around. There was no trace of him. The old lama seemed to have vanished off the face of the earth. He couldn't possibly know how to make himself invisible, could he? As she was standing there in total mystification, a noise behind her made her jump.

"What are you doing here sneaking around following people?" Lama Yondon had somehow rematerialised in the shadows behind her.

"I ... I ... I wasn't following you ... I came to talk with you about something," Yuanhui explained herself, unable to keep from stammering.

"You want to talk with me?" Yondon tottered toward the house. Yuanhui followed him. "Okay, then, go ahead, I'm listening."

"That nephew of yours is still here. He's down by the sand-well stalking the animals."

"I knew he wouldn't leave. He is possessed by evil and will not easily cease." The old lama sighed.

"Then are you going to stop him?"

"Stop him? He is the kind of person who will not give up until he hits the wall of fate." Yondon started to cough. After awhile, he said slowly, "In Hell, there are a great many monsters and devils who shout loudly for salvation. The Buddha used his discerning eyes to review the life of one big monster among them. He discovered that even though this monster committed all sorts of evil acts in his life, he did suddenly show mercy once when he lifted his foot over a spider in the road just as he was about to step on it. Buddha then lowered the silk spun by this little spider into Hell to pull him out of the abyss of misery. The monster joyfully seized the silken thread and started to climb up. But many other monsters and devils tried to follow him. The monster screamed, 'This is mine! Let go! The spider can not bear the weight!' He took out a knife and severed the thread below him. However, when he tried to climb up after that, the spider could no longer lift him. The silk broke, and the monster fell back into the byss of misery. The Buddha shook his head, sighed and departed from the scene." At this point in his narrative, Lama Yondon himself took a deep sigh. He continued, "My nephew is just like this monster who cut off the path to salvation for the other monsters and thus ended up cutting off his own way out. Good or evil differs only in one momentary thought. My nephew will surely cut off the spider's silk. This is his destiny. Other people can not help, and I have done my utmost."

Yuanhui, deeply moved, quietly contemplated this Buddhist allegory.

"Should you not leave tomorrow, you may seek refuge here in my mud house. The tent is too risky." These words Yondon murmured as he looked into the infinite ineffableness that was the heavens and the earth in their mysterious manifestations.

"I am very grateful to you, Older Brother. But I would like to ask, from what am I trying to escape?"

"From that which you should escape."

"Can we really escape?"

"That would depend on each individual's luck."

"What exactly is going on? Is a disaster coming?"

"You really don't feel it? Even the animals have sensed it, and here you are, asking silly questions. Of course, it's clear as a bell, an unprecedented disaster is headed our way."

"Older Brother..." Yuanhui, seeing that Yondon was about to enter the house, cut off what she was going to say.

"What now?"

"You should tell me about what happened to Whitesea..."

"Yes, yes. Tomorrow. I'll tell you tomorrow... By then, everything will be very clear." Yondon stepped over the threshold, but then he thought of something and turned back to Yuanhui. "Can you help me out by filling up the two water vats in the house?"

"Sure. Tomorrow, Aoya and I will be over to do that for you."

"No, it needs to be done now."

Yuanhui could not but comply. Forcing a smile, she said, "Okay, *now*, then. I'll go get Aoya. It's impossible to sleep tonight, anyway."

Aoya rubbed her sleepy eyes and said, "The old lama's out of his gourd. Such a lot of crazy nonsense — don't believe him! Just go to sleep, and we'll carry water for him in the morning."

"No, I already promised, and I can't go back on my word. Come on, Aoya, please? You have to go with me, because I'm afraid to go down there to the sand-well by myself."

"Well, I must say! You're a nut yourself — how can you be so superstitious! Okay — might as well join all the crazies, lugging water in the middle of the night!" Aoya, unable to dissuade Yuanhui, got out of bed in a huff.

They walked over to the edge of the sand-well, where they had been earlier that evening, and immediately felt that something was not right.

"Help ... help..." A feeble-sounding plea for help was coming from the surface of the water.

Taken aback, they strained to see its source, and there sticking just above the surface was a human head.

"Why, isn't that Commander Tieba?" Yuanhui asked. "How'd he get in the well?"

"Hurry up and get me out! It's pulling me in — the mire, it's pulling me in..." Tieba had seen them coming — his saviours, he'd felt — and he'd mustered up all his breath to shout for their attention. With one hand, he was holding onto a thin branch of a willow leaning out over the water, the only thing that had kept him from sinking out of sight. Laughing loudly, Aoya extended her carrying pole toward him.

"Grab hold of the hook at the end of the pole, and I'll pull you out. You scoundrel — you got what you deserved!" Aoya was quite strong and with several pulls dragged the soaking, muddy Tieba up onto the bank.

Tieba crawled and rolled on the bank like a drowned, muck-slathered rat. As soon as he reached solid ground, he collapsed, gasping for air and cursing between breaths, "Mother-fucking filthy fox! It eats my bait, then jumps into the water to drown!"

"Oh, so you slipped into the muck when you went to fish out the fox, hmmmm?"

"That right, nearly did me in! Fortunately, there was that willow branch. Scared the shit out of me, it was terrifying... Who would think that such a nice clear shallow well would have a sink-hole in the bottom. It's really weird — and I walked right into it."

Yuanhui suddenly recalled Lama Yondon's story about the monster and the spider's silk thread. She sensed that the story and the present incident were connected in some way. Could it be that the old lama could really foresee things, and that's why he insisted on her coming to fetch the water tonight? She was greatly puzzled.

"What are you two doing fetching water in the middle of the night, anyway?" Once Tieba recovered his strength, he began to see the oddity of their midnight excursion.

"It's all because of your crazy uncle," Aoya answered. "He insisted that Yuanhui come and fetch water now. He couldn't wait for the morning."

"He did? How'd he know I fell into the muck and couldn't get out?"

"Well, if you go around hunting the creatures that drink from his sand-well," Aoya rebuked him, "how could he not know — it doesn't matter how sneaky you are about it. That uncle of yours is no ordinary person. You really got yourself a second life tonight, and you have him to thank for it."

"It's really a pity," Tieba said with much regret in his voice as he stared at the tranquil well water, "that the fox sank into the mud hole."

Yuanhui's heart constricted. "That spider's thread is going to break," she said significantly.

Her two companions looked at her in bewilderment.

A nebulous sun rose painfully out of the south-eastern sand piles. Enveloped in a thick layer of storm-dust which gradually turned purple-red, it was like a disconsolate ball tightly wrapped in cotton cloth which failed to stanch its bleeding and became soaked through, smearing blood over the entire lower half of the south-eastern sky. A little while later, this bloody ball began its ascent, straining against the heavy white curtain like a newborn infant struggling to cast off its hateful white swaddling dyed with the blood of its own birth. With the increasing intensity of this struggle, the air grew ever drier and more stultifying, with the heat of a blazing oven.

Yuanhui stood at the door and saw Aoya and Tieba off.

When Aoya had sheepishly broken the news that she was leaving with Tieba, Yuanhui had smiled and given her blessing. Recalling the responsibility she had taken on in coming here, Aoya strongly urged Yuanhui to go back with her. But the latter refused categorically, stunning Aoya with a courage and stubbornness that belied her tiny frame, scholarly mien, and the self-effacing look of her uncertain "certain age". Aoya boarded the *lele* cart harbouring sympathy for this perplexing woman.

Yuanhui gazed at the reddening south-eastern sky and found herself steeped in admiration. "Oh, how beautiful," she could not help but say.

She went inside and boiled herself some rice porridge. When she'd done eating, she packed up her things to move to the old lama's mud house.

She emerged from the tent to find herself facing a massive, elongated wall, a great churning tidal front whipped up from the depths of the western desert and bearing swiftly down upon Viridity. Terrified, she broke into a full-tilt run for the old lama's mud house, screaming, "Brother Yondon, save me!"

That broad, turbid yellow tidal wave caught up with her halfway to the house. A viciously powerful sandstorm thrown up by a mighty wind across the horizon, it whirled the sand around with noisy, high-pitched, sand-blast force, sucking feathers, leaves and plant debris high into the sky. Through this screen of chaos, the nearly noon-day sun became as a dark red plate fired to a deep purple hue. The branches of the sand willows thrashed violently against each other, producing a loud whistling sound. A blast of hot wind struck her from behind, dousing her with a heat so intense that her shirt felt as if it had burst into flames. Her mouth was full of sand and sand scraped her eyes so that she couldn't open them. Birds whizzed by her head like bullets shot toward the east. Suddenly she tripped and sprawled into the sand all of ten yards from Yondon's house, a distance that seemed to her a thousand miles. She would never be able to crawl to it. Sand clogged her throat. She couldn't breathe. She couldn't call for help. Just at this moment, she felt herself being lifted, and dragged into the house.

She discovered that all her possessions, her luggage, her bedding, her book bag, her wash basin, and everything else, had been sucked into the maelstrom and were rolling around like balls or twirling around in the sky, up and down, up and down.

"Thank you, Older Brother. Thank you for saving my life." Yuanhui gasped for breath and watched the world outside the door in horror. "What is happening? What has heaven come to? What has earth become? Is this the disaster that you spoke of earlier?"

"Hot sand storm! A frightful disaster sent down from high heaven! The specter of Death for all creatures in the sandland!" Lama Yondon's face darkened, his fragile body trembled. He was squatting on the ground and seemed to be totally spent.

"So horribly frightening! I've read in various places about these hot sand storms, but I didn't know they were so terrifying." Yuanhui shook her head. She had not yet recovered fully from her fright.

"This is just the beginning. Horrors of even greater magnitude are yet to come. You'd better go quickly;

put lids on the water vats and then cover them up with quilts, otherwise, the water will be totally evaporated in no time. You won't survive without water." Lama Yondon had fixed his eyes upon the outside, as if he were expecting something.

"What do you mean I won't be able to survive? What about you?"

"There will be no me. My end has come. I will not see the conclusion of this storm." Yondon spoke calmly, as if he were referring to such mundane matters as eating and sleeping. He was tranquil, relaxed, unemotional.

Yuanhui was overcome with sorrow. After a moment of silence, she said with uncertainty, "Old Master, you seem to be waiting for something…"

"Yes, I'm waiting … for her."

"For her? Who?"

"Whitesy."

"That white wolf?"

"She's a dog Whitesea and I raised together back then, a very intelligent dog. She should come now. It's time for her to come." Yondon was murmuring with confidence as he searched in the murk of the sandstorm for anything unusual.

Indeed, there was an unusual movement. It turned out not to be Whitesy, but Tieba and Aoya. Holding onto each other for support, they tumbled into the house. Neither could speak. Their mouths, eyes, and hair were full of sand. Their faces were blistered from the heat of the scorching wind, and their lips cracked and oozing blood. They hardly looked human.

Yuanhui gave them water, and they slowly recovered some strength.

"What are you two doing back here?"

"*Hai*!" Tieba uttered in disgust. "We hadn't got very far when this damn sand storm caught up with us. Damn fucking sand storm!" Tieba cursed as he spat out sand.

"Humph! It's all your fault, you bastard!" Aoya railed at him. "You just had to hang around the old village because of those foxes. You wouldn't leave and you wouldn't leave. Wasted all that time! You damn son of a bitch, you practically killed me!"

Tieba was reduced to shamed silence. They had lost their opportunity to get out of the sandland before the storm struck and had had to turn back for refuge.

Tieba stood up and tottered toward the water vats for a drink.

"Don't touch that!" Yondon shouted.

"Huh? Why not? Can't I have a drink?"

"From now on, no one's to drink any time they want." Lama Yondon made this declaration solemnly. He looked at Tieba and Aoya. "What water I have stored here was not meant for you to share. Now that you've come back, there are two more mouths. From now on we have to use it frugally — and equally."

"Such huge vats of water — how can there not be enough for the four of us?" Tieba muttered in total disbelief.

"It's not just the four of us. There are also them..." The old lama pointed out the door.

Everyone turned to look outside. Only then did they discover that along the wattle fence, under the eaves, and on the window-sills had gathered a menagerie of desert birds and beasts. There were foxes, jumping hares, sand grouse, hawks... The creatures who lived in the vicinity of the sand-well had all come running here. In the violent wind and sand, each and every survivor was curled up there trembling in terror, with pitiful eyes focussed on the door, throwing themselves on the mercy of men, who were a little bigger and stronger than they.

"It would seem that the sand-well has been buried in the sand," the old lama said. "Even if it hasn't, it can not protect them any longer. Alas, they have no choice but to come close to humankind. Their instinct to survive demands it. How could we refuse them!"

"This is not the time to be worried about them!" Tieba burst out. "We humans are more important!"

"Humans are more important? That's your own point of view. From the fox's point of view, are you important? All creatures on the earth are equal. All lives in the desert have the same value. There is no differentiation in rank or status." Yondon stared straight ahead. He took a deep breath. "It is incumbant upon us humans, who are the wisest of all the creatures and possess greater skills, to lead them to refuge from this disaster that has befallen us all. We should put a stop to all enmity and killing and find a common path to survival. This is the will of Buddha!" Lama Yondon's eyes glowed vividly. His serene face exuded kindness and the transcendent wisdom of the sage.

Yuanhui's heart quickened at his words. She felt as if she'd realised a kind of universal truth. She looked at with with increased respect and said in earnest, "Old Master, although I am not a believer in Buddhism, I do sincerely wish that this will of Buddha, this Buddhist ideal, can be realised."

"Thank you," Lama Yondon responded gratefully.

Silence followed.

After awhile, Lama Yondon, who had been intently looking out the door, suddenly shouted with joy, "Look, everybody! It's Whitesy! My Whitesy has come back! Whitesy, oh Whitesy!"

And indeed, a streak of white lightning was flashing through the turbulent sand, slicing through the tidal wave, streaking like an arrow straight for the mud house. With her flying legs thrusting her form vigorously forward, in the wink of an eye she landed at the door, giving out two barks.

Yondon, forgetting his weakened condition, opened the door to receive Whitesy into his welcoming embrace.

"My Whitesy, my Whitesy, my Whitesy ... you've come back. Oh, how wonderful, you've come back. Wonderful, wonderful..." Yondon murmured to her on and on. Like one who had been long awaiting the return of an absent child, he pressed his face against Whitesy's head and caressed her neck and back with his trembling hands.

Whitesy wagged her tail, stretched out her neck and opened her mouth. She rubbed her head on Yondon's hands and feet. She stood on her hind legs and went into his embrace. In her throat she made low groaning noises, as if she were murmuring endearments or sobbing out her joy. Though she could not use human language to express herself, she was fully submerged in emotions attending reunion after a prolonged separation.

This emotional scene palpably moved Yuanhui,

Aoya, and Tieba. They could never have imagined that a man and a dog could form such a true, pure, and faithful friendship, a friendship to survive intact and unaltered throughout long years of vicissitude; a relationship scarcely found between two humans.

Whitesy suddenly discovered Tieba standing in the corner.

Her throat filled with a single rolling syllable, and she flung herself upon him.

"Help!" Tieba screamed in soul-departing terror. He skeetered wildly off to the side, trying to escape, but Whitesy's explosively savage attack came like a bolt from the sky. She'd landed on top of him before anyone realised what was happening and was ripping through his pant-leg and clawing into his flesh. Blood began to flow.

"Get her off me!" Tieba screeched like a pig being slaughtered. "Save me, uncle! She'll kill me!" He flung his arms upward to shield his head and face.

"Whitesy, come back!" Yondon ordered. "Have mercy on him. Your old grudge remains fresh in your memory, I know; but just let it go now, call it quits. Look how scared he is — it's so pitiful!"

Whitesy obediently loosened her grip on Tieba and returned with her tail wagging. But her unquelled anger continued to rumble in her throat as she kept Tieba fixed in her menacing glare. Tieba clutched his leg and shrank into the corner, not daring to look at her.

Outside, the hot sand storm had increased in virulence. Tons of yellow sand were whipped through the sky in massive ravaging turbidity. The Temple of Viridity, that little green isle in the sea of sand, was now like a tiny sliver of a boat being tossed on a wrathful ocean. Helpless lone target of the hot sand storm, it shivered to its core. The pitiful creatures who'd gathered in the yard dashed back and forth in rising panic, seeking sanctuary from the ever tempestuous onslaught of the wind-driven sand. Hungry, thirsty, exhausted, and suffocating in the hot sand-filled air, their tongues hung out as they tried to breathe. Gradually, they converged upon the door of the mud house, pushing against it with their heads and scratching at it with their claws.

Lama Yondon dipped an earthen bowl into one of the water vats. Holding it in his trembling hands, he pushed upon the door. With Yuanhui's help, the door opened a crack, and he slid the bowl of water outside. The animals rushed upon it, emptying it in a flash. Though that small amount of water couldn't quench their thirst, it was enough to keep them alive. Meanwhile, each person in the house was allocated equal parts of one cup of water. No one spoke. Each was filled with the fear of nature. Each sensed their own insignificance and fragility in the face of nature's mysterious and awesome powers. With untoward arrogance, humans have styled themselves the wisest of creatures. They arrogantly puff and strut and proclaim all subject to their whim; heaven is theirs to conquer at will, the earth theirs to subjugate as they please. But at this moment they appeared so puny and powerless, completely stripped of all influence, cowering in their pitiful frailty, no better or wiser than those little animals.

The sand-gale shook Lama Yondon's mud house. The mud plastered on the roof began to give way and the exposed sorghum stalks beneath, now thrashed noisily. There was a sudden sharp crack as one of the poplar trees by the door snapped in two; its severed crown carried off in the wind. Then with a roaring rip, the entire roof of the house was lifted up! Sand and dirt cascaded down upon their heads as the roof mud and sorghum stalks went whirling high into the sky, scattered out of sight. Sand poured from the sky into the gaping maw of the roofless house. The now vulnerable walls began to sway.

"We are finished! We are finished!" Tieba wailed in despair.

"Follow me," Lama Yondon said in firm, no-nonsense voice. "Come now, to the back of the house."

"The back of the house?! We'll die there all the faster!" Tieba howled.

"I have a cellar there at the base of the dune!" Yondon cried as he stepped resolutely over the threshold of the collapsed door. Yuanhui helped him. Whitesy followed them, and Aoya followed Whitesy. Tieba, finding himself alone, shouted after them in fear, "Wait for me! Don't leave me behind!" and limped along after them.

Yuanhui stepped outside into immediate suffocation as her mouth and nose filled with hot sand that felt like scorching cotton stuffing. She lowered her head, trying to avoid the driving dry wind and the pounding hot sand. She was stupefied by the scene that greeted her eyes. The whirling brown sand had dealt a most deadly blow to the green vegetation around the Temple of Viridity. All the low-growing artemisia clumps had been buried in the torrid drift. The sand willows, the elms, the oleasters, and the calligonums were being bashed about, their withered leaves plucked from their branches and scattered like soap bubbles, dancing in the violent wind and vanishing into the yellow, sand-bloated sky. The hot sand storm had drained them so mercilessly and so swiftly of the green colour that symbolised life. Truly it was something that no one could have imagined. The tougher leaves of the elms still retained a greenish tint, but then a renewed blast of whirling hot sand hit them, instantaneously blackening them, and in the next instant blowing them all away, leaving nothing but bare black trunks and branches whistling in the wind.

Yuanhui couldn't bear to see all this and shut her eyes in terror. She could feel the air temperature steadily rising, as intense as a kiln. She had a prickling, burning sensation on her skin. A horrifying image flashed through her mind of herself being reduced to ashes in this dry hot sand storm. All she would have to do was tarry outside a few minutes more. The hot sand storm would annihilate them all as it had the trees and bushes.

She and Lama Yondon took one step and then another, struggling toward the back of the house.

Their mouths became drier and drier. High in the sky, whorls of reddish-brown dust roiled vertiginously, while the fiery sun twirled like a gyrating top whipped ever faster by the hot sand storm. The violent currents swallowed up that helpless orb and spat it out, over and over, heaping upon it an endless stream of abuse.

At last they reached their destination. Lama Yondon, gasping, stood at the base of the high dune, reached out his hand to feel for the cellar door and opened it. This was a storage room dug from the base of the dune down underneath. Immediately upon entering the subterranean room, they felt the succouring freshness of a cool, moist stream of air. Whitesy, Aoya and Tieba filed in behind them. Yuanhui discovered that a few desert creatures — the lucky survivors — had followed them in. Only larger animals had made it, the smaller, weaker ones having been blown away by the wind or dropped dead in the drifting sand. A black wolf was in the lead. No one knew just when this ferocious beast had joined the group of animals. All his awful majesty and vicious aggression had vanished, replaced by an abject bearing of exhaustion and defeat: tail tucked between his legs, head drooping down, red tongue hanging out in a desperate wheezing bid for air. Nature had endowed him with strength and power, and now nature had taken them back. When Whitesy espied the black wolf, she moved to rush upon him, but Lama Yondon called her back. Tieba, taking up the rear, jumped to shut the plank-door when he saw these animals were following them in.

"Open the door and let them in," Yondon said to him. "There is room here for us all. And you needn't be afraid of them. They won't hurt you." Tieba opened the door and scurried into the room to get out of the way of the animals shoving frantically through the door. They, however, did not dare venture any further than the vicinity of the door where they sat upon their haunches or lay down, as far away as possible from the people, whom they still feared.

Actually, the cellar was quite spacious. Holding a lamp, Lama Yondon continued on ahead straight into the room. They'd gone about ten yards when they saw another door. It was padlocked. Yuanhui and the others marvelled at this unexpected surprise.

"Old Master," Yuanhui asked, "what room is this?"

"Come with me, and you'll see," Yondon said.

This room turned out to be a hall for worshipping Buddha. In front of the wall facing them stood three golden statues high on a platform, Lamaism's Trikala Buddhas: the Buddhas of the Past, the Present, and the Future. Each was as tall as a man, and in front of each was burning an eternal jula lamp. The walls on either side were completely carved with Tibetan and Mongolian script. On the floor were placed various accoutrements of Lamaism, a *damaruu**, an ox horn, a prayer wheel, and several padauk chests which likely contained scriptures and other objects of Lamaism.

"Old Master, is this where you conduct religious ceremonies?" Yuanhui asked.

"No, it's not. I have not conducted ceremonies for a long time. This was the cellar of the original Temple of Viridity that was torn down. Because it had been sealed up long before, few people knew about it, and so it luckily escaped the disaster back then, and the golden Trikala Buddhas and some of the scriptures and accoutrements were saved. During the "cultural revolution", I suffered all kinds of indignities on account of these statues. But I didn't let them down; I made sure they weren't desecrated at the hands of the impious. *Om mani padme hum!*" Yondon folded his hands and devoutly chanted.

"Oh, my gosh! The golden Buddhas! The three golden Buddhas!" Tieba's astonished voice rang out.

---

*A miniature drum shaken in the hand.

His eyes had lit up with greed at the sight of the scintillating golden Buddhas. "Uncle, you are really something! The three golden statues were in your hands the whole time. You fooled them all, those "cultural revolution" interrogators and torturers. You're terrific! These are priceless treasures!"

"You get out of here! Avarice is your name and evil is your game. Your very presence is sacrilege! Whitesy, get him out of here!" Whitesy shot toward him with a menacing bark. Tieba scrambled out of the worship hall for the safety of the outer room.

"Ah, those sinners! So ignorant! In actuality these three golden Buddhas are molded out of clay. They're only coated with a thin layer of gold dust. But laymen refuse to believe this. They were relentless in trying to acquire these Trikala Buddhas, they just wouldn't give it up. Ai! Such sinners!" Lama Yondon shook his head and sighed.

Yuanhui gave a wry smile.

Then, Lama Yondon opened one of the padauk chests and took from it an old package, which he handed to Yuanhui. He said with deliberation, "These are the things Whitesea left behind. Some journals, a pair of glasses, a few books, some odds and ends." Yuanhui quickly opened the package. She leafed through the journals, which were devoted entirely to information and figures relating to the local sandland vegetation and weather conditions. "He went to dig up the root of a Chinese peashrub so he could draw it for his *One Hundred Illustrated Plants and Their Root Systems*, and the sand collapsed into the pit he dug and buried him. It was very untimely. There were many more things he wanted to do here. But ... *ai!*...

good people have short lives...and he was just gone, and he hadn't even had time to tell me what to do with his things. The possibility of death had simply never occurred to him. But ... *ai!*... death came ... buried in the sand, he was. I found the address of his work unit in his journal, and that's how I was able to send the telegramme. He was the only real friend I ever had in the world, and to tell the truth, I am really reluctant to hand his things over to you." Yondon's eyes moistened.

Yuanhui listened as she hugged her husband's things to her chest. Tears silently trickled from her eyes and dropped onto her lapels. Then no longer able to restrain herself, she began to sob forthrightly. Remorse and pain tore into her heart.

"I buried his body in the sand, along with that peashrub and its roots. By now there won't be anything left of his body, it will all have turned to dust along with the peashrub and been absorbed into the roots of the living plants that are there. And so he continues to exist in the desert. This is the best way, really — you come into the world without fanfare, live out your life in an ordinary way, and depart without a to do. The grassroots man returns to the root of the grass. He always kept himself aloof from the ways of the world, and so the way he died was in accordance with his own principles for living." Yondon fell silent. He closed his eyes as if a heavy burden had been lifted from his soul.

Yuanhui, too, embraced the silence and gave herself over to contemplation.

At this time a commotion erupted in the outer room. Since they'd entered the cellar, sand had been drifting onto the cellar door, and now the air inside was becoming thin. Most of the pitiful animals were at their last gasp and had flopped over onto the floor to await their deaths. The bigger animals who still had some strength left, such as the black wolf and some foxes, instinctively sensed that though they'd escaped the ravaging attack of the hot sand storm, the threat of an altogether different kind of death now faced them. Thus, the big black wolf staggered to the cellar door, nudged it open with his nose, and clawed his way with all his might through the high-piling drift sand. Finally, he broke through. He sped through the opening in desperation, and all the foxes and the others still able to move followed.

The sand continued to drift into the door — at a speed which would fill the entire outer room of the cellar in next to no time.

Tieba looked in horror at what was happening to the door, then glanced at Lama Yondon and Yuanhui in the inner room.

Lama Yondon stated to cough. He was breathing with great difficulty. He wheezed to Yuanhui, "My time has come. I am going to be buried here in my Hall of Buddha along with the Trikala Buddhas which I worship. You had better get going — there may still be hope for you to survive."

"No, I don't want to leave either. I will stay here with you and my husband." Yuanhui spoke resolutely.

"*Ai!* You are a complete fool, just like your husband." Yondon coughed violently. His face turned livid. Yuanhui walked over and pounded him gently on the back.

Hysterical howling suddenly came from Tieba. "No, no, I won't die, I won't die. I want to live! I want to get out of here, I want to leave!" He stood up and rushed to the cellar door. He pulled it open and, just like the black wolf, dug with all his might into the blockade of drift sand. He turned his head toward Aoya and shouted, "Aoya, do you want to die here? Come on, come with me!"

Aoya looked at Tieba, then glanced at Yondon and Yuanhui, who showed in their faces neither fear nor pain. They appeared calm and serene, expressing total acceptance of what nature had in store for them. Finally, Aoya stood up. She followed Tieba and crawled out of the cellar. Both of them disappeared outside. With their departure came silence. There was only the hot sand storm torturing and tearing the world apart.

"You should go too," Lama Yondon said to Yuanhui. "It's not for you to emulate me. It's not for you to wait here to die. You should grab your ray of hope and fight for your life — for the sake of your husband, for the sake of the valuable materials he left behind. It is for you to make sure that his *One Hundred Illustrated Desert Plants and Their Root Systems* — into which he poured his life — is put to good use. So he will not have died in vain."

"Old Master, going out is also death. I can't take one step in the desert, knowing not in which direction to go."

"No, there is still hope for you. I'll have Whitesy lead you out of the desert. She knows the way." Lama Yondon reached down to Whitesy lying at his feet and patted her neck. He pointed to Yuanhui, then pointed toward the out-of-doors, and said, "Whitesy, remember, from now on, she is your mistress. You take her out of the desert!"

Whitesy seemed to have understood. She looked at her master, then looked at Yuanhui. She wagged her tail to indicate her obedience.

"You have to dress for combat. Put on clothing of heavy material to avoid being burned. Wear a belt and tie your trouser legs at the ankles. Cover your face so only your eyes are showing." As Yondon spoke, he was searching through his chests. He found clothing and a head wrapper.

"No, Old Master. If I go, we must go together. I can't just leave you behind." Yuanhui spoke through her sobs.

"Enough of that! No more argument!" Lama Yondon raised his voice in sudden severity. "I know how long I've been alloted to live, and this is it for me. The end is rapidly approaching. So hurry up and get dressed and don't waste any more time. I haven't got any time to waste but you haven't come to the end of your road yet, and you can't just quit in the middle!" As he rebuked her, he took out a bottle of water. He handed it to her, saying, "I stored this water here to wash the dust off the golden Buddhas. You take it with you, and use it frugally."

Yuanhui felt very sad, but dared not refuse it. She looked at the bottle with a heavy heart.

Silently, Lama Yondon placed it on the lid of the chest and said, "May Buddha protect you. *Oṁ mani padme hùm!*" He extended his hand and touched Yuanhui's forehead, devoutely bestowing a blessing. Then he turned and walked slowly toward the Trikala

Buddhas. He lowered himself down upon the round mat before them and sat cross-legged. Closing his eyes and folding his hands, he chanted, "Oṁ maṇi padme huṁ, this old lama now takes leave!" And thus he passed away. And a pure and holy light shown forth from his infinitely kind face; a smile of timeless wisdom hovered about his lips, imbued with forbearance of the world's profane ways. It was the final countenance of a man satisfied at having finally reached the end of his long journey through life.

Yuanhui silently prayed for him. This ordinary lama of the sandland had unswervingly kept his faith all his life and in the end passed away in keeping with this faith, peacefully, without struggle or remorse, in an atmosphere of solemn dignity and detachment from the world. Her heart swelled with boundless esteem for this man of undying belief. Yes, a system of belief was a powerful thing. She felt deeply its moving influence and mysterious appeal. No wonder every people in the family of man came to forge religious beliefs with the first glimmer of civilisation and had nurtured them right down to the present. For generation after generation, they've kept the incense burning, maintaining their own logic of existence and development. This too, in its own special way, is a manifestation of nature. For human beings need something to believe in.

A tear spilled out from each of Yuanhui's eyes and slid down her cheeks.

Whitesy, too, seemed to have sensed the passing of Lama Yondon. She stood beside Yuanhui, not daring to approach the lama and rub affectionately up against him as she used to do. She really was a perceptive, intelligent dog. She was afraid of desecrating the purity he deceased.

Yuanhui rubbed Whitesy's head and said, "We, too, should be going. We must get on with our unfinished journey. Yes, we shouldn't fear what lies ahead, we can not fear what lies ahead..."

According to Lama Yondon's instructions, she dressed herself for combat, tucked the water bottle in her clothes, and slung her husband's things on her back. Then she bowed in farewell to the old lama's remains. With Whitesy at her side, she stepped out of the cellar and into the boundless chaos of the sandstorming world.

The cellar they left behind was soon buried in the drifting sand. Not a trace of it remained. If Yuanhui hadn't just stepped out of it, she would have doubted that it ever existed and that it contained the three golden Buddhas of the past, present and future along with a deceased old lama still sitting before them. She would have thought that in this world there was only the yellow-brown desert, the master of all throughout the millennia.

"I will be back. I will return to plant the hundred desert plants and to restore the Temple of Viridity to its original colour — green. And at that time I will hold a ceremony in memory of you both..." This Yuanhui vowed to herself and then she and Whitesy set out courageously on their way.

EPILOGUE

Three days later.

On that vast tract of sand over which the hot sand

storm had just swept across, two figures unusual appeared: a large snow-white wolf-dog and a half-conscious, sand-battered woman, whom the dog was struggling to drag through the wind-blown sand. Staggering and bellying along, the wolf-dog pulled and tugged at the woman who had a white package strapped around her neck, whose face was a mass of blisters, lesions, and bleeding cracks. Her mouth and nose filled with sand, the woman was barely alive.

Though the white wolf herself had reached a state of exhaustion and could barely stay on her feet, she carried on indomitably, and with unswerving loyalty to her mistress took one excruciating step after another toward the east, pushing on ... ever pushing on...

Translated by Josephine A. Matthews

Spring on the Horqin Sandland

Ji Cheng

In 1985, the young Mongolian writer Guo Xuebo published "The Sand Fox", his first short story about the desert, in *Literature of the North*. The work later appeared in English in *Chinese Literature*, (Winter 1987) and in the American publication *Short Story International*. Guo Xuebo is now literary director of a publishing house.

"The Sand Fox" marked the beginning of a series of desert fiction: "The Desert Wolf", "Sand Burial", "Sand Rites", "The Fiery Residence" and "The Goddess of Xiling River". Guo's fiction portrays the hardships, dangers and complexities of life on the Horqin Sandland of Inner Mongolia, and extols the tenacity and strength of life.

I asked Guo why he sets his fiction in the desert. "The first thing I saw when I came into this world was sand,"he replied pensively. "The women in my hometown would spread a layer of dry, comfortable sand on the *kang* when they gave birth. That's probably why I have an affinity with sand. I know the desert all too well. When I was a child, I would run naked after hares on the dunes, dig out edible roots and break off thin branches of willow to make a horse whip; I'd cover myself all over with yellow sand and splash in small pools in the low-lying land — childhood is unforgettable."

Guo Xuebo was born in Kunlun Banner on Inner Mongolia's Horqin Sandland in 1948. His Han forebears from Shandong Province had married with Mongolian people and coexisted on the land with Mongolians, Manchurians, Huis and Koreans. In the past, the local economy was based mainly on animal husbandry, but today is largely agricultural. In the 1920s and '30s there was an uprising against oppression led by a Mongolian named Gadameilin. A long narrative poem of the same name is popular in the area.

The social environment, therefore, with its dominant Mongolian culture, is complex and full of ethnic conflict. The "Andai" dance described in "Sand Rites" is a traditional Mongolian folk dance popular in eastern Inner Mongolia. This bold, free dance is usually performed for an exorcism or sacrificial rites, to cure disease or dispel disaster, or at celebratory gatherings. The Mongolians are renowned for their dancing. Guo Xuebo's father was a painter and balladeer who spoke and sang in Mongolian. People would often gather around to listen to the stories his father told. This kept the budding writer informed about village affairs, and was no doubt his earliest source of literary inspiration. After graduating from a technical school, Guo Xuebo worked for seven years in Kesuoshou Banner about two hundred kilometres from Kunlun Banner. In his seven years there he worked as editor at the county broadcasting station and as a scriptwriter at the cultural centre and for the prefecture's song and dance ensemble. He also did physical work in a village. Here, on this desolate stretch of land, he dug up edible wild plants and herded cattle, and even encountered wolves from time to time. His spirit of adventure, his love of desert flora and fauna and his passion for riding frequently led him to perilous places. One day, while he was out hunting, he shot a wild duck that fell into a lake. He almost fell into the lake himself when he tried to pull it out. On another occasion, he fell off his horse and would have been dragged to death had he not clung to the saddle. Such experiences forged his strong, brave character. During this period he published his first work "High, High Ulanhot" in *PLA Art and Literature* in 1975.

In 1977, Guo Xuebo entered the Beijing Central Institute of Drama. After graduating in 1980, he was awarded a research fellowship at the Literary Research Institute of the Chinese Academy of Social Sciences, specialising in Mongolian history, culture and literature. Two years later, circumstances and his love of creative writing forced him to return to Horqin. But the serious desertification of the area worried him greatly. He wrote: "My homeland, the so-called Horqin Grassland, used to be quite well known. The waves of green plants, the white clouds, the cattle, the vast and wonderful grasslands stir the soul with their beauty. Now they are all fading away, transformed into a sea of sand that stretches for four hundred kilometres, one of the twelve largest deserts in the country. The United Nations has referred to it as a 'terrible miracle'. Who created this miracle? That question had baffled local officials and farmers. People have to live; they have to plough up the grassland to grow grain. As the thin layer of vegetation is dug up, a dormant monster, the desert, is unleashed. As a result, the wind has blown away the clouds and the rain, reducing the land to a land of drought. The yellow sand has swallowed the green wilderness and subjected life to the most savage destruction. The life-and-death struggle with wind and sand has caused relationships between man and man, man and animals, and between animals themselves to become ever narrower and cruder. "Survival of the fittest' is a true description of the situation," said Guo Xuebo. In his anguish Guo embarked on a philosophical examination of man, nature and the meaning of existence. His own domain — the desert — provides the stimulus for his creativity. He is now settled in Beijing, but his persistent interest in the desert prompts him to make annual visits home with his wife and child.

The desert is not solely the concern of those born there, but is the concern of all mankind. As civilisation advances, man becomes increasingly ensnared in the predicaments of existence that he has created for himself: farmland, forests, flora and fauna are being decreased drastically. Thirty-seven percent of the world's land area has already been swallowed by desert. As Whitesea, the desert control expert in "Sand Burial" says, "I think of people more in terms of a colony of ants. They excavate one place to exhaustion and then move on to another, until they've laid waste to all places." The gradual destruction of the remaining land haunts mankind.

The desert theme sets the tragic tone in Guo Xuebo's works.

"The Sand Fox" is the story of Old Sandy Man and his eighteen-year-old daughter Willow who have spent a lifetime looking after the surviving desert plants and whose sole companion is an old sand fox, the natural enemy of the rats. If the rats multiply, the dune plants that have been cultivated with so much difficulty will be eaten up and the desert will grow larger than ever. Unfortunately, Beardy, the chief of the Forestry Centre, does not understand the importance of the sand fox and the relationship between fox, father and daughter. He insists on hunting in the area and in the end the fox is shot, which leads to the worsening of the environment.

"The Desert Wolf" is about Old Jingad, the hunter, and his family. When some of the hunters killed five wolf cubs, the mother wolf steals his two-year-old grandson Gouwa and brings him up as a wolf child. When the boy is ten years old, he is captured after becoming drunk on chicken steeped in wine which has been laid as bait by his grandfather. The grandfather ties him up and keeps him in a cage. Although the child becomes tamer under his mother's care, the she-wolf harasses him with her calls. Just as the child is about to throw himself into the wolf's embrace, the grandfather, in his rage, shoots him. Old Jingad himself later perishes in a deadly fight with the mother wolf. The story arouses many thoughts and feelings, but however you look at it, it is a tragedy.

The main theme in "Sand Burial" concerns the search by Lama Yondon for his pet dog Whitesy. Driven by starvation and hunted by the militia chief Tieba, Whitesy runs away and lives wild as a wolf. Whitesea, a banished intellectual, is buried under an avalanche while digging up a grass root needed for his research. The protagonist, the seemingly apathetic but kind and wise Lama Yondon is buried in a terrible sandstorm.

Most of Guo Xuebo's other novels are also tragedies caused not by the desert or any mysterious force but by man himself. They impart, therefore, a profound and serious message to mankind.

But Guo Xuebo's tragedies are not at all commonplace. There is much to meditate upon in his novels, which inspire rage, respect or admiration for the strength of ordinary men and women. His tragedies are unique because he has incorporated the philosophy of religion in his narration. At the beginning of one novel he quotes the following words from a Buddhist scripture, "There is no peace in the human world, which resembles a fiery residence". The "fiery residence" of his novels, the desert, is dominated by men's struggle, care, anxiety and fear, bound up with a desire for survival, yet in the end destruction is inevitable.

Guo Xuebo describes the desert flora and fauna in detail, not just because they are rare and precious or because he likes to use them as a foil for his characters, but because "all lives in the desert have the same value", as Lama Yondon says in "Sand Burial".

Guo Xuebo's realistic fiction arises from both his particular life experience and his solid foundation in literature. He has read and appreciated Jack London, William Faulkner, Turgenev, Prosper Merimee, etc. He is also much influenced by structural realism. In competition with the film industry, structural realists adopt a multi-layered approach, with the narration taking different points of view in order to achieve a three-dimensional effect. There are three entwined themes in "The Desert Wolf": Old Jingad, Ahm and the desert wolf a technique he has also used in other stories. The style is well suited to the complex life of the desert.

As Zeng Zhennan, a famous literary critic, commented on his desert stories, "Guo Xuebo is a writer in possession of both special knowledge of nature and life experiences. His works, in a language brilliant and vigorous, convey to readers strength and thought-provoking connotations." Gue Xuebo says, "Life is indomitable. There is in the sand dunes a grass, 'soury', as locals call it. No matter how the sands try to cover it, it manages to poke its head through the surface of the desert. The harsh environment forces every life to adopt its own particular mean of survival. In front of my family's house runs Yangximu River, which originates in a small shallow pool at the foot of a sand hill. In the pool is a spring with a mouth the size of a camel-eye from which the spring flows out as thin as a silk thread. Sometimes it seems to stop flowing but at other times it is alive again; or it may be hidden by water grass or covered by fallen leaves. However, it is this small sand brook that breeds the grasses and reeds around it; and it is this small sand brook that sacrifices part of its water to be evaporated into the dry air, part to satisfy the sucking of drift sands on its banks and part to move away the sand dunes in its way. But it braves its course across the sandland, a hard journey of eight hundred *li*, flows into the Xiliao River and finally into Bohai Bay, into the ocean. This small stream, of a tenacious spirit, is representative of all lives that struggle for survival in the desert, and the people that have lived on the Horqin Sandland for generations..."

Guo Xuebo is just like the spring at the foot of the sand hill: and his desert stories embrace the world just as the Yangximu River flows eventually into the sea.

Translated by Wang Chiying

图书在版编目(CIP)数据

沙狼: 英文/ 郭雪波著. — 北京: 中国文学出版社, 1996.3
ISBN 7-5071-0344-7

I. 沙… II. ① 郭… ② 马… III. 中篇小说 — 作品集 — 中国 — 当代 — 英文 IV. I247.5

沙 狼

作 者 郭雪波
中文责编 徐慎贵
翻 译 马若芬等
英文责编 陈海燕

熊猫丛书

*

中国文学出版社出版
(中国北京百万庄路24号)
中国国际图书贸易总公司发行
(中国北京车公庄西路35号)
北京邮政信箱第399号 邮政编码100044
1996年 第1版(英)
ISBN 7-5071-0344-7
01800
10—E—2899P